House of Secrets

The Bloodborne Trilogy

M.E. Evans

Capybara Media

Copyright © 2024 by M.E. Evans

All rights reserved.

No portion of this book may be reproduced in any form without written permission from the publisher or author, except as permitted by U.S. copyright law.

contents

	VI
	VII
1. A SHADOW AT THE GATE	1
2. LOOK AT ME	14
3. THE GAME	21
4. A GOD OF SHADOWS	34
5. SAVE THE LAST DANCE	43
6. WHAT DON'T YOU TRUST ABOUT THAT?	55
7. NO BOOZE AT THE PLAYGROUND	68
8. A UTERUS OF HELLFIRE	81
9. THE BETRAYAL	88
10. BLOTTO	97
11. TELEPHONE GAME	123

12.	DAGGERS FOR EYES	132
13.	THE INVADER	137
14.	SISTER, SISTER	149
15.	PHO KIT	159
16.	A SECRET	169
17.	TOO MUCH TO PONDER	188
18.	FAE SMUT	195
19.	GOODBYE, STEVEN	207
20.	MIND-WEAVING	213
21.	IN HIS ROOM	226
22.	FAREWELL, REBECCA	234
23.	GHOSTED	246
24.	RUBBLE AND RUIN	254
25.	THE MOST BEAUTIFUL WOMAN IN HIS ROOM	260
26.	MEMORIZE THIS PICTURE IF YOU WANT TO LIVE	280
27.	EARL GREY VERSUS THE SADIST	290
28.	COZY LITTLE CABIN	296
29.	THE LORD OF TORTURE	302
30.	A LOVER'S PURR	315
31.	FOR FUCK'S SAKE, JANET.	322

32.	THE HALFLINGS ATTACK	340
33.	SNOW-CAPPED CARNAGE	349
34.	A FITFUL SLEEP	365
35.	THE WAY HOME	376
36.	EVERYONE'S SECRETS AND LIES	385
Conclusion		390
Acknowledgments		391

To all who feel stuck, your story is just beginning.

When it all began, I'd already been dead for a while. On the outside, I looked and acted like everyone else—alive, functional, whole. But inside, I was nothing more than a hollow shell. I tried to pretend everything was fine, throwing myself into the endless tasks of motherhood. But when night fell, and the house plunged into silence, a forgotten part of me stirred, restless and demanding. I ignored it as long as I could, but eventually, I had no choice. Power can be hidden but never snuffed out; it pulses, transforms and endures, waiting for the right moment to set the darkness ablaze.

A SHADOW AT THE GATE

I slid in my thick wool socks, cutting off my daughter, Victoria. "GOTCHA!" I yelled, hoisting her up to kiss her flushed cheeks–not so easy since she'd turned eight.

"Ria, where's your sister?" I asked, setting her gently on the ground while searching for my six-year-old.

Victoria shrugged and shoved her curls out of her eyes before turning on her heel and skipping away. Just then, hard little feet thundered across the hardwood as Olivia, ever-active, rounded the corner and slammed into the wall with a thud. She grunted and shook her head before spinning around to announce herself.

"Hello! It's me!" she called out, giggling, her green eyes wild with delight. Olivia was a miniature version of me, with the same wild dark hair, the same eyes, and the same chaotic energy. Throwing out her arms like bird's wings, she leapt onto my chest, forcing a grunt out of me and nearly taking me to the ground.

"There you are!" I wrapped my arms around her tight and kissed the top of her head. I set her down gently, her feet barely touching the floor before she took off after her big sister, with me hot on their heels. All three of us dashed through the house, this way and that, howling with laughter.

My love for those two tiny people swelled in my chest with every cackle and guffaw as I roared behind them, doing my best monster impression. It was this love that allowed me to push through the unyielding exhaustion each day, hour after hour–picking up around the house, packing organic lunches, stumbling through meltdowns and backtalk. The endless appointments, and endless worrying, and cooking, and cleaning, and baths, and battles–over, and over, and over. But times like these, the love, the belly laughs, make it all worth it, and there's no place else I'd rather be.

I snatched a stack of pajamas from the arm of the couch as I sprinted past, tucking them under my arm like a football while in hot pursuit of my little ones, who were headed for a dead-end in the hallway. They slid to a stop, whirling, eyes wide with amusement and mock horror as I closed in on them, creeping ever so slowly and growling. Once their anticipation reached a crescendo, I dropped to my knees, and we fell into a group hug, pajamas tumbling from my arms to a heap on the floor.

"Can you guys keep it down?!" barked my husband, Steven, from inside his office, where he'd holed himself up for the past twelve hours and for pretty much every day over the last two miserable years. I rolled my eyes and felt my jaw ache.

"Nope, caan't. Life's happening out here!" I called to him through the wall, trying my best to temper the rage building inside of me. Heat spread through my belly and chest, burning up the joy.

Steven yanked the office door open and stuck his pinched face into the hall, "I'm in a MEETING!" he growled through his teeth, eyes narrowed to two hateful slits.

"Daddy! Play with us!" Olivia cried.

"Take them somewhere else!" he snarled. Then, without warning, he slammed the door shut in our faces.

My blood roiled. I balled my fists at my side until my nails dug into my palm, then relaxed them, focusing on the lingering throb. In that moment, I hated him so much it was blinding. And I imagined what it would feel like to punch him in his stupid face, how my knuckles would feel grazing the shadow of his light brown stubble. I blinked, forcing my rage down to a simmer. I sucked in a deep breath, *in for four, hold for four, out for four*, then turned my attention back to my girls, who were still smiling, though their eyes were watchful. *What do I say?* I made eye contact with Victoria and then Olivia, shrugging, "it looks like your dad is upset. It's okay to be mad but not okay to yell and slam doors, right?" They nodded. "Okay. Let's get you into your pajamas so we can read your new books! Does that sound fun?"

I smiled, pretending that Steven's explosion hadn't rubbed off on me, leaving a film of unsteadiness. I handed each girl a pajama set. Victoria politely thanked me. Olivia hugged hers into her chest and bounced on her toes.

"After getting yourselves all cozy, can you each choose one book and meet me on the couch?" I asked, tapping my chin and pretending to mull it over. "Who is faster? Is it Ria? Or Liv? Hmm."

They squealed and then raced toward their room, exchanging competitive taunts back and forth. When they were out of sight, I whirled toward the wall that separated me from my husband and dragged my hands down my tired, puffy face, exhaling forcefully. I would never *actually* harm my husband. But! I *could* beg the universe to do it for me, and so I did just that for the fifth time that day. I hoped that the next time he boarded a plane, it would, I don't know, accidentally eject him. Then guilt gripped me and I banished the thought. I'd never wish anything like that on my little ones, especially not after the way I lost my father. A few minutes later, I sat with my girls curled into my body on the blue velvet couch in the living room, their limbs this way and that, soft little bodies and hard elbows sunk into my belly, bruising a rib. Olivia's head rested on my chest, her legs straight up in the air to admire the different bugs printed on her gray pajamas. Victoria lay to my right, her head on my shoulder, where she could no doubt smell the fragrance of the dry shampoo I used so frequently that sometimes I worried my head might catch fire. Olivia pointed to the illustration of a spider on her knee. Victoria judgmentally scrunched her nose and smoothed the lines of her purple nightgown. I took stock of the state of my house: a small laundry basket was parked on the vintage media center below a painting of a woman giving birth to a clock; the chandelier over the dining table needed a few new bulbs. At least the girls were mostly clean and dressed well (at least in the early part of the day), although Olivia was often speckled in dirt or mystery debris. I, on the other hand, almost always looked like I was coming off of a bender, wearing the same three-days-in-a-row stained black lounge set, my hair corralled into a crunchy pile on top of my head, eyes perpetually bloodshot from a never-ending string of long days. At only thirty-five, I felt somewhere around nine hundred. I yawned, and Olivia followed. We read the two books a million times each until their eyelids were heavy, and the only sounds in the house came from the hardwood creaking like it was stretching and relaxing after a hard day of being trampled.

It was only seven-thirty, early by most standards, but my body sagged beneath the pressures of the day. Hand in hand, I walked my groggy girls up a small flight of stairs to bed, my back aching just above my hips from the strain of their weight as I lifted each into bed. I kissed each of them on the head and then leaned in to whisper, "you are loved, you are safe," before double-checking the windows and turning on the low hum of the sound machine–a magical invention that allowed the girls to practically sleep through an earthquake. I closed their door slowly.

In the kitchen, I paused to pour myself a comically large glass of red wine, swiped the nanny cam from the counter, and headed towards the back door, where I nabbed my beanie from the coat hook with my pinkie finger. A few drops of Malbec hit the floor. I shrugged and stepped over it on the way to my little studio, which was attached to the garage in the backyard. The cold nipped at my face. Shriveled leaves shook in the oak trees, and a fat squirrel raced along the power line with a massive acorn clenched in its teeth. Despite the long day, a smile pulled at the corners of my mouth.

I kicked the door to my studio open and it crashed into the wall behind. "Shit," I muttered. I breathed in the pungent smell of wet oil paints and used my elbow to switch on the lights before placing my wine and the nanny cam on a small desk. I stretched the green beanie over my head, bun and all, then plopped down in front of my easel. A wall-size canvas, my painting in progress, loomed over the space.

"Hey there, cutie," I cooed.

The giant face of Rebecca—a differently-abled elderly Shih Tzu—stared out at me. Her little fuzzy body posed in front of Fleur De Lille wallpaper. With the space heater on full blast, roasting my right side straight through my wool loungewear, I surveyed the full scope of the ancient dog with her crooked head and glossy eyes.

"Oh, Rebecca, you're a hot fucking mess,"

I chuckled to myself, shaking my head in amusement. The dog I saw in front of me was missing teeth and probably wouldn't make it to Solstice. Nevertheless, her owner, Barbara, had commissioned a portrait every year and for the past five years, each one a little larger than the last; the canvas grew because Rebecca's spirit grew, although her aging body shrank and withered.

I loved my job. It wasn't the one I'd envisioned for myself, but I did enjoy it. I'd never planned on painting pets. But I liked dogs, and it was easy to do after the kids went to bed.

After adding some finishing touches to Rebecca's crooked right paw (a glossy Fuchsia toe polish), I noticed the time. *Ten already?* I arched my back and raised my arms to breathe deeply. My lungs inflated to their fill, stretching my rib cage in a dull and glorious ache.

Back inside the house, I checked on the girls, lingering for a moment in their bedroom doorway to watch their chests rise and fall, adoring the way their dark hair framed their light olive faces–a gift we all received from my late father's deep brown Persian complexion, along with mauve lips, and an impressive unibrow–and resisted the urge to kiss them goodnight again. Humming to myself, I wandered toward the kitchen, pausing briefly at Steven's office door to listen to him pound on his keyboard, before continuing on to pour myself *a titch* more wine before going out to the front porch.

The porch swing squeaked beneath me; the brisk air kissed my cheeks as I settled into my happy place, rocking back and forth. The dim street lights were the only lights on at this hour, the sky so black that it seemed to swirl like smoke around the new moon and few visible stars. I pulled my phone out of my pocket and typed a text to Steven.

"It's pretty out. If you get a break, come hang out for a bit."

I swung a little, hoping that maybe he'd come out, and maybe he'd be nice.

"In meetings with the project managers in China."

I swallowed my disappointment and frustration and slipped my phone back into my pocket. The night was silent as a tomb. I scanned our front yard and the road beyond it for signs of life before I reached under the cushion to claw out a pack of cigarettes and a lighter. I lit one and took a drag, leaning back to let my mind wander.

Steven and I had bought the porch swing the same day we closed on the house. I'd insisted we put it together right away, too, so we could have a glass of champagne to celebrate on our porch "like a sweet old married couple." After finishing the bottle of champagne, we'd had sex in the living room and slept on a mattress on the living room floor. Steven had laughed a giddy laugh and rolled into me. He'd looked into my eyes and touched the tip of my nose gently with his pointer finger, mouthing, "I love you." I'd leaned in to kiss him, flicking my tongue into his mouth, before falling asleep next to him.

But we hadn't sat together on the porch for *years*. Hell, we'd barely spoken for years—not since his career took off. Sometimes I ached for the life I'd had before he shut me out, before the loneliness crept in and stayed. For all its joys, being a parent was by far the most isolating thing I'd ever done. Most days,

I barely interacted with other adults. Most days, all I did was direct little people in the ways of the world, coaxing them to eat and clean themselves, playing, praising, and singing songs about a goddamn spider that wouldn't stop climbing up a fucking spout. So much time spent on my knees naming feelings, taking deep breaths, and occasionally blocking tiny flailing bodies from slamming into me with their small, swinging arms.

I was lonely. I was bored. And I was so fucking tired all the time.

My phone vibrated with another message, this time from my sister, Jess.

"Whatcha doin' sis?" she'd written.

I quickly typed out, "Nothing."

"You lying filth," she scolded, "You're smoking. Put that shit out."

I grinned and sent a picture of me flipping her off.

"Ha!" she replied, then sent one back. "Whatever. Twat. See you tomorrow!"

As I slid my phone back into my jacket, it vibrated again. This time, it was an email alert from the PTA at the girls' school. I huffed. "It's Socktober! Don't forget! Accepting donations!" I groaned, then added "socks" to my shopping list and hoped that this week, unlike last week or the week before, I'd remember to grab them for the drive.

Footsteps sounded on the sidewalk, and I panicked, plunging my cigarette deep into the shadows behind the swing. Gods forbid someone see me smoking, especially one of the parents at

Ria and Liv's school. Those blood-thirsty soccer moms would come unhinged, and, I didn't feel like doing the justifying and apologizing, "I only smoke once in a while and never in front of the girls, and I always wash my hands carefully in a vat of bleach but not *actual* bleach, I use organic chemical free vinegar" thing.

It was true. I only smoked once in a while, and never in front of the girls, or anyone else. The only person who knew about it was my sister, who knew everything. It was a dirty, guilty pleasure, but I *needed it*. Once in a while, I needed to live a little dangerously, to feel a little un-mom-like, a little wild. My adult life had become nothing but caution and anxiety as I fumbled to hold on to myself, while also moving into the many new roles of motherhood. Maybe it was harder for me than others because I'd always been a little on the feral side—a little wild. And the all-consuming monotony, mixed with the anxiety of wanting to be perfect–to do better than my parents, specifically–ravaged me.

The footsteps grew louder, closer, closer, until a tall man with short, dark hair came into view. *Oh, it's him;* I'd seen this man before. My stomach fluttered a little. Over the past month, he'd walked by several times, always a little before midnight and often with someone beautiful on his arm, someone equally as striking. Tonight, he was dressed elegantly in a slim-cut wool coat, and holy *stars* was he gorgeous. Hooked on his arm was a woman who looked like she'd just stepped out of a movie screen, so lovely it should be illegal. Tall and lean and curvy, her hair sang in a satin zinc-white bob that caressed her golden shoulders.

I tracked them as they strolled past. Inhaling, I absentmindedly took a final drag from my cigarette, forgetting that the cherry would flair that bright orange. The gorgeous man's head suddenly jerked towards me, fast and animal-like, and his eyes, the most gorgeous and fierce sapphire eyes I'd ever seen--like the crashing waves of the Caribbean–bore into mine. It was predatory, that stare, and it sent a bolt of lightning through my chest. Then he turned his attention back to his date before they rounded the corner and disappeared into the night. My breathing steadied. I had no idea how he saw me so clearly up there in the shadows of the porch, clear enough to look right at me, right into my eyes, right *through* me.

Or maybe I was just so godsdamn lonely, so bored, that a part of me hoped he'd seen me, that somebody would see me.

I hissed as I rose to my feet and wandered down the steps to the garbage cans, carefully pinching out my cigarette and dropping it into the abyss, away from prying eyes, before tip-toeing back into the house, pausing once or twice to look over my shoulder. I could feel eyes on my back, and I wasn't sure if it was just my paranoia from sneaking around, or if my intuition was tickling the flesh on my neck to let me know that someone, somewhere, was watching me.

***

In bed, alone, I let my left leg stretch into Steven's side of the bed, a 400-thread-count Egyptian cotton desert. A small part of me wished he would finish early just once so he could lie next to me like he used to. But then again, having his arms around me would feel so foreign now, almost icky, like sinking into the sticky unknown of a stranger's hold. And the resentment was there, too, from both of us, creating an invisible barrier between us. It had been so long since we'd gone to bed at the same time, touched, or even laughed together, that I could barely remember it. I groaned and focused on the breasts of the nude portrait I'd painted in college that hung above the headboard. I followed the delicate curve of the woman's back, her round hips and full ass, down to the Persian carpet beneath her, a replica of the one in my parents' house, bought on my father's first trip back to Iran after the revolution in '79, when he'd fled the country like countless others. The people had wanted change; I'd heard they wanted a leader who wouldn't exploit the land for western gain. But, after the revolution, once the Shah had been exiled, a group lurked on the fringes, organized and ready. Instead of a leader who would protect them, they ended up with something else.

The moonlight made the colors of the painting glow, and I couldn't help but think of the man who passed by earlier, that beautiful face and confident stroll. He moved like an aristocrat from another time, his open coat punctuating his height and displaying his flat muscles, and his dark blue eyes that had seemed to burn into mine. My lids fluttered closed, and I slid my hand under the cool, crisp sheets. My fingers slowly searched for the slickness of my sex, the oasis in this desert, and I went to work.

LOOK AT ME

It was early morning. The golden hue of sunrise peeked through the blinds, gently warming the breakfast nook where I sat with my family eating. Cupping a mug I'd bought from an artist friend that said, "The Tears of the Patriarchy" in inky black letters, I inhaled the coffee's chocolate and caramel notes and took a sip. Heaven. Olivia copied me with her mug, a small blue enamel cup filled with orange juice.

"Eat your waffles, Liv," I urged, smiling.

"Yeah, eat your waffles, Liv!" Victoria parroted, proudly, forever thrilled that she was the oldest and, therefore, the one with all of the life experience and authority.

"And you too, Ria." I winked at her. Try to enjoy being a kid and leave parenting to me, yeah? Victoria scrunched up her face. "Okay, mamma," she said flatly.

I noted the personalized acrylic family calendar on the wall and scanned over my last name, the hyphen, and his. *If I leave him, do I buy a new one? Change the name? How many other things will I need to change? What will this house look like with half of everything gone?* I glanced at the clock and set my coffee down a little too hard.

"We've got to get going, girls. You both have soccer this morning, then we'll get lunch, then the grocery store, and we can go for a walk before dinner."

"Okay!" Victoria and Olivia chimed together.

"Are you coming to soccer practice?" I asked Steven.

He had a mouth full of waffles and an iPhone glued to his face.

"Steven?"

"WHAT?" he snapped.

He broke focus from his phone just long enough to glare at me. The muscles in his jaw flexed and tightened.

I had to refrain from rolling my eyes. "I asked you if you're coming to their soccer practice?"

His chestnut brown eyes fixated on me coldly and it made the hair on my arms stand up.

"I don't know, " he said, low and clipped, not even trying to hide the contempt. "I'm bu-sy," he enunciated each syllable for emphasis. As if he needed to be as clear as possible so I'd finally understand that he didn't have time for me, them, or anyone. He dragged his eyes to our daughters and his chilly expression softened a little. "I'll try to come, okay, girls? I just need to get ready for my flight tonight."

He turned his attention back to the screen.

"Steven," I began.

He huffed and, without looking at me again, mumbled, "one of us has to have a real job."

His words landed in my gut like a fist. The air left my lungs, and the whole world shifted under me. Ouch. That son of a bitch. *How could he?*

"Excuse me?" I demanded, barely a whisper, already regretting the decision to snap back in front of the children. "I take care of our children twenty-four hours a day, seven days a week. And I do commissions at night, *Steven*." I said his name slowly, like a curse. "How is that not work?"

His eyes shot to me and then back to his phone in a silent dismissal. I wanted to throttle him, to throw my coffee in his face, to scream and cry and pull my hair out in wild frustration. We'd agreed I'd only work part-time so I could be there for the girls because he traveled so much and he wanted me to be with the girls as much as possible like Steven's mother had been home with him, unlike my "terrible" mother, who'd hired a nanny. So even though we'd both agreed that being a stay-at-home mom made sense, he liked to use my "not working" as a way to put me in my place from time to time. I hated to admit that it worked more often than not because the truth was that I felt ashamed for not earning more money. Under the table, I bawled up my fists until my nails bit into my palms.

Resentment swelled in my belly like an ulcer. *Don't react, it's not worth it.* I shoved the hurt down, down, down, into the vast emptiness inside, feeling myself die little by little. If I kept making myself small, eventually I'd just disappear or maybe I already had. I barely recognized myself. Before I became a mom, I had plenty of insecurities but overall I think I liked myself. I didn't anymore. You can't like someone you don't know. The cost of keeping the peace is high. A small piece of us withers each time we resist the urge to fight back.

My younger self would roll in her grave. Folks had labeled me a weirdo, a witch, "that rich girl who found her father in ribbons," but never agreeable or passive. Once, in high school, I'd noticed a young man take a barely conscious girl into a back room at a house party, and I'd stormed after them in a rage and planted myself between the tall, gangly man-boy and the glossy-eyed girl as though I weren't a full foot shorter than him. With death in my veins, I'd barked, "Get the fuck away from her, you gross piece of shit." I must have looked absolutely unhinged because he'd dropped the girl like a sack and scuttled away with his head down as he passed through the murmuring crowd. What would that version of me think about who I'd become? Would I have the courage to help the girl if it happened now?

The muscles tensed in my jaw as I continued to study Steven. *How has it come to this?* I took a deep breath, in and out. His stone-cold expression fixated wholly on his phone filled me with this volcanic, bottomless fury, and I wanted to punch him in his statue-like face. A voice in the back of my mind whispered to me, *"You turned out just like your mom, angry and unfulfilled."*

We'd fallen in love, hadn't we? We'd been happy once. Right? Everything good felt too distant to be real anymore. A few years ago, I couldn't have imagined a life without him. I'd called him my best friend and spent all of my free time with him. Now, every minute in his presence felt like a tiny torture.

My therapist once said marriages have ups and downs and go through phases of disconnect. How long does one wait to see if they are in a "bad phase" or if it has all gone to shit forever? At least I had my girls. My beautiful, spirited, pain in the ass, wonderful girls. I breathed in for five seconds and out for five seconds. Forced myself to sit taller and forced my chin up, then reached into the air and stretched, concentrating on my muscles and the dull ache along my spine and biceps as I pushed towards the ceiling. My watch dinged.

"Oh, shit," I muttered. "We're going to be late for your game. Time to go! I'll scoot out of here and grab your bags and snacks. Finish up, then meet me at the front door."

I nodded at Steven, "Can you help them finish up?" He glanced up, his chin dipping down just once before his gaze settled back on his phone screen. My eyes rolled so hard they ached in their sockets; I slid out of the window seat and stalked around the house like a tornado, collecting a water bottle here, a snack cup there, and a shoe. I yanked on my black Chelsea boots before swinging a long taupe wool jacket over my shoulders. My girls bounded towards me; Steven herded them absentmindedly, still scrolling on his phone. I waited for them to put on their sneakers, doing my best to resist the urge to harass them to move faster. Two hundred hours later, I shoved their backpacks towards them as they burst onto the porch to sprint towards my embarrassing car: sporty, posh-y, and showy, an unexpected marriage gift from some great aunt I'd never met. It embodied all the things I was not and didn't want to be. Standing on the porch, the light hit him just so. He looked handsome there, and for a moment, it was just him, the cute man who used to make me coffee in the morning, who would scream and run from spiders. I leaned in to kiss Steven on the cheek, but he cringed and tilted his head just out of reach.

"Oh...sorry." I fumbled an apology and hopped down the steps.

"Hurry, you're going to be late," Steven hollered to the girls.

So stupid. Why did I do that? My cheeks heated with shame, but I forced myself to shake off the small rejection as I crunched through the fallen leaves to my car.

Pressing the gas with a little more force than necessary, the car lurched forward and we were on our way. The radio buzzed alive with the news, "another body found in the mountains as police continue the search for what they believe to be a serial ki—". I changed the station. Classic rock filled the car, and the girls got some of their pre-game jitters out by aggressively fist-pumping to the music. I tried to concentrate on my hands gripping the wheel, on the music thrumming around us, but I just kept thinking about Steven and his comment, "One of us has to work," and the way he jerked away from me when I'd tried to kiss him goodbye.

Steven wasn't violent, but I was afraid of him. I was afraid of how he made me feel, like I was beneath him, wrong somehow, like my needs were an intolerable inconvenience, a character flaw, something broken in me. I'd seen the aftermath of disembowelment up close, but I knew for a fact that you could gut a person without ever laying a hand on them.

THE GAME

"Yes! Yes! Ria, go! Go!" I roared from a plaid blanket on the grass. My skin vibrated with excitement for my girls, so fearless and strong, as they zig-zagged in cleated feet across the astroturf. They each played separate games simultaneously on fields right next to each other, so my attention was split from one game to the other.

Ria dribbled across the field, keeping the ball close, her legs in constant motion, her little face pinched with determination while she effortlessly wove around the other kids on the field as if they weren't there. She paused only momentarily when she reached the goal, her leg shooting out like a missile to sink the ball into the back of the net, stretching the weave to the limit before landing with a thud on the ground.

There was a pause, and then her team and the crowd erupted into a cacophony of cheers. I bolted to my feet, mentally tethering myself to the grass to refrain from bouncing up and down on my toes (something Ria had once called "embarrassing"). "You did it!" I yelled. "You did it!" I smiled proudly at my oldest daughter, who grinned right back at me before being engulfed by her teammates. The group dispersed a few moments later, returning to their respective positions on the field.

I plopped back on the blanket, my frame tingling with joy. That part of motherhood came easy to me: the cheering, the support, the unconditional love. I loved my girls, and I'd celebrate them every second until the end of time, effortlessly and happily. It was just every single other aspect of motherhood that I struggled with: the routine, the monotony, the anxiety, guilt, worry, and the expectations that made it feel like the walls were caving in around me. I crossed my legs and turned my attention to Liv's field.

It was easy to spot Liv. She was fast as a bullet and looked mad as hell as she cruised toward a mob of children on the soccer ball like flies on a carcass. Her ponytail shook, heat blazed in her cheeks, mouth tight, eyes narrowed on the ball with a ferocity that always made me a *little* concerned. She went for it; her arms shot out for balance as she put all of herself into the kick. A child screamed out from the mob and then began howling in pain. The hoard broke apart to reveal a small boy sitting on the ground, rocking himself back and forth on his bottom, clutching his shin. Tears poured down his face and oh no, oh shit. *Shit. Shit. Shit. Not him. Anyone but him.*

"You kicked me!" The little boy, Bryce, hollered.

"On accident!" Olivia protested. She crouched down next to him. "Sorry, I was trying to get the ball. Do you want a hug?"

"NO!" Bryce wailed. "Don't touch me! I hate you and your weird, stupid family!"

Watching, my first instinct was to rush over to Olivia to save her from the embarrassment and discomfort of her mistake. I wanted to rescue her. But all of the parenting books were like, "Don't rescue them because they need to sit in discomfort sometimes, and if you rescue them, they'll never move out and will join a cult from your basement at age fifty-two." But where is the line? I could never figure out the nuances of those damn books. Love and support, they say, but let them struggle, let them solve their problems, or at least try, but also make them feel safe, seen, and heard. My heart broke as I watched her little face twist with guilt and try to make amends but fail. I didn't want to fill her head with our family's past and drama, but part of me wanted to tell her that there was no use trying to fix a damn thing with Bryce. He was cute and wholly innocent, but he was *her son*, my childhood arch nemesis, Bethany. The queen of bitches, the countess of cunts, and the head of the fucking PTA.

Sweat dripped down my ribs. Olivia was my bold and spirited child, who acted first and thought about it later. Kind, sensitive, and sweet, but impulsive and filled to the brim with hellfire. Where Ria wove around the mob to get to the goal, Liv would go straight through them. It was not the first time Olivia's enthusiasm had gotten the best of her, and I hated, no loathed, the way it labeled her, the way the other parents would tsk and shame her for childhood mistakes, for character differences, for not being smaller, quieter, and softer like the unicorn and pixie girls. An accidental kick in a sea of private schooled and stoic Anglo-Saxons was the social equivalent of killing a box of kittens, and it was made worse by kicking *that specific child*. Bethany, a tall blonde woman with a steely posture that was part ballerina, part Orc, made her way over to Bryce and pulled him into her arms.

I let out a low groan as she turned over her shoulder to eye me. It took all of my restraint not to roll my eyes, but a child had been hurt, and I did care about that, even if he would probably grow up to pass on the monster DNA that was their family legacy.

When we were younger, Bethany and I had been best friends, primarily due to proximity. Her parent's estate was across the road from ours, so we could wander down the spiraling driveway through iron gates to reach her property in minutes. My sister and I spent many summers riding horses with Bethany, creating fairy kingdoms in her family orchard at the edge of their property and wandering the halls of each other's homes. Then we were made enemies, thanks to our parents and their petty HOA war, taking turns to sue each other for violating "community guidelines." One day we were little girls giggling together in an orchard, the next, Bethany wouldn't speak to us. Then middle school began, and she became one of the popular girls at our private catholic school, The Mother of Immeasurable

Suffering. By age twelve, she'd mastered a serpentine smile and the ability to spit words like venom. In high school, it only got worse when the incident happened.

After what felt like an hour, the coach arrived on the soccer field, and Bethany crawled away to the sideline towards her husband, who looked like a Ken doll come to life with his pressed Khakis and side-combed golden hair. The coach helped Bryce to his feet. He squatted down to his height to chat with the children before sending them back into the field. Olivia glanced at me, and I smiled reassuringly at her. "Try again," I mouthed and gave her a thumbs up.

From the corner of my eye, I could see something move, a flash of white. My eyes slid towards the object and locked onto Bethany's face. She flipped her honey blonde strands over her blush pink luxury loungewear-clothed shoulder before slithering towards me. In a few heartbeats, she'd reached my spot on the grass and loomed over me while she smoothed the front of her Lu-Lu leggings and examined my blanket. She scrunched up her nose before sighing and, without invitation, crouched down next to me, rocking back on her haunches like she was about to shit. I stiffened.

"There you are, Danielle!" Bethany said, stretching my full name into a hiss. "How are you?"

Her mouth curved up, but the smile didn't reach her cold gray eyes, the color of a three-days-old corpse.

"I'm doing well, Bethany," I replied flatly. "What can I do for you?"

I searched her pretty face for whatever she was about to say. Surely, she'd start with something about Olivia and Bryce on the field where she'd try to mask an insult, and then, knowing her, she'd pivot PTA demands for upcoming school events, volunteer opportunities, and all of that. I chewed on the inside of my cheek and turned back to the soccer game, to the little bodies moving with intention across the field.

"Good! Good! Just wanted to come chit chat for a minute and see how you and the kiddos are doing."

She said in a voice that was three octaves too high. Her grin was more threatening than friendly, like a wild animal showing its teeth before launching an attack. I groaned. I knew this game as well as the curves of my own body, the shape of my hips, and my round Persian ass. My mom *invented* this game—the gorgeous on the outside, evil on the inside soccer mom who wielded blinding white veneers like a weapon. *Terrifying*.

I forced my face to stay neutral, "That's so nice of you to check in, Bethany. We're doing great. The girls are great."

"Great! That's great! Anyway, did you see my email on the socks? And are you going to sign up to help with the winter festival at the school? All of us will take a class to learn how to hand-carve sculptures from ice blocks for the decorations. You won't want to miss out. We're also raising money for this organization called Healthy Bellies Global to bring Kombucha to children in Uganda. You should sign up! I haven't seen your name on the register. We could use the help!" She crooned.

"Oh, wow." I had to bite my lip to stop myself from cackling. Ice sculpture classes? Kombucha? Is she fucking serious? What is with these disconnected sycophants thinking that they were going to save the world with *Kombucha*?

I coughed to hide a chuckle, "I'll check my emails when I get home and let you know what I have time for," I managed to say with some seriousness.

"Yes! Do!" Bethany said.

Then she leaned in a little closer and cleared her throat. Her shoulder nearly brushed mine as if we were girlfriends, buddies, gossiping at the park, laughing together like when we were kids.

"So I noticed that Olivia is being her little firecracker self!" She whispered, "She just has so much energy, doesn't she? You must have your hands full. But then again, I guess you're used to it. That kind of, uhm, character runs in the family, doesn't it?"

"Watch it." I bit out, staring into Bethany's dead eyes. What I really wanted to do was head-butt her right in her perfectly smooth botoxed face. I knew what she was getting at, knew what she alluded to. Bringing my mother and father into this? Too far.

Bethany's smile spread even wider, proud of herself, no doubt, that I'd reacted to the jab at my family.

"Anyway," she said, rising to her feet, "so glad everything is going well! Let's get together soon! Okay?"

I wanted her to choke. But she just smoothed her hands over her pants again and flashed her great big laser-blasted chicklets one final time before strutting away to rejoin her circle of petty hags.

"Have a good day!" I called after her, then feigning concern, "I hope that yeast infection clears up on its own! Keep me updated!"

She spun around, fists balled up at her side, and scowled before disappearing in line with her friends.

My sister, Jess, plopped down next to me, resting her head on my shoulder. She pushed her thick black-rimmed glasses up her nose and adjusted the tie on her blouse.

"Did you just get here?" I asked her.

"Uh-huh."

"How much did you see?"

"Enough. That bitch will never change."

I reached up to pat my sister's head.

"Did you hear her jab at Mom? The "fire runs in our family" shit?"

"I mean, she's not wrong. Our family is mixed, and passions run high–"

"–But you know that's not what she was talking about."

"I know. Gods, she's boring. Everything having to do with *that*, with mom and dad, is old news."

Victoria stopped running abruptly mid-field to wave enthusiastically and scream, "Hi, Aunt Jess!"

Jess waved back. Then cracked her knuckles. She rearranged herself to sit cross-legged, angled toward me.

"Steven leaves tonight, yeah? Wanna do something this weekend? Park? Lunch? Divorce lawyer?"

She waggled her eyebrows playfully.

"Ha-ha." I deadpanned.

"Okay," Jess sang. "Also, feel free to tell me to shush whenever," she went on, tracking Victoria and Olivia as they walked off the field to gather around each of their coaches. "But when was the last time you saw your friends? I know you're going to ignore me, but you should plan a night out, too. I can come over to watch the girls, or you can take them to mom's house for their monthly lesson in the delicate art of being judgemental as fuck. Think about it. Yeah?"

I rolled my shoulders. My instinct was to say no. My girls didn't need to spend time with my insane mother, and I didn't *need* a break. I loved my kids. However, the stiffness in my neck and the knot in my throat told another story. I heard my therapist's voice in my head: "Taking care of yourself is taking care of them."

"Okay. Yes. I will take you up on the offer and call Cruella to watch the girls. I'm not entirely against fun, sis. I'm just *busy*."

Jess nodded slowly to let me know she really empathized.

"Uh-huh. You're not just busy, you're also really anxious and maybe a little sad? You panic every time the girls aren't with you."

"Well, yeah, because mom's a little–"

"Uptight? Crazy? A cold frigid twat and possibly a murderer?" Jess shrugged. "Yeah, I've met her. But we turned out mostly fine and the girls will be fine, too. Maybe she killed Dad, but she'd never hurt *children*."

"Not helping. And Mom didn't kill Dad. Probably." I mumbled.

"Oh! And speaking of things that are not okay, how's our favorite decrepit dog, Rebecca?"

"Rebecca is good! The real dog is a thousand years old, and I'm pretty sure my paintings house her soul to keep her alive. Her bark is like a death rattle. The painting of Rebecca is not finished, but it's the size of a palace and almost done."

Jess grinned, bumping her side against me playfully, and I pulled her into a hug before reluctantly letting her go. Most of the siblings I knew were polite at best and mortal enemies at worst, but Jess and I had always been best friends despite being undeniable opposites. Where I sought stability, she almost seemed terrified of it. Where I people pleased and tried to keep the peace like every oldest daughter, she seemed happiest when being a contrarian little bitch. Different as we were, she was my best friend, my ride-or-die, the person who understood me best in the world. You'd think our parents would have been excited to have two kids who loved each other, but it was almost like it worried them. Did they think we'd gang up? Stage a coup? Unclear.

I remember once after school, Jess and I were standing around the kitchen in our dumb navy blue uniforms, talking amongst ourselves while our mom cooked rice and Gheymeh, a Persian stew with lentils my father loved. Mom was English through and through, like tea and crumpets in the afternoon every day kind of English, and she hated to cook for the most part, but she'd learned to make Persian food for our dad, and she was pretty good at it, too. It was the only type of food that either of our parents cooked themselves, letting Nancy, their chef, do everything else. On this particular day, Mother wore an oversized black apron over her light blue pantsuit that swayed as she hummed along to Mozart or something. We'd just come home from school and were still wearing our blue Catholic school uniforms–they'd chosen the school for its rigorous academics, not religious teachings, because our family leaned more Zoroastrian-ish than anything else–in our beliefs and in our holiday celebrations. Mom was Catholic, but a shitty one who hadn't been to church in decades and honestly might catch fire if she crossed the threshold of one.

Jess and I were standing at the counter while Mom cooked, chewing on dates stuffed with feta cheese, when Jess cracked a joke about Bethany. We both erupted in laughter, and our mother whipped her head towards us, spatula raised instinctually in the air like a sword. Then she launched into a lengthy lecture about how we needed to take our lives more seriously because life was not supposed to be "fun," and one day, the world would be in our hands (kind of intense way to think about a career or whatever) and how if we didn't stop we'd end up dead with our La-Di-Dah attitudes. The "joking to crack" pipeline was real in our home. Jess, of course, retorted with some smartass remark that got us sent to our rooms. Whenever

Jess and I joke around, I often think of my mom's strong reaction to joy.

Liv and Ria finished with their coaches and walked towards us, taking slow, tired steps. Their rosy faces glistened with sweat despite the overcast and the cool fall breeze.

I turned to my sister,

"Do you ever wonder if mom was always cold and weird? Or did motherhood and marriage do that to her?"

"What could possibly go wrong when a narcy workaholic marries a robot?" Jess joked. Then she leaned closer until our shoulders touched and whispered, barely audible, "And you're not Mom."

I blew out a raspberry to lighten the mood. Jess picked up a single blade of yellowing grass and twirled it in her fingers before flicking it at me with a devilish grin. Ripping up a handful of turf, I sent it flying at her, curling blades floating over her like a veil before settling across Jess's short hair and shoulders. Liv and Ria laughed and sprinted the rest of the way to join in, squealing and running in circles around us.

Bethany glowered as she passed by with her family. I'd arranged my face in a fake smile. "Dude!" I hissed when Jess flipped her off, grabbing her hand and pushing it down. "There are children."

"Children who need to learn how to handle bullies."

"What, no!"

"Come on! You know you wanted to do it, too."

I tried not to smile, but it was useless. Before I knew it, we were laughing. Once we calmed down, Jess hopped to her feet and shook the lawn off of her blouse and out of her thick curls. She reached out to help me up. The girls were running after each other, heading toward the parking lot. We walked after them, watching Bethany's white SUV back out and lurch forward. "That bitch is totally going to make your life hell for eternity, you know?" Jess said, gesturing to it.

No truer words had ever been spoken.

A GOD OF SHADOWS

I floated on the porch swing; my neck craned to take in the other-worldly glow of the crescent moon after another long evening laboring over the painting of Rebecca. I tugged on the knit blanket around my shoulders to keep the cold out. It was almost Halloween, and snow had already capped the mountains. A saner person might go inside when it's cold as hell, but I lived for this weather, for the cold mornings, the beautiful colors in the mountains that seemed to flicker like a hearth, the burnt orange, vibrant reds, and mustard yellow for miles and miles.

I held a lit cigarette up in front of my face and mumbled to no one, "You need to stop this." I waved the cigarette in the air, the smoke rising and swirling from the ember, "And stop talking to yourself. You look fucking nuts." And I did. My fingertips and knuckles were paint-stained. My fingernails were dyed a deep ghoul green. Frowning, I took in how the colors had settled into the lines in my palm, like irrigation canals in arid farmland.

I was so focused on the painted lines of my flesh and the fact that if I stared long enough, they blurred, revealing images of trees, that I didn't notice the shadowed figure at my front gate watching through the cast iron bars.

"Excuse me?"

An accented male voice called out from the darkness, startling me half to death. I screeched and lept in the air, sending my cigarette flying where it landed on the opposite side of the porch and rolled.

"Jesus, fuck! Fuck!"

Diving to the ground, I scrambled after my cigarette before it started a fire and burned down the whole goddamn neighborhood. Fall or not, with the drought, it could easily turn the entire suburb to ash, and all that would be left to remember us by would be melted big-screen TVs and the remnants of power tools that nobody ever actually used. I snatched the still-glowing cigarette up and raised myself onto my knees, shoving my long dark hair out of my eyes to scan the perimeter for the man attached to the voice. The street looked empty but just beyond my yard, yes, there, next to the gate, the hint of a tall figure. Whoever it was took a step back away from the shadows of an old pine and into the moonlight, illuminating short, nearly black hair and a strong jawline. I knew if I looked closer, I'd see dark blue eyes. A classically beautiful face. *Him*. My heart stilled, then began to pound like a steady drum. Then I remembered that he had asked me something.

"Sorry?" I called out, slowly climbing to my feet. Though my belly fluttered with a thousand phantom wings, I sauntered over to the top of the stairs, pushing my chin up and rolling my shoulders back. Why was I posing? I relaxed.

"Is there something I can do for you?" I asked calmly as if I hadn't just scuttled around the porch on my hands and knees.

"I didn't mean to startle you." He said, in what I now recognized as a posh British accent that possibly placed him somewhere in southeast London, where my mother's side of the family was from.

"Are you sure?" I asked, crossing my arms and raising one eyebrow skeptically, "you did just pop up at my gate out of thin air in the middle of the night. Honestly, who does that? Scary people, that's who."

He let out a low chuckle, revealing perfect, bright white teeth. I gave him a crooked smile in spite of myself.

He bowed his head, "You're right. I apologize. I was just wondering if it might not be too much of a bother could I possibly have one of those?" He said, pointing through the iron bars.

"This?" I held my cigarette in the air.

"Yes, that."

"Yeah, sure."

I turned to the swing and pulled the pack out from my hiding spot under the cushion, then sauntered down the porch steps and tiptoed along the cold stone path that led to the gate where he stood. I tried to hide my surprise when I reached him, but shit, he was even more beautiful up close. Eyes like two radiant sapphire gems that seemed to shine, skin smooth as a brand new canvas, stippled with five o'clock shadow, and dark hair that looked like hands had recently been tangled in it. No, like hands were *regularly* tangled in it. I couldn't help imagining my own hands, dirty with paint-stained fingernails, gently pulling at it, too. My cheeks warmed, and I realized that I was fully staring at him and, for possibly the first time in my life, utterly speechless. He must have realized it, too. The smug bastard grinned at me. I angled my head and narrowed my eyes at him as if to say, "oh shut up," because I refused to be ruffled by his ethereal beauty and honed swag. The pressure of the cement pavers under my heels was an excellent momentary distraction.

"Here ya go."

I extended the cigarette to him through the bars of the iron gate. He gracefully lifted it out of my fingers barely grazing the tip of my thumb and I could have sworn that I felt a literal spark there, like when you walk across a carpet then touch something metal. He placed the cigarette between his full mauve lips, and I couldn't help but stare at them and wonder what they might taste like. He smiled and looked at me expectantly.

"Oh, shit, the lighter!" I chuckled, then shook my head, freeing a few waves from the clip that kept part of my hair pulled back. "Follow me!" I said over my shoulder as I turned on my heel towards my house, then paused, remembering the lighter was in my pocket, and turned back. "Oh! Nevermind! I have it here."

I located the lighter in my cardigan pocket. He grinned again when I handed it to him, his fingers intentionally grazing mine this time. I inhaled sharply and pulled my hand back, which only seemed to amuse him. He cocked his head to the side, the cigarette still between his lips, and his lashes dipped as he swept his eyes over me from toe to top, not even trying to be sneaky about it. No, he wanted me to see, to know that he was looking me over, part appreciation, part predatory, and would have been incredibly gross if I weren't doing everything in my power to stop myself from looking at him the same way. The urges I felt towards this man were surprising; it had been years since I'd felt anything so carnal for another human.

"Thank you." He said, exhaling a swirl of smoke into the chilly night air.

"So," I cleared my throat, "where are you coming from or heading to? I must have been completely spaced out because I didn't even hear you coming or, you know, you just materialized here like a ghost."

He chuckled.

"I was just walking down the sidewalk here on my way back home. But I have a knack for being quiet, I suppose. And yes, I picked up on your subtle way of indirectly calling me creepy twice now."

"Oh, did you?" I asked, feigning innocence, "Well, I'm home alone a lot, and it makes me a little anxious…" I trailed off. *What the fuck are you doing? Why did you tell him that?* "And I should not be telling strange men in the middle of the night that I'm always here by myself."

His eyes went to the house behind me.

"Are you a murderer?" I asked.

His eyes snapped back to mine and he raised his eyebrows, lips twitching in amusement. Then he broke eye contact to glance down the sidewalk into the darkness.

"No, not currently." He said with no hint of sarcasm.

It sent a literal shiver down my spine the way he stared off into the distance as though he were thinking of something far away, something in the past. His eyes slid back to mine, and his lip tugged up at the corner,

"You are aware that killers aren't required to disclose themselves to you just because you asked, right? There's no code of ethics that dictates if you guess someone is a maniac, they have to just come clean about it."

I held his gaze, refusing to be the first to look away.

"Anyway," He continued after a moment, "I definitely don't plan on coming back here to kill you. I just moved in down the street, and I've been taking walks around to get acquainted with the neighborhood. Sometimes I stroll to the restaurants or bars there." He gestured down the street with this hand that held the cigarette, one he hadn't taken a drag from since he lit it.

"Yeah, I've seen you walk by with the wom–".

I stopped mid-sentence.

"Ah, now, who's the creepy one?" He clicked his tongue against his teeth. "You do seem to be out here quite a bit."

He said, looking toward the porch. "I see you, too, you know, watching me from the shadows there."

My heart started to pound in my chest, and I could feel my cheeks heat. Suddenly, the trees, the grass, and the fence were all fascinating. I tried not to think about it, but my mind went straight to the other night when I'd seen him and thought about him while I lay in bed, hand between my thighs.

"Uhm, yeah," I stammered, "I hide out here to have a glass of wine and an occasional shameful cigarette after I put my kids to bed and finish work. It's quiet."

Changing the subject, I ticked up my chin towards his hand, "Also, I noticed you're not smoking that."

He glanced down at the half-burned cigarette between his fingers.

"That's because I don't smoke." He said, smirking.

I narrowed my eyes. "Then why did you—"

"You're a mother?" He smiled sweetly, "That's interesting. And unexpected."

What the hell did that mean? Unexpected? What exactly had he been expecting? And how could someone go through life with his face? It was almost hard to concentrate because he was so hot, and that smirk, with that fucking smirk, he knew it. He absolutely knew it.

I would not give him the satisfaction of being a simpering idiot.

"Is it interesting?" I asked flatly.

"Yes. It is. I wouldn't have guessed that you're a mother."

"Why? What does a mother usually look like?"

I crossed my arms over my chest.

"Fair question. I am putting everyone into a rather large box. I simply mean that you have a sort of fire about you, something I can't quite put my finger on, something different."

"It's strange that I have a fire about me because most mothers are dead inside?" I asked, feeling suddenly defensive. A warrior out to protect all mothers.

He barked a laugh and angled his head as if to say, yeah, good point.

"Of course not. But the world expects a lot from mothers, don't you agree? And carrying the weight of the world can have side effects in terms of one's spirit."

"Ah," I said, nodding. My lips barely twitched up at the corners, "so not completely dead inside, just barely alive and dragging around a guttered soul. Like the flickering flame of a candle. I would argue that the hardest part of being a mother is not carrying the weight of the world, as you put it, but rather being burdened with the expectations of society and the invisible shackles of those expectations."

He let out a low laugh and looked up to the sky, then back to me. We searched each other's faces for a moment, and I observed that the whites of his eyes seemed brighter than normal, and the tiny red veins stood out a bit more, too. Kinda weird. I also noted that the silence felt oddly comfortable like we could just stand there for hours looking at each other in some non-awkward standoff.

I shifted my weight onto my freezing toes, rising up, then back down, noticing that even at my highest point, he was inches taller than me. A shiver swept over me as an icy autumn wind cut through my lounge pants and sweater.

He tossed the cigarette. Then slid his hands into his pockets.

"I just realized how incredibly rude I'm being. I'm out here bumming fags and insulting you and all mothers everywhere, and I haven't even introduced myself. My name is Andras, by the way. And you are?"

"Danny. Er, Danielle." I stammered, "I go by Danny."

"Nice to meet you, Danny." He said, looking at me like he was assessing something, "I should be off, but I'm sure I'll see you around." He looked just past me towards my house. Then his eyes slid back to me, my mouth and neck. My blood pumped harder, heating every single part of me. He inclined his head before he backed away and prowled into the shadows. I lingered until the scent of him, something warm and woodsy, dissipated in the air, then tip-toed back towards my house, my head swirling with excitement. Excitement. Something I had not experienced for myself in a very long time.

As I reached my doorstep, I paused and had the unmistakable feeling that I was being watched. There was nothing in the street and the darkness beyond. Still, I moved inside quickly and bolted the door shut.

SAVE THE LAST DANCE

My daughters lay prone on the sofa in a food coma brought on by Taco Night, their little faces glued to the cracked iPad–from tantrum number 9,456–watching a video. An arm's length away, I sprawled across my favorite armchair, comforted by the scent of old leather. The cushions were worn, so soft I sunk deep into them, where I sketched a craftsman house blurred by rainfall. The cooler weather always brought out a certain part of me, the part wrapped in melancholy and drawn to darkness.

It's a little morbid if you think about it, the way we become positively joyous and drawn to all things cozy–warm sweaters and hot coffee–the moment the natural world begins to die. A coping mechanism? Dead leaves fall from dead trees while the air turns cold as a corpse so bring on the cute beanies and pumpkin spice.

Victoria whispered, "Pretty" to herself. Then gasped, "Mamma! Is that you and daddy!"

She craned her neck to look at me, mouth agape, corners turned up like Jack O' Lantern. I gently set down my sketchbook and leant over to see what she'd found.

"Ah," I said, "That's the video from mommy and daddy's wedding." The right side of my mouth curled up at the memory of our small wedding at my parent's estate, the toasts that had been given that night through slurred speeches and tears, some more embarrassing than others.

This video was of our first dance together as husband and wife. Our closest friends crowded the dance floor, swaying and hopping. We melted into each other's arms as we swayed back and forth to the piano music, my head on his shoulder, eyes closed, and a content smile on his face as he looked down at me, his new wife. We were so young and full of fire and booze, and the skirt of my airy mesh gown slid across the floor like a goddamn dream.

I'd put off buying a dress for some reason, and just weeks before the wedding, I stumbled across a tiny bridal shop in downtown Denver and fell in love with the off-shoulder ivory dress with its delicate eyelash lace that peaked out from the bodice. I bought it right then and there without even bothering to send a pic to my sister like I normally do when I shop alone. It fit perfectly around my small breasts and waist and spilled to the floor in airy mesh layers that made me feel beautiful and powerful like I could twirl on a throne right before leading a legion into battle on horseback–it's a feeling that's kinda hard to explain. Unless you were raised by a father who waxed poetic about the female soldiers of ancient Persia while expecting you to "be ladylike."

On the day of the wedding, Jess gasped when I stepped out of the dressing room in the bridal suite. Her green eyes, like mine, like our father's, were glassy when she hugged me. My mother did her best not to combust. It wasn't designer and didn't have a train the length of a school bus, so she wasn't over-the-moon, but aside from a "is that what people are wearing these days?" She stayed quiet. At the ceremony, I felt joyful despite the small tug in my body that told me something was wrong. I loved Steven. Yet there was a noticeable sliver of doubt, a voice that whispered, "he isn't the one" in the far recesses of my mind as I made my way down the aisle and into his arms. The voice rose from a whisper to a chant of, "no, no, no!" that bellowed in my head as we read our vows. But Steven looked so handsome in his black suit, standing before me with his hands clasped together. A reassuring and kind smile met the flicker of doubt in my eyes, and I wondered why my brain was trying to ruin the moment for us. I told myself to stop. Just stop. *You're just afraid of being happy.* Turns out what I'd mistaken for anxiety was my brilliant intuition waving a giant red flag to save me from myself. How is one supposed to know? I just assumed I was freaking out due to my general distrust of marriage caused by years of watching my parents in their odd union (up until my mother possibly unalived my father). At least, that's what the police implied, but honestly, it could have been anyone. Dad was a weirdly private man, always off tying up secret business deals with the Gods knew who. My mother was a lot of things, but a murderer? Honestly? I wouldn't be that shocked.

A loud thud in the hallway jolted me upright in my chair.

"Steven? Is that you?" I called out.

Silence. I leaned down and kissed the girls on the cheeks–both of them still utterly engrossed in our first dance. "Stay here. I'll be right back." They hardly noticed as I skulked up the stairs into the hallway to peer into the darkness. Empty. Nothing and nobody lurked in the shadows. But I couldn't shake the feeling that something was wrong. I turned on the light, but nothing, no sign of humans or monsters, no footsteps, no force coming to destroy my family. I checked the bedroom. Nothing. *Where is Steven? It's like he's reached a new level of absence where he's now haunting the house instead of living in it.* I went back to the girls and plopped down next to them just in time for the camera to zoom in on my mother's scowl. I shook my head at those eyebrows knit together, that down-turned mouth, and the general air of discontent that seemed to waft off her. My mother had spent most of that night gripping her pearls and looking like she was at a funeral. "You're making a mistake," she'd crooned a thousand times leading up to the wedding, and I hated that she might have been right, that maybe she knew something that I didn't.

Olivia shouted, "Grandma!" And enthusiastically pointed at the screen.

"Why are you watching this?" Steven asked.

"Shit! Fuck!" I screamed. I held my chest, "Jesus! You scared the shit out of me. Have you been here the whole time? Where were you?"

He looked around defensively like he'd been accused of pissing in the ice dispenser, "I was in the bathroom. Showering. Packing to leave."

"Oh. The girls found our wedding video while looking at pictures of themselves on the iPad. I forgot that we danced to a piano version of Fleetwood Mac at the reception."

"Oh, that's right." He said flatly, his face unreadable and cold. He pushed off of the door frame. "Anyway, I'll finish packing and then take a car service to the airport. I should be back in two weeks, three at the most. Let me know if you need anything."

I nodded absently. He had stalked towards the stairs and started to climb them two at a time when I jumped to my feet and followed him to the bedroom. He already had his overnight bag slung over his shoulder and was reaching for his black suitcase when I got there.

"Hey," I said gently like I was speaking to an unknown wild dog. "So before you go," I paused to consider my wording. Have you given couples therapy any more thought?" He raised his eyebrows slightly, then pulled his luggage to his side, setting his overnight bag on his suitcase and securing its strap around the handle.

"Steven?" I pressed, clasping my hands together to stop myself from fidgeting.

Steven pulled his phone out from his pants pocket to check the time and slid it back in place. He huffed and looked down at me, absently, as if he were bored.

"We don't need couples therapy. You're the one who has a problem."

Suddenly, I felt hot. My tethered rage snapped. "I have a problem," I ground out, wrapping my words in fury and thorns and broken glass, "with how you treat me." My eyes met his and held.

Steven looked away, pulled his bags past me as if I weren't even there, and headed down the hallway. I followed him, my hands balling into fists.

"I have to go." He said as he hoisted his bags up with some effort and ambled down the staircase. I could have offered to help, but then again, a horrible part of me hoped he would trip and fall. The stairs were carpeted. He wouldn't be seriously maimed or die.

"Steven," I whispered from the top of the stairs, "we need to talk about separating. I can't go on like this for—"

"—Fine. Jesus Christ, Danny. Make the appointment for after I get back and I'll find a way to make time for it."

Well, don't do me any favors, I thought.

A voice in my head tried to warn me. *If he wanted to do the work, he would. Push for a separation, do what has to be done.* But then hope crept in, kicking my intuition to the curb.

He reached the living room and put his bags down to bid farewell to the girls. I leaned against the doorframe to watch, to breathe, to let all of the emotions wash over me.

"Kiddos! Give me a hug! I'll Facetime you when I land! Okay?" Steven called over to the girls who were still watching wedding videos.

"Okay, Daddy!" Victoria and Olivia leaped to their feet and bounced towards Steven. Olivia headbutted him in the balls on accident, and after he howled, swore, and recovered, he scooped them both up in his arms and gave them a big hug, then kissed their cheeks all over. He sat the girls down and nodded to me, "Have a good week," he said, like he absolutely did not want me to have a good week at all.

The front door opened and closed. I felt relieved he'd gone and I wouldn't have to tip-toe around his moods for the next few weeks. I felt confused that I wanted to be loved by a man who clearly could not love me in the way I needed to be loved. I felt stuck, out of control, and always anxious. There were two choices and both were shit: Trust the devil I knew or the one I didn't.

An hour later, with my daughters fast asleep, I unceremoniously readied for movie night with my sister. I threw blankets and pillows on the floor in front of the television to make a giant nest because I wanted to hunker down in it and die. I turned on the fireplace and set out the blood-red cocktails and small bowls of popcorn, candy, and fruit. Then, I lay on the couch and wept.

By the time Jess arrived, I'd stopped crying, but my eyes were swollen and an amaranth shade of red. She looked me over, hugged me tightly, then pulled back and raised her brows in question. Do you want to talk about it, her expression asked. I shook my head and bit my lip to stop myself from breaking down and bawling again. "Okay," she mouthed silently. She took my hand and gently led me to the pile of blankets. We lowered ourselves down, pulling a white comforter over the top of us, fluffing the pillows around us to form a cozy spot, and bringing the snack bowls a little closer. Jess fumbled for the remote while I let myself sink into the warmth of the blankets, into the calm, supportive energy of my sister, where I could just breathe. The music started and we both grinned at each other.

Every month, for decades, this had been our thing. We watched the same vampire movies over, and over, and over again. We'd catch up on life between reciting the dialogue from memory. Ever since we were kids, we'd bonded over our love of fantasy books, Faeries, elves, and quests. As teens, we were obsessed with any YA vampire series in book or movie form. Even when we were fighting, full of hormones and rage, we never skipped our night. We'd sit six feet apart in silence, but we never skipped it.

"Look, Detective Lennox, Jerry Dandridge is a vampire!" Jess and I said together in sync. We howled and rolled around on the blankets. I reached for a handful of popcorn and shoved most of it in my mouth. *Did I forget to eat today?* Jess had a candy bar in one hand and a ruby drink in the other. She took a sip of the cocktail and a bite of the candy bar and smiled.

"What is this again?" she asked. She gargled, the weird mixture of candy and liquor swirling in her mouth. I scowled, "That's so gross." She shrugged one shoulder, held her glass up to the fireplace light, and examined it.

"Blood-red oranges, ice, vodka, pomegranate, and I think that's it," I answered. I uncurled my legs, stretching them out in front of me, then dangling the left one over my sister's right.

"Delicious." she complimented, then tipped the glass to her mouth to finish her drink in one greedy gulp, the ice slamming into her teeth, ruby liquid oozing down her chin. Jess held in a laugh, set the glass down gently, and patted at her chin with the back of her hand.

Reaching for a napkin to hand to Jess, I said, "I can't believe that nobody will listen to Brewster. The only kind of person who could look that hot in an eighties man-blowout is a vampire. That's a scientific fact." I handed the napkin to Jess without looking away from the television. She wiped her face and went right back to devouring her candy bar.

"Would you believe someone if they told you that their neighbor was a vampire?" I wondered. On screen, a teenage boy and his sweet-faced girlfriend frantically ran in the street.

"Yes." Jess said, matter of fact, her mouth full of chocolate.

"You're the most skeptical person I know."

"Yes. But still, yes."

"I don't know what I'd think, honestly."

In unison, we recited in a low growl, "You have to have faith for this to work, Peter Vincent!" Jess pretended to hold a crucifix in the air. I couldn't help but to beam at my sister. I fucking loved her.

Jess grimaced, "Not a fan of his goblin face, though."

"Yeah, kinda gross." I agreed. "But that dance scene, damn, it almost brings me to orgasm. I remember in Junior High when we watched this for the first time, and I fell in love with him. I was the only teenage girl who was scanning middle school the next day for a hottie in a cable sweater. And this is why girls are so into douchebags."

"And women. Women are just as bad in movies. All the hot ones are evil, pick me's, or vapid."

"Yeah, I can see that." I stretched, "I'll be right back. Going to grab a refill." I shook the ice around the empty glass and got to my feet. Jess shoved her empty glass at me without pulling her eyes away from the movie. I took her glass, then padded into the kitchen. It took less than two minutes alone before the silence had my head spinning with rage and disappointment again. I got ice from the freezer absentmindedly, my sadness pressing in all around me like a cage. Inhale. *I can't breathe*. Exhale. *I can't breathe*. I reached for the decanter of blood-red cocktail mix and filled the glasses slowly with an unsteady hand, staring at the ice and how the ruby juice traveled across it. The floor felt like it was sliding under my feet. *This is just anxiety. This is just anxiety.* I pressed both of my palms into the counter, focusing on the cold marble, on the smooth steadiness of it.

Then the hair on my neck stood up, the muscles in my back tense and hard, as if the emotional frustration had materialized in my body and invoked a sense of dread. I felt scared. Like something sinister watched me through the window. I spun to look, but there was nothing, just darkness and the subtle reflection of me, face pinched and tired. Stress and exhaustion marked my posture, shoulders curved inward like I subconsciously wanted to hide from myself. I didn't recognize this version of me.

Pacing, I shook out my hands and tried to understand myself. Steven had agreed to therapy. Begrudgingly, but he'd agreed, and that was good, right? So why then was I so hurt? A voice in the back of my mind quipped, "Because you shouldn't have to beg and damn him for making you." I knew that he wouldn't change and that we were done but I just didn't want to accept it. We couldn't spend a few more decades in emptiness together. And if I was being honest, I didn't even know if I loved him anymore. Still, the thought of him moving out, of the girls feeling devastated, of co-parenting...oh Gods. I wanted to strangle him.

I had loved him once. I'd fallen for him in college after I'd wholly shattered from years of grief and the horror of my father's passing, during a time when I needed to feel stable, safe, and cared for and Steven had been all of those things. He was kind and, well, predictable to the point of being utterly boring. Our life together wasn't exciting at all, but the monotony meant no traumatic surprises either, and I loved it. Then, I got pregnant, and the moment my attention shifted away from him to our child, he changed. He became critical, distant, cruel, and angry. Once I started therapy, the more I healed, the less I was willing to give and the less I was willing to take. And the divide only grew. I didn't need to be taken care of anymore, I needed to be seen and heard, proof that I existed, and mattered.

I took in one last deep breath and promised myself in a whisper, "This is it. If therapy doesn't work, I file for divorce. I will let go. I will be okay." Then I grabbed our drinks and returned to my sister.

Little did I know that Steven was about to be the least of my worries.

WHAT DON'T YOU TRUST ABOUT THAT?

My eyes burned as they focused on the white linen curtains that framed the floor-to-ceiling windows of my bedroom. The aggressive Colorado sunshine–sunny for 300 days per year!–tinted them a pretty golden-white that energized the room, even at five a.m. Pigeons cooed outside and spackled my driveway with their trash bird scat. *Did I get any sleep at all?* I'd been up half the night grieving my marriage in between thinking about Andras, going over our conversation the day before in my head, and dreaming about him. I'd had so many vivid dreams of us naked, entangled in each other, that I kept waking confused that he wasn't actually there. I reached for my phone to check the time, yep, five a.m. and saw an email from the PTA.

"Ugh," Timestamp, three a.m. "Seriously?" I said, groaning. "Are you doing meth, Bethany?" I mumbled into the phone screen before begrudgingly scanning the email.

"Hello, parents! We love our community here, and who is responsible for this warm and wonderful community? Our teachers, of course! We'd love to show them just how much we appreciate them, so choose a gift! Thanks so much!"

The next email was a confirmation for the couple's therapy appointment I'd made with a woman my personal therapist had recommended. I added it to the digital family calendar, Steven's work calendar, and our acrylic wall calendar in the kitchen. Steven would be back soon, then two days later, we'd have the appointment, and hopefully, hopefully, we'd get things figured out, whatever that might look like. Maybe I'd magically get the strength to leave; maybe he'd magically see that he was hurting me and stop. Maybe he'd just disappear and save me the heartache of asking him to pack his shit up and go. I was a coward and fuck if I didn't know it.

I stuffed the phone under a pillow and groaned into the white sheets, then rolled to my back and stretched, feeling the soft cotton against my shoulders and legs, and took a slow, deep breath, concentrating on the sensation of my chest expanding towards the ceiling like I do every morning, or at least try to. I exhaled and noted the sensation of my lungs deflating towards my spine. I'd learned how to meditate from an app to help manage my stress and keep the depression away, too. And it worked, coupled with therapy, bullet journaling, mindfulness apps, yoga, time to myself after the kids go to bed, smoothies, screaming into the void, regular masturbation (if I can get the alone time), and as-needed anxiety medication. Deep breathing also made me significantly less stabby towards Steven. And while slow breaths wouldn't save my marriage, it seemed to hold me together while I ambled towards divorce or a mental collapse.

A low creak sounded down the hall, a door yawning ajar. *Any moment now.* I braced for the ambush. I wiggled my toes and fingers and tried to hold on to the quiet stillness of my bed, these few moments that were mine, unencumbered by Olivia's tiny bladder and her need to pee two thousand times per day or Victoria's spirited refusal to eat white foods. Any minute. Then I heard it, stomping down the hall, a light scratch at my bedroom door, and the screaming creak of the stubborn old hinges as the door was thrown open. A thud as the knob bumped into the dimpled wall. Olivia stood in the doorway in her blue shark pajamas, grinning with Beatrice, the stuffed Narwhal dangling upside down in her left hand.

"Mamma? Hello?" Olivia called out, her big green eyes dancing at the sight of me. And Gods, I loved the way the girls lit up when they saw me. Olivia launched Beatrice onto the bed, then seized the white comforter in her tiny hands, hauling herself up.

Another set of footsteps with a wider gait approached. "Moooom! Wake up." Victoria whined as she entered the room and effortlessly climbed onto the bed, flopping down next to me and immediately burrowing her face into my neck just like she did when she was a baby.

Victoria had always been my nuzzler, smashing her face into my skin as if she were trying to get herself absorbed back into the womb. Olivia, on the other hand, I was lucky if I got one hug every couple of days most of the time.

"What should we do today, my little Jelly Beans?" I asked.

I stretched the blanket over us like a fort. Olivia clapped, giggled, then reached up to touch the blanket above her. Victoria tried to smooth her wild hair back, pushing rogue strands off her forehead.

"We have all morning and afternoon before you go to your grandma's house, remember?" I asked. The girls nodded as they remembered. I looked at their little faces. They adored their grandma, even though Jess and I could barely stand the woman who had birthed us. It's not that we didn't love her. It's just that we realized a long time ago that life was a lot easier when her impossible standards were kept at a digestible distance.

"Let's make pancakes!" She said, "Pancakes!"

"Okay, sounds good," I agreed, letting go of the comforter that floated down over all of us.

Victoria laughed, trapped under the blanket, and threw it back, bathing the three of us in clouded sunlight. I winced and reached up to my wild hair to untangle Olivia's hands from my twisted waves.

"So we'll make pancakes," I said, finally freeing Olivia's fingers from my head, "And then?"

"PARK!" Victoria yelled, bouncing.

"Okay, okay, go grab your aprons, and I'll be right out," I said, pulling my daughters in for a hug, squishing their soft round cheeks into mine. The girls wiggled out of my embrace and flopped and bounced to the edge of the bed, shrieking with laughter.

Olivia and Victoria slid off the bed and ran out of the room, screeching, their hard little feet pounding into the old floors, thumping and creaking their way toward the kitchen.

Seventy-thousand hours later, all hell had broken loose. The quartz countertops of the kitchen island dripped with pancake batter and maple syrup, and I leaned against them with a half-empty cup of coffee in my hand, trying to rally some calm into my body. Olivia flailed on the ground, screaming at the top of her lungs, mouth agape, eyes squeezed shut, legs kicking every which way. Victoria sat at the island counter, silently eating a pancake as if her sister wasn't losing her shit a few feet away.

"I wanted to pour it myself!" Olivia shouted. "Why did Victoria do it?" She sobbed. Then she got to her feet, charged Victoria's legs, and missed.

"Don't do that." I said firmly, trying to remember what I'm "supposed" to do when my youngest turns into a homicidal football player. Then it came to me. I set the coffee cup down on the counter while Olivia backed up to charge again, her face wet from crying, her hair sticky with maple syrup.

"I wanted to!" She yelled again.

Olivia barrelled towards her sister again, but I calmly dropped to my knees and blocked the attack with my arms. I gently held Olivia's arms down by her side and made eye contact.

"You're frustrated and mad because your sister poured your maple syrup. I feel mad sometimes, too. It's okay to be mad. I will not let you tackle your sister, though."

Olivia continued the tantrum for a minute, and then her arms relaxed as she backed away from me, still crying. She turned on her heel, scanning the room for something to destroy, spotted something and went for it. Before I could catch her, Olivia knocked a stack of papers from the counter on the way to the stairs and headed toward her bedroom. White stationery floated to the floor like leaves on the wind scattered across the hardwood.

I swallowed hard and tried to remind myself that I loved my children.

"Nothing in the damn books about what to do when they do that," I grumbled as I dragged myself towards the papers on the ground, dropping to my knees to gather them up.

"Liv is so rude," Victoria said flatly.

"Ria, we're all learning." I reminded her.

I crawled around collecting papers.

Was that the right thing to say? I wondered, searching my brain for an article or book or social media post about how to talk to your older kid about being a shamey asshole. While I reflected on this, the sound of spilled liquid came from somewhere nearby. I sat up on my heels like a meerkat, scanning the kitchen for the culprit. Ria stared at the counter as a river of orange juice flowed across the quartz and onto the floor. "Sorry, mom!" Victoria said, "it was an accident! I'll clean it up!" Then I heard splashing and Olivia growling, "puddle!" When had she snuck back in here?

"Mom! Olivia is jumping in the orange juice!" Victoria growled.

"Olivia, I want you to stop that," I commanded, my voice low and slowly turning hostile.

Olivia took off running, a trail of sticky orange juice footprints behind her.

"Shit!" I cursed.

"Mom! You said a bad word!" Victoria accused.

"Jesus Christ, Ria, I know. Can you just give me a minute?" I snapped and felt guilt barrel into me immediately.

Ria's eyes met the countertop, and her bottom lip quivered. She began to cry softly.

"You're being mean to me," Victoria whispered.

Shame washed over me in nausea-inducing waves. I had to remind myself that everyone makes mistakes. It's fine. The rage I felt daily continued to surprise me, even years into my parenting journey. And I knew that a big part of it was because I didn't have support which made me that much more angry toward Steven.

I had expected to feel tired, have long days, struggle, but nothing could have prepared me for the white-hot rage that felt like I might set fire to the world. I counted in my head, 5,4,3,2,1.

Then got to my feet. I set the paper stack on the counter and slid onto the stool next to Ria.

"Ria? I'm sorry I yelled. I felt frustrated and let my emotions get the better of me. I'll manage my feelings better next time. Okay?"

I offered her a hug. She accepted, and while my arms were wrapped tightly around her, I kissed her head and held her a moment. We finished breakfast on the porch. It was early and chilly, but I had to get out of the house. I sipped my coffee with too much cream and sugar, cupping it like a precious goblet, while the girls made fart noises at each other and told the same "knock-knock" joke a hundred times. They slowly migrated from the table to the floor, from shoes to bare feet, and then from the steps to the cold, soggy grass to play tag. I watched and waited for the sensory overload I felt to dissipate. I wandered down from the porch, mug still in hand, to gather herbs from a narrow garden bed on the far side of the yard to dry. It was fall, and I wanted to have plenty dried before winter. Olivia and Victoria buzzed underfoot, fled to the opposite side of the yard, then disappeared around the back. I gathered some dill and gently placed it in a small pile on the edge of the planter. I smelled my fingers, inhaling the lemony, earthy scent. It reminded me of Bahgali rice, of lima beans, of my father cooking in the kitchen on a weekend night while Jess and I read in the tea room. I carefully tugged off a few stems of fennel and some rosemary, smelling my fingers between each of them.

"I love the smell of lemon balm." A man said in a low voice that reminded me of red wine, linen sheets, and late nights.

Andras smiled at me from the other side of the fence, hands in his pockets. Where was he going so early in the morning dressed in black trousers, a black wool sweater, and a long gray overcoat? Many men in Denver tried to pull off the "elegant man about town" look, but most of them missed the mark. Andras, well, he looked like the designer had made the clothes with him in mind. He was the perfect opposite of me in my loungewear speckled with pancake batter, and brown slipper boots. I wished I could run into this man just once when I looked, well, *better*.

"How long have you been standing there?" I asked.

I absentmindedly plucked a lemon balm leaf and handed it to Andras, who gingerly took it and brought it to his nose.

"Smells so lovely. Reminds me of tea." He said. "I used to drink some before bed to help me sleep a long time ago."

"I practically freebase it on nights when I'm anxious."

Andras laughed, low and throaty. He placed the leaf on his tongue, a simple act that he somehow made sensual, and swallowed.

"And how is it?" I asked.

"Doesn't mix well with the coffee I just drank. At Twilight–that new cafe down the street. Have you been? It's quite lovely."

I shook my head.

"Well, maybe at some point I'll see you there?" He smiled, "How are you?"

I tracked ducks flying south in the sky. The day was sunny but a little cold, and I appreciated the sun on my face. The herbs perfumed the air. I folded my arms across my chest and leaned back a little.

"Honestly? I don't know. Marriage is, well...and parenting is tough. It's like no matter how many books I read, no matter what I do, I feel like I'm constantly flailing. I just want to be a good mom and have them grow up to be okay, and sometimes that feels impossible."

Andras tilted his head as if he were confused. I assumed I'd freaked him out by oversharing.

I continued, "I'm aware that I just unloaded a lot, and I don't know you at all."

"Can I ask you a forward question?" He asked.

I nodded.

"Do you like your girls?"

I frowned and crossed my arms.

"Of course I love them. I'd die for them. I'm biologically wired to throw myself into traffic for them."

"Admirable. But I didn't ask if you love them. Of course, you love them, or you wouldn't be fretting over your parenting mistakes. What I asked is if you like them. Do you like who they are when they're not a bit of a challenge? Do you like their personalities? Their true character."

I focused on the stones around the garden beds while I pondered the question. My girls were funny and kind. Victoria always wanted to do her best and enjoyed rules and telling everyone else how to follow them. Olivia was strong-willed and focused. They both had brilliant imaginations, laughed loudly, and questioned endlessly.

I liked both of them immensely.

"I do."

"So," Andras searched my face for something, "What don't you trust about that?"

I blinked.

"I don't know," I said, barely above a whisper.

He smiled softly down at me. His head cocked to the side.

"Speaking of, I think your little ones are coming this way." He said.

Just then, my daughters came squealing around the side of the house, running straight into me, nearly knocking me off the planter box. I grunted, then wrapped my arms around them.

"Who is that, Mama?" Victoria asked, eyeing Andras. "I heard you talking to someone and came to see."

"This is our new neighbor," I said.

"Hi! I'm Olivia!" Liv offered up.

Andras smiled warmly at each of them. He extended his hand to shake Olivia's, "Very nice to make your acquaintance, Olivia. My name is Andras."

"Nice to meet you!" Olivia beamed and reached through the iron fence to shake his hand.

"And you are?" He asked Ria.

"I'm Victoria," she said suspiciously. It's nice to meet you, Andras." She kept her arms firmly at her side.

"So, your mother and I were just talking about plants." Liv and Ria looked between Andras and me. Andras continued, "Would you like to weigh in? Do either of you have a favorite plant? I'll go first, Lily of the Valley. Because it can thrive in even the harshest conditions."

Victoria's brow knitted together as she considered. Olivia hopped from one foot to the next, then yelled out, "Death Camus!"

Andras's eyes went wide with surprise, then he threw back his head and laughed deeply, "Death Camus! Why is that your favorite?"

"It's pretty, but you can't touch it because Mom said it will kill you. It's cool."

"Yeah, that's true," I added.

"Well, I think your knowledge of plants is very interesting. You're so young to know so much already." Andras said to Liv.

Victoria stepped forward, not willing to be overshadowed by her little sister, "Horehound. Because mom gives it to us when we're sick, and it makes us feel better."

Andras glanced from me to Victoria, "Wow, that's an excellent plant. Healing plants are very important, and again, I'm utterly impressed by how much you know. You're both brilliant, I can tell."

Victoria smiled and twirled. Andras glanced back at me, "And what about you? What's your favorite?"

I didn't have to think about it. I'd been obsessed with the same flower since childhood, the one they made perfume and rose water from. The one we saw over and over again in Persian paintings and tasted in Persian dishes growing up.

"The damask rose," I said, smiling. I gestured across the yard to a rosebush. "I had it imported from Iran. And honestly, it would have probably been easier to import a tiger. It's nearly impossible to find someone on this continent that sells it."

"Beautiful," Andras said, holding my gaze until I felt awkward and looked at my hands.

"Can we get a tiger?" Olivia asked, hopping from foot to foot faster now.

"No." I said.

Olivia pouted. Victoria turned to her sister, annoyed, and demanded to know where in the world we would keep a tiger. They were heading towards a fight. Gods help me. Andras slipped his phone out of his pocket and checked the screen.

"Well, it was so lovely meeting both of you." He said to the girls, "Have a lovely day, Miss Olivia and Miss Victoria." He bowed his head to each of them.

"It was very nice to see you, too, Danny."

I cleared my throat, "Uhm, yeah, you too."

Andras slid his hands back into his pockets, smiled warmly, and sketched a bow before casually strolling off.

NO BOOZE AT THE PLAYGROUND

I swung my car into a narrow parking spot at the park. "We're heeere," I sang to Liv and Ria as I tucked my hair behind my ear. Sliding out of my seat, I commanded my phone, "Call Jess." I adjusted my left earbud before pulling on my backpack, filled to the absolute top with snacks and water.

Free from her seatbelt, Victoria eased forward to the edge of the seat and then slowly turned to face the open door before setting her feet on the asphalt, standing in one smooth movement, careful not to fall. I rolled my eyes. My mother had clearly given my girls lessons on the "proper" way to exit a vehicle in a dress. Then Victoria wandered to the grass and stopped, waiting patiently for me to free her sister.

Jess's voice boomed in my earbud, "Yes?"

"Hey, I'm here," I said.

"I'm sitting at the north edge of the park."

"K," I said, and hung up.

Tracking my oldest daughter, I scanned the horizon for potential threats, because that's what you do, apparently, when you're both a mother and unbearably anxious. The playground was surrounded by massive trees with leaves of green, red, and gold, changing with the season. Olivia's face had turned red from her intense scowling and thrashing as she tried to rip her seatbelt off her chest. I leaned in to pick her up. " I CAN DO IT MYSELF!" Olivia screeched and kicked her legs until she wiggled free from her seat. She lurched forward, chocolate-colored curls bouncing on her forehead, then plopped onto the car floor. She stood slowly, extended her hand, and waited for me to help her. Olivia then dragged me toward her sister, who stood patiently watching the clouds from where I'd told her to stay.

"Let's go find Aunt Jess," Olivia said to her sister.

My girls turned to me for approval and when I nodded they sprinted towards the playground, laughing and yelling indecipherable words, Victoria in the lead, Olivia forcing her legs to go as fast as they could but still falling further behind. Jess sat on a bench near the sandbox, holding a can of something. Her head rested against the back of the bench with her face turned up towards the sky as if she were sleeping.

"Sorry, we're a little late," I said, plopping down next to my sister. I shed my backpack, letting it slide to the ground with a thud next to a disgusting blue-speckled mess of something wet and sticky.

Jess straightened up, then leaned over to kiss me on the cheek, her red lipstick no doubt leaving a mark. She flipped her chin-length hair to the side. "Oh, it's fine," Jess said, "I'm just sitting here being one of those incredibly off-putting people at a playground without kids. So far, I've been given the stink-eye by no less than four mothers. And a German Shepard."

Wrinkling up my nose, I said, "Yeah, I can't imagine why anyone would find it odd that you're draped on a bench at the playground in a half-sleeping position at noon with a can of," I reached over to spin the aluminum can around in my sister's hand, "beer, a can of beer."

"It's gone," Jess said, "and I am a childless graduate student in perpetuity, so once in a while, I get to day-drink."

"At a playground," I deadpanned.

"Sure. I mean, I'm not putting it into anyone's sippy cup. And I'm also not even remotely buzzed. Although I wish I were..."

Jess sat up tall, groaning as if just coming out of hibernation. She yawned, dragged herself to the recycling bin, tossed her beer can inside, and then paused to survey the place. Two men in their late twenties were shirtless just beyond the garbage cans, tying each end of a rope around two adjacent trees to attempt tightrope walking. They growled and flexed at each other casually. Everyone else at the park wore a jacket and participated in various park activities–dog walking, jogging, and frisbee-throwing.

Jess returned to the bench and plopped down next to me. Her eyes trained on her nieces throwing mulch at each other, her brows raised in mild concern. Then she extended her legs, which were a little shorter than mine, and crossed them at the ankle.

"So, how are you? The other night, you were upset."

She searched my face for a lie, for honesty, for any tiny sliver of emotion that might settle there. Those hazel eyes of hers were full of concern.

"Don't give me that look. That sad, pitiful look, like I'm a puppy that just got kicked or something," I said, leaning forward to pull my laces tighter on my right high top.

"Don't bring a puppy into this," Jess said. "You really are your mother's daughter, ya know."

She grinned.

"I resent that."

"Me too."

I crossed my legs at the knee and leaned back. Olivia and Victoria played Dinosaur tag. Their contagious guffaws tugged at the corners of my mouth.

"Everything is about the same as when I saw you at soccer practice. I'll be fine."

Liv and Ria stopped running to argue about which was the T-Rex and which was "it." For the love of Gods, couldn't they just get along for five damn minutes?

"Just practice taking turns being the T-Rex!" I called out to Liv and Ria.

"Alright," Jess conceded.

I chewed on my bottom lip, considering.

"Steven is out of town for another week, and when he gets back, we'll try therapy. He said he'd do it, so we might as well give it a go, but I'm losing hope. We haven't even texted since he left, and honestly, I don't miss him at all, and that's probably the saddest part. I'm a little burned out, sis. Being a mom feels endless sometimes, even if you love it. Fuck, *especially* if you love it. The more you care, the harder it is, and sometimes I feel like I'm being swallowed whole."

A pause. Then Jess sighed wearily,

"I'm sorry." She put her hand on my thigh. "It seems like being a parent nowadays is really hard. Remember when we were kids? Not a care in the world. We were tossed to the nanny; adults smoked in cars with the windows rolled up while kids played games in the back-back. Hell, I don't think I wore a seatbelt until college."

"Ah! The back-back!" I exclaimed.

I remembered being on the highway as a kid and seeing children piled into the hatchback of a car in front of us, little mouths and noses pressed against the window to make faces.

"And," I remembered suddenly, "they sent us to camp or had Aly take us to all the activities so Mom could have a martini or ten in peace. Thems were the days to be a mom."

"Aly." Jess's eyes widened, "Wow, I haven't heard that name in a while."

"Me too. Our parents were the worst, but at least we had the best nanny. Too bad she got spooked and left after dad was, ya know," I said.

Victoria and Olivia climbed the steps of the giant slide, Victoria gracefully bounding and Olivia clamoring behind her on all fours with the grace of a newborn rhino, just like Jess and me at their age. Jess acted as my shadow for the better part of our childhood because she was two years younger and didn't want to be left behind. Sisters, I thought, what a strange and magical kind of love.

Hopefully, my kids would stay friends, protect each other, and make it to adulthood without me being accused of murder. Lofty goals. It was hard enough to lose our father and ten times harder to wander the halls of our high school to the cacophony of gossip. The talk was brutal. "Did you hear? Did you hear? Daniele and Jessica's mom killed their dad with a hunting knife. A tennis racket. With an evil glance. A curse. Did you hear? She was taken to the police station for questioning last night."

What happened to my father was devastating, and not a day had passed since when some part of me didn't feel uneasy or anxious, the shock of the whole thing having fused itself to my nervous system. It reverberated through me every now and then as a reminder that things were not okay.

Jess cleared her throat and ran her hand over the buttons on her blouse, carefully considering her next words.

"So what are you thinking?" she said softly. "I don't want to tell you what to do, but I don't want you to be unhappy forever, either."

Jess put her delicate hand on my shoulder and squeezed gently before resting it back in her lap.

"I know," I groaned, "It's complicated. And it's not." I exhaled loudly. "I'm unhappy, mostly because of my marriage, so the easy solution would be to get myself out of it. But I don't *want* to get divorced. I don't feel like I can handle the aftermath of piecing Liv and Ria's lives back together. Of losing time with them on holidays, every other weekend, and over the summer. It just breaks my heart to think about it. But it's not good to model bad love for the sake of good parenting. And I'm so incredibly lonely."

What I didn't say because it might worry her, but felt in my bones, was that the resentment and loneliness were breaking me day by day. The endless, icy absence of love, the pain of being ignored, of not being valued, hollowed me out.

The distant mountains were beautiful; snow-capped peaks jutted into the pale blue sky. I knew I'd held on for way too long, hoping Steven might do a one-eighty, become kind again, or, ya know, he could get a lobotomy so we could keep the family together and avoid the painful untangling of our lives. I feared I'd waited too long. Worse, I feared I'd made a horrible mistake in marrying him in the first place.

Jess yawned again, then shook her head, her bob swinging around her jawbone.

"He's turned into a miserable ass," she said dryly. "You have a lot of valid reasons why you want to work it out, and I get that, as much as a childless person can, and I even applaud you for it. But I hope you know it's not a personal failure to recognize when something isn't working. That's a strength. That's bravery. Two qualities you have always had in spades." She smiled tightly and I smiled back. Jess adjusted the collar of her shirt then continued, "and you're not repeating our upbringing by divorcing that shitweed. I know you want it to be more stable than what we had and it will be no matter what. Mom was forced into single parenthood because someone tore dad apart in our childhood home. If they'd simply divorced, well, we'd be fine. I think."

I whipped my head to Jess.

"That's kinda brutal."

"I know, but it's the fucking truth."

"Yeah."

I paused to scan for the girls and couldn't find them. I lept to my feet, unable to catch my breath. I took three steps toward the playground, and the knot in my throat felt like a noose. Then I spotted Victoria standing off to the right of a blue slide, and something about her sneaky posture told me enough.

"RIA!" I yelled, "are you being nice to your sister?"

Victoria turned and smiled sheepishly at me, then slowly moved aside to let a furious Olivia off the slide where she'd been trapped. Victoria took off running with a red-faced scowling

Olivia right behind her. Once I felt pretty sure Liv wouldn't catch and beat her big sister, I found my way back to the bench.

"If Liv catches her, she's going to kick her ass," Jess mumbled.

I huffed a laugh.

"Luckily, she can't catch her."

I patted my sister's slender, marble-hard rock climber's leg that felt like it had been chiseled from stone.

"Anyway, it's your turn. Let's talk about you for a minute."

Jess pursed her lips and squinted into the distance.

"Hmmm. Okay. Uhm, life is dull on my end. I'm good, just working on my dissertation and staring at my living room wall, mostly." She brushed her short, glossy hair behind her right ear, revealing a little tattoo on her neck, a series of triangles symbolizing earth, air, fire, and water, the four elements. Fire, especially, was a big one for Persians but all of the elements were important to both ancient Persians and witches.

"Still not dating?" I asked.

"No, not really. Everyone is terrible. You'd think being queer would mean more options but like, no, everyone is gross," Jess said. "I have a date this week with this really beautiful woman I've been chatting with a little in an app. She sounds really fun, but she's only here temporarily to visit a friend, so maybe I'll have a short fling to look forward to."

"I think if things don't work out with Steven, I'm going to buy an epic vibrator and never date again. My goal is to be a bog witch because I can't fathom ever being in another relationship."

I stretched my arms to the sky, wiggled my fingers, and arched my back to release some tension in my joints.

"Join the club," Jess said, sighing.

"Oh!" I whipped my face to her. "But I forgot to tell you!" I grabbed her arm and shook it, "I met a new neighbor. And holy fucking shit, he's one of the hottest men I've ever seen. He's got this intense British creepy arrogant prick thing about him. I'm not making him sound great, I know, but seriously, he has this intoxicating-to-be-near thing about him."

Olivia and Victoria bolted from the slide to the climbing wall.

"Stay in my sight," I called to them.

Jess angled her body towards me, pulling her knees into her chest.

"Do I smell infidelity coming your way, hmmm?" she sang, winking.

"No, no. I don't think he'd be into a soon-to-be divorced mother of two. Although he did say that he was surprised I'm a mom. Whatever *that* means. Also, I've seen him walk by a few times, and he's always with different women and sometimes men, all gorgeous. There's something about him, though, I don't know. It's like, it's going to sound weird to say out loud, but it's like something about him calls to me."

Jess let out a large breath to let me know that she was annoyed and then glowered at me.

"Danny, you have children, not the bubonic plague. Anyone would be lucky to have you. Maybe you'll run into him again, and at the very least, you can have a fuck buddy who is nice to look at and less boring than Steven."

I rolled my eyes.

Victoria and Olivia bounded towards us, holding hands, their eyes ablaze with mischief. The forever back and forth of the spirited child, the expression that changes from one second to the next, from fire to twinkle. They scrambled onto the bench and crowded Jess's lap. Jess smiled and wrapped her strong arms around the girls, pulling them into her chest, where they happily snuggled in. A knot formed in my throat, and the tears swelled to the corners, taking it all in: my sister, my girls, my people. I inhaled shakily before breathing my feelings out in a subtle gust.

When we got home from the park, my mother's black Mercedes sedan loitered in front of my house. She had a key, but she'd planted herself on the sidewalk to examine my yard, her lips turned down at the corners as she surveyed every square inch of the place.

I freed the girls from my car so they could bounce over to my mother for a hug or something that resembled a hug. My mother adored the girls but always embraced them as if it were her first time touching another human being. She patted each child gingerly on the back with the tips of her fingers, smiling warmly while doing so.

"Run and get your things! Beth is making your favorite tonight! Chocolate cake!"

Liv and Ria squealed, running for the front door.

"Give that poor woman a Friday night off once in a while," I mumbled.

She rolled her eyes and waved her gloved hand at me.

"Do you have their things ready?" She asked, scrunching up her nose at my house again.

"I do. Come in. I'll grab their bags. And why do you keep looking at my house like that?"

"Like what? I like your house. It's so cute. Very quaint."

"You said that like I live in an outhouse in the middle of a forest."

"It's just so *small*. Doesn't it feel a little, I don't know, suffocating?"

"No," I said flatly. "Not everyone can live in a mansion in Cherry Hill, Mom. It has four bedrooms and two bathrooms. What else do I need?" Then I thought about it and knew a laundry list was about to pour out of her. "Actually, don't answer that. I like it. It's perfectly fine for us."

"Suit yourself," she said, making her way up the front steps to the porch, where she seemed to be searching for a rodent infestation by the way she frowned, dragging her gaze over every inch of the swing, the chairs, the cement of the porch itself.

We stepped through the door and I gestured to the two small suitcases in the entryway before peeling off my boots to wiggle my toes. I tossed my long wool coat over the console table, then threw my beanie on top of that. My mother watched me with a horrified expression as if I'd just squatted and shat in my hand.

"What?" I asked, gesturing to my things, "I'm going to put my coat and stuff away in a second. Do you want a cup of tea?"

"You're an adult," she said, shooing me away with a hand. "You can live in filth if you want. And no, thank you. We should be going so we can be on time for dinner."

I pressed my lips into a tight line to keep my mouth shut.

Before I could say something I'd regret, Liv and Ria came running back downstairs, clutching their stuffed animals. They paused to hug and kiss me before grabbing their suitcases to drag to my mother's car.

"See you soon," she said, her back to me. Then, much more quietly, she whispered, "Love you."

A UTERUS OF HELLFIRE

A wave of pain hit me as I shut the door behind my mother and leaned against it, groaning. I doubled over and clutched my lower belly. Fuck! Ouch! I growled. The pressure had been building all afternoon, and a dull ache had come and gone for an hour or so but the discomfort had turned into something much, much, worse. Of course, I had the night all to myself, with horrible, gut-wrenching cramps. And without a warning, a wave of warm, sticky, wet soaked my underwear. *Damnit*.

I waddled like a toddler to the bathroom only to realize that I was completely out of tampons, and my period underwear was nowhere to be found. I did what any respectable woman would do when randomly starting her period a week early with nothing on hand, and shoved a wad of toilet paper into my underwear, where it immediately got to work chafing my vulva. I grabbed my beanie and keys off of the console table in a huff and drove to the neighborhood store, hunched over my steering wheel, troll-like, and tortured, to stock up on essentials.

In Heymans, I grabbed two boxes of tampons, a box of pantyliners, pain reliever, a bottle of wine, a pint of chocolate fudge ice cream, and a scented bath bomb, all precariously balanced in my arms because I'd lied to myself when I'd got here about not needing a cart just like every other time I'd ever been to a grocery store in my life.

The cramps worsened by the second. I couldn't stand up straight. My body slowly forced me into a partial fetal position while still on my feet. Pace quickening, I hobbled around a corner without pausing, too distracted by my murderous uterus to spot the tall figure blocking my path until it was too late. I plowed into him, *hard*, and bounced right off as if I'd collided with a cement wall. Stars flickered behind my eyes and I lost grip on my evening's bounty. In helpless horror, I witnessed my poorly balanced grocery items spill out of my arms.

"Ouch. Shit, I'm so sorry!" I muttered, confused. As tampons, ice cream, and Midol crashed to the floor.

"Danny?" A low, sensual voice asked.

I froze. I knew that voice.

The wine bottle, bath bomb, and pantyliner box remained clutched against my chest. My cheeks heated as I bent down to pick everything else up, and my eyes slowly raked over the black boots in front of me, the black trousers, sweater, the long black coat, then finally flicked up to sapphire eyes that danced with amusement.

"Andras," I said, flustered. Of course this is when I'd run into him, with my undies full of wadded toilet paper, my face pale and twisted in pain, looking like a goblin who just raided a period trove and was running off to hoard it.

I tried to think of a way to escape as quickly as possible while balancing all of my items precariously on my forearm. Andras held a bottle of wine in one hand, another tucked into his coat pocket. He smirked at me.

"Fun night planned?"

"Does it look like I have a fun night planned?"

I lifted the pitiful bounty in my arms just so.

"I'd say it looks bloody fun to me."

His eyes went to the box of tampons, the wine, and then down, below my arms, below my belly. Did he just glance at my crotch? He smiled widely as if he'd just opened a present. I scrunched up my nose. Ew! *Weirdo*. I prepared to say something devastating, but my lower stomach twisted, and I lurched forward instead, wincing and groaning.

Andras's expression softened, the grin and amusement gone.

"Are you okay? Do you need help? Here, let me carry some—" He took a step toward me, sliding his hand free from his pocket.

"No thanks, I have to go." I said, "Sorry again for bumping into you." I waddled past him towards the cash register.

"I'm not sorry." He looked over his shoulder, "It was good seeing you, Danny. Feel better, love."

Love? Love! I practically hurled my items onto the conveyor belt and jammed my credit card into the machine to get the hell out of there as quickly as possible. At that point, the pain had me nearly doubling over, which provided a horrible little reprieve from any embarrassment I might have felt for looking so godsdamn unhinged. *Fuck.*

I just wanted to be home, hopped up on pain relievers and half drunk while binge-watching rom-coms with *much better* meet-cutes until either the booze or the cramps knocked me out. Thanking the cashier with a dip of my chin, I headed for the exit without so much as glancing up from the scuffed white linoleum floor. I scrambled into my car and texted Jess what had happened. She sent back a meme of a woman cry-laughing.

"I hate you," I replied.

The fake-fur throw felt like heaven against my ultra-sensitive goose-pimpled flesh. The pain slammed into me in nausea-inducing waves, but I knew that the pills would work soon enough and the movie would be a nice distraction. I chose the sappiest one I could find, with a predictable plot, so in my tortured state, I wouldn't have to pay much attention while I rocked myself gently, pausing only to take a sip of wine straight from the bottle.

The house was so quiet without the girls; it was both a relief and a sting. But they were happy with my mom, getting pedicures and watching a cartoon in the theater room. And thank the Gods they weren't here right now when sitting upright felt like an impossible challenge (not that I hadn't done it before–I'd had to parent while actively vomiting and shitting my pants before). Now, though, I could just lay on the couch and writhe and groan and wait for the meds to work.

A faint knock at my door woke me. My cramps were gone but I must have been out for a while because the movie had finished and a new one had started, some reality show. I pulled my robe closed tight as I rose to my feet, padding slowly to the door in a sleepy haze. It was dark out but still early enough that I wasn't worried about someone being at the door.

"Who is it?" I called out.

I pressed an ear to my thick oak front door, rising onto my toes to peer out of the ornamental-colored glass at the top of the door. Dark blue eyes met mine, and I stared into them as if in a trance. Without thinking, I turned the deadbolt and swung the door open.

Andras leaned against a porch pillar in his black suit, his hands in his pockets. He smirked at me with a knowing gleam in his eyes. No matter how much I tried to hide my fierce attraction to him, he knew better.

"Andras," I said, clutching my robe to my chest. What are you doing here?"

"Are you alright?" he asked. "I just wanted to come and check on you and tell you that you look beautiful, and I can't stop thinking of you."

Thoughts emptied out of my head and my throat went completely dry. I swallowed hard and it was like trying to gulp down ash.

He pushed off of the pillar and closed the distance between us until he was no more than a handbreadth away. I could feel him exhale against my cheek, his warm breath like a phantom caress, as he looked down at me, eyes burning with predatory focus. He reached out and gently took my hand, bringing it up to his mouth, where he kissed the backs of my fingers with unbearable tenderness. I inhaled sharply and he smiled wickedly down at me. Then he brought my hand up and placed it behind his neck, holding his own hand on top as he leaned in to kiss my cheek, his mauve lips so soft, so gentle. I leaned into him, into the embrace, then slowly turned my mouth to his and—".

Banging. There was banging somewhere in the distance. I lurched forward on the couch, patting at my sweat-damp nightgown, panting. My fingers went to my lips to caress them gingerly. Another dream of him. It had been another dream. I was still in my living room, still a little drunk, and the movie was still playing on the television. A gruff male voice yelled from my porch, "Delivery!" and I jumped in my skin. Then something thudded against the door. At least the cramps were gone, but godsdamnit, why did I have to wake up from that dream? I smiled to myself and electricity swirled in me. I wished I could go back to sleep, back to that moment, and drag him into my house to kiss, and kiss, and kiss.

Retrieving the package from the porch, I smiled at the pillar where Andras had been standing in my dream until a shadow caught the corner of my eye, and my head jerked towards it. Nothing, there was nothing, just the darkness, the chill of the night air, and some rustling pine cones in the neighbor's trees. I dragged the box back into my house, a box full of ten dozen socks of various sizes for children who needed them in the community. I closed the door, locked it, and set the box on the counter, debating if I wanted to go to sleep or try to finish the movie. In my dreams, though, there might be someone waiting for me. I smiled.

I wanted to cling to the delicious joy of being desired. It was only pretend. I could pretend that Andras and all of the sharp lines of his handsome golden face had really shown up at my house to delicately kiss my cheek. Even if a part of me felt ashamed. I was actively trying to save my marriage while fantasizing about another man. What kind of a person did that make me? Probably not a very good one, I supposed.

Padding up the stairs on my way to bed, I thought about Steven, who was on a plane heading home. We'd fallen apart, and I couldn't help but wonder if we'd heal or stay broken.

THE BETRAYAL

My hands were shaking in my lap while the couple's therapist, Stephani, observed me carefully from her worn armchair. The throw pillows pushed into my back on the burnt orange sofa and I resisted the urge to fall over, pull my legs into my chest, and scream.

Steven, the bastard, had not shown up to our appointment.

He came home from China and went back to work. Then Friday came around and after school, I sent the girls to stay with their grandmother again–two weekends in a row, which I did *not* love–so Steven and I could make this Saturday morning appointment and then have the rest of the day, and part of Sunday, to process. I'd imagined a nice scenario where we met with the therapist, grabbed brunch, and talked about all of the ways that the therapist was totally right. Over omelets and coffee, we'd make a plan for how to fix all of it in a big black notebook that was essentially a marriage to-do list. Do the things, check, move forward, check. This morning, I'd even called out to him before leaving to do some early Solstice shopping to remind him of the appointment. "I'll see you at eleven!" I hollered at him through his office door. He gruffly replied, "Yeah, okay." I went shopping and bought a few nice outfits for the girls and an amethyst ring for my sister for protection. I'd stopped by a coffee shop and sipped a latte while I checked in with Ria and Liv, who were apparently on their way to get a haircut with my mother. Great.

I added a new listing to my personal website— one of my own paintings, not my commissioned animal work —a piece I'd named, "There's No Place Like Home," an oil painting of a woman sprawled out on the floor, half of her painted brown, the other half white, with each half of her body in a differently decorated room. One half was a traditional British home, the other half a Persian one with ornate carpets and gold details glittering on the shelves. Catholic symbols mixed with the elements of nature. Mixed. A dichotomy of two colliding worlds, two pieces of a whole.

The clock ticked loudly on a nearby shelf in Stephani's office as if it were taunting me. Tick tock. Tick tock. Like a tongue clicking against teeth in disapproval. She shifted in her chair, papers rustled, a pen scratched across a notebook.

"Are you alright?" She asked, gently, as if I were about to break.

"Yes. No." I said, without looking up from my hands.

"Do you want to talk about it?"

I fought against the sting in my eyes. My voice cracked, "I've been asking him to come to therapy for four years. He's always said no. But he finally agreed and I was relieved and hopeful. And this was the last shot. I know it might not seem like that big of a deal; people miss appointments, but Steven doesn't. He's the most punctual person I've ever met. He's been in China until a few days ago…and…I'm tired. I'm just really tired. And I wonder if there's something wrong with me that I haven't given up until now."

She exhaled, "Of course, you held on for as long as you could. It sounds like you really wanted it to work. That's understandable. All of this must be really hard. Would you like to wait a little longer?" Stephani asked.

I inhaled sharply, flicking my gaze up to meet her doe-like emerald eyes. She tilted her head in question, and her auburn bob shifted with the movement. Her office was painted a pretty dark blue that complemented the strands of orange in her hair, and two still-life paintings of flower bouquets hung above where she sat. I chewed on the inside of my cheek.

"It's been thirty minutes. I don't think he's coming." I said, quietly. Swallowing hard, I tried to dislodge the knot in my throat.

"I don't think so either." She said with a sigh, "Would you like to reschedule?"

I shook my head. Panic struck hard as the finality set in. When I left, everything would be different. Everything. My life was about to fall apart. Closing my eyes, I inhaled deeply, counted to four, exhaled, and counted to four again. It didn't help. My skin began to crawl.

I opened my eyes slowly.

"No, thank you."

I forced a polite smile and tried to muster the strength to pull myself from the couch. I needed to get up, get to my car, and drive home. So many difficult conversations lay ahead to start the slow, painful untangling of our lives. But I was so exhausted–not in a sleep-deprived way, but worse, like I was tired in my soul.

Stephani gently cleared her throat,

"Danny? Would you like to do an exercise for the next ten minutes? It might be really helpful to get you centered right now."

"Okay," I whispered.

"Get comfortable and close your eyes."

I leaned back against the soft cushions and let them envelop me, hugging a taupe throw pillow into my chest. I held it like a baby. Stephani spoke soothingly, like a low, lulling, song, instructing me to feel the weight of my body, telling me to let go and be in the moment, but her words were swept away by my frantic thoughts. All I could see behind my closed eyes for those ten minutes was a montage of things to come: Steven's face when I asked for a divorce, telling my daughters, being a single mother from this point forward. *Fuck.*

Afterward, I thanked Stephani and left the appointment bleary-eyed and confused.

Driving home, every song on the radio seemed to validate my rage. Not even K-pop could dim the red I saw or cool the fire roiling in my veins. Images swarmed in my head of our life together, seeing him on campus that first time, our first date at that pizza place, our wedding dance, and the look of awe on his face when our girls were born. And then the moments of us drifting away from each other. How the past few years of disconnect had all come down to this one moment, this one crucial opportunity to heal it. But he'd left me there, alone, to crumble in front of a stranger as I realized my marriage was officially over.

Motherfucking rage. I felt unyielding rage at that moment and my foot became leaden as I pressed down on the gas so hard my car lurched forward like a bullet. How could he do this to me? To us? To them? Changing lanes, I cut someone off and they laid on their horn. I bared my teeth, flipped them off and gunned the gas again, weaving in and out of cars on the freeway, zipping around trucks, as if I were trying to outrun the hurt, the inevitable pain. I was speeding past a diesel truck, jerking my car into the lane in front of it to exit the freeway, when I caught sight of Olivia's empty booster seat in my rearview mirror. What the fuck was I doing? I let off the gas, let the car slow to the speed limit, and allowed the rush of sadness to hit me. Pulling into a supermarket parking lot, I swung my car into a space. Anger, disappointment, rejection, fear–all of it consumed me as I crossed my arms over the steering wheel and wept.

Ugly, heaving sobs poured out of me. Salty trails covered my cheeks and arms. Snot leaked in a big sticky mess as I let myself come undone. As I let the truth hit me, again, and again, in waves.

I was truly, irrevocably, absolutely, heartbroken. And I was terrified. Would I be okay? Had I failed my children? Could I really do this alone?

That had always been my fear, the one that lurked in my subconscious, the one that had kept me from leaving last year, or the year before that. The fear that I couldn't handle it all alone, that I couldn't handle the reality of being alone in the vast demands of adulthood and parenting.

But then again, I'd already been doing it alone, hadn't I? Steven and I were not a team. We were an illusion. If I was being honest, all he contributed was a sticky fog of negativity that clung to me day and night, slowing me as I made my way through this life.

I pulled a baby wipe from the glove compartment to clean up my face, dabbing away at the tear lines, the mascara stains under my eyes, and the snot that clung to the skin around my nose. I chucked the wipe onto the floor behind my seat, put the car into drive, and slowly made my way home.

Steven was on a conference call when I flung open his office door, my face a mask of horrible calm. Startled, he jerked back into his chair, then relaxed. His face twisted in rage, eyebrows knit together, teeth slightly bared, as he mouthed, "I'm in a meeting."

"I don't care." I mouthed back.

Then, without much thought, I bent over and unplugged his computer. When he lunged forward to grab the cord from my hands, I pulled them back and growled,

"We need to talk. Now."

He got to his feet and stood over me.

"Whatever it is that you need to say, hurry up. I can't miss this meeting, it's—"

I glared up at him.

"—more important than the couples therapy you agreed to and then didn't show up for?"

"Oh, Jesus Christ. Is that what this is about? It's not the end of the world, Danny. I said I'd think about going; I never even said I'd go for sure. Just reschedule."

He turned as if to say, "Conversation over."

Oh, but the conversation was not over. I flung the cords down on the floor, fighting against the ache in my chest.

I growled through my teeth, "You did not say you'd think about it, Steven. You said to make the appointment and I did. And I sat there waiting for you."

"Whatever, Danny. Can you get out of here now so I can get back to work? You know one of us has to wor—"

A voice in the far recesses of my mind whispered in an otherworldly tone that was both angel and demon. "Easy, child, easy," it said, "Breathe and be done with it." It would have terrified me if I weren't burning with fury. I bared my teeth and ground out a demand to Steven.

"—Look at me. Look at me!"

He turned, rolling his eyes, before looking into my face.

"I am fucking done. I am walking out of here and filing for divorce. We are done." My vision blurred as my eyes filled with tears, "I told you that therapy was the final straw, and I meant it. I needed you to be there," my voice began to crack, "and maybe you didn't take me seriously or didn't care. But I will be filing divorce papers." Steven's mouth had slackened as he watched me, silently, surprise written all over his expression. I turned to leave the room but paused, and without looking at him said quietly, but not weakly, "Please, start moving your stuff to the mother-in-law above the garage. We can work out the details later and talk with the girls when we're ready, but just start doing that."

Steven's chair shifted underneath him.

"Danny, I just got back from China. I'm sorry, I–" He started.

I didn't turn to look at him as I shook my head emphatically. "No. Nope."

My legs began moving. My body buzzed with uncomfortable energy, my hands twitched and ached from wringing them, and my heart thundered so fast I worried that I might be having a heart attack. I snatched my phone from the counter and texted my sister on the way to my studio in the backyard.

"Jess, what was the number of that lawyer friend of yours? The one you said is cutthroat and amazing?"

"Oh, okay. I'll call you when I leave the library. Sending!" Jess responded.

In my studio, I plopped onto my stool. I breathed in deeply, inhaling the sharp fumes of oil paint and thinner. I exhaled slowly, letting go of the tension in my back and shoulders. With a brush in my hand, Rebecca seemed to smile down at me, and I felt a kernel of pride for how she'd taken form on my canvas and now appeared before me in all of her larger-than-life, albeit a bit broken, glory. A few more strokes, a few more shadows, a touch of highlight, and she would be whole.

My phone dinged. Jess sent the phone number for her lawyer friend. Brush in one hand, phone in the other, I waited for someone at the law firm to pick up.

"Yes, hello," I said to the receptionist. I'd like to make an appointment with Lara as soon as she's available. Yes, I'd like to file for divorce."

BLOTTO

Aside from the silk dancers and shimmering old-timey costumes, Blotto was a warm and unassuming place with exposed wood rafters and straightforward cocktails. The amber lights were dim, and the decor was minimal, with only a few carefully hung expressionist-style paintings. In the center of the room, hung from the rafters, two cadmium-red silk drapes cascaded to the floor. A woman with iridescent copper hair in pin curls wrapped them around her thighs, two hundred feet from the floor. A drum roll thundered from the small band in the corner. The room fell silent as everyone in the bar craned their necks up towards the aerial dancer. The drumming stopped, and she let go. She writhed, twisted, turned, down, down, down, bound in red, her body extending horizontally and then vertically and then horizontally again, speeding towards the floor and certain death. The room froze. She caught herself with the flick of a wrist, belly down, her face only an inch from the ground. I exhaled, having no idea I'd been holding my breath in the first place. The crowd hooted and clapped. The dancer took a bow and sauntered to a table with the other dancers.

Sitting on my right, I turned to my ridiculously beautiful friend, Sebastian. He wore pants with suspenders like a giant paperboy to "match the theme of the bar." His shoulders bounced as the jazz started, a broad toothy smile on his handsome face,

"I seriously love this place. I will never get sick of seeing them fall."

His chestnut eyes danced with excitement.

"Same." Sam agreed, flipping her platinum hair over a shoulder and adjusting the fringe on her ruffled blouse. She crossed and uncrossed her legs at the knee, then examined something on her leather pants, scowling at it. Sam was the kind of woman who didn't look like she should exist in the real world, with her creamy pale skin and full, kissable lips.

"It's been so long since I've been here," I said.

"We know." Sam said, coldly, "Happy to have you back and appearing in person for once."

I glared at her. She smiled back sweetly.

Blotto attracted everyone from college students and middle-aged folks filled the massive room, a hodgepodge of age, race, class, and style seated at the high-tops and square tables for as far as the eye could see. When we were teenagers, we'd gotten in with fake I.D.s, and Jess and I spent an entire night trying to get a waitress to break character and give her real name or the tiniest detail of her real life. But every time we'd asked something, she'd laugh and say in a perfect nineteen-twenties Chicago accent, "Oh, now honey, I told you—name's Daphne. Born and raised in Chicago." Then she'd touch her pin-curled blonde bob and saunter off with an exaggerated swing of her hips that made her sequined dress catch the light. Years later, we saw "Daphne" in the food court at the mall in a pair of gray joggers trying to soothe her angry toddler, and it was *unsettling* to hear her real voice, lower with a heavy Brooklyn accent. I thought about that a lot. If any one visual contrast could represent the stark realities of parenthood, it might be a video reel of Daphne being herself without her child in tow versus Daphne playing the role of mother at a food court.

I often found myself lost in thought here. What would it be like to wear those amazing flapper dresses, smoke cigarettes with abandon, and chug booze in a dark Chicago speakeasy? I could picture myself with Sam and Sebastian hopping on and off the dance floor, laughing and carefree. We'd been through so much together. It broke my heart sometimes to think about how much space had grown between us since I'd married and had kids. They were both perpetually single and traveled, partied, and drank while I parented, painted, and sipped glasses of wine on my porch alone in the dark. Although, honestly, becoming a sort of recluse had more to do with anxiety and depression than it did with being a mom. I didn't like to be in a crowd or away from home. I needed time to work on my own projects—paintings and mixed media pieces that examined otherness and belonging and grief. Time alone in the shadows every night gave me space to think and dream and get my head on straight, to soothe my anxiety, and to process my day. I worried, almost incessantly, that something might happen while I wasn't at home that would haunt me for the rest of my life. Because in the midst of ordinary days, tragedy waited. Misery lingered between laughter and love. That was the lingering effect of trauma.

Sebastian put his large hand on my shoulder, rubbing lightly. "It's been a while. But here you are, dressed up to boot. I mean, look at you. This backless top and these trousers are fire. Couldn't bother with heels, though?" He looked down at my Oxfords and tsked.

Cocking my head, I glared up at him through my lashes, then held my foot to the light, "I'm wearing pretty lace socks, though."

Sebastian examined the delicate sheer black socks and nodded in approval, "I do love the socks."

I felt a light tap on my spine and turned and wished that I hadn't. There stood Kim, a petite redhead, waiting, her gray eyes darting from me to my friends like she could not wait to be introduced. She wore jeans, brown boots, and a wool sweater. Her fingers fretted with the hem. Kim's daughter went to school with Ria, and she was on the PTA and probably one of the people who would not stop sending me sock emails.

"Danny!" she gushed, opening her arms wide and pulling me into a hug like we were the very best of friends. I stiffened, then slowly relaxed and wrapped my arms around her to briefly squeeze back.

"Oh my God!" She exclaimed, letting go and backing up a step to take us all in. "It's so crazy to see you here! I never see you *anywhere* outside of the drop-off lane or coffee shop near the school."

"You and me both," Sam muttered.

I shot her a disapproving glare.

Then something strange happened. I became possessed with what could only be the PTA spirit and, without meaning to, sat up a little taller. The corners of my mouth lifted into a wide smile that felt really unnatural for my face as if my muscles were being strained.

"Kim! Hi! Kim, this is Sebastian and Samantha." I introduced them. Kim beamed at Sebastian and Sam, who both offered a tight smile and echoed, "So nice to meet you," like they were, in fact, not happy to meet her at all. *Assholes*.

Kim nodded to each of them, then whipped her head back to me.

"How are the girls? We need to have a playdate! Genevieve just got a brand new tea set! Oh my God, and did you see that email from Bethany about the gift cards? Is it just me or are we slowly being nickel and dimed to death?" Kim threw back her head and cackled at her own joke. Her coppery red hair swayed behind her.

"I thought the exact same thing when I saw that email," I said, but my voice sounded odd, fake, higher in pitch and the tone gentler than usual, like I was talking to a young child. "Ria would love a tea party. Liv, not so much, but she can play in the yard, right?"

"Definitely. Perfect! Okay, I'll text. So good seeing you! Oh, and let me know if you sign up for any of the upcoming PTA events! Have a good night." Kim patted my shoulder and waved to Sam and Sebastian before heading off to a booth of women who all looked exactly like her. Some I recognized vaguely, others I didn't.

Sebastian stared at me judgmentally, his eyes narrow and brows knit together. "Okay, who are you? Seriously. That was so eerie seeing you like that; it's like you morphed into an infomercial for magic mops or something."

"Fuck off," I said, rolling my neck. "I know..."

Sebastian laughed out loud and smacked the table with his tattooed hand covered in delicate lines depicting planets, moons, and stars.

"Okay, so back to what I was saying earlier." I started, "Did you know that the majestic Orca speaks a familial dialect?" I said, enthusiasm tinging my words.

"Honey, why are we talking about whale languages again? I want to talk about the weird peppy person you just morphed into when that woman Kim came over just now." Sebastian said.

Why were we talking about sea life? Other than the fact that it was fascinating? (Which it totally was). To avoid talking about the end of my marriage. Obviously. I knew that and they knew that.

Sam sighed dramatically.

"Why are you surprised by the weird whale facts?" she said to Sebastian. "How long have we all been friends? Since high school? You know this is what happens when you let Danny spend too much time by herself, she gets obsessed with things. Sparkly vampire movies, that K-Pop group homeless men, or–"

"Stray Kids," Sebastian interjected, "And honestly, I'm kinda obsessed, too. Have you listened to them?"

"Anyway," Sam continued, "I want to talk about your weird reaction to that woman, too. You normally have a raspy deep voice thing going on that sounds hot and bitchy. That other voice is, well, just bad. Who did you just morph into?."

Sam rested her hand on my arm.

Glancing back and forth, I took a sip of my wine.

"Dolphin," I added.

"Pardon?" Sebastian asked.

"Orcas are dolphins," I corrected him. "Not whales."

"Oh my God, kill me now!" Sam threw her hands up and rolled her eyes. "You avoidant bitch. Fine. We'll pretend like we didn't just witness you birthing a whole separate personality. Fine. But can we please talk about something other than the social-emotional world of ocean creatures? Like sex? Or honestly, anything else?"

I leaned back, folding my arms across my chest. "Alright, fine. I'll stop. *Begrudgingly*. And I don't know why my voice did that thing with Kim, okay? I want those moms to like me, I guess so that my kids aren't exiled like we were when we were growing up."

Sebastian put his hand on his cheek, sighing. He shook his head disapprovingly. Sam frowned, then tipped her drink up to finish it.

"That's sad." Sebastian finally said. "Danny, they're not you and Jess. Their mother isn't being investigated for murder. At least, not that I know of. Where is Steven, by the way?" Sebastian smirked.

I shot him a dirty look, then grabbed my purse off of the chair and swung it over my shoulder. I wanted to say that he was at home, hopefully packing up his shit and moving into the small guest space above our garage, but I wasn't ready to tell everyone yet. Soon, but not yet. Not before I had time to sit with it.

"I'm gonna grab us one more round so I can poison you." I flashed them both a nightmarish grin, "I can't stay too late though, the girls are at my mom's again, two weekends in a row, and tomorrow morning I have to pick them up. I don't want to look hungover." I turned my nose up and arched my back, forcing my shoulder blades together. In a deep and monotone voice, I mocked my mother, "You're a disgrace."

"Well that's eerie, you sound just like your *terrifying* mom. Anyway, whiskey on the rocks for me." Sebastian sang.

"Same!" Samantha chimed in, lifting her right hand lazily and then letting it fall back onto her lap.

At the bar, a handsome bartender in a nineteen-twenties outfit greeted me with a nod while dramatically flinging a towel over his shoulder, performing "the mysterious bartender" character. A heartbeat went by before he finally asked, "What can I get ya?"

"Two whiskies on the rocks and a glass of pinot grigio."

"Comin' right up, ma'am!"

Ma'am? When the fuck did I become a ma'am? Something that felt a lot like my youth dried up and died inside of me.

My eyes drifted up to the rows of liquor bottles that lined the back wall. So many bottles, each one occupying its own cubed shelf, and the shelves went as far as the ceiling beams. It must have taken a carpenter hours, days, and weeks to finish each little square. It was beautiful. Why didn't I come here more? I used to have so much fun back when I saw Samantha and Sebastian every week. Life was busy, sure–running errands, packing lunches, going to school events–but was I really too busy to have a life outside of those things? Was I really too busy to enjoy myself?

I was still focused on the bottles when I felt someone step into the empty space to my right.

"Hello, again." A sensual male voice drawled.

My spine went rigid. Turning slowly towards the voice, my heart kicked hard in my chest, boom, boom, boom, until my eyes landed on a man's pecs and had to travel up a few miles to his perfect face. Andras. Right there in the flesh, leaning against the bar, smirking down at me with those hypnotic sapphire bedroom eyes. He had the face of a God, or a demon, a face that could convince just about anyone to commit just about any sin. Even slouching, he was so much taller than me. We locked eyes until I remembered the grocery store encounter and suddenly found my nails to be *very interesting*. At least I didn't look feral for once, that was a plus. But then I also remembered the dream where he'd pressed his full mauve lips into my cheek and the lust-filled fantasies that had crept into my head while I did the dishes, washed my face, or cleaned the bathtub, and my cheeks grew warm.

Andras's body tightened, and his eyes narrowed on me, a slow, wicked smile on his lips.

"Danny. What are you thinking about?" He crooned.

I went still. He sounded like he knew exactly what I was thinking about and worse, he seemed to be gloating about it.

Forcing my face into neutrality, or at least trying to appear aloof, I looked up from my nails. But then I caught the faintest scent of him–woodsy and warm–the kind of scents that brought to mind a man covered in car grease wrestling a tiger shirtless or an impeccably dressed man sitting in a smoke-filled bar in Prague drinking amber-colored booze on the rocks. *Damnit*. My entire body heated like a traitorous bastard.

"Are you feeling alright?" Andras asked, with mischief and mayhem written all over his expression. "A little better than the other night?"

I exhaled loudly and angled my head.

"Yes, definitely better than the other night," I shook my head like I was waking up. Then I looked around the bar, making a show of it, "And where the fuck did you appear from again? I swear, you just pop out of nowhere every time I run into you. And if you keep doing it, I'm going to have a heart attack. I'm *old*, you know?"

His mouth dropped open and his eyes widened as he feigned shock.

"I literally just walked over and stood here but you were staring–quite mesmerized, I might add–at the bottles. You were a little distracted." He glanced up at the glass and the cubes, then leaned forward as if to tell me a secret, "And I fear I'm probably older than you."

"I doubt that," I countered.

He looked about the same age as me but without the typical wear. His golden skin seemed to glow, not a sign of stress anywhere.

"I'll place a wager on it." He murmured. Then, glancing up again to the bottles above us, "So what's so interesting about that wall?"

I winced. "I don't know, they're pretty? And I just do that, I guess. I get lost in my thoughts a lot and it's almost like I leave my body entirely. I have an overactive imagination or something. I was thinking about life, things, and what it would have been like to be at a real speakeasy decades ago and trying to picture the room back then. I am one hundred percent sure that disappearing in thought is some kind of coping mechanism of mine"

I nodded to the bartender to thank him as he set down my drinks in front of me. Then I slid a twenty dollar bill to him. He thanked me by placing it over his heart, fluttering his eyelashes, and smiling playfully.

"Anything for you?" The bartender asked, gesturing to Andras as he slid the twenty into his pocket.

As Andras surveyed the bartender's face, his muscles tensed, and his midnight blue eyes narrowed and fixated on him, and I could have sworn there was a flash of something menacing, something that promised pain.

"Yes, I'll have another of these," he said coldly, shaking the ice in his glass, "and another round for the lady and her friends. Also, when you get off of work, I want you to punch yourself in the fucking face repeatedly, you piece of shit."

I flinched. His words were sharp but delivered with a calm cool that made my skin crawl. I looked back and forth from the bartender to Andras.

The bartender blinked sleepily, "Okay," he said as if he hadn't just been aggressively insulted and threatened. Then he went back to making drinks.

My chest tightened as my head whipped to Andras, who was watching the bartender make our drinks smugly amused.

"Do you know him? Or are you just completely fucking insane?" I demanded.

"Let's say I do know him in a way," Andras's eyes slid to me, "and he's not a particularly good person. He did something unforgivable to a woman very recently," Andras said, his expression settling into something cool and calm. No sight of those fury-filled eyes. "He deserved it. And worse, honestly."

He had such a lovely face but what kind of monster lingered behind it? Or maybe the bartender *had* done something terrible, maybe to someone Andras knew? I considered telling him to fuck off, and thought about storming away.

Andras quietly surveyed my face, and then his eyes flicked to his empty glass and lingered there for a few heartbeats. The silence would have been awkward if the look on his face wasn't so pensive and almost sad. Almost like he'd been swept into a memory and held there by heartbreak or grief.

He cleared his throat.

"I'm sorry for saying that in front of you."

I glared at him. My throat tightened and I felt my pulse quicken.

"Maybe you shouldn't have said it at all?"

"No, no, I definitely don't regret saying it." He said sternly but not unkindly, "Just saying it in front of you. I'm sorry if I scared you or made you uncomfortable."

I slowly nodded while I tried to wrap my head around what was happening.

He studied my face again for a moment, then focused on the far wall and the crowd, then back to me.

"The real speakeasies, back in the day," he began, "were much like this in some ways. Smaller spaces, though, were usually dark and underground." The bartender set a new glass in front of Andras, who didn't bother to acknowledge him even when he took a drink from his glass, and continued, " They had this sort of dangerous, unsettling feeling about them that was really...exciting."

Andras flashed a grin that lit up his face and was bright enough to cast evil from the shadows of Hades. How do people like him just walk around looking that perfect like it's the most natural thing in the world? I felt like a honey-badger on a good day, on a bad day, I felt like one of those cocaine addicted sharks off the coast of Mexico. The chandelier danced in the deep blue of his eyes and I let myself get lost in them. I was simping for him like a teenage girl. What the hell was wrong with me? I stared and stared, and stared, and couldn't stop. Heartbeats later, my brain came back online.

"Like what you see?" He asked, smirking.

"Your description," I cleared my throat, "is oddly specific." I took a drink from my glass, "Did you used to work in a theme bar? Or wait! A bachelor's degree in history?"

Andras chuckled, "No, no. I'm just kind of a history nerd, I guess."

He took another sip of his drink. Then glanced up at the ceiling as if trying to remember something that might be written there.

"I think I saw it in a book somewhere. It had lots of pictures. Felt almost like being there." An eyebrow rose playfully, and his lips kicked up at the corners. I had to remember to breathe. Every hair on my neck stood up and tingled. My mouth–my evil, backstabbing mouth–seemed to fall open for him as if beckoning him there. Jesus, I had just barely decided to get divorced and it was like I had no control over my response to his pheromones, as if the universe wanted me to bed him. I took a step back.

"I get that." I said, clearing my throat, "I love to read, too. And research things. I spend a lot of time falling down rabbit holes about honestly anything. I don't know why but I'm really into Orcas right now. It was angler fish for a while because the female is made of testicles, and tomorrow, it will be something else. Who knows. I just really like to learn, I guess, then I use it to torture everyone around me. I'm a real hit at cocktail parties."

Andras huffed a laugh.

"But honestly?" I went on, "It's how I distract myself from …things."

"Interesting." He said, angling his head, "I like that."

"That I distract myself?"

"That you recognize why you do it and are willing to talk about it so openly."

I looked away, embarrassed. My cheeks flushed hot. I licked my lips, a nervous habit. Andras stared at my mouth with blown-out pupils. The world seemed to close in around me, shadows enveloping us, shutting out the entire world then they receded. It took actual effort not to lean towards him. *What is going on with me?* I'm an adult woman swooning–yes, swooning–over a man in a bar.

In a panic, I blurted out, "I'm married." Instant regret. *Oh, fuck. Why did you say that?* But I had to say something, my blood pulsed *everywhere*. It felt electric and delicious and utterly *wrong* and I could feel myself standing on the precipice of a shame spiral. I was not single yet, not legally, and wouldn't be for at least ninety-one days, according to Colorado law. But at that moment, I didn't want to be tied to Steven anymore in any way, and that felt bad and confusing and so *scary*. Then a sharp grief overtook me and I felt my body sag.

Andras's voice was gentle,

"I remember. When we were talking at your gate, you mentioned that your husband traveled a lot, right before you raked me over the coals for my idiotic comments about motherhood. And then vaguely accused me of being a serial killer."

The corner of his mouth tilted up.

He reached toward my face, then paused, "May I?" He asked.

I had no idea what he planned to do but I dipped my chin anyway.

Long, soft fingers gently brushed against my cheek and then curved over my ear, sending a shiver down my spine, as he tucked a loose tendril back in place, where it must have escaped the small gold comb I'd used to pin my hair back on either side. My mouth went completely dry.

"There." He said, resting his forearm back on the bar's edge.

"Thank you." I whispered.

"Are you alright?" He asked, looking me over.

"I-I think I'm just tired," I lied. I *was* tired. But also anxious and heartbroken because things were complicated. I chewed on my thumb nail for a beat to think. "I'm having a great night, honestly. I haven't been out with my friends in a long time, and I love them so much…" I trailed off, and turned to glance behind us at Sam and Sebastian, who were unapologetically gawking in our direction. Andras followed my line of sight, smiling and nodding to them. They smiled back but did not look away. *Weirdos*. I shook my head at them and turned back to Andras, to our conversation. "And, it's been nice talking to you, I mean not when you're being insane to the bartender, but the rest of the time. When you showed up I was staring at the bottles, and thinking. Sometimes I feel like adulthood has dragged me into the dregs until the highlight of my week became shopping for a new duvet or finding a new anxiety med that worked, and I just can't help wondering if this is it? Is this my whole life?"

Cradling my drink to give my hands something to do, to act as a sort of buffer between us, as if having an object there would stop me from grinding on him like a cat in heat. After a long pause, Andras asked,

"Are you not happy?"

Instead of answering, I took a giant gulp from my wine glass.

"You know, Danny," He dipped his chin, "you make life sound absolutely abysmal. Are you aware of that?"

I rubbed my temple and winced. "Oh, Gods," I groaned, "I do make life sound awful, don't I?" I shook my head, trying to gather my thoughts, "I don't feel like my life is awful. It's not. It's just that with every new responsibility, I feel like I have to give away tiny pieces of myself, over and over until I'm no longer whole." Andras only tilted his head slightly in silent question. I sucked in a breath, "Or maybe," I went on, still fumbling to organize my chaotic brain, "I just haven't figured out how to be all the things at once, how to let all of my parts co-exist peacefully in a way that feels…balanced."

Andras's expression was kind as he searched for something in my face, although what, I had no idea.

"You're sad. And scared," he said quietly, without breaking eye contact. It was not a question or a judgment. My body leaned forward as if I were being gently swept toward him by some invisible force.

"I don't know if this is true for you," Andras went on, "but it certainly has been for me. I know that when I'm feeling caged, it's because I've unknowingly built the bars myself."

That was sobering. My spine straightened and as if a floodgate had been cracked, a cascade of truths crashed against my skull. The floor seemed to be the least distracting place to focus my attention while I imagined the myriad ways my playing into cultural expectations, traditions, and gender norms–all of it–had created or contributed to my unhappiness.

"Yes," I said quietly but not weakly. Not shamefully. "I think you're probably right. At least, this once." I smiled up at him and he laughed.

"If I'm being honest," the corner of his lip curled up, "You're really odd."

"Hey, buddy," I glared.

"Not in a bad way. You might be one of the most interesting people I've met in a really long time. You're so," a pause, "easy to talk to, so openly vulnerable and honest. It's not common, you know? Has anyone ever told you that you have a way of making people feel at ease? Even when you're being completely morose."

I stifled a laugh, "It's because I'm non-threatening."

"I wouldn't say that." He said, shooting an incredulous look at me.

Silence.

Then I realized, to my embarrassment, that my lips had parted, and I found myself practically panting at him like an enthusiastic Labrador. I rocked back on my heels to once again compose myself. Gently clearing my ash-dry throat, I said,

"Thank you. And...I don't know. I think maybe I'm just too lazy to be dishonest. What's the point of anything else? If we become friends, you'd figure me out anyway, and if we don't, it wouldn't be worth the performance, right? I'm too tired to knit a different narrative. Plus, I grew up with parents who could've won awards for their acting; everything–and I mean everything–was about appearances and doublespeak, and it got even worse after..." I trailed off. *No need to go into detail about your father.* "Anyway, my sister and I were never very good at any of it to begin with."

Andras smiled wide, his eyes creasing at the corners, "Ah," he purred, "so we are going to be friends?"

I shrugged and looked up into his face, "We'll see."

"Ah, yes, of course."

He leaned down close to me, his face directly above mine, and I could almost feel his breath on my forehead as he playfully whispered,

"Am I no longer creepy?"

I stared up into his face, my neck aching from the angle.

"Oh no, you *definitely* are."

Andras stood tall again, towering over me, and laughed a deep, warm laugh. I grinned. A faint buzz came from his pocket, and he reached in to pull out his phone. He read something quickly on the screen, then slid it back into his pocket.

"And it looks like my date is here, so I'll let you get back to your mates, and I'll see you around?"

He grabbed his glass, brows raised as if to say, "You know how it is," and I nodded in return: yes, I did know. I knew that more than once per week, he took someone home with him, and I guess he met them here or at one of the other bars or restaurants nearby. Andras sketched a bow in jest and turned to prowl towards the front of the club, straight up to a gorgeous brunette with long, sleek hair that reached the middle of her back and full breasts that peaked and swelled out of her skin-tight black dress.

The woman looked Andras up and down in approval, delighted by what she saw, as if she'd just opened a gift and it was exactly what she'd wanted. They were clearly meeting for the first time, but how? A dating app? I couldn't picture Andras swiping left or right in search of a one-night stand. What would his bio even say? "Absolutely stunning mystery man from somewhere in England will show you one wonderful night then never see you again." Ugh, is he the kind of guy who sends dick pics to women to "entice" them into meeting? Gross. I shook the image out of my head.

I gathered up the drinks I'd ordered and the ones Andras had ordered for me—minus the one I practically guzzled at the bar while chatting with him. Five glasses balanced among long, thin fingers spread wide and hooked in strange directions around them. Sam and Sebastian, the bastards, watched me precariously balance the drinks and navigate the crowd with morbid delight. It was as if they'd made a bet on whether or not I'd make it back without dumping the whole lot down the front of my shirt. I narrowed my eyes into tiny slits at them, which made Sam's smile widen. I stole a glance or two of Andras and his beautiful date, already cozied up at a booth near the stage. Damn, he moved fast. He was leaning into her, smiling lazily as he whispered something into her ear that she seemed to be eating up. Good for her.

When I reached my table, Sebastian and Sam quickly relieved me of the drinks that were cramping up my hands, offering teasing bits of praise while I jokingly scowled at them. They each pulled a drink towards themselves and—as if they'd choreographed it—leaned forward eagerly like two co-conspirators waiting for crucial intel.

"Who's the hot guy?" Sebastian demanded, turning to look behind him, towards Andras and his date.

"Stop staring!" I ordered, sliding onto my chair. "And that? That's Andras. He just moved into my neighborhood. We met the other night and—".

"Danny, he's fucking gorgeous!" Samantha interrupted, tracking Andras like a cheetah stalking prey as he made his way back to the bar again, no doubt to order a drink for his date, who was now sitting solo, scrolling on her cell phone in the booth.

"Yeah, he is," I mumbled. "But he's almost too hot, right? He definitely knows it. Just look at how he's prowling over to the bar like some kind of dark God." Sebastian, Sam, and I all studied him. "It's annoying."

Andras's head whipped towards us, and I went still. His eyes immediately shot to mine and held for a moment. He smirked. And winked. As though he'd heard us talking about him over the music and the murmuring crowd. I shook my head at him then turned my attention back to my friends.

Samantha's eyes were wide, full of delight and intrigue, "Did he just look at you and wink?"

"Yeah. Almost like he heard me, but that would be impossible. I think it was just really obvious that we were gaping at him."

"Well, there's no way he heard us. What is he, a bat? But he definitely turned to look at you," Sebastian waggled his eyebrows playfully.

Samantha tilted her head, "You can't just be friends with someone who looks like that and remain faithfully married, Danny. It's scientifically impossible. Your vagina is going to detach from your body and seek him out like a...what's that ugly fish that you wouldn't stop talking about a few months ago? A male," she chewed her nail for a beat, then slapped the table, "Angler fish! The one that attaches to the other one and–"

I interrupted, "I get it."

She waved a hand dismissively.

"So if you're not going to fuck him, I will. Introduce me."

I huffed a laugh and briefly considered telling them that I was filing for divorce. But I didn't want to talk about it or think about it. I wanted to have fun, to feel joyful, to find release, not grieve or mourn or explain my heartache and fear. Tonight was about letting go.

"I *am* friends with Bash," I said, angling my head toward Sebastian, who chuckled at my compliment, "and despite his terrible personality, he's pretty easy on the eyes." He absolutely was. Sebastian was classically stunning, tall, muscular, with an angular face. "And yeah, I'll introduce you next time."

Sebastian held his glass in the air, "To a beautiful night with beautiful people and their terrible personalities."

Samantha and I raised our glasses to meet Sebastian's. We exchanged loving glances and sang "CHEERS!" in unison, the glasses clinking together.

A stage light beamed onto the silks. A man in a tweed three-piece suit stepped up to the microphone in the center of the room, "Ladies and Gents, Scarlett!" He gestured to the center of the floor. Applause erupted in the room as a woman in a silver, sequined bodysuit appeared behind him, bowed, and began her ascent up the lustrous fabric. I casually scanned the room for Andras, but he must have left because the booth was empty and no sight of the gorgeous woman he'd been with either. I bet they were at his house by now, and the woman was slowly peeling off his perfectly tailored trousers and springing free his giant cock—it had to be huge, given his swagger—and I could almost feel what it would be like to be her, to straddle him, my thighs hugging his hips. I raised my arms in the air and stretched my back to clear my head and the images there. Well, good for her. Good for him. At least somebody is getting it tonight because I certainly wasn't. Steven was somewhere in Asia, and even if he were home...we were too distant, too...broken. For that. Loneliness seeped into my bones, and my heart hurt. Dread and icy uncertainty crashed like a seaside storm in my chest, anxiety flooded every inch of my body, and I couldn't breathe, couldn't think. I focused hard on the table and tapped my fingers against my thighs: five, four, three, two, one.

Sebastian slid out of his chair to stand next to me, gently slipping his arm around my shoulders and resting his chin on top of my head.

He whispered, "You look like you've gone somewhere else, honey, like you're in pain. I love you. What do you need?"

I sunk back into him, reaching up with my right arm and hooking it around his thick, tattooed neck.

"Thank you," I whispered.

Sam leaned forward from where she sat and mouthed, "Love you," her aqua eyes glistening a little. Then she sat back in her chair, still searching my face, looking into my eyes. Her chest rose and fell for a heartbeat before she reached for her drink.

My phone vibrated against the table. I lazily unwound myself from Sebastian to check the screen, just in case it was something about my little ones. Instead, it was a message from Kim, the PTA mom from earlier in the night, that read, "Okay, dish. Who was the hottie at the bar that you looked so cozy with?"

"Uuugh," I groaned.

By morning, every parent I'd ever met within a fifty-mile radius of The Forest Excelsior School would be gossiping about me talking with Andras at the bar, just like the game of telephone we all played as kids. Every person would add their own flair and embellishments. It would start with, "Danny talked with this gorgeous man at the bar, I wonder who he is," then turn into "Danny is having a full-fledged affair with a South American Drug Lord and has run off to Jamaica to marry him."

Of course, I could tell Kim the truth—that Andras was just my neighbor and I didn't even know him. But I was attracted to him, and we'd been talking for at least fifteen minutes, something that would be noticeable to anyone, especially someone like Kim, who lived for scandal. At one point, he'd been inches from my face, and I'd stared up into those luminous blue eyes, inhaling his scent as if it were cocaine. Trying to defend myself or minimize it would make it worse. Once Bethany found out—and she would find out—that bitch was going to have a heyday.

Sebastian gently removed the phone from my hand, a low laugh escaping him as he read the message. I shot him a look.

"This will be fun," he shrugged.

I exhaled loudly. He showed Sam, who groaned and said,

"Oh, God. I hate them,"

While Sebastian and Sam didn't have children, they knew the game. We'd all gone to the same private school together; we all had similarly performative, dysfunctional families. We all knew what the gossip train looked and felt like. I slid my phone back into my purse.

"I'll deal with it tomorrow. Maybe let's just have one more drink? Or ten?"

Sebastian winced, "Don't go all Moms Gone Wild on us, honey. You can not show up hungover at your mother's tomorrow. She will eat you alive."

"She won't kill me. I don't think."

TELEPHONE GAME

The four cups of coffee did not make me feel more alive. The painkillers barely dulled the thrumming in my head, and dread beat like a drum in my gut—which certainly didn't help the nausea—as my car crawled through the obnoxiously high iron gates of my mother's estate. It felt like I'd spent the night being trampled by wild animals, and it didn't help that it was barely eight in the morning. I spilled out of my car as though my limbs had turned liquid, and then I wobbled toward the sprawling stone manor, doing my best to act normal. Halfway up the cobblestone walkway, I spotted the girls and my mother trotting around the grounds on Spider and Rex, mother's prized quarter horses. Liv rode with my mother. They'd be at it for a while, so I ambled over to an old oak tree in a grassy area and slid to the ground, tugging my scarf a little higher on my neck to block out the dawn chill. The early morning frost on the ground bit into my jeans, and the slight breeze whipped unruly strands of hair across my eyes, but at least the fresh air kept me from retching. I swore that the next time I ventured out with Sebastian and Sam, I'd drink less, go to bed earlier, and avoid Andras at all costs. Or at least not swoon over him in public.

Maybe I should have responded to Kim's text. But what could I have said? Nothing but the truth—that I was a hoe who found myself swept up in Andras's sex king vibe like an idiot–would be believable. I had no intention of telling Kim or anyone that Steven and I were getting divorced, not yet. Anything I said would be used against me in the vicious court of sycophant suburbia. Not that I cared what any of them thought of me, but the rumors might hurt my girls, and that mattered. Parents talk, kids talk, and everything comes back to them full circle in the classroom. Cheating rumors would be especially brutal—would fuel taunts, teasing, and shame. I cracked my knuckles. I hated that Andras had an effect on me, but I could barely admit it to myself, let alone the world.

Last night, when I got home, the window of the small mother-in-law apartment above the garage glowed with light, signaling that Steven was settling into his new home and working unencumbered well into the next day. But I didn't think about him, or my broken heart, or dividing our assets. Nope, I crawled into bed and thought of Andras, how he'd been inches from my mouth, the scent of him in the air: whiskey, tobacco, cedar, and something metallic that seemed to cling to my clothes and hair.

Groaning, I scrubbed my hands down my face. Coffee. I needed more coffee but didn't want to drag myself to my feet and stumble in *there*. The manor stood tall enough to block out the sun and large enough to sleep a small village. Despite growing up in this house, it didn't feel like a home. A home has laughter. A home doesn't feel like a mausoleum. The 15,000-square-foot manor was too pristine, too quiet. And, of course, there was the dark truth that our father had died inside, right on the first floor. But he didn't simply die. You say someone died when they had a stroke, or their heart gave out, or they tripped down the basement stairs on the way to the laundry room and snapped their neck. Bob died, sounds like, "he grew old, and then that thing happened that happens to all of us one day." Dad didn't simply pass from this life one night in his sleep. He had been torn to ribbons. He'd been murdered here, on this property, and it would forever taint the place. The unprocessed grief stuck like a film over the brand-new paint they'd used to cover the blood splatter. I shuddered. Images of how we'd found him filled my head and haunted my thoughts and my nervous system. Then, there was our mother, in a Burberry dress, being led away in handcuffs. We'd been questioned relentlessly for weeks by detectives who had no business questioning traumatized teens.

Our lives would never be the same after that. We wrestled with grief, fear, loss, and the unnerving possibility that our mom had been the one to do it. To be honest, I don't think anyone would be shocked if our mother, the ice queen, had killed someone. But the way he'd been killed was so disturbing that there was no way she'd done it—she was too squeamish for that, too clean. She couldn't even look at raw meat in the kitchen without wrinkling her nose or turning away. The detectives said that all of the evidence pointed towards her, all of it, but they couldn't quite prove it. So they let her go and no other suspect was ever found. It was bad enough to lose our father, and though Jess and I were positive Mom had nothing to do with it, there were moments when we subconsciously wondered. How could you not? Imagine being asked to do your homework by someone who'd possibly disemboweled your father in his study down the hall. Best not to take any chances.

I shut my eyes hard to clear my head and raked my fingers through the dead grass, letting the frost burn my fingertips. Hooves pounded against the earth and then abruptly stopped in front of me. I opened my eyes to see the long legs of a bay-colored mare, a mere foot from my knee, and my gaze flicked up to my mother hovering there in her riding clothes, poised tall and unmoving like a statue on the back of Rex. Liv sat nestled between my mother and the saddle horn, smiling down at me.

"Hi, mamma!"

I blew a kiss up to her.

My mother was the picture of her posh British background, with pretty gray hair pulled up in a French twist, polished thigh-high riding boots resting in stirrups, and her high-cut cheekbones flushed a rose pink against her pale face. Liv wore an almost identical outfit to my mother's, her curls in a low ponytail at her nape, just below her riding helmet.

"Daniele," Mom said, looking down her nose at me, "why are you sitting on the wet grass like a dog? If you're not going to ride, why don't you take yourself inside and have Elenor, or whoever is working today, make you a cup of coffee or tea?"

"I'm fine here." I grumbled, "I'm enjoying the morning and don't mind sitting on the grass like a dog, Mom."

She exhaled dramatically, the sound of the burdened and suffering, and shrugged.

"Do as you will, Daniele, as you and your sister always do. Don't let comfort get in the way of your decades-long brooding."

She clicked her tongue against her teeth and Rex jerked his head up but began moving his powerful brown legs forward, the muscles tensing and bulging with every stride. I glared at her narrow back and flipped her off when she was halfway across the field. *Brooding*. Brooding is how my mother referred to mourning as if it had been odd and annoying that we'd reacted negatively to–or even noticed–our father's brutal passing. That alone might have convinced me of her guilt if it weren't for how incredibly non-violent she'd been all our lives.

She was no saint. She had a wicked mean tongue and was a master of guilt and manipulation, but she'd never laid a hand on us and rarely lost her temper. Our mother's weapon of choice was cool, calm calculation, not brute force. She was strong from years of tennis lessons and endless pilates, but not strong enough to do *that*. Plus, Mom had always been too squeamish, too posh, and too clean to ever put herself in any situation where she might be sullied in any way, let alone becoming drenched in another person's body fluids. I can say with absolute certainty that whomever, or *whatever*, killed our father would have ended up soaking wet in sticky crimson. I swallowed hard.

In the distance, Ria bounced on top of a trotting Spider, his blonde coat glowing, her face a mask of cool focus and confidence. Seeing them out there, I remembered Jess and me at about the same age, in the same style of clothes on horses long dead, and our riding teacher, a squat, severe man, barking orders at us the entire time. I shivered; the cold had finally reached my bones.

In the kitchen, I made a cappuccino with the espresso machine and cozied up on the chaise in front of the fireplace with some House and Home magazines that I found on the end table. My mother and the girls came inside shortly after. Ria and Liv waved to me as they were shooed upstairs to the guest rooms by my mother to shower and change. They came down a half hour later in clothes I didn't recognize (surely gifted by their grandmother), their dark wavy hair in braids and headbands, most likely styled by Elenor, who was probably cleaning the rooms upstairs. The girls ran to another part of the house to do who knows what. I called after them, "Five more minutes! Pick one last fun thing to do, and then it's time to go!" My mother's eyes danced as she watched them bound down the endless hall across the marble stone floor. She cooly prowled to the armchair closest to me and lowered herself gracefully onto it. Crossing her legs at the ankle,–Gods forbid she wrinkle her white pantsuit–she straightened her spine like a queen on a throne, her gaze sweeping across my face then dipping to my feet and slowly creeping up to settle on my eyes. I bristled as she silently judged.

"How are you?" she asked, resting her hands in her lap.

"I'm doing well," I said.

I spread my legs and slunk down in the chair. I didn't know why I had to irritate her on purpose, but I couldn't help it. My mother's eyes narrowed on me and she inhaled sharply but held back whatever it was she wanted to say. A pause.

"How is your sister?" she asked.

"Good."

"Good."

"How are you, Mom?" I asked.

"I'm doing well, thank you."

"Good."

Then, we sat in silence for what felt like a million years. She watched me. I let my eyes roam around the room. The paintings were the same ones that had hung on the dark green walls when we were young: a forest at dusk, a vase of peonies, and a massive portrait of a nude woman staring at something off to the right. The ceiling was flawlessly white without a dust particle or cobweb in sight, meaning that someone regularly climbed a very tall ladder to clean the thing. A few loose tendrils fell over my eyes when I leaned over to examine the rug–the same vibrant blue, green, and red Persian rug I'd painted in the piece above my bed at home. Liv and Ria screamed and laughed somewhere across the house, but other than that, the place was as silent as a tomb.

It had always been dead quiet unless they threw a party or my mother put on some of the jazz or classical music she liked so much. Once in a while, our dad would listen to old Persian music, and a smile would tug at his lips as he spread his arms out wide to snap his fingers and move his broad chest back and forth to the beat. This usually happened after he received good business news and had one too many tequila shots to celebrate. Jess and I would join him, moving our hips, shaking our shoulders; our mother would watch with raised brows, being way too Anglo-Saxon for ass-shaking. Despite these moments, despite the Persians being a warm people, our father was typically quiet and distant, his bushy black brows forever knitted together and forehead creased in an expression of deep contemplation as he mulled over work while silently judging everyone. Obsessively. Still, I missed him. For some reason, that always seemed to bother our mother. Her refusal to comfort us or even talk with us about what had happened had deepened the divide between us over time.

Victoria burst into the room with Olivia right behind her.

"We're ready!" Victoria announced.

"Thank Gods," I muttered under my breath.

"I heard that," my mother accused, looking bored.

I rose to my feet, my back aching from slouching in the chaise. I supposed I deserved it. I bent down and hugged Olivia and Victoria. We walked towards the front door together, the girls practically under my feet and my mother directly behind us, gliding.

"We had caviar again!" Victoria said.

"It was disgusting," Olivia added.

"It was not disgusting," my mother countered.

We turned to face her at the large, black, medieval-looking door in the foyer.

"Goodbye, Grandma! Thank you!" Victoria said, stepping forward to hug her grandmother gently around the legs. My mother patted her on the head, careful not to upset the headband.

"Thanks, Grammy!" Olivia waved.

"Thank you, mom," I said, smiling tightly.

My mother dipped her chin.

"Of course, darling," she said, barely a whisper.

DAGGERS FOR EYES

They stared, stared, stared as I stepped through the doors of The Forest Excelsior School on Monday morning, one daughter on either side of me. I tried my best not to notice the judgemental gazes of every single parent in the hall; the looks that some of them shot in my direction felt like daggers. Kim's lips pressed together in a thin line as I ushered Victoria and Olivia past her in the hall, and I shot her a look that read something like, "You're a fucking twat." Two mothers off to the right, both in nearly identical high-end workout gear, whispered something to each other while glancing at me sideways. Another mom, Layla (who I actually liked), flashed an approving smirk when my yellow-green eyes met her aqua blues as if to cheerlead, "Yesss, get it." I forced an uncomfortable smile before continuing on my way to Ria and Liv's classrooms. I double-checked each of them, scanning their blue and green uniforms to make sure everything was in place and kissed them on the head before handing each one off to their respective teacher. Then I made my way out of the school, pausing only momentarily in front of a window for a heartbeat to take in my outfit: black sweatpants and white sweater, mocha hair down to my shoulders in a wild, wavy mess that refused to stay out of my tired face, and yesterday's mascara still flaking onto the skin around my eyes like a raccoon. Damnit. I looked like I'd just survived forty-eight hours of sorority hazing. I shrugged at my reflection and continued on.

I considered my to-do list as my feet moved forward–grocery shopping, wine store, then pick up dry cleaning, buy new cleats for Liv, go to the paint store for some new canvas and maybe the bookstore to wander aimlessly for a while. I was lost in thought when I hit the parking lot and looked up to find Bethany positioned in front of her white SUV, arms folded over her chest, parked directly next to my car.

"Good morning, Danny!" Bethany sang.

She smiled like a serpent and waved with her gloved fingers. Her face looked flawless even first thing in the morning, with winged eyeliner and neutral pink lipstick applied by a masterful hand. Bethany's blonde hair tumbled over her breasts, ending in large curls.

"Hi, Bethany," I mumbled flatly. I walked directly towards my car without pausing to chat, knowing full well that she wanted to prod and chide. I didn't have the patience for her or the games—not today.

"How are you?" she cooed, slithering away from her car to follow me; her fur-lined snow boots—probably from a litter of kittens—crunched in the slush behind me.

"Fine, thanks," I mumbled.

I didn't even attempt to hide the bite in the words, my utter annoyance with her for the past two decades coming to a head. Fumbling in my bag for my keys, I picked up the pace toward the door of my car.

"So everything at home is okay, then? Are you and Steven okay? Because I heard that—"

I whirled to face her, and she stopped dead in her tracks, rocking back on her heels, eyes wide with surprise.

"Bethany, I know what you heard," I spat. "Yes, I was out with Sam and Sebastian on Friday night. Yes, I ran into my neighbor who I don't even fucking know. And yes, he's painfully fucking hot, and no, I am not having an affair, and my marriage is just fucking fine, Bethany. It's fucking great."

I lied. Blatantly lied. My marriage was not fucking great. We were getting fucking divorced. In fact, I had an appointment later in the day to sit down with my lawyer and Steven's to sort shit out. I felt myself flinch from the lie, as if my body itself rejected it, but until we sat down with the kids, until we'd told our parents and friends, I sure as hell wasn't going to tell Bethany anything.

Bethany's eyes settled into a deep scowl, her chest rose and fell, and she gripped her keys a little tighter, but her mouth stayed shut in a tight, thin line. *Good.* I spun away from her to face my car door and hit the key fob to open it.

"I don't know why you're being so defensive. I'm just checking on you. And Steven. Wanted to make sure things weren't on the rocks and he wasn't in...mortal danger."

I balled up my fists and growled low, waiting for my car door to open. I'd known Bethany forever, since before we were even in training bras, and she'd been exactly the same since Junior High. Serpentine. It was like she fed off of the discomfort of others and, therefore, needed to fan it with her vicious tongue, which she hid behind her lovely, fake smile and perfectly manicured Stepford wife facade. Pretty face and a demon soul, just like her parents. Her eyes bore into the back of my head and I tried for the life of me to calm myself down, to stop myself from responding to her insult. In the end, I lost the battle and heard the words come out of my mouth before I realized I'd spoken them.

"Oh, fuck off. Don't you get fucking sick of this fake passive-aggressive shit?" I said, barely a whisper, while I bounced from foot to foot waiting as the car doors inched open. They were so slow as they hinged up that it was comical, and I could feel her glare branding my backside.

"What did you say?" she said coolly. "I couldn't hear you."

But there was an edge to her words, a challenge that told me she had heard me and wanted more. I exhaled loudly. *The godsdamn wraith.* My car doors finally opened enough for me to squeeze in. They hung in the air like a bat, ready to launch skyward. I groaned. *I really have to get a new car soon.*

"Have a good day, Bethany," I said through my teeth.

Glancing over my shoulder with one eye while I slid into my car, I could see the storm beneath her skin, and her eyes narrowed barely to slits. I threw my purse blindly over the backseat. Then I waited for the stupid doors to lower so I could drive away while she stood her ground, unflinching, shooting daggers at me with her blue-gray goblin eyes. Once the doors clicked shut, after what felt like an eternity of being cornered by a cobra, my engine silently came to life, and she slid back to her SUV, texting manically as if sending an SOS to anyone who might listen.

The story being spun was old news. "Danny is an unraveling psycho," she'd write to whatever group chats would listen, positioning herself as the angelic martyr who only wanted to be helpful. In the past decade, I'd experienced enough gaslighting to cause the atmosphere to combust. I could imagine this same back and forth between us decades from now when we took turns paying people from the grave to alter the epitaph on our tombstones. "This cunt lies here." Maybe one day, I'd finally snap and cut the brakes on her Jazzy and send her into traffic.

I chuckled to myself and pressed my middle finger to the window as my car glided past hers and she glared.

THE INVADER

A crash somewhere in the house ripped me from sleep. The bedroom was dark except for a small sliver of moonlight peaking through the curtains. My eyes strained to focus as they searched the space, my brain still foggy with dreams. A sharp crash thundered from somewhere in the front of my house that had me up and balancing on shaky legs in an instant, wobbling like a newborn fawn. My head spun as my feet instinctively moved toward the baby monitor on my nightstand to check on my little ones. My shoulders relaxed a little when I saw them there fast asleep, snug in their beds, the low thrumming of the sound machine off in the distance. *What was that sound?* My mind raced. *Steven just left on a trip. I'm here alone. Did a picture fall off of the wall?* Then something clinked and clattered. *Chimes? No. Glass.* The sound of glass shattering to the floor. Then heavy boots hitting the hardwood, stalking slowly, and carefully somewhere not too far away. I went wholly still. Then the frozen terror melted into fury, my shaking hands balled into fists, as those heavy steps started up the staircase, towards me, towards *my girls*. My body lurched into action, and I pulled my joggers on and reached for my phone on the nightstand.

"This is 911. What is your emergency?" A woman asked, even-toned, almost robotically.

I whispered, "Someone is in my house. I have two children here. Please send help. They're coming." My voice cracked.

"Stay on the line with me. I'm dispatching a car right now. They'll be there in just a few minutes. Stay with me." She commanded as if she had the power to protect me through the satellite signal.

I disobeyed, setting the phone on the bed to scan the darkness for an object that could be used as a weapon.

The footsteps grew louder and heavier until they made it to the hallway, and the floor groaned outside my bedroom door beneath the weight of whatever massive thing loomed there, listening, searching. I crept cautiously toward the dresser, careful to avoid the loud boards, the ones I'd memorized while up all night rocking Olivia to sleep when she'd been an infant. Inhaling sharply, I reached for a glass mug with shaking fingers. And waited.

The bedroom door cracked open, hinges moaning a warning. I sucked in tiny gulps of air, my heart pounding against my ribcage. In a flash, I leapt forward, swinging the mug with desperate precision. It connected with a sickening thud against the side of his bald head. The dark figure growled, a guttural sound of pain and fury, as he staggered back into the hallway. *Get to the kitchen. Get a knife. Get to my kids.* The frantic thoughts raced through my mind as I bolted from the room; but his large, strong hands shot out, snatching a handful of my hair and yanking me back.

My feet flew out from under me, and in an instant, he was dragging me down the stairs away from my daughters. Good. My heels thumped and scraped against the steps as I struggled for leverage, his grip on my hair unyielding. My hands clawed at his fist, flailed, and punched in wild desperation.

He threw me across the living room floor, where I collided with the sofa, breath knocked out of me. Scrambling to my feet, adrenaline surging, I charged at him with every ounce of strength in my body. My scream, raw and primal, pierced the air as I hurled myself at the dark mass, determined to protect my family at all costs.

"GET THE FUCK OUT OF MY HOOOOOUSE!" I roared as I collided with his muscled body.

Despite his size, he grunted and fell back. I kicked and punched and scratched at the large head and those wide eyes as arms the size of logs closed around me and tightened, forcing the air from my lungs. Rage. Blind, murderous rage took root inside of me, and I went wild with madness. *I'd kill him, I'd kill him!* My skin seemed to burn with wrath. It must have been the adrenaline, but my hands that were pinned to my sides started to tingle, as if electricity danced across my palms. "Let me go, you piece of shit!" I shouted curse words as if I could somehow weaponize them. Then something happened, and my body just took over like it knew what to do, how to fight, and I head-butted any reachable surface, snarling, spitting like a rabid dog until I landed one solid blow to his nose with my forehead and felt a cool smear of blood on my face as the grip around me loosened.

I pulled my knees up into my chest between us and shoved my feet into his ribs, pushing off until his arms were forced open. He snarled as I flew backward out of his grasp, my back and head slamming into the floor. I inhaled raggedly. White lights clouded my vision as I gasped for air. A door opened and shut. Had the girls come downstairs? I whirled, searching the shadows through blurred vision. Did this man have friends, more horrible bastards coming to end me? Or worse? *I would kill them all.* The Ogre-sized man stalked towards me, teeth bared.

A warm breeze blew my hair across my face. My vision cleared just as he reached for me. I cried out as I scrambled backward and scuttled across the rug, trying to get away, get away, get away, and get to my feet. Then, as if propelled by the shadows themselves, he was airborne, thrown by some invisible force. His body slammed into the far living room wall, head snapping back with a crack as he sagged to the floor, lifeless. I frantically searched the living room, eyes darting from one wall to the next, combing the darkness for someone else. Someone had to be here with me, someone or *something* capable of throwing a man the size of a refrigerator across the room.

"Hello?" I whispered, barely audible, as I rose on shaky legs.

The chandelier light came alive, temporarily blinding me. When my eyes adjusted, they found a pale, three-hundred-pound man with a goatee and bald head lying unconscious on the floor, his body at an unnatural angle. Blood pooled under his nose and slid down deep, weather-worn frown lines. The blue and white peacock wallpaper above him was dented and shredded, like it had been hit with a wrecking ball. My fingers went to my mouth to stifle a small cry working its way up my throat.

"Are you okay?" asked a low, gravely voice, an otherworldly tone enveloped in rage and wrath.

The voice was familiar but strange. I froze. Then, slowly, so slowly, I turned towards it.

Andras leaned against the wall nearest to my dining table, his hands in his black trouser pockets, head angled in question, his expression unreadable. *Am I hallucinating?*

"Andras?"

I blinked hard, but he was still there.

"Yes. It's me." He tilted his head. "Are you okay? Did he hurt you?" he asked gently, in a way that sounded more like the man I knew.

I wrapped my arms around myself, "Why are you...how did you get..." I took a slow, deep breath and tried again, "Where did you come from? And him?" I stammered, unable to slow the cascade of thoughts and questions crashing into me, unable to form a full sentence.

Andras glanced sidelong at the brute. "I don't know who he is. I was walking by and I heard you yelling, heard a struggle. Are you hurt?" His eyes raked over my body and face.

My hands went to my hair and touched my face gingerly, then ran them down my body. Everything was numb.

"I–I don't know. I don't think so." A pause. And then terror flooded through me. "Oh no! Olivia! Victoria!" I spun, then sprinted towards the stairs that led to the second floor, to their room, taking two at a time I clamored up them. My bare feet smacked the polished hardwood as I flew down the hall and braced myself for something horrible as I swung open their bedroom door. The room was dark except for a small night light in the far corner. The quiet lull of a fan and the crashing waves of the sea poured from their sound machines and both girls were fast asleep. I breathed a sigh of relief, then double-checked the windows and the closet before closing the door and checking the rest of the upstairs, then padding back downstairs cautiously to where Andras still stood in the same spot, unmoved. I slowly entered the living room, eyeing the unconscious man, hating him with a depth and severity that unnerved me. He'd entered our safe space, he'd put his hands on me, he— Was he breathing? A dark and cruel part of me hoped he wasn't.

"Are your daughters alright?" Andras asked, dipping his chin to levy his eyes at me.

I nodded once. "Is he alive?" I asked. I gestured to the unconscious behemoth.

"Barely," Andras responded flatly, a hint of disdain in his voice. "We should probably call the police to get rid of him."

"I already did. I called 911 for help, but...I'm sure they'll be here any second."

I went to the couch and collapsed onto the cushions. I ran my hands through the wild, tangled mess of my hair.

"I can't believe this. Thank Gods the kids weren't hurt and didn't see anything."

Jess and I hadn't been so lucky when we were younger, when we'd come across our father twisted and flecked with blood. The image would torment me forever, and I never wanted my girls to experience anything like it.

Andras's focus shifted to the floor.

"I remembered that you had children so I checked on them first when I got here, that's why it took a second for me to get to you."

Sliding my hands down my face, I narrowed my aching eyes on him,

"What do you mean you checked on them first? How would you have done that? I heard the door open, and then this man was airborne. There wasn't enough time...and how...how did you throw him like that?"

I panted between words, struggling to get enough air into my lungs.

He nodded as if to admit that it did seem strange. His hands slid out of his pockets, and he rolled his shoulders before prowling towards the man and crouching down to examine his face.

"Maybe it seemed faster than it was because you were in the middle of trying to gouge out his eyeballs. I heard struggling from the sidewalk, came in and saw you both, and worried that more men might be in the house. Since you seemed to have the situation here under control, at least for a moment, I ran up and checked on the girls, sniffed around for more of him, and then rushed back to you. Just in time, it seems." He smiled tightly at me. "I'm not exactly small, Danny. We are about the same height, me and this bastard."

He smiled again, with his teeth this time, but the smile didn't reach his eyes, which seemed darker than usual, darker than midnight blue, almost black. Maybe because the room was dimly lit? But no, that couldn't be it, poor lighting wouldn't turn sapphire to obsidian. I was so tired.

Andras was tall, and even beneath the dark gray sweater, you could see that his body was strong and muscled. Still, he'd have to be a fucking giant to toss someone that size like a sack of potatoes. I opened my mouth to tell him that but stopped when I noticed a change in him. He was still crouched to examine the man, but his head was now cocked to the side, eyes wide with shock or confusion.

"What is it?" I asked, getting to my feet.

"Have you ever seen this man before?" Andras asked, without taking his eyes off of the giant.

"No. Why? Do you recognize him?"

My heart thundered against my rib cage, boom, boom, boom, and I wrung my hands so hard the knuckles ached. Andras slowly stood, eyes still trained on the man. His hands were balled into fists so tight that his knuckles were white.

"Andras?" I asked.

His eyes, full of worry, slowly slid to meet mine.

Red and blue flashing lights bounced across the living room window. Andras's gaze darted about the room as if he were on the verge of panic. I went to the curtains to peer out. Three police cars had stopped in front of my house, parking in the middle of the street. Officers slowly exited the cars, hands on their guns as they crept towards my house. I turned to tell Andras that the officers were about to reach the front door, but he was gone. There were no footsteps leading away from the room, no sound of a door opening or closing, no trace that he'd ever been there at all, like he'd evaporated or like I'd imagined it.

I pulled open my front door to twirling blue car lights and three male police officers with their weapons drawn on my porch. They eyed me carefully, armed and on edge. Carefully, so carefully, I put my hands up and said, "This is my house. I called 911 because a man," my voice cracked, "broke in. He's in here. I have two children asleep upstairs. They're safe." I angled my body away from the door so they could see inside the house. The police officers crept slowly past me, and once inside the living room, they paused, their shoulders relaxing as they exchanged confused glances with each other and then turned back to me.

One of them, a man of average height with a mustache, snuck towards the lump on the floor, then squatted down to check his pulse.

"He's alive," he said, "But he's out cold. Call an ambulance. We can cuff him to the bed." Another police officer, a woman with strawberry blonde hair and kind eyes set into a freckled face, came up to me.

"Ma'am, do you want to start from the beginning and tell me everything that happened?"

She took a notepad out of her pocket.

Tears rolled down my cheeks while I answered the police officer's questions. No, I'd never seen him before, and no, I had nothing particularly valuable to steal. How did he end up on the floor? I didn't know. The details were fuzzy. I'd charged him and fought him off like a rabid honey badger, a partial truth, and that's how he ended up there. He must have tripped, I lied. I left out the part where Andras had appeared out of nowhere, like a godsdamned archangel, to save me. I wasn't really sure why I decided to leave it out, other than I had no idea how to explain it without sounding insane. He came in like a breeze, knocked out the man on the floor, and then disappeared into thin air. At that point, it felt entirely possible that I'd imagined him, a kind of stress-induced hallucination, if such a thing existed.

The officer explained, "There have been a string of break-ins in this area. Usually, the houses are vacant, though. Something tells me that this is the guy responsible for them. He probably cased your place, saw your husband leave with luggage when he was staking out the street, and assumed your house was empty."

She tapped her notebook with her pen.

"My guess is you surprised him by being here."

"I had this weird feeling like I was being watched all week," I said, hugging myself.

"Because you were." The officer said.

They were kind enough to quietly check the girls' room without waking them.

"The house is clear," an officer yelled from the kitchen.

I stood aside as two EMTs wheeled the burglar out of my house on a stretcher, still unconscious. He groaned as they went down the stairs, and I shut and latched the door behind them, watching from the window as they carted him toward the ambulance. They fanned open the ambulance doors and without warning, the burglar rolled off of the stretcher and landed on his feet like a cat. I brought my hand to my mouth and tried to stifle a scream as panic struck. A police officer near him lunged for the man, but he took off in an unnaturally fast sprint with two police officers in pursuit on foot. One of the cars lurched forward, lights on, siren wailing, before it disappeared out of sight.

A knock sounded at my front door, and I startled. When I cracked it, an officer stood there with a sorrowful expression on her face.

"Ma'am, I'm so sorry." And she looked sorry, face pinched, and mouth turned downward, "The suspect regained consciousness and fled the scene. Our officers are in pursuit and shouldn't have too difficult of a time catching him. But just to make sure he doesn't try to come back here, I'm going to stay through the night. If you need anything at all or see anything strange, I'm parked right in front of your house. I'll keep you updated."

I nodded, unable to form words or articulate the ten thousand questions and fears plaguing me. How did he get away from them so quickly and easily? Did they think he'd come back here? I thanked the officer for staying to watch the house then closed and locked the door. I shuddered as my house fell dark and silent again.

I swept the broken glass from the floor and taped the window shut with some plastic bags I found. I phoned my sister, then made tea with hands that wouldn't stop trembling, the whole horrible thing playing over and over in my mind. I thought of Andras. Something about the burglar had spooked him, and then he'd vanished.

Sitting at the top of the stairs, I slowly sipped the chamomile tea I'd made and listened to the sounds of my house resettling. Every creak and bump nearly brought me out of my skin and to my feet.

SISTER, SISTER

"I should probably shower." I rubbed my eyes. "The girls will know something's wrong." Jess swiveled to look at me, to take inventory of the damage, and I could imagine what she saw: wavy hair in frizzy tendrils around my pale olive face, not in a "messy but hot" way, but in a "my head was nearly pulled from my body by a psychopath" way. My face felt sticky, and I could sense where my mascara had left crusted black saltwater trails down my cheeks.

I shifted uncomfortably on my oak bar stool where Jess and I had been hunched over the white marble counter in my "light and airy" kitchen for a while. At least, that's what Sebastian had called it when he designed it. When they did the renovation, I'd repeatedly said that I wanted a home that felt "awake" and "alive," but after what happened the night before, after a giant man forced his way into my home, the rising sun and its warmth pouring in through the windows could only remind me that I had way too many fucking windows. Each one a possible entry point.

"Maybe you could just say we had a slumber party and stayed up all night binge-watching sad nineties movies and hysterically sobbing. They'd probably buy that. Tell them you watched The Notebook and One Day back-to-back." "Jesus Christ! I look *that* bad?"

"Yeah, you fucking do."

Jess had been in a fitful sleep when I'd called her at two a.m. after the police had left. When she heard the quiver in my voice followed by a breakdown into a dark, unnatural pitch on the phone, she must have sprinted for her car, plaid pajama set, fuzzy boots, and all, because she pulled up less than fifteen minutes later, pale-faced and shaking. This is where we'd been for a while now, hunched over our coffee cups, shoulders touching, the house still and ominous, even as the sun came up over the horizon.

Jess gently patted my knee.

"Do you want to get a little sleep, sis? It's five, and I can watch the girls when they get up."

"I can't. I'm too anxious to sleep. I keep replaying the night over and over again. I keep imagining a million different horrifying scenarios."

"Yeah, of course, someone just broke into your house and attacked you."

"Like dad." My voice nearly broke, "I almost ended up like dad."

Jess's hand went still on my leg, heavy, and the light in her eyes dimmed just a little at that. She tried to hide it, but I noticed the deep, shaky breath she took. She cleared her throat, and her hand began moving on my knee again.

"Did the police have any more info on what happened and why? Or were they just totally useless?"

"No," I croaked, "just what I told you, that there have been a lot of break-ins around here recently and that man probably thought the house was empty."

I started to rock slowly back and forth to soothe my electric nerves.

"They said he probably saw Steven leave with bags. He panicked when he realized I was in the house. That's probably why he attacked me. But how the fuck do they know? Maybe he's a murderer. Maybe the guy had lead poisoning. I read that lead poisoning leads to aggression. But then, so does poverty. Maybe he's struggling to pay bills. Maybe he injured his back skiing and is now addicted to heroin. Maybe our family is cursed, and he was here for me, intentionally. Who the fuck knows." My eyes darted around, brows knit together. "And Andras, my neighbor. The one I told you about before? It was weird enough that he just showed up and saved me and then literally disappeared. But I could have sworn that something flashed in his eyes when he got close to the man, when he leaned over to look at him. Almost like fear and recognition. But maybe I'm going crazy and imagining it. Maybe he was never even here at all."

"You're not going crazy. You're traumatized, and I'm sure it's triggering as fuck given all of the stuff we've already put behind us. But yeah, him just taking off, that's weird. That's "wanted by the FBI" weird,'" Jess agreed. "But it's not that strange that he came to help. You said he walks by all the time. It's definitely possible that he just heard struggling and came to help and left…honestly…who knows? Maybe he's a drug mule."

I frowned. She grinned in an attempt to lighten the mood, to ease the anxiety.

"I'm super grateful for him, but I don't know, something was off. He came running in like one of the X-Men with super Hulk strength and—"

"Hulk isn't one of the X-Men, sis."

I glared at that.

"I mean, it makes sense that you don't feel extremely trusting right now. But you don't know his background, right? Maybe he was in the Marines? Or maybe he's a retired MMA fighter. Or maybe he did that weird, ole-timey sword-fighting bullshit you did when you were a kid, and he's really into gallantry, or what the fuck ever? Maybe he's on steroids."

"It's called fencing, *asshole*. And Dad made me do it, along with the decade of martial arts he forced on both of us. And I don't know. It was more than the crazy strength. He looked off, somehow. His pupils were all giant and black."

"He probably did too much cocaine at the club."

I ignored her attempt at levity this time. My eyes flicked up towards the ceiling and stayed there as I left my body for a moment, the details of the night playing out. The fear and anger still lingering in my body seemed to anchor themselves deep in my flesh; I could feel myself being branded by the experience in real time. I shook my head, trying to dispel the images.

I scrubbed at my face and turned to Jess.

"I don't feel safe. I feel like my seams are going to break. I can't take any more right now." I rubbed my hands through my hair and let out a growl of frustration. A strange pressure expanded in my chest, an electrical storm about to burst. As if any minute, a thread would rip, and the nervous, chaotic energy that made up my insides was going to erupt from me and destroy the world.

Jess rested a slender hand between my shoulder blades. A warm smile appeared on her face as if to say, "I'm here. It's going to be okay, I promise." I tried to return the look, but my lips turned up weakly, my eyes too full of exhaustion to sell it.

"Well, that's a terrifying sort of expression," Jess said, chuckling softly. "I'm here, okay. And I'm not leaving until you kick me out of your goddamn house."

"Thank you."

I knew all of this was hard for her, too, knew it brought up memories of our father and that she wouldn't leave because she loved me but also because she feared that someone else she loved might be ripped from her if she wasn't diligent and present. It was the same way I felt day after day after we lost our dad, like every moment was fragile and like everyone I loved could be ripped away. I fell forward to rest my forehead on my arms on the counter.

"I need to text Steven," I groaned. "He's in New York or something."

"I'll do it," Jess said, picking up her phone and quickly typing out a message to Steven. She read it out loud, summarizing the events of the night, followed by a terse, "Everyone is okay and safe."

My voice was surprisingly raspy as I said into the counter, "as soon as they wake up, let's just get out of here. Let's go get a vat of fucking coffee and just get out of this house."

"Okay, just rest. I'll watch the monitor and keep the girls safe." I heard her pull the little screen over to her, heard the stool shift as she leaned back, getting comfortable for the long haul. Jess sighed and whispered, "I seriously need to get me one of those sleep machines. They're fucking magic if even Liv slept through it all."

A horrible buzzing sound coming from somewhere nearby jolted me awake. It felt like my skull was being compressed like a sponge being wrung out by two meaty hands. My eyes flew open and my neck and cheek stung as I peeled my face from the counter. "Oh Jesus," I said, rubbing my skin where an angry pink mark had formed. I looked around my sunny kitchen, bewildered, my mind in the thick fog of exhaustion. Then it all came flooding back to me, the break-in, the man, all of it.

The room spun. My hand gripped the counter to steady myself while I listened for my sister. The buzzing came from my phone vibrating against an empty coffee mug on the counter.

"Hello?" I answered nervously.

"Danny, what's going on?" Steven demanded, panicked, his voice scratchy and higher than usual. "I got a text from Jess saying that someone broke into our house a few hours ago and I haven't heard anything from either of you! And she's not answering her fucking phone. Are the girls okay? Danny? Danny! Are you there?"

"The girls," I scanned the kitchen for the monitor, but it wasn't there. I walked into the living room. Empty. My stomach twisted, and I sprinted towards the staircase.

"Danny?" Steven yelled into the phone.

"Hold on!" I snapped back.

"Jess? Are you up there?" I called up the staircase. No response, no footsteps, no movement.

I climbed the stairs, three steps at a time, and just as I nearly reached the second floor, I heard a faint giggling coming from out back. I scrambled to my feet and ran towards the back door, bursting through the screen, my cell phone still in my hand and Steven's voice, small and far away, calling out to me. In the backyard, Olivia and Victoria were zipping around, squealing, while Jess growled in hot pursuit.

"Girls!" I called out, louder and more shrill than I meant to. Olivia and Victoria's heads craned around to see me frazzled and wide-eyed with a red welt the size of an orange in the middle of my forehead from the nap, like a psychotic narwhal.

"Mamma's awake!" Olivia announced, clapping and jumping up and down. Both girls ran towards me and each one tackled a leg, hugging and yanking my kneecaps in an adorably painful show of love.

"Hi, my loves," I sang, reaching down to run my hands over their soft, messy tendrils. My shoulders relaxed with every passing second that I could see that they were safe and secure right in front of me.

Jess wandered over, "You're up! How was your nap? Who is this on the phone?" She poked the screen in my hand that was just kind of dangling at my fingertips.

"Oh shit!" I said, holding my phone back up to my ear, "Steven? Are you there?."

He was gone, so I slid my phone back into my pocket and reached down to grab Victoria, who was sitting on my foot, wrapping herself around my leg.

"Come here, darling," I said, heaving just a little as I picked her up for a big hug, nuzzling my face against her tiny neck. Victoria giggled.

Jess bounced around the yard like an airplane, holding a cackling Olivia in her arms. Olivia zoomed off the moment her feet hit the ground as if some motor inside of her kept her legs going at all times.

Jess tilted her head, pressing her lips together. "You okay, sis?" She asked.

I kissed Victoria on the head before setting her down.

"Yeah, I just woke up in a bit of a panic because as soon as I opened my eyes, everything flooded back to me, and I couldn't find you. And then Steven called. I guess he's coming home as soon as he can grab a flight. How terrible is it that I'm actually surprised he's coming home for this?"

"That's pretty fucking depressing, is what that is." Jess's wide eyes were trained on mine. Then her face relaxed and she blew a raspberry to break the tension. "How are you feeling? Do you want to see the cameras I had installed while you were zonked out?"

"Cameras? How?"

"I know a guy!" Jess said, huffing a laugh.

Jess grabbed my hand and led me around to the side of the house. There were four cameras that captured every imaginable angle. Even one pointing to the sky. "Is that in case someone tries to parachute out of a plane onto our roof?" I joked. Jess nodded her head and we exchanged a smile before she grabbed my hand and led me to the other side of the house to see the other nine-hundred cameras.

Jess showed up for people by getting shit done, and there was absolutely no one better. She had a knack for knowing when and how to take charge like she could see inside of people, partly because she was genuinely fascinated with folks and could sit for hours listening to anyone go on about anything and everything, no matter how mundane. She also had ironclad boundaries. Jess didn't do anything that she didn't want to do, ever. So while I slept with my face smashed against the cool kitchen counter until one p.m. (the longest I'd slept in since college), Jess managed to dress the girls, have the broken window repaired by "some guy," install security cameras, because she had "a friend," and do a coffee and pastry run so there would be caffeine and sugar when I woke up.

"It's kinda creepy, honestly," Jess said.

"Yeah, it is. And thank you," I said, a knot forming in my throat. Maybe I didn't win the lottery in the parent or husband department, but I sure as fuck had the best sister in the world.

PHO KIT

The reclaimed wood table in my dining room was crowded with paper cartons and soup bowls from a local restaurant comically named Pho Kit. Olivia pretended that a Triceratops was eating her soup noodles, and Victoria tried to master her chopsticks, picking up two or three noodles, then growling in frustration when half of them plopped back into the broth. I tried to master my nervous system, stay calm, and not have a complete fucking meltdown over the insane mess they were both making.

"You're trying really hard!" I said to Ria, drawing from an article I'd read that week on the importance of positive reinforcement and the advantages of praising effort. I'd tried to remember it all and employ it when I could, along with a laundry list of other tips from an essay that should have been titled, "How To Not Screw Up Your Kids Like We Were Screwed Up (But Different!)."

"Seriously," Jess was saying, "it's absolutely barbaric out there, and I already had trust issues to begin with, but now I don't believe anything. If I'm chatting with someone on the app and they claim to be a zoologist, what I picture is a person living in their parents' musty garage with a massive reptile collection, including a Python bestie named Kyle. And I can't tell you how many people have asked me over to watch them play video games on their vintage Nintendo in a poorly furnished studio that reeks of farts and old beer."

I huffed a laugh.

Jess nodded in agreement.

"I'm *never* dating a Zoologist," Ria mumbled.

Jess and I erupted in laughter; wine dribbled out of my mouth, beading down my chin.

"Well played, Ria," Jess winked at her.

"Well," I said to Jess, "I guess that's one good thing about getting married right out of college. I never had to use a dating app. And that's all anyone uses now, right?" Ack, what would I do now that we were splitting up? I'd have to vow to never date again, which seemed easy enough at this point, or be forced to meet someone like that. I pressed my thighs together to keep all of that reptile-loving phantom dick at bay.

I reached for the box of wine and held it over Jess's glass before filling my own. Thanks to my sister and her random security connection, the comically large monitor on the far wall now displayed live feed videos from each security camera, twenty-four-seven: A black night landscape, a cat sauntering past the house, our shaking aspen tree swaying in the breeze.

"What band is this again?" Jess asked.

"Vampire Weekend," I responded, "we used to listen to them in high school, remember?"

The music played softly in the background, a pretty male vocalist singing, "Look outside at the raincoats coming, say oh, look outside at the raincoats coming, say oh."

Jess smacked the table. "Oh, that's right! Sorry, I blocked out most of high school, and pretty much everything that led up to it." She sighed and adjusted the collar of her white blouse.

Wine swirled in my glass. It burned sweetly all the way down my throat with every sip. Smiling wryly, I joked, "What? You didn't want to cling to the billion hours of studying? Or mom and dad's soul-crushing expectations? Or all of the...very specific teasing?" I was alluding to the endless taunts about mom murdering dad, careful not to say too much in front of my kids.

Jess rolled her eyes and blew a raspberry.

The security system came alive with a low "beep, beep," and my head jerked towards the screen as a tall, lean figure entered my yard through the iron gate, closing the distance to the front door in determined strides. My stomach twisted until the figure glanced up at the camera, and I recognized my husband's square chin and short, light hair. I exhaled a large gust of air, realizing I'd been holding my breath the whole time.

"Daddy! Daddy! Daddy!" Ria began to chant.

"Daddy!" Liv joined in.

Steven came into the dining room, slowly, wearily. "Hey," he said, eyes red, face blotchy and lined with exhaustion. His gaze met mine, and he winced an apology as if saying, "I'm sorry I wasn't here." He set his bags down at the front door, rubbed his jet-lagged eyes, and went straight to the table where the girls sat, kissing each of them on their curly heads, lingering for just a second. Then he unexpectedly went to Jess to hug her awkwardly from behind, causing her eyes to flare wide. She smiled tightly and patted his shoulder. He said, "thank you, for everything," and she dipped her chin just a little in a silent "you're welcome." Steven walked over to me. I craned my neck up at him, "Welcome home." I said. He smiled tightly, then put his hand on my shoulder, squeezing gently, as he leaned down to kiss my cheek. It was the first time he'd done that in more than a year. He sat next to the girls and made eye contact with everyone, his brown eyes sincere, searching, as he looked around the table at each of us. Then he cleared his throat,

"How is everyone doing?"

"We're okay," Jess said gently. The softest voice I'd ever heard her use with him, absent of the usual edge of contempt and challenge.

"Good," he said quietly. "Danny? Will you pass me the potstickers?"

I grabbed the takeout box and handed it to him. He took a big bite and smiled widely. Despite my efforts to fight it, my lips curled up at the corners in response. I'd filed for divorce and things were underway, but maybe we could be friends? I imagined a wand bonking him on his sandy brown head in a sort of Cinderella moment. But instead of a ballgown and an updo, he would get his fucking priorities straight.

***

Steven's soft snoring woke me. He slept in my room, not as my husband, but because the guest room felt too far away after what had just happened. Then, the birds outside of the window kept me from falling back asleep. I rolled over to face him. His long eyelashes quivered as his eyes twitched behind his eyelids. Pushing up into a seated position, I started to slide my feet gently into my slippers when large hands grabbed me around the waist, dragging me back under the covers. I barked out a laugh and rolled over to face Steven, his hair matted from sleep, and a wide toothy grin that made his brown eyes wrinkle at the corners.

"Are you okay?" He whispered.

"Yeah."

"When Jess texted me what happened, I felt sick at the thought of losing you and I couldn't sleep, or eat. I just needed to get here. I still can't believe it. And the girls in the house…I'm just so glad that the police got here as fast as they did and that the girls somehow slept through it all. I'm going to invest in that sound machine company, those things are life-savers." He buried his head in my hair and held me tight. It felt nice to have a warm body hold me again, to connect, but it also felt all wrong.

"Yeah, thank Gods for the police," I agreed.

I hadn't told him who had really saved us because it sounded absurd and unbelievable. I didn't really understand why, but I didn't want Andras and Steven to meet.

A long wave broke free from my hair clip and fell across an eye. I tucked it back behind my ear, and let myself relax into the bed, into him, just one last time, just to see.

Steven turned his face towards me, his dark brown eyes transfixed on my lips. And I shrank away from him. I'd just been horribly traumatized and he wanted to get laid, the only confirmation I needed to know that I'd made the right decision in choosing to end the marriage. Hurt flashed in Steven's eyes but it was gone as quickly as it appeared.

"Do you want coffee?"

Steven sat up, twisting to glance at me over his shoulder.

I nodded that yeah, yeah I did. After throwing on a black fleece lounge set, I met him in the kitchen to make coffee and pancakes together. While I whisked, he told me about the business deal he'd been working on, and I caught him up on the girls, the weird things Olivia had said recently and Victoria's favorite game that week. He even laughed a few times and added to the conversation. Our interactions felt like they did when we were dating, when we were friends. Back then, he wanted to know me, really know me, and at the time I needed that more than anything. I needed to be known for me, for who I was, unattached to my family and the things that had happened to us. Back then, I'd started a new chapter of my life with Steven and now I'd start a new one again, alone.

As the time went on, I began to feel a flutter of something in my heart, a warmth, an ease. Could we forgive each other, start over, and be friends again? Was that even possible after divorce?

Victoria and Olivia came around the corner and pitter-pattered toward us with sleepy red eyes and frizzy curls shooting in all directions. Ria climbed into her daddy's lap and smashed her cheek into his chest. He kissed the top of her head while taming her waves a little with his hand. Olivia padded up to me and laid her head on my knees face down, and I wondered how she could breathe like that. It brought back memories of waking up every ten minutes when Liv was a newborn, making sure she was still breathing, still okay. So tiny, so fragile. I still worried about her, about them, but I worried over different things. Was I being too strict or too permissive? Did they feel loved? Did they feel safe? What was I supposed to say when my child was being bullied? How could I explain the socio-economic complexities of homelessness in a way that was age-appropriate but taught compassion? Should we tell them that a scary man broke into our house, or not? For fuck suck, was anything ever an easy answer?

The home invasion awakened my worst fears, and my anxiety had become a living thing, palpable, charging every nerve in my body, as though human skin had been stretched over a thunderstorm.

"I want pancakes, too," Olivia announced into my leg.

"Pancakes?" I asked, caressing her back. "Perfect! That's what we have! Sit at the table and I'll grab your plate."

After getting the girls settled, I plopped down at the table. Steven rubbed his hands together, "Let's dig in!" My lips kicked up at the corners and I couldn't help but beam, and beam, and beam. This was the scene I'd imagined when I'd found out I was pregnant with Ria. Sunlight in a breakfast nook, the whole family seated together, telling stories, laughing. The smell of coffee and maple syrup hanging in the air, a potpourri of wholesome morning memories.

My phone buzzed in my robe pocket and I slid it out absent-mindedly to check. A message from Jess read, "So I did some light stalking, and Andras lives like two blocks from you in that big white house we've walked by a million times. The one you love."

So close. He was so close. That's why I always saw him walking in front of my house, that's why he always took our street to get to the restaurants, cafes and bars, and why he was probably walking by the other night when the man...

"But why are you stalking him, you creep?"

"You wanted answers. Let's go talk to him."

I slipped my phone back into my pocket and reached for my coffee but it tasted like ash in my mouth. I did want to know what happened the other night. But the thought of walking over there and knocking on his door made my insides knot up. Knowing where he lived changed things, somehow. He went from a mysterious gorgeous God who I couldn't stop daydreaming about to a fellow neighbor, a man who mows his lawn (or at least hires someone else to do it).

"Everything okay?" Steven asked.

"Yeah," I said, noticing that I was staring at the table intensely, brows heavy in thought. I tried to push it out of my mind, to stay present, to enjoy the lovely breakfast with my family, but try as I may, I couldn't stop thinking about *him*.

***

So Andras lived in my favorite house in the entire city. A large, white, two-story home with a huge porch and two rocking chairs, straight out of a t.v. show. The second story had a large, black-rimmed window that looked out over the street, and every time I jogged past it, which was often, I'd imagine myself up there with an easel, looking out over the oaks and maples.

I bent down to tighten the laces on my running shoes, grabbed my black bomber jacket from a hook on the entryway, and yelled to the kids and Steven, who were playing in the living room.

"I'm leaving for a run guys," I called, peaking around the corner to make sure Steven heard me. He stayed focused on the crooked block tower he'd been constructing with the kids, "okay, have fun."

I burst from the front door and ran in the opposite direction of the big white house while I worked up the courage to go there alone. Jess wanted to go together, but I couldn't wait, couldn't keep wondering what had happened that night, how he'd disappeared into thin air, and why. I wanted to thank him, truly thank him, because he could have ignored the sounds coming from my home, could have made the choice to stay out of it like so many did. The "bystander effect," they call it, is where we're conditioned to mind our own business so much that women are taught to scream "fire" instead of "rape" to get help.

I took a sharp turn at the corner and headed east, pushing for the hills, gritting my teeth through the burn so my head would stop spiraling. A mile, two miles, three miles, up, up, up, then right, and right, back down, and full speed until I gasped for air and nearly puked. Then the flooding stopped and my thoughts felt like my own again. My eyes swept over the house in front of me, the black window frames and white shingles above the massive second-story window, and the looming oak trees.

I panted, holding my side, taking in the newness of the place. There were two spherical porch lights on either side of the new glossy black front door that used to be red. The drapes behind the large windows were new, too. The dark green floral pattern that used to scream "Traditional French" was now a more modern heavy gray linen. I could see inside the house, see movement as someone crossed a window. Thoughts eddied out of my head as the front door swung open and a distractingly beautiful man in gray slacks and a navy blue sweater stepped out.

A SECRET

My mouth went completely dry as Andras crossed his arms over his chest, leaned against his door frame, and smirked. *Ugh. Why was I here again?* My brain broke. All that remained was a circus monkey banging on symbols.

"Well, this is unexpected," Andras purred, existing there in all of his tall and perfectly sculpted glory, like a high-fae male or some other creature from one of the hundreds of books I'd read over the years that described preternatural beauty.

A pause. He cocked his head to the side, and I realized he was waiting for me to speak.

"Hey. Uhm," I swallowed hard and clasped my hands together in front of my chest, "I'm sorry for just showing up like this but, uhm, I wanted to talk with you about the other night, and I don't have any other way to contact you."

"How did you know this is where I live?" A single eyebrow quirked up.

"Light stalking," I mumbled, shrugging.

He clicked his tongue against his teeth.

"Do you want to come in?" He asked, pushing off of the door frame and gesturing inside.

"Sure," I said. I took out my phone and typed Jess a message about where I was and what I was doing.

Andras cleared his throat, "sorry, would you prefer to stay out here? As I said before, I'm not currently homicidal. I just opened a bottle of wine, and I've got the fire going."

I arched a brow at him.

He rubbed his hand down his face, "...oh piss, not to make it sound romantic. It's just cold in my house. I was reading."

I examined him skeptically. "Yeah, I'll come in. One drink. I'm just texting my sister real quick to tell her exactly where I am in case I go missing."

"You're joking?" He huffed a laugh.

"Absolutely not." My fingers flew across my screen, "dropping a pin aaaand... sent."

"Okay. That's fair," he nodded. "My entire gender deserves that. You reap what you sow and all."

"Exactly." I slid my phone into my coat pocket.

Andras turned to the side and gestured for me to go ahead of him, "please come in."

My stomach fluttered as I strode past Andras and took in the woodsy scent of him. Stepping over the threshold and into the foyer felt strange–it was as if I'd just come home. Jesus, I thought to myself, I *really* love this house. The door clicked shut behind me and Andras prowled to my side, smiling like a cat. Shit. *Shit*. I was playing a very stupid game. My sister's taunts echoed in my ears about the many reasons why he might have fled my house as the police arrived the other night. "Wanted by the FBI." I couldn't fully trust him, yet I was so painfully attracted to him. And now I stood, alone, with him, in his house.

I blew out a breath and took in the space while he quietly watched me, hands behind his back as if he were on a casual stroll in a museum. I don't know what I'd expected of his house, his style, but it wasn't this. Artwork was everywhere, and fresh-cut flowers filled two enormous vases at the bottom of the staircase. Warm spice candles were somewhere, invoking images of cozy blankets and mirth.

"You have a beautiful home," I said.

One wall was filled with a mid-century modern credenza with abstract art, and the adjacent wall featured a well-lit painting of a ravenous naked woman feasting upon a bushel of apples.

Andras leaned in closer to study my face.

"What are you thinking about?" He asked.

"I don't know. I guess I was expecting something more dark and broody. Like a bachelor den."

"Ah-ha, I see," he chuckled. Sorry to disappoint. Would you like to sit down?" He led me towards the living room off to the side, where navy blue paint covered the walls, to an inviting brown leather sofa under a series of white continuous-line Picasso prints in thick, almost museum-grade unbreakable glass. I lowered myself onto the sofa and twisted to inspect the prints, the thick paper, and the ink.

"Would you like me to take your jacket?" He asked, still standing.

"No, thank you," I answered without looking away from the artwork.

"Alright. Make yourself at home. I'll grab the wine while you look at those," he said as he walked out of the room. I shrugged my jacket off and draped it over the armrest.

Andras returned holding two stemless wine glasses, a bottle of wine, and a corkscrew. He set everything gently on the wooden, mid-century coffee table.

"I hope a Pinot Noir is alright."

"Didn't you say you already had a bottle open?"

I turned to eye him suspiciously.

"I did. I do. But it's not nearly as good as this bottle here." He tapped on the neck of the bottle, click, click.

I grunted out an approving thank you, before twisting back to the drawings. "These look like originals," I mumbled to myself.

"Mmm." Andras hummed.

I turned back towards him.

He elegantly lowered himself into the leather chair across from me and worked to uncork the bottle of wine.

"They're not, though, right?" I asked.

Silence.

I pressed, "They're not, though, *right*?"

He glanced up from the wine bottle and cracked a mischievous smile.

I glared at him and turned back to the drawings.

"You gonna tell me about them sometime?"

"Sure." He said, unable to hide the amusement in his voice. "Your wine."

Andras held out a glass to me and I took it, nodding in thanks.

A record player hummed classical music from the far corner, and hundreds of books lined the floor-to-ceiling shelves.

"You have so many books," I observed, in awe of every single one of them. "I love to read..." I trailed off.

"I'm relieved that you've finally found something about me that isn't entirely off-putting." He smirked.

I studied his face. Fierce blue eyes, flawless olive skin, five o'clock shadow, and a cocky glow that seemed to radiate from him. His soft, pillowy lips seemed to have their own gravitational pull. *Come closer*, they beckoned.

I drank from the glass in my hand, crossed my legs, and leaned back into the sofa.

"So are you going to tell me what happened the other night?" I asked.

The proud grin wholly vanished from Andras's face. He set his wine glass down with a clink and leaned back in his armchair.

"Yes, of course. What would you like to know?"

His fingertips silently tapped the armrests.

"Well, everything, I guess. I guess to start, how did you know something was wrong? How did you get into my (locked?) house and..." I shuddered, "and, and how did you grab that man and throw him into the wall like that? You did it like he was nothing..."

"You were fighting him, which was impressive by the way, and you were preoccupied so maybe that's why it seemed like I did more than I actually–."

"Don't do that. Don't bullshit me. If you don't want to talk about it, that's fine, we can talk about something else, or I can go. Just don't try to convince me that I imagined it."

I rose to my feet and grabbed my jacket.

"You're right. I'm sorry." He said.

I paused, facing him in his chair; he tipped up his chin to look at me, concerned.

"Thank you," I started slowly. "Regardless of how you did it, I might not be here, my girls might not be here, if you hadn't helped us, and I will always be grateful to you for it. I just wanted you to know that."

I started for the front door, and just as I reached the foyer, Andras called to me.

"Please don't go. Look, I..." He began.

I hesitated, my hand hovering just above the front door handle. *He doesn't want to talk about what happened. He's hiding something. You thanked him. That's enough. Go.* I turned the handle and stepped back to pull it open when a gust of wind lifted the loose tendrils around my face. And then Andras was next to me.

I screamed and lurched backward, but a large, gentle hand caught me at my lower back and righted me to my feet. Andras removed his hand and took a large step back away from me.

Andras's eyes were wide. He raked his hands through his hair and blew out a breath. My heart thundered in my chest as panic took root. He must have noticed my chest rising and falling quickly because he put his hands up in front of him as if trying to talk down a scared animal. "I can explain," he spoke softly. "You have nothing to fear from me. I'm not going to hurt you. Can we please sit down and talk? I'll tell you whatever you want to know."

There was nowhere to go. Nowhere to go. Nowhere to go. If he could move like that, from one place to the next in a blink, I was trapped, and he was probably going to murder me or keep me in some dungeon of horrors. I had to stay calm, had to think. I nodded slowly, reluctantly, my eyes owl-like as I tried to survey my surroundings.

I plodded to the couch like a woman heading for the noose and lowered myself to sit once more, keeping my eyes trained on the coffee table, scanning, scanning, scanning for a weapon. Andras sat on the chair again, forearms braced against his thighs. The record had finished and the room was painfully quiet, except for the rhythmic whirl of the turntable going around and around, a million miles away.

"I'm so sorry," Andras began, his voice quiet, and shaky. "Thank you for letting me explain." I could hear him talking and even sorta make out the words below the pounding pulse in my ears from my heart slamming against my ribs, pumping adrenaline through me like a drug, begging me to move, to run, to fight, to get out, get out, get out. And then I saw it, the wine bottle barely within reach on the coffee table. Maybe I couldn't outrun him, but if he were stunned....I planted my feet on the floor.

"I know all of this is going to sound crazy," Andras began. Then he glanced towards the window, towards the street just beyond the wall, and I knew I wouldn't get another shot. I lunged for the bottleneck, wrapping my fingers around it tightly, pulled back and swung it as hard as I could at that beautiful line of his jaw. The bottle broke upon impact as if it had been thrown against a wall. It sent Andras toppling off his chair, his hand going to his face. My forearm stung but I ignored it as I clambered over the coffee table and raced for the front door, my feet slipping across the tiles in the entryway so I crawled on hands and knees, reaching up, grabbing the door handle and yanking it open. Then a gust of cold air rustled my hair and skittered over my face, the scent of someone warm and woodsy, hit me, and Andras was there, eyes full of shadows. He rubbed his jaw.

"Ouch." He whined, "that bottle fucking hurt."

I flung myself backward, away from him, whatever he was. Whatever *this* was.

"How the fuck are you doing that? LET ME GO!"

"That's what I was trying to explain. And you can go. I won't stop you."

Andras dropped to his knees and put his hands out again, like he was trying to calm a scared animal,

"Seriously. You can leave," he said, "I'm not going to hurt you. I just wanted a chance to explain. To really explain. I just–"

Andras stopped mid-sentence and blinked. His eyes changed from sapphire to gold, and I startled, sliding back further away from him. He frantically looked me over, the ravenous gleam of a predator in the tilt of his head, the color of his eyes. Then his head jerked suddenly towards my arm, where blood was pooling and slowly falling to the parquet as if in slow motion. I must have cut myself on the bottle, but it didn't hurt, not yet. Andras squeezed his eyes shut tight and exhaled slowly. When he opened them, they were blue again. I stepped back.

"Your eyes," I whispered.

A pause. Then Andras ground out, "can you cover that? I have bandages in the hallway drawer."

"Your eyes just changed color. And you move so fast..." The beauty, the old-timey grace, the way he seemed to prowl through the world like a goddamn animal looking for a meal, and he'd tossed that man as if it were nothing. No. Not possible. Do I need to get my Prozac checked?

"Oh, my fucking Gods. What are you?" I whispered. "Are you a...a...?"

I cringed, unable to get the words out, because it sounded way too crazy to mutter out loud. Every movie I'd ever watched with Jess on movie nights flickered through my mind. It wasn't possible. I mean, we'd always talked about it, fantasized about it, but that's all it was–a fantasy.

Andras kept his head turned slightly away from me. "I'll explain everything. Can you please just cover that?" he pleaded.

Slowly getting to my feet, I kept my eyes trained on him and backed away to the hallway closet he'd nodded towards. Careful not to turn my back to him, I rummaged for a heartbeat through old cords and other riff-raff, until I found the first aid kit that appeared to have never been opened. I quickly applied a large band-aid to a small but deep cut on the underside of my forearm, eyes glued to Andras, who remained kneeling ten feet away, grimacing. Was it possible? Was he really *that*? Or maybe he was just some psycho who wanted to be one and took steroids and wore contacts that magically changed color.

But what if it were true? What if the world was more vibrant and dark and diverse than I'd ever imagined? What if it was as magical as I'd dreamed of, once, a long time ago? Tossing the kit back into the drawer, I walked past Andras, still kneeling as if he were afraid to move for fear of scaring me off. In the living room, I plopped onto the couch for the third time and waited for a whole two seconds before Andras was across from me.

"You seem strangely calm," he said, concern flickering in his eyes.

"I am. Call it a gift or a curse, but I seem to do okay under pressure. And maybe it's because, like everyone my age, I grew up obsessed with vampire lore and fiction, and it doesn't seem that scary anymore. Which is probably stupid, but I think if you wanted me dead, you wouldn't have saved me, and you could have killed me like the second I swung that bottle at you."

Andras only tilted his head as if to say, yeah, true.

Continuing, I said, "But I have a few questions. Are we talking Anne Rice, or Dracula, in which case I'll start to be properly afraid, or like Vampire Diaries? What are we talking about here?"

I folded my arms over my chest and waited for a response about what kind of vampire he was and the thought of how ridiculous it all was made my lip kick up at the corner.

Andras winced a little, then dragged his hands over his face. "Hmm, well, definitely not Dracula, I don't have a harem of demon vampires trapped in my basement." His eyebrows knit together as he mulled it over, "Anne Rice, hmm, we don't sleep in coffins, and sunlight is fine, I mean, a bit draining, but fine. There are some people who are every bit as evil as some of her characters but I'm not one of them, currently. I'm sure there are novels out there that come close but honestly, it's a genre I try to avoid." He chuckled. "I'm sure you can understand why. Also, I think your being unfazed might have something to do with your character. The fire I so rudely brought up the night we met."

I threw up my hands, "Maybe? But I mean, I did just hit you and flee. Let's stay focused on you, for a minute, okay? Like how is this even possible?"

"It's not that strange, is it? I'm not made of magic, the things that I can do are pretty standard for most animals. A wolf can hear your heartbeat, smell what you had for lunch. A hummingbird can be twenty feet away one minute and next to you an instant later."

"You're really minimizing this," I said, annoyed.

"I'm really not trying to." He cracked his knuckles, then clasped his hands together, "I guess after all this time it doesn't feel that big. I'm a predator. So I'm built like one. Now, are you going to ask me *the really important questions*?"

"Like what? Like, are you planning to kill me? My sister knows that I'm here, by the way. What else is there?"

"Let me just answer the things that I feel might come up. Yes, I drink blood from human bodies, not blood bags from a hospital. That's not a thing that I know of, and I can't even imagine the logistics of it. I haven't killed anyone in decades. Yes, I have killed people, regrettably, and many. Yes, there are others like me, but I only know a few. No, I can't control you with my mind, per se, but I can be *incredibly persuasive*. No, I've never done it to you, but you'd really have no way of knowing, I guess. I can catch glimpses of thoughts, sometimes, and I do have a fancy sort of gift, mind weaving, where I can pull someone else's mind into mine and it feels like reality for both of us."

I grunted in approval, "Well, that's cool." Then it occurred to me that he was probably old, like really old. I wrinkled my nose, "Ew, you're like a hundred, aren't you?"

He threw his head back and howled. Howled! "Give or take a few centuries. And yes, thank you. Ew is always a favorite thing to hear from a beautiful woman."

My cheeks flushed at that.

"Thank you."

"You're welcome."

Andras grinned.

"So, is it hard to be around people? Is it hard to be around me without, you know, like, eating me?"

He leaned forward, resting his forearms on his thighs, and looked directly into my eyes.

"What do you mean by eating you? Specifically?" He smiled, "Yes, it is difficult to be around you and unable to devour you, lick you, be with you." He said this with feral delight, as the color left my face and I forgot how to breathe. For just a second, a specific sort of hunger flashed there, a burning sort of need.

My breathing returned to normal. I rolled my eyes, "You know what I mean."

"Yes, it's difficult. Or, I suppose it can be. I don't walk around wanting to sink my fangs into everyone. In general, I hardly notice humans anymore unless it's been too long, and I'm famished. Unfortunately, today is one of those days. But also, I like you, quite a bit. I'm attracted to you in a way I haven't been attracted to anyone in a long time, or maybe ever. You're beautiful, obviously–nobody can argue with that–but you're also tender, funny, kind, and strong. Admittedly, there is a bit of that unfortunate side effect, a drive to...uhm, consume you. In the carnal sense, but also literally. However, I'm not going to attack you. I have self-control. I'm not a frat boy at a kegger." He winced playfully.

He thought I was beautiful? I mean, when I was younger, I knew that, but these days...well, I hadn't felt that way in a long while. Hard to do when you're constantly nursing two children back to health every other week. But what he'd admitted about liking me sent molten fire through my veins. Power flooded from somewhere inside of me, not from his validation, but because of the reminder of who I was, who I am, deep down: My own person in my own right.

I uncrossed my legs and leaned forward *just* so, positively pulsating with sexual energy. Andras's lips kicked up at the corners in pure feral delight as though he were more than happy to accept my challenge. A wine glass sat before me on the coffee table, having somehow survived my attack on Andras. I grabbed it and took a long drink–anything to avoid thinking of Andras and the body beneath that sweater. Gods, I just knew that he tasted even better than he looked. I took another drink, focussing on the spines of the books behind him, anywhere but at his smirking lips. Those full, soft lips. His tongue and teeth. *His teeth.*

"Your teeth," I blurted out, sitting up tall as I came out of my sex-charged stupor.

"Sorry?" Andras asked, one eyebrow raised.

"Show me your teeth."

"Hmmm."

I grinned.

"What are you up to?" Andras asked.

"Nothing. I'm just," stretching my neck to the side, drawing attention to my jugular, "really sore."

Andras's eyes transformed into an incredible shade of deep gold, an enthralling mix of angelic purity and animalistic ferocity. He tilted his head back, parting his lips just enough for me to see his top canines as they descended slowly, morphing into razor-sharp fangs. I leaned in closer, captivated by the raw, magnetic energy emanating from him. Magic. The air crackled with it, making me dizzy with a heady blend of excitement and fear. I felt an irresistible pull towards him, a visceral connection that thrummed through my veins and felt hot in my chest and fingertips. He exhaled deeply, closing his mouth and eyes, and when he reopened them, they were that beautiful serene blue once more.

Andras ran his tongue across his top teeth.

"I feel like I'm at the dentist," he joked.

"Do you go to the dentist?"

"No. I don't get cavities, and I don't know how I'd explain all of this," he motioned to his mouth, "after an x-ray."

"Fair. Does it hurt?" I asked, a flutter of guilt.

"No," Andras said, "it's more of a pressure. A pinch, but it's brief."

"And all of those people you're with?" I asked, remembering all of the pretty women and one rather attractive man one night.

"Dates. When you've lived as long as I have, there's not much to do to entertain yourself. There's sex. There's blood. There are books and music and the occasional hobby. Once in a great while, there's vengeance or love. Or are you asking me if they were my dinner?"

"Yes."

Andras chuckled, "Oh, yes. But they're very much alive and back on whatever dating apps I found them on, I'm sure. I only take a small amount," he said, attempting to show me on his fingers, "when they're..." he searched the ceiling for the right words, "...preoccupied? I can make it quite pleasurable and I heal the marks so there's no evidence."

A clock chimed somewhere in the house, marking the hour. Has it been an hour? More? It would be easy to stay all night, asking question after question about his long life, and the secret world that existed within, yet beyond, ours. But I couldn't. I needed to get back home, to Liv, to Ria, to dinner, to books, and to bedtime.

"I have so many questions about all of that, and more, but I have to go. My girls are with my husb–." I trailed off. What was Steven? We were getting divorced, so calling him my husband felt like a charade. Still, being here, in Andras's home, also felt wrong. It was too soon. We had just ended things and there I was sitting in some hot guy's living room, swooning over him. *Cool. Great.*

Andras watched my face closely, watched as I processed so much.

"I'm a mess."

I tossed back the rest of the wine in my glass and popped up, swaying, then stumbling. Andras appeared instantly at my side, one hand on my lower back and the other behind my shoulders, hulking around me for support with strong, gentle hands. His slightly stubbled chin slightly grazed my cheek, sending an intoxicating rush of blood to the apex of my thighs. *Is my mouth watering?*

"Thanks," I said, into his face. "My iron is always a little low and sometimes it makes me dizzy to stand too quickly."

I gently pushed off of him, "I haven't told anyone but my sister this, and honestly, I don't know why I'm telling you, but I'm getting divorced. And it's not final, but I shouldn't be here feeling, ah, things," I said.

"I understand," he said, barely a whisper. He forced a small smile that did not reach his eyes, where shadows seemed to swirl.

I nodded, slowly.

If I don't get out of this fucking house, something is going to happen that I will feel guilty about for the rest of my life or at least until the inevitable dementia from too much screen time.

He offered a crooked smile, and I realized it was because he was reading into how I felt, what I wanted. I glared at him and smoothed the front of my shirt.

"Thank you, again, for everything." I said, genuinely, looking down.

"Of course," he said, stepping back.

Andras walked me to his front door, stalling a heartbeat before pulling it open for me. On the porch, the sun was setting, a bright orange burned in the sky, and it was like the world, my world, had completely changed, yet also somehow hadn't.

"I feel like this comes without saying but–" Andras said.

"–don't tell anyone. I know."

"No, I was going to say that I want to see you again."

I searched his face. No smirk, no crooked grin, just him, sincerely, waiting. I smiled a little at that, then forced myself towards the porch steps. Calling quietly over my shoulder, I whispered, "I want to see you again, too."

My legs carried me forward, as I stepped from one world to another. As I wandered from his home towards my own, towards my family, my thoughts shifted from Andras to them. One moment, I'd been ready to pounce him, to taste him, to press into him, and the next, all I wanted was to sprint through my cozy warm home with my two little girls on my heels. I wanted to snuggle their delicate little faces and delight in their curious eyes. Andras was a hard man to leave, but my girls pulled me towards them, without a second thought. But as I made my way down those last few streets towards my house, a chilling sensation crept up my spine again, like someone was behind me, watching. This was the third time I'd felt that way recently and with the break-in, oh Gods. I ran as fast as my legs could carry me back home.

TOO MUCH TO PONDER

The last thing I needed was too much time to think. After the break-in, Steven's sudden kindness and learning that Andras was...I didn't need time to sit in silence and obsess. Yet there I was, trapped in my car in the school pickup line, early, with nothing to do but listen to radio advertisements for erectile dysfunction meds and remember the terrifying beast of a man in my house—who had been taken care of by my vampire neighbor— the vulnerability I'd felt.

The fear that had radiated from my gut into every part of my body and soul that night flooded back to me. His giant body engulfing mine, the smell of sweat on his skin, and my fury and rage as I pushed, clawed, and kicked at every part of him. My breath escaped me as I shuddered. Then my mind went to Andras and his golden eyes, which had been full of death and rage as he'd appeared out of the darkness. His handsome face, framed by parted mauve lips, revealed unnervingly white teeth and razor-sharp fangs.

How did any of this happen? Was I going crazy?

The car in front of me swung out of its parking space into the road, engine roaring as their black SUV disappeared out of sight. And now, directly in front of me, of course, sat Bethany's giant white SUV.

Not now.

A bell rang. The large glass doors of the school swung open. Two administrators pushed and held the double doors open for the students pouring out in a sea of blue, green, and white uniforms. Ria and Liv were among them, their wild curls bouncing as they walked together, holding hands, surrounded on either side by elementary school children of every size, color, and character. Some of the children sang, laughed, played; some wore somber expressions, weary from the day; and others rubbed the sleep from their eyes. Liv bounced, her mouth moving quickly as she prattled on to Ria, who stared straight ahead, her eyes sweeping the car line then settling on mine. I turned off the car and got out. My lips parted and curled up at the corners as they padded towards me.

I dropped to one knee, arms open. "My girls!"

"Mamma!" Olivia beamed.

"Hi, Mom," Ria said, flatly, "did you comb your hair today?"

I shrugged off her tiny insult, pulled the girls into a hug, and asked if I could kiss them on the cheek. They nodded, and I kissed them both, then sat back on my haunches, arms dropping to my side for balance.

"What was the funniest thing that happened today?" I asked as I rose to my feet, taking each girl by the hand and leading them toward the car.

"Jasper farted," Olivia howled.

"Ew," Victoria scoffed, but her mouth pulled up at the corners.

I opened the car doors, bouncing from foot to foot as they clicked open and up. Parents turned to watch.

Out of the corner of my eye, I saw the blonde heads of a grown-up and a child moving toward the white SUV and did my best not to make eye contact. To my surprise, the girls climbed into their seats easily and did themselves up, something that almost never happened with Liv, who I still had to bribe regularly in public, to my chagrin. I walked around the car, just as Bethany opened the door to her SUV and began to climb in. She saw me and stopped, bringing her leg back down to the road.

"Hi, Danny." Her lips peeled back in a wide smile that didn't reach her eyes.

"Bethany," I mumbled. I nodded to her and started to get into my car when she stepped towards me, her mouth open to speak.

I paused. "What is it, Bethany?" I ground out, not at all trying to hide the irritation.

The smile faded from her face, and for once, her eyes softened. She actually looked genuinely decent for a moment.

"I just wanted to ask if you're okay. I heard what happened—the break-in. News travels fast. I'm sorry—truly. And I'm glad that you and the girls are okay."

Totally caught off guard, I stared at her for a heartbeat. I blinked.

"Thank you," I said, studying her face, "But why?"

"Our families don't like each other, Danny, but it doesn't mean that I want you to die, Jesus. And I certainly don't want anything bad to happen to the girls. I'm not a monster."

I chewed on my lip. Did I believe her? Not really. Sorta? No.

A pause. Then her eyebrows lifted, and the serpentine smile returned like she'd just thought of something.

"Oh, and while we're chatting," she said, flipping her blonde hair over her shoulder, "I should tell you that someone sent me a photo of you coming out of a big white colonial-style house recently. A night or two ago, maybe? And the man Kim saw you with at the bar, the really cute one, owns it, I guess?"

"What man?" Victoria demanded from inside the car.

"Nobody," I said, reaching into the car to turn on the radio.

Nothing had happened. I had no reason to feel the rising wave of guilt. But Andras was, well, a fucking vampire, and the last thing he needed, or I needed, was for Bethany and the rest of her cunt club to be acting like some kind of neighborhood paparazzi.

"Bethany," I said, straightening my spine, "this is creepy on so many fucking levels. Do you think that it's okay to film and photograph people while they're going about their lives? What is it that you want from me? Ever since we were kids, you've been like this. Is the goal to be a fucking twat in perpetuity? That's so *boring*."

Her candy-pink mouth fell open. A few parents leading their kids to their respective cars looked at me sidelong as they ushered them past.

"As I said," she spat, "we don't like each other. And honestly, I was just trying to warn you. But you're being a real bitch, so maybe I'll forward the photo on to Steven."

I shook my head and tsk-ed at her, then climbed into my car and turned the radio up while my ridiculous doors descended and clicked into place.

A pop song filled the car, and I turned back to my girls, "I love you both so much!" Then I spread my arms and shook my shoulders, kicked my head back, and belted out the tune with Ria and Liv as I pulled away and shot forward past Bethany.

"Burning down the HOUSE."

***

When we got home, I was surprised to see Steven's car there and a little excited to see him, too. We felt like friends again, and it was nice. Victoria and Olivia rushed into the house with backpacks in tow, squealing and screeching, "Daddy! Daddy!" Steven leaned down to hug and kiss each of them before asking them to go put their stuff away in their rooms. He and I watched them run up the stairs, their boots stomping and thundering as they disappeared out of sight.

"They're so crazy," I huffed, laughing.

Steven turned to me, crestfallen.

"What's the matter?" I took a step forward to close the distance between us.

He didn't say anything, just flipped his phone over on the counter so that the screen was up and gestured for me to look at it. I squinted at the blurred image of me in running clothes, leaving Andras's house. My throat felt tight.

"Is this where you went the other night?" He asked with eyes that were utterly dead, unfeeling, empty.

"I went running," I said, and it wasn't a lie. I had gone running first. "Then I stopped by to chat with our neighbor because he had some art he wanted to show me." Also true, technically, and who says that fangs aren't a work of art? It seemed like a smart idea to leave out the part where he's an old as fuck non-human who nearly killed the man that had attacked me in our living room. Steven's eyes raked over me. Then his lips quivered.

"You're not already moving on? I know we're...not together. But..."

"No. No, I'm not moving on...not yet. But honestly? It's none of your business anymore," I said, quietly.

He nodded reluctantly.

"I mean, who else would put up with you?" he said, chuckling.

I blinked.

"I have to pee," I said, turning to walk away but then stopped cold. I spun around and reveled in his confusion.

"A lot of people would put up with me, Steven, in fact, a lot of people would even go as far as to fucking enjoy spending time with me. You dick."

Closing the bathroom door, I sat on the edge of the tub and breathed deeply. *Who else would put up with me?* Prick. And Bethany? What was I going to do about Bethany? My hands curled into fists and I breathed, and breathed, and breathed.

FAE SMUT

"Can't believe you went to that guy's house without me," Jess reprimanded, referring to Andras.

"In retrospect, I'd probably wait for you if I had to do it again so it doesn't look like I'm fucking him." I sighed.

"I hate Bethany," Jess grumbled, taking a huge bite of her strawberry croissant, pausing for a heartbeat to scan the coffee shop from the table where we sat. "And I hate that she's so awful that I *have* to hate her. Women supporting women, and all that, but it's impossible with her. I didn't think she was all that great back when we were kids, but I swear, puberty made her actually evil."

"I blame her parents. Mom and Dad were bonkers, but they never tried to turn us against anyone."

Jess raised an eyebrow, "Mom and Dad?"

"Okay, they did, but her parents must have held a brainwashing meeting that included a ten-year plan for all the ways she should terrorize us."

I exhaled and rolled my shoulders back. The barista, a pretty blonde woman with a nose ring, set a latte down in front of me. I nodded a thank you.

"I feel like I'm being stalked," I said, taking a drink from the blue mug, savoring the vanilla-flavored foam of the oat milk. "And actually, I keep getting this feeling that I'm being watched. Even before the break-in."

"You are being stalked. These bitches have nothing better to do than meddle in everyone else's lives. And the funniest part is that it's not like Bethany's life is picture perfect–fuck, we know that better than anyone growing up across the street from her," Jess shook her head. "None of them have perfect lives, so they've got some nerve judging everyone else." She pressed her lips together tightly for a beat. "Do you know who took the photo?"

"I mean, there's only one person it could be. Kim is the *only* one who lives in our neighborhood–everyone else lives on the hill."

"Kim, huh?"

"Kim," I shrugged. "Such a bummer, too. She didn't seem so bad."

"People will do crazy shit to be accepted, Danny. I mean, not us–we seem to enjoy being outcasts. But everyone else likes to be liked."

I huffed a laugh.

Jess cocked her head, her glossy bob glistening under the cafe lights, "It's true, you know," she added, adjusting her blazer.

"You look nice," I complimented her. My sister was forever a beauty, timeless but modern and quirky all at the same time. She'd basically worn a uniform all her life, first in Catholic school, and then she created a sort of business casual uniform for the rest of her life: blouse, blazer, and slacks–what she had referred to as Queer Professional in high school. And damn, did she make it her brand and pull it off every day for a decade.

"Thank you. I like your outfit, too." She said, eyeing my jeans and sweater, "especially the oxfords with the ankle socks."

"Mersi," I said, thanking her in Persian.

She winked, then asked, "What's the plan for Bethany?"

"I don't know. Hex her?"

"Hasn't worked in the past," Jess said casually.

I frowned, "Can't tell if you're joking or not?"

She shrugged and popped the last of her croissant into her mouth, and I wondered what in the hell she'd tried to do to Bethany. Jess glanced at the clock on the wall and stood up, gathering her keys, wallet, and phone into her leather tote bag. She leaned down to kiss me on my cheeks: right, left, right, three times, the way Persians do.

"Meeting with a professor about my dissertation, gotta run. Then I have a date," she bemoaned. "But I'm sorry again, about everything. I know you're going through so much right now, and I'm here for you. Always."

I waved her away, "I know. Love you."

Pulling a spicy novel, which could easily have passed for Fae porn, from my bag, I got cozy in my chair. I should have been grocery shopping, cleaning, and completing all manner of menial adult tasks while the girls were at school, but I'd decided to take a half day to have coffee with my sister, whine about the assholes I'd had the recent displeasure of dealing with, and read for pleasure in this cozy coffee shop. I cracked the spine, leaned back, and let myself be swept into a magical world that no longer seemed all that far-fetched. If vampires were real, all bets were off. For all I knew, this godsdamn book in my hands full of fae lords fucking their partners *to the hilt* might not be fiction at all. Could be a High Fae memoir. "Rhysand, Unveiled."

The book hooked me right away, pulling me into its action-packed plot of shadows, romance, and fate. I didn't notice the man standing next to me with arms crossed, simpering, until he tapped me lightly on the shoulder. I whirled in my seat, eyes snapping up to Andras looking down at me with eyebrows raised. I exhaled loudly, my shoulders relaxing a little.

"Good book?" he asked. "Do you mind?" He reached over and turned it to see the cover. He pressed his lips together, trying to stifle a laugh.

"I see."

I rolled my eyes.

"Yes, it has plenty of *that* in it."

"Yeah, I know. It's very good."

He flashed a knowing smile.

My curiosity was piqued.

"Oh?"

"Yeah, I can't remember if I told you or not, but I edit books. Mostly nonfiction, but commercial fiction and such, too. I'm friends with the woman who edited this particular book" he tapped the cover with his finger. "She said she had to commit herself to many cold showers to get through it. And apparently, she broke more than one vibrator. So, naturally, I had to read the entire series. Big fan." He smirked, "You'll be surprised to find out who the main character ends up with in the end."

The man never ceased to surprise me and I couldn't help but love that about him.

"Well, I guess we have Fae smut in common. And it sounds like I have a lot to look forward to," I said, tilting the book to examine the girth.

"May I sit?" he asked, chin dipping towards the empty seat at my table.

"Oh, Gods. Uhm, shit. Sure, but I have to tell you something, and maybe you won't want to stay long after."

"Well, that doesn't sound good," he said, sliding elegantly into the chair.

"So," I cleared my throat, "apparently someone saw me leaving your house, I think the same person who also saw us talking at Blotto that one time and blabbed it to everyone."

I winced, "How pissed are you?"

"At them? A lot."

"At me?"

"You? Not at all. It's not your fault, Danny."

"Hmm."

"She sent the picture to this woman, Bethany, who is like my arch nemesis. It's a long, boring story, but essentially our parents spent the better part of a decade suing each other over community guidelines in Cherry Hill. It's some twisted, modern-day Capulet and Montague shit that I don't even want to get into because it's humiliating and gross. But Bethany sent the picture to my husband. Or ex-husband, or whatever. He seems to believe you and I are having an affair."

Andras frowned. A pause while his jaw worked.

"Hmm."

"Yeah."

The corners of Andras's lips kicked up slowly into a wicked grin, "I mean, I'm not opposed to having an affair with you."

My lower stomach fluttered. But I put on a big show of groaning and rolling my eyes, rocking back in my chair as the perfect picture of cool disinterest.

"I'm sure you have plenty of folks already warming your bed at night."

"I do," he said, flashing that cocky grin. "And yes, I know you're not interested, and I don't want to be beaten with a wine bottle again anytime soon, so…"

I put my hand on my chest in mock horror. He nodded at me as if to say, *yeah, you, exactly*. He inhaled sharply and tapped his fingertips quietly on the table.

"I don't like someone watching my house and taking photos for obvious reasons," he said flatly.

"Yeah. I figured as much."

A couple of young women sat next to us, pausing their conversation briefly to stare, or rather gawk, at Andras. If he noticed, he didn't let on, but I imagined that being drooled over was a daily sort of thing for him and probably had been for a long time. Fuck, centuries. Centuries! A part of me felt smug to be sitting with him, to even be friends (if that's what we were becoming) with this striking man. I knew his secret, his world-altering, incomprehensible secret. I wondered what the young women would do if they knew the truth.

Andras rested his forearms on the table. He angled his head in question.

"You're lost in thought again. Everything alright?"

"Yeah," I breathed.

He studied my face for a moment, and I could have sworn he was scenting the air, too. He subtly perked up an ear as if he was trying to smell the lie, searching my body for telltale signs of upset: a racing heart, a chemical change. Weird. I'd ask him about it later when we didn't have a table of fangirls hanging on his every word.

"So," he began, "what are you going to do about this awful person?"

"I don't know. Nothing. Something. What is there to do?"

A barista swung by and set down a mug of black coffee in front of Andras, who smiled up at him.

"Thank you," he said, sincerely.

"Coffee, huh?" I asked.

"It's not my drink of choice," a wink, "but I do enjoy it."

He took a small sip and set down the mug with preternatural grace.

"You could poison her," he resumed. "I mean, that's how important families used to settle this kind of thing back in *my* day."

"Hilarious," I deadpanned.

He shrugged.

For over a decade, I'd fantasized about myriad ways to get back at Bethany for her bullshit. Like when she told everyone in Miss Laru's chem class that my dad haunted, yes *haunted*, our house after his death. Or when she told my ninth-grade boyfriend that I was a witch who summoned demons on the regular and had been possessed multiple times (laughable, when you don't go to a private Catholic school), and he stopped speaking to me overnight. Or in seventh grade, when our poodle died, and she told everyone that my sister had killed Tom-Tom in a fit of rage. I'd daydreamed about getting even but never did. It just never seemed worth it. I didn't really care what other people thought enough back then to take action, plus I had Jess, Samantha, and Sebastian to soften her blows. Now that I was in my thirties, petty gossip and revenge seemed absolutely fucking ridiculous and I couldn't understand for the life of me how my parents and Bethany's parents had spent so much time as adults plotting to fuck each other over. But Bethany had gone too far this time. Revenge would be had.

"You sure you're alright?" Andras pressed, reaching out to tap my hand.

"Yeah. Just trying to sort all of this shit out in my head."

"You know, in my experience, she's probably just trying to hide from her own problems by casting the spotlight on yours. Maybe she's a hoarder"

"Of what? Rat turds? Actually, I could picture it. They'll write about it in her obituary one day."

Andras perked up.

I rolled my eyes, "Like in a long time when she dies from old age. Not right now."

He waved me off.

"Here lies Bethany Nilsen and her menagerie of shit."

"Bethany...Nilsen," Andras repeated, narrowing his eyes.

"Do you know her?"

"No, not at all. But..."

Andras clasped his hands together, grinning with evil delight like a Bond villain.

I narrowed my eyes at him suspiciously.

"What is that look? You look like you're *plotting*. Don't plot. I appreciate the sentiment, but I'm a grown-ass woman, and I can handle this by myself."

He huffed a breath and leaned into the table to close some of the distance between us, his expression sober.

"No doubt you can handle it alone, love. But you shouldn't always have to," he whispered.

Something in my chest cracked open at that. I couldn't think of anything to say, so I just offered a warm smile.

We said goodbye at the cafe door and parted ways. I plodded through the newly fallen snow towards my car parked a block away, turning only once to glance back at Andras, crouched down on the sidewalk to hand a stack of money to a homeless woman wrapped in a dusty pink blanket.

I tossed and turned in bed that night, alone, the house quiet and dark. Steven had resumed sleeping in the guest house, and while it was close, every sound and shadow rattled me. My phone buzzed. The too-bright screen blinded me temporarily, but once my eyes adjusted, I could make out enough to see that I'd received a text from an unknown number. Assuming it was going to be some aggressive reminder about the various volunteer opportunities at Liv and Ria's school, I almost shoved the phone under my pillow. I didn't need one more thing bouncing around in my head. Then again, I wasn't sleeping anyway, so why not? I tapped the screen. The message opened to a single image that was hard to make out until I expanded it. I gasped. Clear as day, I could see a blonde woman with long hair dangling out of a window in the freezing cold, wearing nothing but her underwear and snow boots. I knew that window. It was around the corner, right across from Andras's house. I knew that hair and body, too.

Bethany. Bethany looked like she'd been caught in the middle of something indecent and tried to flee the scene in secret without enough time to fully dress. I gasped. No way! Holy shit! I couldn't believe it.

"Is Bethany having an affair with Kim's husband?" I asked the anonymous number that I deduced belonged to Andras.

"Close. But no, he actually just got home, and then Bethany launched herself from the window. I'm guessing that she's having an affair with *Kim*. At least now you know why she's obsessed with finding dirt on you."

What! I sat the phone down and covered my mouth. A very cruel part of me wanted to destroy her, to blow up the picture of her dangling out of the window and put it on a fucking billboard. However, an affair with Kim? No matter how much I wanted to throttle her, I wouldn't *out* her. That was her secret to keep. But it might have been the leverage I needed to get her out of my life for good, so I hatched a plan in the lamplight, like a supervillain. I couldn't risk confronting her in person in case someone overheard. So instead, I'd wait until she'd dropped her son off at school and pulled away, alone in her blinding white SUV. Then I'd send her this picture and tell her that it was time to stop this fucking madness. And that's exactly what I did the following school day.

I sent the message and watched her slam on her brakes a moment later, nearly hitting the curb. Bubbles started and stopped on my screen. They started and stopped again. And again. And again. Finally, the word "Okay" appeared. Then her SUV lurched forward, taking her and her secrets with it.

GOODBYE, STEVEN

A perky waiter set a glass of white wine on the linen tablecloth in front of me. "Your order will be right out," he said, looking from me to Steven, before buzzing across the patio to another table. We hadn't been to that restaurant together for years, but at one time, a lifetime ago, it had been our favorite weekend brunch place. My throat tightened. I reached for my glass of wine and drank half of it in two gulps before setting it back down on the white tablecloth with a muffled clunk.

Steven pursed his lips together and ran his fingers over the salt and pepper stubble on his left cheek.

"Are you okay?" he asked, his voice a little higher than usual.

I nodded, inhaling so deeply that my chest swelled, popping the top button of my black cashmere cardigan. I rolled my eyes in a self-deprecating way; look at me; I'm an idiot, in hopes that I'd beat Steven to the punch. Over the years, he'd criticized me so much and made so many comments on my imperfect clothes or my chaotic way of being that I had a hard time being perceived by him at all. My fingers worked to push the pearl button back into its slot.

"Wow, this is really hard," I chuckled nervously. The papers finalizing our divorce had arrived, and we'd agreed to sit down and talk about what to do moving forward, how to co-parent and co-exist, together but separate, until the girls were grown and beyond.

"We have a lot to talk about, and it feels a little overwhelming," I admitted. We'd already sorted out the big things in mediation and basically just agreed to split assets, finances, all of it, evenly. We agreed on a sixty-forty split for custody because his job didn't allow him to be there half of the time. Easy peasy. But the smaller things, like how to best communicate, or how to tell the kids, we had yet to discuss. In my naivety, life after divorce could be easy, we both just needed to accept that it was the best thing to do, make a plan, and execute that plan to raise our kids as two platonic friends.

"I just hope we can find a way to be friends." I said earnestly, "We clearly aren't meant for marriage, but we've shared a lot for a long time. We share children. And at one time, I think we were in love. We should try to remember that, right?"

Steven squeezed his eyes shut and opened them wide like he was double-checking to make sure the world was real. He cleared his throat, opened his mouth to speak, and then closed it. He confused me.

The perky waiter once again bounced up to our table. "Here you go. Salad for youuuu!" He placed a fennel and orange salad in front of Steven, who glared at him for the interruption, "and the carrot ginger soup for you!" He set the small ceramic bowl in front of me. "Enjoy!" he sang, and skipped off, the whole restaurant his personal runway. I had no idea where the positivity or energy came from, but I *wanted* it.

"I know it's too late," Steven said carefully, his eyes big and doelike. He poked at his salad with a fork, "but just for the record, I still love you. I think we could still make it work. Honestly, it started as jealousy; I felt neglected after you had the girls, and I think I became resentful. I know I can do better–."

"–Steven. No." I shook my head, "that's not why we are here."

He dipped his chin once, begrudgingly accepting the rejection of his last ditch effort, then put a finger in the air, signaling the waiter to bring him a glass of wine.

"I love you, too." I admitted.

Should I be totally honest or keep it amicable? It wouldn't do anyone any favors to hold back but fuck I didn't want to say it but I needed to.

"I'm just," I searched for the words, "I'm just not in love with you anymore, Steven. You haven't been good to me. You had a million chances to do better, and you didn't. It's too late for us to fix that; I can't get past it; I've spent a billion hours in therapy trying. But I don't think it's too late for us to build a friendship."

He stared into his lap, sniffling quietly, and when he looked up, his eyes were glossy and red.

"Okay," he whispered.

I forced a smile, lips tight and awkward as I battled internally. See, I cared about Steven, so I wanted him to be okay. And I was so sick of his shit that I wanted to slap him. Because after *everything*, I had to sit across from him while he cried or performed crying when all he had to do was care enough to do better for all those years.

The waiter brought wine, and we sat quietly for a while, nursing our wounds and sipping from our glasses. Steven ate a few bites of his salad, I swirled my soup, and the silverware clanked, a choir of church bells within the silence of our miserable little world.

A toddler at a nearby table yelled, "Oh shit, man!" His horrified parents turned crimson and frantically scanned the perimeter to see if anyone else noticed. Steven and I looked at each other and lost it, our laughs bouncing off of the walls, carrying our collective joy and sorrow with them, until the tension dissolved within me, and I pictured it traveling out of my body like a black cloud, gathering in my chest and billowing out of my mouth like a smokestack. Like a dragon.

"Oh damn," I dabbed at my eyes, "I needed that." I chuckled. "Remember Ria's swearing phase?"

Steven cleared his throat.

"Mmhm. Who knew a preschooler could drop the F-bomb with so much conviction."

"And in the right context, too."

He nodded, "Yep."

It felt *good* to laugh together again. It had been *years*. A weight lifted off of us–and there we were, under all the muck, two old friends reminiscing about our beautiful children together.

And just like that, we slid into the semantics of the divorce, agreeing that he should stay in the mother-in-law apartment above the studio in the backyard since he traveled so much. It didn't make sense for him to pay rent, which would only take away from the girls' college funds.

It was better, immediately better. The anger I'd been carrying around diminished, because we were treating each other with respect for the first time in a long time. He couldn't afford to take me for granted, and I didn't feel like I was walking on eggshells.

We grieved the relationship over the main course–scallops for him, halibut for me–and we both cried, laughed, mapped out our lives, apologized, and after a glass of dessert wine, walked back to our cars happier than we'd been since the girls were born. I had no doubt that many battles lay ahead of us. *But damn*, I thought, *I should have done this a long time ago.*

Back at the house, we sat the girls down in the backyard next to the playground we'd all built together and told them that we had decided to raise them together as friends, instead of as married folks. Victoria cried and ran to her room, then Olivia panicked and followed. We spent the rest of the evening outlining what life would look like moving forward, ensuring them that we would love them exactly the same, forever. Seeing the girls upset made me wonder, more than once, if I'd made a huge mistake. But I reminded myself of what my therapist had said about how "everyone's hard comes for them at some point in their lives, and divorce would be their hard. I could love them through hard, but I couldn't prevent hard from happening." It became a sort of mantra. That and "don't model bad love for the sake of good parenting," among a dozen others. When I got really desperate, I just chanted, "What would Dolly do?" Because Dolly Parton, patron saint, y'all. Our lives were changing and it terrified me, I'd bit my nails down to the quick and had gnawed my lip raw, but for the first time in years, I felt hope, too, that I'd get to wake up one day not too far off, and feel like myself again.

MIND-WEAVING

In the back corner of Blotto, I sat at a small table illuminated by two tea candles arranged near a small vase of fresh wildflowers. I stared into the flame, feeling the heat radiate off of it while it danced and balanced atop the wick. I was painfully aware of a number of things: it was very early in the evening, and I was one of only five patrons, which made my reckless plan more likely to fail (this might have been subconsciously intentional); Annette Hanshaw's song, "I've Got A Feeling I'm Falling," rang from the speakers, and that music, mixed with the dim lights and smell of "locally made" gin, was incredibly romantic, maybe *too* romantic. I'd showered, done my hair and makeup quickly, and chosen an outfit that made me feel powerful and sexy. I knew that I looked good in the drop V-neck and high-waisted jeans, my back straight and tall, eyes sweeping the room. I hoped, almost painfully, that I'd run into Andras. After all, this was one of the places he came to meet dates.

It had been a few weeks since I'd run into Andras in the cafe and chatted with him about Bethany. A few weeks since he'd somehow–I didn't even want to *know* how–snapped a photo of Bethany shimmying out of Kim's window in a lacy thong and snow boots. And one week since my divorce was final. Ever since, I'd been successfully fighting the urge to go to Andras's house for some kind of distraction, some kind of release. Steven was in China again. Victoria and Olivia were home with Jess, watching a Santa movie, and I had fuckall to do. So here I was.

I'd have two drinks alone, and if Andras didn't turn up, I'd call Sebastian or Sam, go get dinner, and spend the night dancing, laughing, and filling the hole in my chest with friendship and mirth. I needed it. Not just because of my new single status but because I needed to carve out a place in the world that was just for me. Since having the girls and my marriage tanking, I'd been stuck in survival mode, in routines, in unhealthy habits, just going through the motions to get through each day. I loved being a mother but *was* unhappy with how I'd abandoned myself in the process. Not that long ago, Jess, Sebastian, and Sam had all not-so-subtly pointed out that my eyes seemed empty, shadowed, at times, that I'd stopped laughing and resembled a storm cloud in a jogger set. At the time, I'd ignored them and smugly wrote them off as "clueless childless folks." What did they know about being a mom and stumbling around in a crumbling marriage? Everything, apparently. I didn't realize just how right they'd been until now. Until I'd stopped focusing all of my energy on holding onto Steven and started thinking about myself and what I needed to be happy, without him.

I could be happy. I could make this life anything I wanted if I were bold and brave. Leaving Steven was the first step in casting fear aside and reaching for joy. Ripping my life away from Steven's felt daunting, yet there was peace in it, and a hunger for love, for touch, for passion, excitement, and life—a drive to make up for lost time.

I tapped the candle's liquid-hot surface with the tip of my finger, then peeled the dried wax off and let the pieces drop back into the candle, where they melted back into themselves. A figure appeared in my periphery, and my gaze slowly drifted up. A waiter in an old-timey uniform, a vest, and nineteen-twenties arm garters flipped open his notebook, asking, "What can I get ya?" I felt a slight pang of disappointment and then smiled, ordering, "A very dirty martini?" He nodded and sped off towards the bar. I turned back to the flame. *It's probably better if he doesn't show up. What am I going to do with him, anyway? Plus, he's going to live for a billion years, and I'll probably die around eighty from some kind of cancer caused by turpentine exposure.* I'd pulled out my phone to text Sebastian, "what are you up to?" when a figure appeared again next to me. I turned eagerly to accept my martini and froze with my arm partially extended, then awkwardly dropped it to my side.

"Well, hello again," Andras purred. His blue eyes raked over me and then flared with delight. He lowered his head and whispered, "What brings you here all alone?"

I crossed my arms and leaned back in my seat.

"You have to know that you sound so creepy right now."

He tipped back his head and laughed with wicked amusement, then took a step toward the empty seat across from me before pausing.

"Can I sit? Or will we cause another scandal?"

I gestured to the chair, "go ahead."

Andras prowled to the chair and slid in. He adjusted his jacket sleeves before resting his forearms on the table's edge. He leaned in conspiratorially, whispering, "You know, the strangest thing just happened. I went outside to take my usual evening stroll, and when I got to the end of my street, I caught a whiff of a very distinct floral perfume lingering in the air, which led me here. You wouldn't know anything about how that scent got there, would you?"

I shrugged sweetly, "I may or may not have gone a block out of my way to rub my wrists on a tree near your house. Like a sloth. I wasn't actually sure that would work, but I was curious about your sense of smell. And apparently, it is *amazing*. How long can you smell someone after they've walked by?"

Andras thought about it, working his bottom lip with his teeth. I tried not to stare.

"Hmm, about twenty minutes, but since you nearly dry-humped that big oak tree on the corner–nicely done, by the way, it lingered for longer." He angled his head like a cat playing with a mouse, his tongue resting between his teeth. "Is there a reason you wanted me to follow you here?"

"First of all, I did not 'dry hump' anything. Ew. And yes. I wanted to buy you a drink for snapping that photo of Bethany hanging out of Kim's window." A partial truth. "I have no idea how you caught that, and seriously don't want to know, but thank you. Thank you so much," I spoke sincerely and meant it. It worked. "Bethany barely even makes eye contact with me at drop off and hasn't bombarded me via text or email, either."

He smiled and inclined his head. "Anytime, love."

The words, thank you, were insufficient. This man, this immortal man, had literally saved my life once and now my sanity, and I had no idea how to ever pay him back. I guessed I could offer to be his snack if he was ever hungry and short on dates at some point. Though that seemed unlikely. My cheeks heated as I imagined his teeth on my neck and hand down my pants, making small circles at the apex of my sex. Pressing my knees together, I shoved the thought away. Still, my body betrayed me, and my underwear dampened.

Andras stilled, and his eyes flashed gold, a startling display of what he truly was beneath the human guise. He dipped his chin down to look up at me through his lashes like an animal about to pounce.

"What is it you're thinking about?" He asked in a low gravely voice.

I died inside.

He grinned, and it was positively feral.

I shifted uncomfortably in my seat. *Gods. Calm down.*

I cleared my throat.

"I was wondering if you're going to order a drink..."

"Oh, were you?" He purred.

"Yes."

"Liar. And yes, I will be ordering a drink."

Andras waved at a passing waiter, who paused mid-stride to take his order: a Manhattan for himself and "a panty dropper shot for the lady." Arrogant, obnoxious, son of a bitch. And yet, I longed to sit on that perfect face.

"So what's it like being, ya know, what you are?" I asked, taking a sip of my martini. The vinegary bite of the olive juice and the burning sensation of the gin washed over my tongue and slipped down my throat.

Andras glanced around to make sure no one was lingering within earshot before continuing, "Exactly like the movies. Love triangles, glitter skin, feeding frenzies." He waved his fingers in front of himself, a gesture that was part spooky and part jazz hands.

I rolled my eyes.

"Seriously," I pressed.

"Okay, but prepare for a very dramatic yet boring story. Being...immortal...can be really lonely. Some decades more than others." A shrug. "Life can feel redundant, and the monotony and loneliness can start to drive you a little insane. Unlike the movies, vampires don't really run around making carbon copies of themselves, unless there's a war. It's rare to meet another. The possibility of having to spend hundreds of years with someone is a really effective deterrent. Plus, even if you do meet someone, or turn someone, well...you know the saying: 'power corrupts and absolute power corrupts absolutely.' And I certainly never wanted to be responsible for adding another psycho to the world."

"But how did *you* become one?"

He went rigid, his eyes darkening as if a haunting memory was dragging him back to a place and time he didn't want to visit.

"I'd rather not talk about it, or *him*. Some things are best left buried and forgotten," he said, his voice an octave deeper and a little hollow.

"I'm sorry. About all of that," I said, reaching slowly for his hand. He looked down at the contact, his eyes now a gilded blue. I couldn't help but chuckle, at which he smiled back sheepishly.

"There are perks, though, of being...*this*," he said, dipping his chin to gesture at himself.

"Like speed and strength and living forever?" I took another sip from my martini. "As a woman, I spend a lot of my time afraid. I can't walk anywhere at night without looking over my shoulder every thirty seconds, especially after...especially after my father died. And again, now, ever since that man broke into my house. I can't imagine feeling that...safe," I admitted.

Andras slowly shook his head, then focused on his drink. "Yes," he said, "there's a certain comfort in it, in that way. There *is* the fear of being found out and ending up in a laboratory or being hunted by human mobs, but that's not your typical day-to-day fear. I feel exceptionally safe most of the time and can keep those I care about safe, too." He paused as if to consider something before continuing, "So your father died?"

I nodded.

"Murdered."

"And you saw him after?"

"Yes. And I've been anxious and fearful of death, of not being able to keep people I love safe, ever since."

"I'm so sorry, Danny."

My glass seemed to glow as the ice floated there, reflecting the light. And then I saw the blood, so much blood.

"He'd been," I breathed in and out slowly, "Torn apart in his office. They were looking through his things. Files and papers were everywhere, and blood splattered..." I swallowed hard. "My sister and I found him."

Andras's soft fingers found mine across the table. He stroked the back of my hand delicately.

"I'm sorry."

I forced a tight smile.

"It was a long time ago," I said softly, "but it affects me every day. Honestly, he's probably the reason I got married to my ex in the first place. I wanted a safe and boring life."

"And now?"

"And now I want it all," I said, meeting Andras' eyes, "Fear be damned."

He pinned me to the spot, his hand still gently caressing mine. His lips kicked up slightly at the corners as he glanced up from his drink to me. "You know, there are advantages to being like this, too. Can I show you something?" he asked.

I nodded, excitement and fear washing over me.

The room around us began to darken. I inhaled sharply, and my spine locked up as shadows expanded like the room was being rubbed out with ebony paint. Then, slowly, the shadows receded to reveal teak bedroom furniture and a large king-size bed with a floral installation around a crystal chandelier hanging above it. A fireplace crackled along one wall, and an end table stacked with old books hugged each side of the bed. Andras and I sat at a writing table in the far corner of the bedroom. My eyes widened, and I darted about the room. My chest rose and fell faster, faster, and faster.

"What's happening," I whispered.

"Our bodies are still in the bar, but I've pulled you into my head. This is my bedroom," he motioned around the space. I wanted to show you this," he said, waving a hand towards the bed.

I raised my eyebrows. "A bed? Seriously?"

"Oh. No. I mean...unless that's what you want?" he smirked. "But, no. Look above the bed."

My eyes climbed the wall and narrowed in on a painting where a headboard would be.

I hopped to my feet and froze. My hand flew to my mouth as I gasped, "Oh shit." I looked down at my body. "Did I just stand up and yell in the bar?"

"No. Whatever we do here stays here. All anyone else can see is just us sitting, hanging out, and time goes by faster here, almost like a dream. So while it might feel like we're here for a long time, it will seem like a few heartbeats out there."

I nodded slowly. "This is crazy," I whispered. Then my feet were moving as I ambled toward the bed and it felt real, impossible to decipher from the real world. Flexing and relaxing my hands, I marvelled at the sensations, while taking in my surroundings in awe.

"Mattise?" I asked incredulously as I came upon the masterpiece that hung behind protective glass on the wall just above his bed.

The nude figure of a woman lying down popped against a colorful background of blues and greens. I inhaled and imagined what it would have smelled like when the paint was still wet.

"Mmmhmmm," he hummed, "I thought you might like it."

"I do. It's beautiful."

My hand ran down the buttery-soft linen comforter, and a warm wave washed over me as a sudden need to be desired caressed, and filled hit me. I spun on my heel to face Andras, still sitting motionless at the table, though something like amusement marked his face.

"Take me back to the bar," I demanded in a sudden panic that I didn't understand.

"Of course," he said.

The room exploded with shadows and darkness, and when they cleared, we were back in the bar; a silk dancer had begun their ascent up the crimson drapes, and the place was suddenly packed with patrons. I pressed my eyes closed to stop the world from spinning. When I opened them, I felt like I might puke. *Reading about fantastical shit could not be more different than actually experiencing it.* For a moment, my reality seemed to hang on a frayed thread swaying precariously in the wind. My delicate human brain couldn't comprehend up from down, left from right, or real from fake.

Andras's expression was sober as he reached across the table to caress my cheek.

"Just breathe," he said. "It's really intense the first time, but it will pass."

"Intense?" I suppressed the urge to glare at him, "I feel like I'm bopping around in Wonderland."

Andras frowned. "That bad, huh?"

"Yeah, probably because I already feel like my sanity is one panic attack away from shattering these days. And you can just...*pull* someone into a different world like that?" I asked, leaning forward against the table to keep my voice low, then muttering, part in awe, part in horror, "I can't tell if I think it's amazing or utterly fucking terrifying. Also, never do that to me again without warning or permission."

"Of course not."

"Okay," I whispered. I needed to clear my head. "Excuse me, I'm just gonna run to the bathroom."

I wandered down the hall towards the restroom and fought every cell in my body, screaming at me to run, run, run. While sitting down to pee, I texted Jess.

"Sis, is it too soon to move on from my marriage?"

Jess replied more quickly than usual, and I was glad for it. "No. You deserve to feel loved. You deserve to be happy. And I wouldn't feel guilty one bit. You guys are officially done, and frankly, Steven checked out of your marriage years ago, so as far as I'm concerned, you've been single for years. Do it. Break the seal."

I read the words over and over again in the bathroom, *Steven checked out years ago.* Truer words had never been spoken, yet I still agonized over him. Meanwhile, out there sat Andras, a gorgeous immortal, waiting for me. A man who had saved my life and my children and helped me put an end to the painfully ridiculous Bethany feud. Sure, I'd only known him for a couple of months, but he made me smile and laugh, which was more than I could say about Steven, who had stomped around the world like a raging curmudgeon for the past few years.

I pulled up my pants, flushed the toilet with the toe of my shoe, and smiled knowingly at myself in the mirror while I washed my hands. I spun around and strutted back to the table, ass in full swing, Persian hips like a honing beacon, turning heads all the way back to Andras.

I hopped into the seat across from Andras, who seemed very focused on a stain on the table. He inhaled as his eyes flicked up to me to say something, but stopped, eyes dragging over me.

He seemed to notice the change in my body where I'd gone from reeling confusion to something else, something primal. He grinned.

"Are you feeling better, then?" He asked. "I'm sorry I didn't warn you about the side effects. To be honest, I forgot, but I take full responsibility for making you feel upset in any way."

"Thank you. I'm fine," I said. "Better than fine." I lifted my chin towards his drink. "Bottoms up," I said, throwing back the rest of my martini and wincing as the full strength of the liquor hit the back of my throat. Then I placed both hands on the table and closed the distance between him and me, staring into his eyes like a fox giving chase to a rabbit (if the rabbit were unable to die and itself a perfectly designed creature of death). My chest rose and fell as I panted–yes, panted. Andras's lip kicked up on one side but his eyes were the color of honey once again, and laser focused on…?. His long fingers curled into fists, his nails carving into the table while he waited, and waited, and waited until finally, I realized that he wasn't going to make a move until I said so. I smiled.

"Take us back to your room," I ordered, our eyes still locked, as I leaned over the table until I was inches from his face.

Andras's pupils expanded, the gilded blue turned a blazing gold, and the world went black.

IN HIS ROOM

I found myself in Andras's bedroom, which was not actually his bedroom but in his mind, where the fireplace crackled and the bedspread practically sang my name. A smell of ash and whiskey hung in the air. I nervously tapped my fingers against the side of my thighs. The man in front of me wasn't human. And it had been a long time since I'd been touched, let alone by someone other than my husband. Would I even remember what to do? Andras breathed shakily, his focus going between my eyes and my mouth, where they lingered a little longer. His full lips parted, and he paused, frozen, until I realized, again, that he was waiting for me. My skin prickled with goosebumps.

My eyes dragged down his muscled body. I slowly reached up and unbuttoned the first button on my low-cut top. Andras sucked in a breath. I unbuttoned another and then another, revealing my black lace bra. Then I took a step forward until we were so close that his uneven exhales warmed my forehead as I gazed up at him. His scent, cedar and whisky, filled my nose. I closed my eyes, taking it all in. I gently laid my hand on his neck and whispered, in a breathy voice I barely recognized, "Can I kiss you?"

"You can do anything you want to me," he whispered back, his voice deep and full of gravel. He wrapped his arms around me and pulled me against him, and my skin, every inch, flushed and heated. My stomach tingled. I pushed up onto my toes as he brought his soft, warm lips to mine. A flick of his tongue had my body tightening and shuddering. "Oh Gods," I whispered against his mouth, and he chuckled darkly in response. He lifted me off the floor with one hand under my ass, and I wrapped my legs around him, pressing my center against the considerable length of him. I writhed and kissed him harder and he responded by opening his mouth for me and running his tongue over mine. I ran my hands up under the hem of his shirt, across his warm skin, the peaks and valleys of his abs, and the pecs that twitched under my palms as he gently laid me on the bed.

Andras sat back on his heels, waiting again, as if giving me time to change my mind. I kicked off my Oxfords, then slid off my pants in one silky movement. My black lace panties hid the faded scar from where Olivia had been cut from my body. The fireplace added a warm glow to my round hips and long legs, and I was thankful for that. I took Andras by the hand and pulled him down on top of me, slowly working my fingers over the buttons on his shirt while we kissed, inch by inch, revealing his abs and the deep carve of his hip flexors that formed a perfect

"V." My underwear were drenched. I unbuttoned his slacks, keeping his pelvis close to mine. The rest of our clothes came off in a flurry of hands, tossed on the floor in a careless pile until we were naked, and Andras was on top of me.

He kissed me slowly, softly, down my neck, pausing at my breasts. "These are beautiful," he breathed before flicking his tongue over my nipple. I bucked and writhed beneath him. He smiled against my breast.

"Is this okay?"

I nodded enthusiastically.

"Yes?"

"Yes," I gasped.

He licked and teased each one until I was moaning and grinding against him, desperate for pressure, for something, anything to relieve the ache building in my lower belly. His hand slid down to my entrance and stopped, "Okay?" he whispered, looking up at me from my chest with glassy eyes. "Yes." A large, long finger pushed into me, and my back arched. "You're so wet," he said into the skin of my belly, and I gasped and begged, "more." Finally, when I thought I was going to die from want, he trailed down further, paying special attention to my scar, his finger still pumping and curling inside of me. Then his mouth, hot and wet, found its way to that little bundle of nerves at the apex of my sex, and I screamed. He licked softly at first, leisurely, drawing the little bundle into his mouth and sucking gently, finger pumping, pumping, pumping. He slid his finger free, and I whimpered, feeling suddenly too empty. *Please don't stop, please don't stop!* Large, strong hands gently spread me open, and he settled between my legs like he planned to be there all night, looking his fill for what felt like hours with his pitch-black eyes. Unable to take it anymore, I reached for myself, but just before my fingers found my clit, he plunged his tongue inside of me, in and out, and I reached for his hair, tangling my fingers in it and almost laughing at the irony. I nearly came.

"Andras!" I moaned and bucked.

"Is this okay?" he asked, pausing, his breath hot against me.

"Yes," I moaned.

"Do you want me to keep going?"

"Please," I begged.

He licked up my center, and my hips rose off of the bed, but he pushed my hips gently back down, holding me in place. He licked again, then settled over the bundle of nerves, flicking his tongue there, then closed his mouth around me to suck gently. He slipped two fingers inside, and I breathed his name as I went over the edge so explosively that I nearly blacked out. My vision went dark, and all that existed at that moment was infinite pleasure, so intense that I felt like I might die. Can an orgasm kill you? My body quivered and shook against his mouth as I clenched around his pumping fingers and whispered filthy things. He pulled away and sat back, his mouth still glossy from me, and curved into a proud smile.

He pressed his tongue into the corner of his mouth.

"Thank you," he said.

I shook my head, still a little out of my mind from the best orgasm of my life. I pushed myself onto my knees, wrapped my arms around him, and kissed him, tasting myself on his lips and tongue. I climbed onto his lap and lowered myself onto his cock, slowly, inch by inch, giving myself time to adjust while I took in the full width and length of him. "You're huge," I whispered against his lips, and he had the audacity to shrug. His head dropped back as I moved a little faster, and his fangs caught the light of the fire. I kissed his neck as I moved up and down on him, feeling deliciously full.

For a moment, I forgot that my body was in a bar. That the sex wasn't real. I forgot about my problems, my anxieties, and my divorce; all that existed at that moment was him and me, and our bodies moving together as he buried himself deep, deep, deep. I kissed him hard, sliding my tongue over his sharp canines. He leaned back, bracing himself with one arm, bringing the other around my waist to lift me enough for him to move under me. He pushed up, up, up, in rapid, punishing thrusts, and I arched into it, finding the little bundle of nerves with my fingers, rubbing in tiny, messy circles. Teeth scraped the delicate skin of my neck.

"Yes!" I encouraged him to bite me. Suddenly, I wanted it almost more than I wanted his cock inside of me.

He focused his eyes on mine. "No," he whispered, shaking his head.

All of my focus went to my fingers, to the fire building there, and I moaned. Andras's breathing became shaky as he thrust, and thrust. He looked down to where we were joined, to my fingers moving there, and whispered in that dark, deep voice of shadows and dreams, "Danny."

I went over the edge again, my head kicking back as my body shuddered. Andras swore, "fuck!" and his cock pulsed inside me as his orgasm exploded from him. Our eyes roamed over each other's faces as we panted there a while, until finally I slid off of him and fell back onto the bedspread in a daze. He lay next to me, smiling sleepily. No sight of his canines.

"You didn't want to bite me?" I asked.

"No."

"Why?"

"Because the effect that I can have, the nice one, won't work here. Your mind would perceive it as painful. And it would bloody hurt. I care about you. I don't want to hurt you."

"Oh..." I said softly.

I had no idea how long we'd been in this room in his mind. Thirty seconds. Six hours. Just like a dream, we were there all night, and I didn't want to leave the warmth of his bed or his breath, the kindness in his eyes, or that body, muscled from Gods knew what. All that I could say for certain was this: being with him was like dieting for a lifetime and then being handed an entire cheesecake.

***

My martini was still cold to the touch when Andras brought us back to the bar, and my nausea and confusion from the mindweaving weren't bad this time. I adjusted quickly, to my surprise. I'd gone from naked in bed to clothed in public, from tousled hair and wild makeup to everything still in place. Andras's espresso hair was no longer disheveled from where I'd dragged my hands through it. He gave me a look that meant something like, "we just fucked," and my cheeks flushed. I needed time to process. I'd had unbelievable, mind-blowing sex with Andras, my lovely neighborhood vampire, and...*what was this life*? I had to parent in the morning.

Andras seemed to read everything on my face. "You look like you're ready to go. I'll call you a car." He smiled, but something else lurked there, some other feeling. Sadness?

"Thank you."

At home, I checked on Victoria and Olivia. Both were passed out in their beds. Jess had crashed in the guest room.

I changed into a silk nightgown, crawled into bed, and was hit with an overwhelming flood of emotions. Confusion, shame, grief, excitement, *everything*, swelled and crashed everywhere inside of me all at once. My throat tightened and the tears came so fast that my cheeks felt wet before I even realized I was crying. They trailed down the side of my face, across my temples, and into my hair. I hadn't thought it was possible to feel so connected to someone like that, let alone so soon after my divorce. Being with Andras felt as natural as breathing. It felt like coming home like we were meant to be, and something about that felt as wrong as it felt right. Curling up in the fetal position, I let myself feel all of it, until I fell asleep.

FAREWELL, REBECCA

"You don't think you could have made it, I don't know, just a little smaller, sis? It's like the size of a fucking movie screen." Jess said, standing in the shadow of Rebecca's portrait in my studio with her head tilted back to take it all in.

"I just did what I was told," I said, shrugging.

Jess shot me a sidelong glare.

It was pickup day, and the moving folks were coming to remove the massive canvas from my life. I had no idea where the owner of this portrait would hang it, but I imagined she lived in a castle–probably in the same area as my mother–and had wall room to spare. That, or she was building a mansion out of these portraits.

Jess and I had woken up before the girls, a rarity (and an indication that Jess had put them to bed way too late last while I was out with Andras), but it was nice to have a cup of coffee together in the living room, cozied up on the couch, both of us wrapped in my favorite green velvet blanket. It took most of my self-control not to tell her about last night, about Andras in the bar, in his mind, in his bed. Thankfully, Jess filled the silence by lamenting over her dissertation and sharing some details about some "super hot" woman she'd been on a few dates with recently, which was a lot for Jess. "And when do I get to meet this super special lady?" I teased. She gave a look like she'd just chugged sour milk and waved me off. Then I got the call that movers were on their way to fetch Rebecca, so I dragged Jess outside to help me cover the canvas in a protective fabric before they arrived.

"And why do you care so much about the size of this monstrosity? How exactly does it effect you?," I mumbled while trying to untangle some rope to secure the portrait, lest it arrive scratched or mangled.

"Because I'm out here, in the cold, way to early in the morning, helping you wrap this thing. If it were a normal size, we'd already be back inside on the couch, cozy." Jess lamented, still standing there, judging Rebecca the Shih Tzu's crooked face, clouded eyes, and tongue that flopped out of her mouth in the space where teeth should be, like a moist beef filet.

I scrunched my face.

"Thank you for waiting with me while they come to pick this up. Also, can you help?" I tapped my fingertips on the canvas, one finger at a time: One-two-three-four-five, five-four-three-two-one.

"I suppose," She said, faking a smile, "if you stop with the anxious tapping."

"Fine." I grunted out, yanking a sheet of fabric free from a shelf, "I have so much to tell you about last night."

"Yeah, I figured. You kept giving me longing looks this morning like you really needed to say something," she chuckled.

I glared, "Well, don't *we* know everything."

"When it comes to you? Pretty much."

"That's fair."

I moved around the canvas to close the gap between myself and Jess and lowered my voice; after all, Steven's apartment was above my studio, and even if he wasn't there, it felt...weird.

"So I kinda had sex. I mean, well, yeah. Listen, I—"

Jess went slackjawed. Her full red lips parted in a silent gasp. Conspiratorial delight twinkled in her eyes.

My phone rang before I could continue stammering on. Jess threw her hands up in the air and mouthed, *now*?

"Okay, I'm opening the gate," I said into my phone and mouthed, *I know,* in return. I stalked to the iron fence of the driveway, unlocked it, and swung the massive gate open with a creak and thud.

Two men in gray coveralls waited for me. We exchanged pleasantries and they followed me to the portrait. One man had a mustache and a large blanket tucked under his left arm, and the other was bald with a crow tattooed on his neck and a spindle of twine in his hand. What a relief–I wouldn't have to bother wrapping the damn thing. The large bald man sent a feeling of unease prickling up my spine; even though he looked nothing like the man who'd attacked me in my home, there were enough similarities to trigger my nervous system, to wake my worry, to have it whisper concerns in the recesses of my mind. *Be cautious, look out, watch him.* As instructed by my therapist, I acknowledged the warnings, reminded myself that this was the voice of anxiety, and then focused on the pads of my feet while I walked.

"There she is!" I sang, pointing to Rebecca. The mustache guy raised his eyebrows at his partner as if to say, *Jesus Christ, rich people, right?* But the bald guy beamed and exclaimed, "A Shih Tzu! Awesome! Check this out!" He rolled up his sleeve to reveal a tattoo of a Shih Tzu with a giant pink bow on its head and the words "Violet Cake" in cursive below it.

"My partner and I couldn't have children, so Violet is our little girl," he giggled.

The mustache guy inspected the tattoo and patted him on the back. "Cool ink, man."

Jess and I smiled at the man with the Violet Cake tattoo. "She's perfect," I beamed, gesturing to Violet. "Let me know if you ever want a painting of her the size of a school bus." He giggled again, then rolled his sleeve back down. The two men immediately started to wrap the painting and secure it with twine. Jess and I moved politely out of the way and out of earshot.

Standing shoulder to shoulder with me, she whispered, "Tell me everything."

"Uhm, right now?" I whispered back.

I listened for the girls to make sure they were still asleep. What had happened between Andras and I was really hard to explain. I hadn't had sex with Andras...but I had. We did. It had felt real–so real I'd even forgotten we weren't actually in his bed at one point. So yes, I guess we did have sex in whatever manner it happened.

"Uhm, so, I had sex with Andras," I said so quietly it took a moment for her to register the information. For a second, I considered telling her that he was an old as-dust vampire, too, but thought better of it.

Her mouth dropped open. Then she threw back her head and cackled, her brown wavy bob quavering around her face.

"What is so funny!" I demanded, crossing my arms over my chest.

"What's so funny? You were so anxious about everyone thinking you had an affair with him, and then you bang him five minutes after ending your marriage? Really subtle, sis, not at all suspect."

"We *didn't* have an affair; we've been officially divorced for months now," I countered. Steven and I were done, the papers were signed, and he technically lived in the guest apartment now, even though he could more often be found in the main house with the girls. Which I didn't mind. He'd become a much more pleasant person since we separated.

"I know, I'm just giving you shit."

"I know," I said, unsmiling, "and I don't know if I have it in me to care what any of those gossiping wanks thinks anymore," I admitted.

"Good," Jess said, with a curt dip of her chin. "So, give me the details. How was it? Tell me everything."

I brought my hands to my mouth to hide my giant smile, feeling a rush of giddiness swell in my chest. "Amazing. Incredible. It's hard to put it into words." My lower stomach tingled and flipped just thinking about it. "He's gorgeous. His body was..." I trailed off. Perfect? Hard? Flawless? Vampiric? "Uhm, and he was so *good* at *everything*. Extremely skilled."

Jess's eyes widened,

"Ha! The look on your face. Your cheeks are flushing. That good, huh?"

"Yeah," I said, my hands roaming from my mouth down to my chest, where they paused to feel my heart drum for a moment. The beat brought me back to my body and the cold reality that I was a human woman with a thrumming heart that could stop beating at any moment, and Andras was a vampire who would outlive me tenfold. That was only one of the *many* reasons we couldn't actually date. Plus, my girls didn't need the additional stress of me being with a new guy after splitting from their father. We were still adjusting to our new life, it was hard enough without anyone else thrown in.

"Sis?" Jess whispered, placing a hand on my shoulder. "What's wrong?"

"It's just," I paused. What could I say? Well, you see, he's immortal, and I'll likely die on a random Tuesday from PTA-induced stress. I blew out a breath, "I like him. The sex was amazing, and we shouldn't do it again. Andras has a *complicated* past. And present? And honestly, I haven't known him for that long. But maybe there's something between us to explore…one day. Down the road. Just not now."

"What? Does he cook meth?"

I glowered at her.

Jess threw up her hands in defeat.

The moving men grunted loudly as they hoisted up the wrapped painting (which looked more like an old mattress than a work of art) and hobbled towards the moving truck, the cold wind pushing and pulling the canvas like a ship's sail. "Thank you," I called out to them, waving goodbye with one hand while I closed the iron gate with the other. After securing the lock, I turned and nearly slammed into my sister, who'd been right behind me, arms crossed, looking bored.

"What the hell?" I exclaimed, surprised.

"I can tell you're hiding something, you crafty bitch," she said, one eyebrow raised.

There was no point in lying. She knew me well enough.

"I am hiding things." I admitted, walking around her, "A lot of things. I mean, he's not married or anything. He's just, well…complicated, I guess? I'm not ready to talk about it."

Jess followed me. I loved my sister in part because she would call me out when I was doing something stupid, but also because I could tell her *anything*. And I wanted to tell her. I was bursting at the seams to spill the tea about Andras–THE thing–because it was every romantic scenario we'd ever dreamed of since high school. Thank you very much, *Vampire Diaries*. Plus, we were, *for all intents and purposes,* witches (if you had to use a name for what we were), and what goes better with vampires than witches?

Jess and I had grown up utterly obsessed with all things magical, elemental, symbolic, and otherworldly, and what was an immortal if not all of that? But we weren't witches in the, I don't know, typical sense. Unlike the goth kids in our private Catholic school who practiced to rebel against their family religion, who were always angry and constantly hexing everyone (good for them, honestly), we were witches in our blood, from birth, in the things we believed, and how we existed in the world.

Like many Persian families, our family had Zoroastrian roots from long ago, before the Arab tribes conquered the Persian empire and made Islam mandatory. The Zoroastrian religion is an eco-religion of sorts, rooted in respecting the earth and its elements. Everything started from there and, over time, became something else for our family. We didn't consider ourselves Zorasts, but parts of the religion were woven into our culture, so as little girls, we celebrated the change in seasons. We jumped over the fire for the Spring Equinox with our parents and their friends to ask for good health–a terrifying sight for our conservative Christian neighbors who believed that every spring, we were attempting to summon demons to burn down their mansions. Bethany's family delighted in calling the fire department every year. The twats.

Jess and I were the kids who wandered around thanking the trees for oxygen. And because of our mom's love of gardening—the only thing that woman did other than ride horses that involved even a speck of dirt—we knew every property of every herb, flower, and weed under the sun and how to use them to heal or harm. Even our dad, who traveled most of the time (and was a cold, critical ass when he *was* around), fostered the ideals that the earth should be respected and treated as a living entity and life force. He didn't teach us about death in terms of heaven or hell, but from the first law of thermodynamics–energy cannot be made or unmade. So when our goldfish, Goldie, died, we were told that the energy that made Goldie, Goldie, left her body and went back into the world to give life to other things. This made perfect sense to us as kids, and we accepted it easily and without question. Witchy-woo shit (whether we called it that or not) was just part of our life, part of our family culture, woven into our genetics. And Andras was crafted of magic straight out of a paranormal romance novel, and I *couldn't tell my sister*. At least, not yet. And it was *killing me*.

"I'll fill you in. Eventually. I promise," I said over my shoulder as I walked towards the studio door to lock up.

"Uh-huh," Jess mumbled.

"Anyway," I said, turning the lock. "A lot is going on," I continued, stuffing my hands into my jogger pockets. "My head hurts, and I'm confused. I mean, I'm finally divorced like I should have been five years ago. But some part of me will always love Steven in a very platonic way. It's just," I sighed, "this is not the life I'd planned, and I'm still mourning that. And now I have a crush on someone?"

I groaned, folding myself into a patio chair.

"I understand," Jess said. "It's a lot."

She plopped down across from me and melted into the chair until her and the cushions were one mass. Her tongue poked around the inside of her cheek while she stared at me, unblinking.

Finally, I got tired of waiting for her to say whatever it was she was clearly thinking. "What?" I asked, more bite in my tone than I intended.

Her lips pursed. "I was just thinking…you're allowed to be happy, you know that, right?" Jess stated, matter of factly. "Ever since we lost dad it's like you just kinda shut down. And once you became a mom it got even worse. You don't have to weather the storm, Danny, if you're a part of it."

We regarded each other for a long while, saying nothing. She wasn't wrong, and the implication of that hit me, hard. When was the last time I felt pure, unbridled joy? When was the last time I just, I don't know, wanted something for myself?

"Fuck, that's cold," Jess hissed, pulling her knees into her chest and crossing her legs at the ankle. "We don't live long enough to be unhappy." She wiped at the knee of her trousers, brushing off a piece of lint.

"I know." I agreed. Although, what if we did? "But what if...what if you could live forever? What would you do differently?"

"Well, I wouldn't want to spend forever miserable," she said, leveling her gaze at me to emphasize that it was obvious. "But, live forever *how*? Are we talking about cool powers? Or exactly like we are?" she pondered.

Jess tracked a bird overhead, her small hand hovering just above her eyebrows to block the sun from her large, round eyes. The corner of her lip kicked up. She whispered, "Robin," to herself. My sister, the twenty-nine-year-old birder.

"For debate's sake, let's say like a vampire or something."

Jess grinned.

"Hmm. *Twilight* vampire or *Fright Night* vampire?"

I huffed a laugh because I'd asked Andras something similar. I loved how much my sister and I, though so incredibly different, were alike.

"*Vampire Diaries* vampire? I guess?" I shrugged.

Her lips twisted to the side, and she hummed some tune, then said, "well, I'd do everything differently and everything the same. I'd do it all. And have a lot of dirty vampire sex."

She smiled and waggled her eyebrows while hip-thrusting out of the chair.

"You're going to fall over," I said, chuckling.

"And you?" Jess asked, arching a brow.

My mind drifted to Andras and his body pressing into mine, those full soft lips parted, breathing against my lips and between my legs. I anchored myself to the freezing chair.

"I'd let myself want. I think."

GHOSTED

An audiobook droned on in my earbuds about the minds of children and how to integrate their brains and get all the parts working together harmoniously to create a solid and stellar human being. Which would be great fucking information, if I could remember any of it. *Would this entire book not be better as a fridge magnet?* I silently griped. Occasionally, I'd lean over my notebook to add a bullet point, a reminder of how to do things "the best way." And with every book I ticked off of my list, I noticed that there were a lot of "best ways," and I wasn't sure how to implement them all, or if it was even possible.

I dragged another laundry basket in front of me and started the task of matching tiny socks. Victoria and Olivia sat at my feet, coloring with paint sticks on a canvas spread on the floor of the playroom, elbowing each other back and forth with increasing hostility. Eventually, one would snap and tackle the other. Then they'd go full-on Thunderdome until I separated them. Five minutes after prying them apart, they'd make up as if nothing had happened and focus their energy on being pissed at me. Repeat a thousand times throughout the rest of the day.

Colorado was covered in snowflakes and frost, the heater groaned, the girls argued, and branches rustled outside. An occasional yap from the neighbor's terrier interrupted the winter ambiance and the calming effect of the classical radio station that I never turned off in the living room. Classical music was not my favorite, and I didn't know much about it, but I hated a silent home and needed something to bring the air to life. I leaned back against a llama throw pillow, noticing the way it softly pressed against my lower back. It reminded me of Andras's powerful and soft hands, of how he'd held me when we had been together.

I must have been smiling, lost in my happy thoughts, because Victoria exclaimed loudly, "Mommy, you look happy!" She tilted her head, her mouth wide, and curved into an adorably, goofy, jack-o-lantern grin.

I brushed Victoria's cheek with the back of my fingers.

"I am! Because I'm here with my two favorite people ever."

"We're not jackasses," Olivia asserted for no reason at all, without bothering to look up from her drawing of what seemed to be a family on fire. *Horrifying.*

"Excuse me?" I asked.

"That's what you call people you don't like when you're driving."

"Hmm, yeah, some people are just terrible drivers and, uh, that's not school language, okay?"

Olivia giggled and went back to doodling.

Groaning, I got to my feet, feeling the strain and ache in my calves from a long run that morning around the glassy, duck-filled lake in Washington Park. A light snowfall had coated the ground to form a slick powder that made it an effort to stay upright. I felt pretty proud that I'd only fallen on my ass once. But the awkward balancing atop the frosted trail had done a number on my legs and they just wouldn't stop throbbing.

"I'll be right back, I'm just going to get a drink of water," I explained before padding into the kitchen in my giant slippers to check my phone for any missed calls or messages. Andras had been on my mind all day while doing dishes, taking a shower, and staring at myself naked in the mirror. I got that drink of water, then checked my phone screen again, blowing out a heavy breath when he still hadn't texted me. Of course, he hadn't. Neither of us had messaged each other apart from that one time he'd sent the photo of Bethany, who now seemed to be pretending I'd died and no longer even sent necessary school PTA information. I pivoted away from the counter and then walked in a circle before coming back, like a dog trying to get comfortable before lying down. *Don't do it!* I admonished myself.

Steven argued with someone on the phone and paced in front of the kitchen window, "can you puh-lease tell me when exactly the units will be finished." He over-enunciated the way people used to with my dad after he'd immigrated from Iran. As if speaking more than one language (albeit imperfectly) somehow makes you an idiot? *Asshole*. I took another sip of my water, a small stream drizzled down my chin, and I used my sleeve to dab it before setting the glass in the sink. Clink. *You cannot text your mind-lover crush while your ex-husband is pacing around the house.*

A powerful wind rippled across the windows, howling into the nooks and crannies of the exterior bricks, filling the house with a goosepimpling draft. I shivered, then padded to my bedroom to grab my robe from its hook. Pulling the plush robe around me, I paused in front of the mirror. A dark tendril of hair hung over my brow, and it looked the way my father's sister's (my aunt Zahra) hair used to look first thing in the morning when she visited. In my reflection, I saw my mother there, too, or at least the heavy tug of loneliness on my features. The silence in my home for the past few years and the lack of companionship had been unbearable. It reminded me of the home I grew up in. I swore I'd raise my girls differently and had envisioned a better life for them: an affectionate space, a safe haven, and a place of acceptance and unconditional love. Shame had been riding me hard for years, for not marrying and having children with someone kinder.

"If it makes you hysterical, it's probably historical," I muttered. It was a mantra I'd learned from my therapist, a reminder that if something triggers big feelings, it's probably coming from the past. I closed my eyes and imagined the pressure of

Andras's body on mine, comforting me like a weighted blanket, enveloping me like this cashmere robe.

I opened my eyes and moved towards the kitchen with purpose, taking the stairs quickly to swipe my phone from the counter on the way back up to the playroom. My sore legs shook from going up and down the stairs so many times. Why did we buy a house with stairs again? I paused outside of the playroom to cradle the phone in my hand and type out a message.

"I'm confused about what's going on in my life. It's messy. But could we see each other again, soon?" Sent. My pulse quickened. I tucked my phone into my robe pocket and went back to my chair to finish folding the mountain of laundry, to bury myself in the smell of "fresh jasmine garden," to keep my mind focused on my hands.

A few moments later, my phone buzzed, and I stilled for a heartbeat before reluctantly pulling it out of my pocket and flipping it over in my hand. When I saw that it was a message from Janet, the peppy as fuck PTA mom who inexplicably shouted in every message she ever sent, the exciting flutter in my stomach turned into annoyance.

"HELLO, PARENTS! IT'S JANET NEWSBIRIED HERE! JUST A FINAL REMINDER THAT IT'S TIME TO VOLUNTEER FOR THE HOLIDAY PARTY! ICE SCULPTURES, DONATION DRIVES, GIFTS, AND MORE! I'D LOVE TO KICK OFF THE FESTIVITIES WITH A STATEMENT OF GRATITUDE. I AM GRATEFUL FOR OUR SCHOOL (GO WOLVES!) AND ALL OF YOU! HOW

MANY HOURS CAN I PUT YOU DOWN FOR? THANK YOU FOR DOING YOUR PART TO GIVE BACK TO YOUR COMMUNITY."

I immediately copied the message and forwarded it to Jess, who responded so fast it was frightening with, "Fucking Janet. Does she just have unlimited free time? Also, my favorite thing she's ever done was the grandparent-themed appreciation ball, where she raised money for a retirement living facility for everyone's grannies. This is a class of toddlers. Their grandparents are barely sixty, lol."

"Dad died way younger than that."

"Died sis, not retired in a senior living community. OMG, do you think she'll raise money for their funerals next year?"

"Probably."

"I've gotta meet this lady."

"Hi, Janet." I replied to the screaming PTA mom, "Put me down for a financial donation and two hours of time. Thanks so much for organizing." I slid my phone back into my pocket and folded a pair of tiny leggings in half.

How did so many parents seem to have it all together while I forever floundered in survival mode? Moms like Janet or dads like Niel and Brandon hosted themed cocktail parties and organized sock drives or retirement fundraisers for people who were not even retirement age. My phone buzzed again, and I rolled my eyes, whispering, "What the fuck, Janet?" Under my breath. I added the little pants to a basket for Victoria and reached for my phone. This time, it was not Janet.

My heart sank.

"I'm sorry," the message from Andras began, "I'm going to be away for a while." I sucked in a breath before reading on, my stomach twisting. "But I'll be in touch. Take care of yourself."

Take care of yourself. So distant and formal. *Oh shit. He got what he wanted, and now he's done. Gods, it would make sense, after all, he has so many people in it, a constant turnover of warm bodies and fresh blood.*

I read the screen again, jaw set, teeth grinding. How had I been so stupid not to see it? The rejection stung. Glancing down at the hardwood, at my toes that had slipped free from the pillowy slippers. The chipped white toenail polish, a reminder that we were in a very different place in our lives; we lived in very different worlds. Andras was a *vampire*. A very, very, old vampire. And I was home folding tiny clothes, for the tiny humans in my care. I inhaled deeply, wiggled my toes, and focused on my body to stay present, to stop the sadness from setting in and consuming me, at least until later when I could grieve in the darkness of my bedroom.

Victoria and Olivia screeched, signaling that one of their paint sticks had successfully been weaponized. For once, separating them was a gift, a welcome distraction until I could figure out how to feel and what to do about Andras. The sane and logical part of my brain wanted to focus on my kids, myself, being single for the first time in a long time, and my art. A petty and proud part wanted to march over to his house to give him the finger. Yet an inner voice whispered concern. Go, it urged. Go.

RUBBLE AND RUIN

Andras looked like he'd seen a ghost from where he kneeled on the floor of his entryway surrounded by rubble and ruin. I might not have recognized him if I weren't staring directly into his house from his porch. His black t-shirt had been torn in more than one place, blood smeared his gray sweatpants, and his hair and face were coated in a fine dusting of debris. The dark blue eyes I so often found myself drawn to were vacantly fixed on a spot on the floor. A beautiful woman with sun-kissed skin damaged by cuts and bruises crouched, panting, beside him, her delicate arm at a strange angle.

Andras' head whipped toward me. I stepped back, startled.

"I'm so sorry." I apologized, "I shouldn't have come."

I turned to go.

"Please don't go, Danny," Andras called out. But there was something unspoken in his tone, something desperate.

His voice sounded too strained, too wounded to be his. I froze and turned, startled to find him already standing at the doorway. He forced a weak smile, his beautiful face covered in pink scratches, like freshly healed cuts. The gorgeous woman slowly reached his side, face neutral and unreadable. She glanced down at herself, as if taking in the damage for the first time, eyes settling on her bent, gnarled arm. She rolled her eyes with annoyance before ducking behind a wall, just out of view. Something cracked, and she swore loudly. Andras frowned. Then she was back at his side, rubbing her arm. It still appeared a little off but was no longer completely mangled, aside from the piece of jagged wood jutting out of her thigh right below her tattered silk nightgown. Drywall chunks and crusted blood decorated her body, and even still, she was one of the most beautiful women I'd ever seen. Her cheekbones could cut rocks.

In a way, two of my suspicions had been right. There stood Andras, disheveled and obviously in trouble but with a nearly naked woman. It stung. But I didn't have the right to be angry; it's not like we were together, and I just got divorced, for fuck sake. Plus, I knew he needed to date in order to feed. The guy had to eat, right? At least, that's what I told myself.

Andras examined my face.

"Danny," he said, gently, "I can see your mind racing. Whatever you're thinking, it's not that." He tried to force a smile to put me at ease, but it came off as manic with his bloodshot eyes and way too-toothy grin. Something had rattled him, scared him. Honestly, it hardly seemed possible–the unkillable man was all swagger and smirk–but something had happened, something bad. I studied them.

"What happened?" I asked quietly but not weakly.

I stepped around them and into the house, knowing that the last thing any of us needed was for Kim to record me, Andras, and this gorgeous woman in a state of duress, so I was quick about it. Bethany had all but stopped her bullshit after I'd texted her pics of her fleeing Kim's bed, but no part of me truly believed she'd drop it off forever. If anything, she'd probably stock up on evidence for a few years before going in for the final kill when I lay on my deathbed.

The front door clicked shut behind me. The house was absolutely destroyed, and the view inside was far worse. There were human-sized dents and holes in the walls, his dining table lay in shreds, and blood had been splattered across the walls and floor. My hands flew to my mouth and I gasped as images of my father flooded back. The room tilted under my feet.

"The blood. Oh, no, the blood," Andras said quietly, as if he were far away.

He rushed to me and gently took my elbow to steady my balance. I looked up at him, and his dust-coated hair and face, thankful.

"Nadia is an old friend," Andras began, while he steadied me. "She arrived a few weeks ago, around the day I sat with you in the coffee shop."

Nadia grinned. "I'm terribly sorry we're meeting like this. I've heard so much about you. Nice to meet you," she said.

"It's nice to meet you, too."

I dipped my chin to her then turned to Andras. "What have you told her about me?" I asked him. "And I thought you were leaving? What is happening? What happened to your house?"

"I told you that I was leaving because I was trying to keep you safe," he held up a hand as if telling me not to jump to conclusions, "because unfortunately, it's not safe for me to see you right now." He gestured around his broken house, "and now that you've come here, you're most certainly in danger."

He paused and turned to Nadia, saying, "there's no way he didn't stop somewhere to see if we gave chase. He probably saw her approach."

Nadia shook her head that she agreed.

"In danger of what? From who?" I demanded.

I turned to Nadia.

"OH, GODS! NO," Nadia exclaimed, chuckling. "No, you have nothing to fear from me. I have nothing to do with this. I don't even really drink human blood. I'm mostly on the puppy diet." Puppies! I scowled. Nadia shook her head emphatically. "Well, not *actually* puppies. I'm not a *monster*," she chuckled to herself, "but I do mostly drink animal blood, like from deer, unless I'm committed to someone, which I haven't been for centuries, although I *have* started dating someone here, and they're lovely, so maybe one day. And unlike this infant *here*," she angled her head to Andras, "I'm old and not really tempted by human blood. Andras, however, must be suffering terribly around you." She beamed at him with absolute delight. Andras rolled his eyes.

"You're also a vampire?" I asked, unable to believe it. "Oh, and..." I pointed to her thigh, "you have a thing sticking out of your leg."

Nadia looked down at the splinter of wood the size of a knife jutting out of her thigh. "Great," she hissed then reached down and yanked it out in one effortless motion. Blood oozed from the gaping hole. Then, the bleeding slowed as the skin knitted itself back together.

I gasped.

Nadia clasped her hands together, waiting for Andras to say something.

Andras exhaled, "It's faster if I show you what happened here. May I show you?" he asked, extending his hand.

"How?" I asked, but just as the words left my lips, I realized what he meant. "You want to show me inside of your head?"

"Yes."

Andras smiled tightly, hand still extended. Slowly, reluctantly, I rolled my shoulders back in preparation for the epic mindfuck about to happen and reached for him, letting his long soft fingers envelop mine. He gently pulled me into him, close enough to feel the heat radiating off of his chest and gently grabbed my chin to tilt my face up to meet his stare. "I'll be with you, don't worry," he promised. I blinked once in confirmation and watched as the onyx of his pupils spread like spilled ink until the blue was gone, the white was gone, and all that remained was darkness. The darkness spread around us, too, shadows eating up the light until the whole world turned black. Then I realized I was seeing through his eyes, as if I were behind them, peering out. Much like a movie, a scene began to play.

THE MOST BEAUTIFUL WOMAN IN HIS ROOM

Andras's mind took us to his bedroom again, and I wanted to smack him for a second, thinking he was trying to be funny. The full moon spotlighted his bedroom window and the veranda, where a dark-haired beauty, Nadia, waited with her hands on her hips in an unmistakable "go fuck yourself" power stance. It was cold out, and I felt something, looking at her. Love? Was I feeling his feelings, too? Or not necessarily feeling them, but sensing them second-hand?

One of Nadia's six-inch heels tapped against the ground impatiently. Andras threw open the double doors and stepped into the light, locking his sights on Nadia. They took each other in for a moment, he narrowed in on her sharp cheekbones and large almond eyes. She was beautiful, absolutely stunning, and I could feel that she knew it from the way she looked down her nose at him despite being a few inches shorter. She stepped forward, her expression resolute and severe. Andras slid his hands into his pockets and rocked back slightly on his heels.

"Nadia," he spat. Then his body began to shake, his lips twitching as a smile broke free, and they both burst into laughter. Then Nadia was on top of him, on top of us, her long legs wrapped around his waist. I tensed. Did I really need to see all of this? Nadia gently cradled his head in her hands, kissing his cheeks all over, leaving sticky red lipstick marks. He set her down lightly, and she sauntered right past him into the bedroom, like she owned the place, with Andras following close on her heels, hands back inside his pockets. If I were able to feel my body at that point, I knew my skin would be crawling, and my heart would drop in anticipation of what might happen next. If they were gonna fuck, I didn't want to see it.

"I've missed you," she cooed, twirling to face him with an ethereal grace that had clearly been honed over centuries; after all, she'd jokingly referred to Andras as "an infant," a reminder that she was so, so much older than him. She reached out and touched his shoulder gently.

"I've missed you," he said, absolutely beaming. "Where the hell have you been?"

"Everywhere," she shrugged, looking down at his pants and wrinkling her nose. "Never thought I'd see you in loungewear," she teased.

My eyes flicked towards a wall mirror and there Andras stood, shoulders back, head high, sapphire eyes twinkling. Okay, was she insane or did she not notice how absolutely incredible his ass looked in those pants?

He followed her disapproving gaze down the length of his body, then smirked. "A sign of the times, old friend," he cocked his head, "and I caught your scent just as I was heading to bed. There simply wasn't enough time to change into something more acceptable."

Nadia's smile faded, and she bit her lip nervously. She clicked her fingernails together a few times.

"Listen," she cleared her throat quietly, "before we catch up." She winced, "I've got some extraordinarily shitty news and you're not going to like it one bit."

Andras's entire body went rigid. Staring at her mouth, he waited for whatever damning words were about to fall from her full red lips.

"Well, it seems you might have some ex-boyfriend problems soon."

"What does that—"

Nadia raised her brows and dipped her chin to indicate that he fucking knew exactly what it meant.

"Oh no," Andras whispered, staggering back. His legs felt weak, and his fear became my fear. I wanted to hold him. He began to pace from his bed to the fireplace and back. "No, no, no," he chanted. "Bloody hell, no. That's not possible." He dragged my hands through his hair. I could feel his face twisting with rage. The room came into hyperfocus, and I knew that meant his pupils were expanding, like spilled ink, rubbing out the blue, just as they had before he'd pulled me into his mind to watch all of this unfold. He clenched his hands into tight fists at his side, still pacing, and his eyes narrowed into two hateful slits focused entirely on the floor.

"Yeah," Nadia agreed as she blew out a breath. "I'm sorry."

She took a step toward him. "It appears that your psychotic ex is free from that lovely cement pit we dumped him in. And apparently, yet unsurprisingly, he's holding a bit of a grudge." She examined her ruby red nail polish, which anyone else would have taken as a gesture of indifference, but Andras seemed to view it positively. He knew her well enough to know that she was focusing her attention elsewhere in order to give him time to process without her eyes on him.

He paced some more, and then we were in a different memory, a darker one, grainy and old. The smell of wet cement overwhelmed my senses, followed by gargling, furious screams and threats of revenge hurled up at Andras from somewhere low, somewhere nearby. A pit, a quickly filling pit. Nadia stood to his right, grasping his hand so hard I thought she might break it off until the rage and roaring stopped. They slept there, seated in the shadows, until the slab was thoroughly cured.

Then we were back in his bedroom, facing Nadia, whose eyes were silver-lined and full of sorrow.

"How?" Andras pressed, his deep voice quiet and steady in a way that promised violence. He gestured to the carpet between them, "tell me how." He quickly scanned the room, then went to the window to peer out. Nothing. Nothing but trees.

Andras whispered quietly to himself, "he could be anywhere. He could be on a branch, on a roof, hiding in a car. Anywhere."

Nadia closed the distance between us, or between them, coming so close I could see every one of her long, sweeping lashes. "Humans," she grimaced. "They freed him. Some students..." She trailed off then threw up her hands, "and that's why they can't have nice things!"

Andras glanced at her disapprovingly.

She scoffed, crossing her arms.

Sauntering over towards Andras's bed, the same bed he'd touched me on the last time he'd pulled me into his mind, she leaned against the mattress, and my heart dropped, thinking of where this might be going. Nadia casually brushed a piece of lint away from her red dress. She scented the air.

"Something happened here recently," she crooned, looking around, distracted for a moment. And...oh, Gods, could she smell that I'd been there? Could there even be a scent from that? Or...had other women been there recently?

I didn't want to know.

she seemed to remember that she was in the middle of delivering bad news. "As I was saying," she cleared her throat, "some archeology students studying the old way of making Roman cement accidentally freed him while excavating the site, and, unfortunately, wound up very dead. There was barely anything left of them, just a mess of husks shredded to pieces after they'd been drained dry."

Andras stalked past Nadia, out of the bedroom, and down the stairs. He moved towards the study, Nadia traipsing behind him like she had all the time in the world.

"I've tracked his mayhem to this continent, Andras," she went on. "He's already here, maybe not yet in Denver, but here." I felt a chill skitter up Andras's spine and neck, and I wanted to cringe, to hide. He was afraid, very afraid, and I wondered: how evil is this person if both Andras and Nadia are terrified of him?

Andras bit back nausea as he beelined straight for the bar cart against the back wall, lifting a whiskey decanter from its place and filling a heavy crystal glass to the rim with the amber liquid. He handed the glass to Nadia without looking up, intentionally avoiding the concern in her eyes.

He poured the same glass for himself before offering the side of his glass to Nadia. The crystal rang out beautifully as their glasses gently collided.

"Cheers." They said flatly, without any cheer at all.

Andras knocked back his whiskey in two enormous gulps, then poured another while still swallowing. For fuck's sake, this man knew how to drown his feelings. Nadia frowned at him, but he didn't seem to care. She made it a point to take her whiskey in small mouthfuls, sending a deliberate and judgemental message with each sip.

"You realize that you need to be sober to deal with this, right?" she gently chided as Andras depleted his second glass. "And considering your black-as-night lord-of-death eyes, I'm guessing that you're not at all in the right headspace for this conversation yet. Carry on, then, keep drinking." She lowered herself to the side of the armrest of the sofa, legs crossed at the ankle.

"What is it?" Nadia demanded. "Something is bothering you. I can feel it."

He scowled at her, then downed yet another glass of whiskey as if it were a cold glass of water in the desert. Adding one more splash of liquor to his glass, he blew out a breath and then turned to face her, running a hand through his dark hair.

"Not too long ago," he began, "I saw a halfling. I wasn't entirely sure because it's been such a long time since I've scented one, but I'm certain of it now."

"You saw a halfling *where*?"

"It's a long story. A man broke into a neighbor's house very close by, and I happened to hear the struggle and went in to help. He was unconscious when I leaned in to get a closer look at him, but his scent was...weird. Human, but not."

"Fuck."

"Yeah. I even tried to find him again after, tried to track him down and couldn't. I've kept an eye on the house, and on the woman he attacked, but nothing so far."

I couldn't believe what I was hearing. He suspected the thing that attacked me wasn't human. And he'd been keeping an eye on my house ever since? I didn't know whether to be flattered or horrified.

Andras scrubbed at his face and cracked his neck.

"It's been what, centuries?" he bit out. "You don't think there's a chance that he might just want to, I don't know, fucking move on?"

Nadia's eyebrows went up at that.

"Weak men have held on to grudges for a lot less than a broken heart, Andras. Well, a broken heart and a knife in the back."

Andras rolled his eyes and scoffed.

"Does it honestly count as a betrayal if he was trying to kill us?"

"In his deranged mind, yes."

Andras paced back and forth on the rug as if his vampire senses had gone haywire, nearly knocking into the coffee table.

"How much time do you think we have?" he asked, glancing at the windows again, tapping his pinky against the glass in his hand like a tiny nervous woodpecker.

Nadia shrugged.

"I don't know. Hours. Or days. He's fast and insane so it's possible he's already right outside of your house. I came to warn you as soon as I found out. It would have been faster to call, but I really don't trust phones, you know that. Never have."

Andras stopped pacing and his shoulders relaxed.

"Thank you," he said quietly, "I have missed you." He smiled with his teeth, "I am happy to see you, even though I wish it were under better circumstances. Please, tell me you're going to stay a bit?"

I felt Andras's eyeballs tingle. I wondered if he was going to cry, or...or was that what it felt like when his pupils shrunk back to normal after his eyes went black?

"Ah, you're calming down," Nadia observed.

Yep, must have been that. I laughed to myself.

Nadia stood before him as beautiful as any model and as proud as an empress, with the same eternal grace as a God.

"I've missed you, too, Az," she said, taking Andras's hand in hers and holding it. "We haven't been in the same place together in centuries, not since we both lived in London, with all its unimaginable indulgences." She grinned like a cat and Andras chortled. "We drank everything and every*one*, danced all night, and were mostly happy. Weren't we?"

"Mostly. Everything would have been perfect if it hadn't been for Callum."

"So you won't leave right away, then?" Andras questioned, peering down into her eyes.

Nadia tilted her head up and smiled wickedly, "Leave? Me?" She clicked her tongue against her teeth, "and miss out on all the fun?" She motioned around the room, "Never. I didn't get enough of you back in whatever century. The Middle Ages? So long ago, gross." She wrinkled her nose at that. "Plus, I'm curious about the life you've built here."

She dropped Andras's hand to turn away from him, pointing a ruby red nail at the bookshelves filled with way too many books, an occasional piece of art, and one succulent shriveled nearly to death.

"Still reading everything you can get your hands on, I see." Her lips curved up in a teasing smile.

"Oh, much worse," Andras teased. "I'm a book editor."

He went to the leather couch to perch on the armrest, resting his forearms on his thighs.

Nadia spoke to the bookshelves, "From feared mercenary to publishing? It's essentially a lateral move, I suppose?"

Nadia sauntered over to join him on the couch. She slipped her heels off, letting each one tumble to the floor with a thud. She flexed and pointed her slender feet, toes painted red to match her fingernails, before swinging them up onto the couch and lying down. Crossing her long legs at the ankle, she pulled a throw pillow toward herself and fluffed it behind her head.

With her eyes closed, she breathed,

"I'm awake. Just need to rest for a minute. I haven't slept in days. I had to get here–to Denver, to you–as fast as possible." She hummed quietly to herself for a time, "I know that this is terrible, Az. I know that Callum is a dangerous lunatic, but something else seems to be weighing on you, too. Something...no...some*one*, is making it all that much worse, no? What's their name, this person you're worried about?"

Nadia briefly opened one eye to peer up at Andras from the couch, then closed it. Her lips revealed the slightest hint of muted amusement as she waited for him to answer.

"You're obnoxious," he said, teasing, "and her name is Danny."

My heart thundered. He was worried about me? I didn't want to see this. It felt wrong to watch this, like an invasion of privacy, eavesdropping on them talking about this, about me.

His jaw worked, and he rubbed at his temples.

"I think about her all the time, almost constantly, since the first night I met her. She's beautiful and curvy, with a full gorgeous ass and modest, beautiful breasts that fit perfectly in my mouth." He smiled wickedly at Nadia, who grinned with her eyes still closed. I wanted to smack him; I was flattered and proud that he thought me beautiful, but I wanted to smack him. The bragging lout.

Andras went on, "Her eyes are sometimes the color of evergreen, other times golden yellow and weary but warm. Her laugh is breathy and sincere, and she isn't afraid of me, even knowing what I am. She isn't scared to rage at me, something that I don't encounter often, as you well know. Not as a mercenary or soldier, and certainly not as a vampire. Well, other than with you, of course, Nadia. You've never had a hard time in that regard." He huffed a laugh, and my Gods, I wondered if my body was swooning back in his foyer.

"I barely know her," he continued, "but she's special. I feel like I've come home when I'm with her."

"Huh," Nadia breathed thoughtfully. "Did you feel that way instantly? Like you'd been infected by her?"

"That's an odd way to put it, but yes."

"Fated," Nadia whispered.

"That's just folklore. It's not real."

"How do we know that?" Nadia raised an eyebrow in question.

"I've never seen it. Have you?"

"Just once. I think just once."

"She's also human." A pause. "And a mum to two little girls."

He tensed as if waiting for Nadia to react as if he expected her to leap to her feet and pummel him.

Her lids flicked open, and she growled.

"You're a bloody idiot," she scolded.

Almost too fast for me to track the movement, she yanked the pillow out from under her head and flung it at him, but he snatched it out of the air and winked at her.

"Have you gone mad?" she hissed, propping herself up on her elbows.

"Apparently, yes," he said, setting the pillow down next to him. "You'd like her, though. She's kind and determined. A real ball buster." He huffed another laugh.

"Well in that case, I *would* like her," Nadia agreed. "But you're still a bloody idiot."

"Yes. And now it's all a mess. Now I'm afraid I've put her in danger."

"You absolutely should feel terrible," she said flatly, but then she grinned. "I'm teasing. Andras, you had no idea this was going to happen. And what a horrible life you'd lead, we'd both lead, if we spent every day thinking about that vampiric equivalent of asbestos we call your ex. I'd rather hoped he'd just rot until the earth boiled and put him underwater."

"Yeah," Andras ground out.

Nadia's smile faded as she studied him.

"Can I ask you a question?" she whispered.

"Anything," he whispered back.

"Alright." She blew out a breath, and Andras stilled, waiting for something terrible. "As an editor, are you specializing in...paranormal romance?"

"Oh, fuck off," he said, throwing back his head to laugh. He grabbed a pillow with vampire speed and hurled it at her, but she curled up like an armadillo to deflect the hit, her red dress hiking up to reveal red panties. He threw back his head and laughed and laughed: a warm, deep, belly laugh. Nadia leaped to her feet and grabbed another pillow, but by then, he was running towards the door. She gave chase, bare feet smacking against the floor, across the entryway, up the stairs, and to his bedroom where he dove onto his bed, howling. She bounced after him and clambered onto his back, as she growled and pretended to nip at the nape of his neck. They shook with laughter. Nadia rolled off of him and removed her leather harness, dropping it off the side of the bed. Andras rolled onto his side and propped his head up on an elbow to watch her. I wasn't sure I wanted to see what was about to happen next, but I kept looking anyway, peering out from behind his eyes. Nadia peeled off her dress and threw it across the room, her ample breasts bouncing in her red lacey bra. Climbing under the blankets in her underthings, she rolled to her side to face him, hands under her cheek, eyes hooded with sleep. She yawned.

"Tell me everything about Danny," she said, barely a whisper.

Everything went black as the memory faded.

It took me a second to figure out what memory we were visiting next. The world lay cloaked in darkness and shadow. When the shadows receded, Andras sat at his dining room table, the room still in one piece, with his face in his hands.

"Andras? You did the right thing, Az," Nadia was saying.

She sat across the table from him, stretching her neck from side to side and adjusting the strap of her white slip. Andras groaned, then dropped his hands from his face. He clasped them together under his chin and watched Nadia drink her coffee. She flipped her hair to one side and angled her head, offering a small warm smile.

"Az?" she said, again.

Andras simply raised his brows in answer.

"I don't know if lying to her was the right thing to do," Nadia said,

"But I guess lying is better than endangering her kids. Her ex-husband, well...I honestly don't care if Callum shows up to disembowel him. He sounds like an ass."

Andras huffed a laugh.

Nadia tapped her long, claw-like fingernails against her mug, as if she were thinking of something more supportive to say.

This must have been what happened right after Andras texted me that he would be leaving. So this was moments before, oh...before Callum came here and destroyed everything, moments before Nadia and Andras were injured and kneeling in rubble.

"Look, you know how I feel about men running around making other people's decisions for them," Nadia went on. "It's not okay. But in this case, it's that, or she ends up torn to pieces. And he'd make it last, too, you know—"

"—I know. You're right. But it doesn't feel good."

"We both know you can handle plenty of pain and somehow be mostly fine. So have all of the feelings you need to have and then—"

An explosive crash echoed from the second floor and reverberated across the hardwood. Nadia and Andras were on their feet, legs wide and ready to fight. They craned their necks towards the ceiling, listening and waiting. Then light footsteps sounded as something or someone made their way to the staircase. Nadia's chin lifted, and she caught Andras's eye, motioning for him to scent the air and mouthing, "Callum." Her canines were already elongated and ready to rip his throat out. Andras caught Callum's scent and I could feel his eyes and gums tingling as his own fangs descended, his pupils widening into hateful blackness.

The footsteps paused at the top of the staircase, and then like lightning something smashed into Andras, sending his body back, back, back until his head cracked against drywall. The sound of bones crunching rang out, along with Nadia's roar.

"Fuck!" Andras spat blood and got to his feet. He scanned the room. Nadia bared her teeth and jumped onto the table with catlike elegance. Callum came out of nowhere–a blur, an icy wind–and went for Nadia, but she was ready. With cat-like elegance, she backflipped off of the table, landing in a crouch. Callum appeared near the back wall, leaning against it like he had all the time in the world. He would have been handsome–olive skin, black hair, dark brown eyes–if it weren't for the bitterness twisting his features into something hideous and cruel. The psychotic, dead eyes. He wore a black suit and a skull cap, like he'd based his look off of a British gangster film from fifty years ago. His arms were folded across his chest. He sneered at Andras.

"Callum," Andras said, with an acidic bite. He took a step forward, "you look well."

"Given the circumstances," Callum spat. His accent was strange and old. He went on, "imagine waking up in a cement block like a bloody dinosaur and remembering that your partner and his *pet* put you there."

"Darling," Andras drawled, wiping dust from his arms, "let's not forget that you tried to kill us first. Some would say you kind of deserved it." Andras squared off his shoulders, chin high.

"Ah, there it is," Callum sang, "the arrogant bastard I once loved."

"Get on with it," Andras ground out.

Callum laughed performatively, letting his head fall back ever so slightly, like he was trying out for the role of villain in a community theater production. Andras glanced at Nadia, a portrait of amusement, as she rested on the table with her arms crossed over her chest, legs crossed at the ankles, and the faintest hint of a smile on her dark rose lips.

"Are you...dramatizing your own brand of evil?" Nadia asked, disbelieving, "you don't have to bloody exaggerate it. You are *actually* a fucking demon from hell, you narcissistic shitbag."

Callum's head whipped to Nadia. "Shut up, whore," he spat. "You won't be so clever after I rip your teeth out of your bloody head and make a fucking necklace out of them."

"Oh, Callum, you say 'whore' like it's a bad thing." She shrugged, "I'm actually quite proud of my history. You, on the other hand," her black eyes fixed on him, cold and damning, "are a spoiled prick. And *that* is fucking tragic, considering how bloody old you are. I mean who lives this long without stumbling into a bit of self-reflection?"

The muscles in Callum's jaw flexed as he narrowed his darkening eyes on Nadia. The absolute hate that radiated from him seemed to seep into the space, eating up all of the light in the room, but Nadia didn't seem to notice or care. She examined her nails and sighed. Callum cracked his neck from side to side. In a flash, he stood face to face with Nadia, their noses nearly touching. Yet she didn't so much as move, didn't so much as blink. Callum's arm shot out, trying to grab Nadia by the throat, but she blocked it with her own arm and climbed him like a tree, positioning her legs around his neck and throwing her weight to the side, slamming his body to the ground. The entire house shook down to the foundation. She rolled away from him, hopped to her feet, and then sprinted for him, but Andras reached Callum first.

Andras's leg shot out, kicking Callum in the ribs and sending him smashing into the beautiful dining room table. Wood and debris exploded in all directions. Nadia was already there waiting when he landed, snatching him up by the hair and dragging him through the house.

"Remember *this* move, you son of a bitch?" she seethed in his ear.

Andras grabbed a broom from its place against the far wall and snapped it into two sharp stakes.

"Nadia!" he shouted, launching one of the stakes to her. She spun, catching it mid-air, careful to keep Callum's midnight black hair in her fist, his back arched, and she slammed the stake down on the center of his chest. It missed by just a fraction when Callum yanked free seconds before the tip of the stake hit true. Nadia cursed. The stake tip scratched down Callum's ribcage, ripping through his jacket and undershirt, leaving a faint blood-red line. Injured or not, Callum struck hard and fast before Nadia could react, grabbing her arm and bringing it down on his knee, cracking bone. Nadia shrieked. Then he smashed her cheek with a fist in a cobra-like strike. He snatched the stake from her loosened grip.

"Nooooo!" Andras roared, his fists clutched, as he began to move toward them.

Just before Andras reached them, Nadia managed to land a roundhouse kick to Callum's jaw. He stumbled back, and

Andras was upon him, thrusting the other stake into Callum's back. A billowing howl escaped him as flesh tore, wood grazed bones, and blood sprayed. Callum stumbled and looked down at the splintered spear jutting out of the center of his chest. He turned to look at Andras, hurt flickering in his otherwise cold, empty eyes.

"I really didn't think you had it in you to do it twice," Callum gasped, reaching for the stake.

Andras relaxed his guard. Callum fell forward. Then, without warning, he whirled, headbutting Andras in the face, a horrible crunch sounded, and sent him sprawling back as blood gushed from his nose. Callum gripped the stake jutting out of his chest and growled as he ripped it free from his body, dark blood oozing from the wound and soaking his shirt. He tossed the blood-soaked and splintered stake at Andras's feet, baring his teeth. Even though I was looking out of Andras's eyes and I knew it was only a memory, I wanted to run, wanted to hide, wanted to claw and kick away from him. A low growl started in Andras' chest as he looked up at his foe, his enemy, his former lover, and he shifted his weight to stand, but Callum whirled, nearly ripped the front door from the hinges, and disappeared into the night.

Andras dropped to his knees, cursing, "Fuck! Fuck!"

Nadia came to his side, crouching next to him and balancing on her heels. She wrapped her arms around him and whispered, "that couldn't have been easy for you, love."

"No, that's not it," Andras whispered. "I loved him once, but that feeling is long dead. I just…" He dragged his hands through his debris-flecked brown hair. "Fuck, we were *so* close to being rid of him. How did I bloody *miss* his *heart*? Now he's out there, and we won't be able to relax, and Danny won't be safe until we—"

"Why am I not safe?"

A familiar voice, my voice, called from the doorway. Then shadows once again filled the room.

MEMORIZE THIS PICTURE IF YOU WANT TO LIVE

Once again, I found myself back in the foyer of Andras's home. Stepping back, I yanked my hand free from his, panting and clutching my chest. Nadia studied me quietly, trying to figure out, I supposed, how I felt about everything I'd seen, everything I'd learned. It was too much. It was way too much. Callum...Calum was a monster. I could feel myself cracking, shaking under the weight of it all.

"Danny," Andras whispered, "I'm so sorry." His sapphire eyes were heavy. "We'll keep you and your family safe, I promise."

"Family?" I asked, my voice hollow. My heart drummed harder and harder and harder. My mouth went ash dry. I wrapped my arms around my body as if trying to physically hold myself together.

Nadia sauntered over to me, as silent as the grave, barefoot and spackled blood and dust. She gently set a slender, crimson-crusted hand on my shoulder.

"Sorry, love," Nadia said, "but we don't have much time. I know you just saw quite a bit, but just in case, here we go: Andras's former lover is a psychotic prick who was a very powerful Roman lord. He threw a spoiled man tantrum a few centuries ago and murdered loads of people, then came after me and Andras. We subdued him, then buried his rotten, demon ass in cement, but he got out, and he's here, in Denver, trying to kill us and anyone Andras has ever cared about. Since you showed up minutes after he left, he most likely saw you if he didn't already have spies watching you. Unfortunately, that means you're in a heap of trouble. But we are *here* and quite capable, and I assure you, we will keep your family safe."

The room spun. I turned and puked my guts up all over Andras's tiled entryway. His large, strong hand rubbed my back and held my hair as I heaved and heaved. Finally, I stopped, bracing my hands on my knees, my breath ragged and catching.

"I have kids, Andras," I whispered, voice breaking.

Andras helped me stand, and Nadia handed me a small washrag that I used to wipe my face. Andras tucked a loose lock behind my ear and smiled at me warmly, then gestured for us to move away from the vomit pooling on the tile. I mindlessly followed, too afraid to feel embarrassed, to feel anything but terror.

"I know, Danny. I know. You have every right to hate me or be sick with worry, but we have to act fast. Listen carefully, I think I have a plan that will turn Callum's usual tools against him. Like me, Callum gets glimpses here and there into the minds of others. They're just random images most of the time, chaotic and jumbled. But if he doesn't know that you know that about him, you can possibly use it to manipulate him into a trap."

"Me? Why would I need to manipulate him? How?" I asked.

A scratching sound coming from the living room had me nearly jumping out of my skin. Andras and Nadia jerked toward the noise, and in a blur, they were gone, leaving me alone for what seemed like an eternity. I waited helplessly for everything to be okay, which took me back to high school—to the year Jess and I found our father on the floor of his office. We'd called 911 and then our mother, who'd already left for her afternoon tennis lesson. We stood outside of his office door, trembling, for what felt like forever while EMTs called out to each other in a language that we didn't understand. Jess and I held hands until the office door opened, and our father was wheeled out on a gurney, a sheet covering his mutilated corpse. Our mother arrived just as they were putting his body in the ambulance, and we watched through tearful eyes as she embraced our father for the last time and wept. It was the only time we'd ever seen her cry, before that day or since.

Andras and Nadia suddenly appeared in front of me, startling me out of the memory.

"It was just a tree branch against a window," Andras said, "but it's not safe here. We don't know when he's going to come back. Probably sooner than later. You need to get your kids out of your house. Is there somewhere they can go for the weekend, with your ex-husband, maybe? Can you fake an illness to stay behind?"

An icy chill ran through me. I nodded robotically, my mind racing with where they could go and what I could say that that might be convincing. I took a deep breath and let it out in a shaking gust. *I would not panic. I would not panic.*

"Can I have a drink?" I asked.

"Yes," Andras said. "Water?"

"Fuck no," I scoffed, "Something *much* stronger."

In the study, I sat in the leather chair, pulling my legs up into my chest, breathing in, out, and in, and out, trying my best to calm the voice in my head that told me to run, run, run. To my girls, to safety, to anywhere but here. Nadia eased herself onto the couch, glancing down with furrowed brows at the soft, pinkish lines all over her bare legs where deep cuts had been not so long ago. Her white slip, dirty, ripped, and blanketed in smears and splatters of blood, bunched at her hips. Andras perched on the armrest beside her, long legs crossed at the knee, hands woven together and resting on his thigh. She'd been plotting something with Andras when I'd come back from the bathroom, where I'd gone to splash ice-cold water on my face, but it had taken me a handful of minutes to calm down enough to think straight.

"What are we going to do?" I breathed, my voice shaky.

"Well," Andras exhaled, rubbing his neck, "he'll come for you tonight or tomorrow. Patience has never been one of his strong qualities; he won't put it off for long. He'll try to get into your house because it's better than plucking you off of the street in public. Don't ask him in, no matter what."

"He can't come in if I don't invite him? Like…that's a real thing?"

"No, he can't," Nadia answered flatly, sounding far away, "and yes, it's a real thing, although honestly, we aren't certain why. We believe it has something to do with the balance of nature. If creatures as strong as us could just wander into anyone's home, frankly, there wouldn't be any humans left." She wasn't boasting or threatening, I realized, just stating a fact.

"How does it work?" I asked, confused, " I didn't invite you in, Andras, so how did you come in to help me when that man broke into my house?"

"You did. Remember the night we met in your front yard at the gate?" He smiled as if he were remembering it fondly, "you said that you needed to grab your lighter and invited me to follow you inside. The intent is enough. The invitation still holds." He pressed his lips together for a beat, thinking about something, "Just make sure that you act like you don't know who Callum is, and try not to think about anything at all," he looked to Nadia, then back to me, "except for this. Memorize it, and then just hold the image in your mind."

He held up his cell phone to show me the screen, a picture of a small cabin in the woods. A sign next to the front door, nailed above the mailbox, read, "Lakewood 7."

"Imagine me and Nadia here," Andras said.

"Why?" I asked, committing the photo to memory like he'd said.

"You'll be pretending that you don't know me or Nadia, but he'll know otherwise." Andras continued, "he'll think you're trying to protect us. So when he sees this cabin in your thoughts, he'll immediately go there, and we will be waiting."

I gripped my knees. "So the plan is...for me to wait around for him to try to kill me in my own house so that I can imagine some creepy cabin I've never been to, hoping that he will take the bait and zoom up after you?" I asked in disbelief.

Nadia smiled up at Andras. "She's a total ballbuster," she said, "and you're right, I do like her."

Andras shook his head as if this were hardly the time or place.

"I know him, Danny. And we trust that he'll see it in your mind and come for us. The cabin is isolated, so we can get rid of him without being noticed by anyone who might call the police. We'll have the advantage of having cased the area and the element of surprise. The hard part for you will be not thinking of anything else."

I lowered my feet to the floor and tapped on my thighs with my fingers, 1-2-3-4-5, then 5-4-3-2-1. Everything sounded totally insane. How could this possibly work? I was a notoriously bad liar and always had been. My mind tended to race, which is why

I spent so much time running, and breathing, and meditating, and...

My spine straightened as it hit me, and I smiled wickedly.

"You know what," I chuckled. It might not be that impossible, after all. "I have ten meditation apps on my phone. I can concentrate on the pressure of my feet for a *very* long time if I have to."

Andras stared at me for a moment as if I'd lost my mind, then threw back his head and laughed.

"Perfect!" he said.

Then the smile melted away, he gazed downward, and when his eyes flipped up to meet mine again, they were full of pain. His jaw tensed.

"I'm so sorry," he whispered.

"You couldn't have known," I reassured him.

And that was the truth. It's not like he could predict the future. Or at least, I didn't think so.

"Whether or not I could have known, I am still sorry that this a burden you don't deserve. I'm sorry for your fear, your worry, for all of it. I will do whatever I can to keep you safe, keep them safe, and to make sure nothing like this happens again."

I smiled softly.

Nadia abruptly sat up, "Let's get you to your house so you can get your family out and somewhere safe. We don't have time for apologies and pish posh."

I nodded emphatically and we all stood. Taking two steps toward the doorway, I paused, and turned to face them. I didn't know why, but something, something...*urged* me to stay with them. A voice in the back of my head, intuition, whatever it was, screamed that I needed to go, too, that I needed to follow them into the mountains to fight this evil alongside them. I needed to see Callum dead with my own eyes. *Kill him.*

"I'll go home and ask Steven to take the girls to the guesthouse at my mother's. Can one of you make the apartment above our garage uninhabitable? Maybe break a pipe or something? Then, they can all stay in Cherry Hill until I'm no longer pretending to be sick. But once they leave, I'm coming with you guys."

"No," Andras ordered.

"It's not negotiable, Andras," I argued, tilting my chin up, our eyes held with equal determination, finding that unyielding part of myself and hauling it out of wherever it had gone to hide for the past few years. "I am coming."

Andras' face was unreadable, a mask of stone and ice and will. But after a few too many heartbeats, that icy mask melted. He nodded only once.

"Let's go," Nadia commanded, spurring us into action.

Nadia and Andras walked me as far as a neighboring house and then peeled away to sneak into the guest house and avoid the cameras. I could feel their eyes on my back as I flung open the cast iron front gate and sprinted up the porch stairs. I threw open my front door and bolted past a startled Steven, who had come over to watch the girls. They were having lunch at the table as I flew past, heading straight into the bathroom and slamming the door dramatically behind me. Once in the bathroom, my hands shook, and my temples pulsed to the rhythm of my heartbeat. Scanning the shelves, I searched for something to pour into the toilet bowl. Then spotted lavender soaking salts and grabbed the bottle. Steven knocked on the bathroom door, "everything okay in there?" he called from the hallway. Pretending to heave loudly, I let the entire container of salts cascade into the white toilet bowl, plop, plop, plop, toilet water splashed onto the floor and all over my black yoga pants. *Gross.* The toilet flushed, swirling the salts around and pulling them down into the pipes and sewer. Sure that all of the evidence of my lie was gone, I went to the sink to splash some cold water on my face.

"No, I'm not okay," I groaned.

I gaped at the reflection in the mirror: pale, pale skin and wild, fearful green eyes. Everything seemed to twitch from head to toe, like my entire body was being devoured by my nervous system, one electrical bite at a time. "Fuck," I whispered. Guilt rose in crushing waves between the bouts of terror. Like most people, I'd leap into the jaws of the hounds of hell for my family without a second thought. But I could not live knowing that I'd put them in danger, least of all because of some ridiculous crush. I would never forgive myself if anything happened to them because of me.

Steven knocked on the bathroom door again, "Need anything?"

"No," I said, weakly, without even having to fake it, "I think I have the stomach flu. I'm so sick. You should take the girls to my mom's and stay in the guest house there for a day or two. You should leave right now, before it spreads."

Steven cleared his throat, "I mean...if you have it, I'm sure we already do too." I yanked the door open, glaring through the one-inch opening. "Don't be a pain in the ass for once in your goddamn life." I rage-whispered, "Just get the girls out of here before we spend the weekend cleaning puke and shit out off of every surface of this home."

"What about our guest house?" Steven grumbled.

"Mommy? Are you okay in there?" Olivia called out from the dining room.

"Yes, honey! Just a tummy ache. I'll be good as new soon," I called back, doing my best to banish the uncertainty clinging to every word.

Steven turned and walked down the hallway, his footsteps growing faint the further he got. I shut the door and a beat later heard him yell, "My bathroom is flooding in the guest house! Damnit! I'll call a plumber. Girls! Let's pack your stuff! We're going to have a sleepover at your grandma's house until mommy feels better." I plopped down on the edge of the bathtub, my hands shaking and my bottom lip quivering for what felt like forever. Finally, when the front door opened and shut and the house fell silent at last, I put my head in my hands and bawled.

EARL GREY VERSUS THE SADIST

A thunderous knock sounded at my front door, and I spun towards it without thinking about the cup in my hand; Earl Gray tea splashed on my fingers, burning horribly. My stomach instantly flew into my throat; I tasted pennies and the acidic tang of too much caffeine and fear, real, visceral, primitive fear. I'd been waiting for this, for him, all day, pacing, drinking cup after cup of tea, texting Steven over and over and again, "Is everything okay? Are the girls okay?" And every time, he'd replied, "Yes, they're *still* just fine." I gripped the mug tighter, letting the heat bite into my palms.

The pain clouded everything, and it was all I could think about. Padding cautiously across the kitchen to the entranceway, I focused on the pain, on my steps, letting my mind cling to those things until I reached the front door.

My body siezed up when the knock sounded again. I took a slow, deep breath and, reluctantly, opened the door. The hinges creaked like they were alerting me of danger, howling for me to keep the door closed. Callum stood on my "Welcome" mat, a crooked smile on his lips. My breathing hitched, but I did my best to refocus on the pain in my fingers. I lifted my eyebrows in feigned surprise as if to say, oh, hello, what are you doing here? And I *was* surprised for three reasons. One, this man was a monster, a murderer, and an immortal former Roman lord. Two, even though I'd already seen him in Andras's memories, I hadn't been close enough to realize just how handsome he was, but part of me expected a sinister-looking monster, a shark-toothed gremlin, a thing of nightmares. Instead, Callum looked like any handsome Mediterranean man with dead psychopathic brown eyes. He wasn't nearly as beautiful as Andras, but handsome just the same. He wore another perfectly tailored suit, gray this time, and a black skull cap.

I steadied my breath. Forced my body to convey calm, curious, relaxed. It was no small thing.

"Hello? Can I help you?" I asked, trying to keep my voice steady, trying not to wince from the burns, no doubt branding my fingers.

"Hello, ma'am," Callum drawled, his accent thick but difficult to place. Unlike Andras's or Nadia's, it wasn't modern British, but something else, something older.

"I'm terribly sorry to drop by like this. But I've heard that you're a very talented painter, and I'd love to commission something for my mother, you see, it's her ninetieth birthday and, well, I'd love a portrait of her with her precious Yorkie."

I nearly laughed. A Yorkie? He couldn't do better than that?

Callum's lips curled up at the corners, but the smile never reached his eyes, which were now dark, piercing, and as endless as the universe. He looked like he'd forgotten how smiling worked. Even if I hadn't known who and what he was, I would have been terrified by whatever he was trying to do with his face. It was the grin of a murderous creature wearing the skin of a man and about as kind and friendly as a mountain lion toying with a meal. I pressed my hands around the mug, harder and harder, fighting against the urge to curse or cry out. Clearing my throat gently, I did my best performance of a casual conversation among strangers. Just an artist and a potential client, nothing more, nothing at all out of the ordinary.

"I'm so sorry," I willed my face into a mask of disappointment, "I'm not able to take any new commissions until after the new year." I swallowed hard, shifting my weight from one leg to the next, willing myself to focus, just focus, a little while longer.

"How unfortunate," Callum muttered, his deep, soulless eyes bore into mine, then flicked behind me into my house, then back to me where they lingered as if trying to hollow me out for a few heartbeats before raking across my body, pausing for a second on my hands. He sighed through his nose.

"Again," I went on, "I'm not taking any work right now, but—"

"—Clever girl," he said, his voice emotionless.

Callum leaned against the door frame, crossing his arms over his chest. "Is that what Andras told you to say?" he asked, a hateful smile dancing at the corners of his lips. Just as instructed, I pictured Andras's face and, to my horror, accidentally slipped into the memory of me kissing him. I stilled as Callum flinched but quickly recovered and forced myself to think of the photo of the cabin and Andras saying, "Come here, and we'll keep you safe." I know he saw it there in my thoughts because he glowered at me and chuckled, a note of smugness in his low laugh. I felt the pressure under my feet and concentrated on that unbearable burning sensation in my fingers.

Callum shook his head, clicking his tongue against his teeth. Then he vanished in a blur of wind.

With one hand, I slammed the front door and locked it, then set the mug on the floor, shaking the heat out of my palms, cursing and fighting back the urge to vomit. I continued to focus on my feet, on the pressure there, as I ran to the kitchen to grab my phone from the counter to text Andras, "He was just here. I did what you told me and he left." Then I sprinted back to the foyer closet to tug on my running shoes. Slinging my overnight bag over my shoulder, I snatched my keys from the counter and paused just long enough to shiver at the thought of what I was about to do. Maybe it was safer to stay here in my home where Callum couldn't get in. Maybe it was smarter, too, but I couldn't shake the feeling that I was meant to go. A force I couldn't explain tugged me toward him. Powerless human or not, I wanted to help him, and when Callum fell, I needed to see it with my own eyes. Opening the door, I scanned the trees, roofs, and yard for any sign of Callum, then jogged towards my car. As I waited for the doors to open, an SUV slowly crept down my street and stopped behind me. I froze. Hands visibly shaking, I turned slowly as a dark-tinted window rolled down.

Janet, one of the PTA moms from our children's school, poked her head out of the window, grinning, her bright whites glistening like new porcelain. *From a toilet,* I thought.

"Danny! I'm so glad I caught you! We haven't received your donation for the valentines celebration, so I just thought that since I'm in the neighborhood, I'd swing by to grab it."

An obnoxious rhythmic base thrummed from her speakers.

I breathed in and out, trying to shove down the growing anxiety that told me to drive, drive, drive to the mountains, to get to Andras, to get there now.

"I'm sorry, Janet, I've just been swamped, and it somehow slipped my mind. I'll take care of it tonight when—"

"—Oh, I don't mind waiting," she said.

I could feel my blood pressure rising. The rage from everything that had happened in the past twenty-four hours—no, the past few months—with Steven and the burglar, and now this nightmare with Callum, my kids being in danger *again*, and Andras being a vampire—it all crashed into me again, and again, and again, until I couldnt take it anymore.

Hands in fists, my chin lowered as I glared into her light blue eyes, auburn hair, and chunky highlights,

"I said I'm busy, Janet."

Janet's mouth dropped open and her eyes went wide with disbelief.

I held her stare, almost hoping that she'd be stupid enough to push it. I *wanted* her to push, to take the bait, practically dared her to, so I'd have somewhere to direct the rage engulfing me. Instead, she gasped dramatically before speeding off into the suburbs. I climbed into my car, trembling as I gripped the steering wheel and floored the gas, heading for the hills.

COZY LITTLE CABIN

The fireplace crackled in the living room of the cabin where I sat with Andras and Nadia. From my place in the leather armchair, I watched snowflakes float on a gentle breeze. Snow blanketed the forest beyond the cabin in a stark, lifeless white, a blank canvas. Aside from the occasional deer wandering outside, the world was silent and seemed to hold still, as if we weren't about to be attacked by an ancient vampire with a flair for bloodshed and violence. The snow brought memories of hot cocoa, the holidays, and giddy excitement, which seemed so out of place as we waited, and I silently pleaded with the universe to keep my daughters safe. To help us kill Callum quickly.

Nadia lay on the age-worn sofa with her legs bent at the knee, her camel-colored trousers comfortably loose but hugging her ample hips and bottom. Her fingers worried the knot on her matching twist-top sweater, her eyes glued to the ceiling, lost in thought. Andras clasped his hands together in his lap, his long legs stretched out in front of him, crossed at the ankle. He focused his sapphire eyes on the fireplace.

"This reminds me of the old days," Nadia said, sighing, eyes still fixed on the ceiling.

"Does it?" Andras asked without looking away from the fire.

"Well, I suppose just the part where we're together and Callum is being an asshole."

She raised her eyebrows in jest and glanced at Andras sidelong.

He hissed, but there was hint of levity there. He leaned forward to rest his forearms on his thighs. The firelight cast a soft, warm glow on his face, the flames dancing in the blue of his irises.

"What a fucking mess," he said, hushed. Then he turned towards me, "I am so incredibly sorry, Danny. Truly." It was barely audible.

I hugged my legs into my chest, resting my chin on my knees. There were a million things I wanted to say to him but none of it had to do with blame. I was scared. Andras couldn't have known that any of this would happen, couldn't have predicted that Callum would get free after however many centuries, with a mind functioning well enough for vengeance. What was Andras supposed to do, live his entire immortal life in fear of the past, trying to control the world and the people in it to protect any potential love interest from some terrible fate?

"It's not your fault," I whispered.

"It is," he muttered.

Incredulously, I shook my head slowly. Then went back to watching the snow because I wasn't in the headspace to convince him.

"How did you guys meet?" I asked, still focused on the forest and its expanding shadows, as the sun dipped behind a mountain.

Nadia laughed softly, drawing my attention away from the woods. She broke focus with the ceiling, letting her cheek fall towards the sofa cushion to observe Andras, still brooding in the chair. Tendrils of her hair fell over her face. She rolled to her side and pushed up on one arm, shaking her hair back.

"Well," she began, smiling to Andras, who regarded her with an unreadable expression, "it was in the street, actually. I was playing an innocent game called Thimble Rig, on the lands that Callum lorded over. Well, I should say, lands that Callum owned and Andras...enforced?"

"By innocent game," Andras huffed, "she means a scam. She was scamming people out of coin. Gambling was very illegal back then to anyone who was not of a certain class. I stopped short the second I saw her. She looked like a queen," Nadia beamed at this, "and she...well, she smelled not human. I realized almost right away that she was like me and..."

"Back then? When was that?" I wondered out loud.

"Thirteenth century, I think?" Andras looked up at the ceiling like he did sometimes, like that's where he'd find the information.

I gasped.

"Thirteenth-century? During Medieval times?" I paused to do the math. Four, five, no, six! No! "That would make you six hundred years old?" I asked, in awe, trying and failing to temper my shock.

"Yes."

"And?" Nadia added, raising an eyebrow. "Go on. What were you just about to say? About me?"

His lip tugged up at the corner, "Nadia was not human and she was absolutely gorgeous," he replied, flatly, "of course."

"I know," she said, "I just like to hear you say it." She smiled devilishly before resuming control of the narrative.

"When I saw that Andras was with Callum, ugh, my heart just ached for him. I knew of Callum, that he was a sadistic prick, and Andras seemed too...good."

"Good? I was an absolute fucking monster, Nadia," Andras grumbled.

"No. You were *behaving* monstrously, but I could feel your compassion and kindness. I saw slivers of it when you thought nobody was watching. Anyway, it doesn't matter. Tonight I feel the same way I did back then: worried about you because of that son of a bitch."

Andras rose to his feet in one elegant motion. He prowled out of the room, then returned a moment later, holding a bottle of wine and three wine glasses. The cork popped faintly, and he filled a glass for me, which I accepted with a faint smile, then for Nadia, and finally himself. He stood by the fire for a heartbeat, staring into the flames again, and I couldn't help but crane my head up to take him in. He looked like a God, like someone forged from magic and dreams, or maybe nightmares. He wore all black: a wool sweater, and trousers that fit him too well. Those piercing eyes were dangerously focused, and his sensual mouth pressed into a tight line.

My phone buzzed. I held my breath while I slowly turned it over to read the screen. A text from Steven, "Putting the girls to bed. Do you want to tell them goodnight?" I exhaled, and a wave of relief rose and fell inside of me. They were still okay.

"I'm unable to talk," I wrote. I'm too sick. Kiss the girls goodnight and tell them I love them so much."

"Is everything okay?" Andras asked. "Your heartbeat sped up and then slowed."

He silently lowered himself into the leather armchair.

I nodded, "Just Steven letting me know that my girls are asleep and well." I brought the wine glass to my mouth and drank, letting it warm my throat for a long moment before I asked, "I need to know what's going on, the full story. Why is he after you? Is he the one who turned you?" I paused, wondering if that's what they actually called it outside of the books and movies I'd consumed. "I know it's all part of your past, and that it's personal, but I think I deserve to know why I'm holed up in a cabin right now worried about my children."

Nadia cut Andras a sharp look, nodding for him to go on, encouraging him to talk. Andras blew out a breath.

He began slowly, "Callum is the person who made me."

His thumb idly stroked the side of his wine glass.

"Where do I begin?" he asked me and Nadia.

"At the beginning."

THE LORD OF TORTURE

"I don't know how familiar you are with the Middle Ages or warfare, so please stop me if this is old news." Andras finished his glass of wine and leaned over to set it on the end table before leaning back in his chair, extending his long legs and crossing them at the ankle. He rested his elbows against the arms of the chair, clasping his hands together. "In the Middle Ages, Lords had armies, and Callum was a Lord, kind of 'The Lord' of the region–powerful, ruthless, and wealthy. He'd been in England since Roman Britain because he was incredibly old. He'd been a Roman general who'd fought the Persian empire before being stationed in England to torture and slaughter the Anglo-Saxons, which he did with absolute gusto. Being a very old vampire made him an incredibly successful soldier because he was stronger, faster, and deadlier. He quickly made a name for himself and rose to power."

A loud sigh came from the couch. "Andras, we seriously don't have all night. Can you get to it, please?" Nadia groaned.

He looked at her sidelong, then rolled his eyes. It was the most human and casual thing I'd ever seen him do, and if it weren't for the severity of the situation and the panic writhing inside of me, I might have chuckled.

"As I was saying, my entire family was killed during the sacking of our village. Almost everyone had been slaughtered; everything burned to the ground. My parents, sisters, aunts, uncles—everyone was just gone. I'd been in the hills hunting, about a day away."

Andras stared straight ahead at nothing like he'd drifted somewhere far, far, away. He inhaled shakily, and my throat tightened. I wanted to hug him, ply him with liquor—anything to comfort him—because I knew that pain, the one where someone you love is hurt, is violently taken from you. And I'd lost only my father. I couldn't imagine the horror of losing everyone, including your sisters. Oh my Gods, if I lost Jess...

My hand rose to my mouth.

"Andras, I'm so sorry," I whispered.

Andras dragged his eyes to mine. His lips tipped up slightly at the corners, and he dipped his chin subtly in a silent thank you. He stretched his neck from side to side, then dropped his hands to the sides of the armchair, wine glass in one hand, fingertips of the other brushing against the leather.

"I was only seventeen and had to learn to fight for survival," he murmured, "I got bloody good at it, so fighting for money just made sense. I had no other skills and was numb after, well, everything. By age thirty, I'd become a mercenary for hire. One night, I was drinking at a tavern with a few other men who were actively peacocking for a small table of women. I spotted a gorgeous man who appeared to be in his late twenties, standing back in the shadows, smirking at me. I'd always fancied men–women, too, and a bit more–but also men. He had elegant, crow-black hair, a sharp Roman nose, and dark eyes under thick dark eyebrows. I could tell by his clothes that he was a landowner–."

"Darling, get to the juicy bits." Nadia cut in, sitting up on the couch and crossing her legs. She fanned the air as if to tell him his time was up, then leaned forward, her eyes wide with excitement, "Andras fell for him right away, then found out he was a Lord, a big shock, and Callum was completely taken with Andras because, well, just fucking look at that face! If I weren't gay, I'd want him, too. Anyway, Callum recruited Andras to fight in one of his horrible demon armies, and Andras accepted because he was a bloody idiot. Enamored with a beast."

"You were a soldier in his army? And lovers?" I asked, amazed.

"Yes."

"And then he turned you? Or, sorry, made you?"

"Yes. But it didn't take long to see who he truly was."

"An evil, tyrannical bastard," Nadia added.

Andras shrugged. "He was. He is. Even after I figured that out, I couldn't get away because whenever I tried to end it, Ca llum...well, there was torture, a lot of torture. I was imprisoned for a decade or two here and there. He killed people I cared about. Once, he threatened to set fire to an orphanage if I left him, and that was one of his milder threats."

"So I stayed, where I witnessed appalling things, did nightmarish things that I'm not proud of..." Andras winced. "Then, one day, I met Nadia. Almost instantly, my life began to change for the better. I'd served Callum for so long at that point, and I completely loathed him. But I was trapped. Tethered. Nadia reminded me of who I'd been before my family...before I lost them and we became very close, albeit secret friends." Nadia and Andras exchanged an adoring look, "Then, a few years later, Callum discovered our friendship and tried to kill Nadia,"

"Tried to gut me, actually," Nadia mumbled.

"And I just snapped. I wanted him dead, wanted to get as far away from him as possible. I'd had one good thing in my life and he'd tried to take it away, and for what? I wanted to end him."

Steven and Callum were not the same, but I could understand how it felt to be mistreated for years and feel stuck. I knew how it felt to break. I could imagine the loathing and rage very well.

"We managed to, sort of, trap him in cement because beheading him hadn't worked. And that's where he's been until recently when some bloody idiots must have accidentally let him out."

My eyebrows came together, and I leaned forward in my seat. "Trapped him?" I asked.

"Yes. Callum was Roman, so he knew how to make virtually indestructible cement with saltwater, limestone, and volcanic ash, which he used for constructing houses and things on his lands. So he might have, uhm, fallen into some uncured mud."

Nadia fell against the back of the couch, crossed her arms, and scowled, then hissed. "I didn't think he'd get out, honestly," she grumbled. "*And,* even if he did, I didn't think he'd be able to even function mentally, let alone track us down and nearly kill us in your house."

"Why didn't you think he'd be able to function? And who let him out?" I asked.

"Some archeology students studying Roman cement removed a chunk to take back to their lab in London and let the fucker out–to their end, sadly, because he immediately ate them. Anyhow, after spending a few hundred years starved in darkness and solitude, I assume he's lost whatever mind he had left. I should have known, though, with his cunning demon soul, it wouldn't take him that long to adjust from the shock of airplanes, cars, cell phones, and the internet."

"You said that you'd known Callum before meeting Andras?" I asked Nadia.

"I'd been made a century before Andras and spent much of my time in the area, mostly picking off the Romans for fun and sport and snacks. So I knew *of* him, and I knew many who knew him, and while I'm not the faintest of heart, I made sure to steer as clear of him as possible," she said.

Nadia cocked her head to the side as if she'd just thought of something, then added, " I'm a vampire. I've been one for a long time, and I have known many truly shitty people, and I have done things that are not...*entirely* okay. But I can say, without a doubt, that he is the worst creature I've ever encountered. He is truly evil if there is such a thing. Ruthless, murderous, vengeful, and a narcissistic psycho. Really. What did you see in him?"

Nadia turned to Andras expectantly.

"It's not like I fell for the real him, you ass," Andras grumbled. "*As you expressed,* he's a narcissistic psycho. I fell for a curated version of him who was lovely, sexy, and incredible in bed. By the time he could no longer keep up the ruse, by the time I realized that he'd been slowly gaining control of my life and taking me apart piece by piece, it was a bit too late. After just a decade with him, I didn't even know who I was anymore."

I didn't see it coming. I didn't even feel it coming. One moment, I sat there listening to one impossible tale after another about their lives as immortals, and the next, I was sobbing into my hands. My wails were so raw and unbridled that I barely felt a breeze as Nadia and Andras appeared next to me in a blur –thinking, I assumed, that I must be having a seizure or a stroke. Small, delicate hands rested on my knees, and a larger, stronger hand pressed against my back. I wept, pent-up sadness pouring out of me until I could function again.

"Are you alright?" Andras asked quietly. His long, strong fingers trailed up and down my spine in long, soothing lines.

A tissue tickled the back of my hand, and I reached for it, drying my eyes and cheeks. Then took deep, aching breaths, nodding slowly, still unsure if I could speak without re-opening the floodgates.

"I–I am not alright," I said. Then I burst out laughing, cackling hysterically as I covered my face again and felt my brain push against my skull. When it stopped, I leaned back in my chair, clutching my shirt in my hand.

"I'm clearly losing it," I whispered. "I'm just going through a lot right now, the divorce, general overwhelm, the Roman sadist who could kill me or hurt my kids..." I trailed off. "And your story, everything from losing your family–which I can relate to on a smaller scale–and your relationship with *him*, where you lost yourself...I just feel all of that so much. I feel it all in my bones, and I've experienced a version of it that has utterly wrecked me."

Andras' hand froze on my back, and he went completely still. His eyes turned black, and then the inky blackness receded like it had never been there.

"I'm so sorry. I very much want to kill your ex-husband. Slowly. After we've dealt with Callum."

I rolled my eyes. "You're unhinged," I joked.

"That's a new one!" Nadia said. "I've never heard anyone call someone unhinged before. I always love my trips to the U.S. for the vocabulary alone."

My lips pulled up at the corners, and she grinned back, her eyes dancing with something I couldn't pin down. It was as if she were full of joy, delight, empathy, and a small, hidden pain.

"I'm going to make some tea," Andras announced.

He rose from his knees in one elegant motion before wandering down the hall to the kitchen. Nadia then sauntered to the couch, smoothly and deliberately, like her movements were a dance. She pulled a knitted throw onto her lap, snuggled under it, and then nodded toward the blanket. Smiling faintly, I shook my head "no" before turning back to the fire.

Not long after, a warm mug of tea found its way between my cold hands, providing a welcome piece of normality and comfort. Until I remembered how it had felt to look into Callum's cold eyes while my fingers thrummed with pain. Wincing, I pushed the memory away to focus on the smell of the chamomile, the delicate floral taste on my tongue.

The three of us sat in silence by the fire as the night crept on. A yawn escaped me, and Andras turned, examining my face. "You should sleep if you can," he encouraged, rising and extending his hand towards mine. I took it.

"Come," he said, turning to lead me down the hall to a small bedroom with a king-sized oak bed. The cream and green comforter was inviting and cozy. Freshly fluffed pillows were stacked high at the head of the bed, guarded by an embroidered throw pillow that commanded us to "Rest Well." I didn't think it would be possible for me to sleep knowing that Callum was out there somewhere. Just the thought of him set my body on fire with the need to fight, to run. Andras must have sensed my anxiety or heard my heart because I felt his large hand on my back again.

"I got you into this, and I swear on my life that I will fix it. I will kill him, and no harm will come to you or your family." He paused before going on, "I know words are pointless, especially when it comes to something like this, but I promise I will make it right."

I turned to look up at him, and his hand fell away from my back. His eyebrows came together almost as if he were in pain, and those shocking blue eyes glistened.

"Are you okay?" I asked quietly, my heart breaking for him just a little.

"I cannot let you lose your family," he whispered.

Andras closed his eyes for a heartbeat and shook his head. So much pain. His life had been long but full of pain: loss, torment, entrapment, anguish, and guilt. I could see it all flashing across his face as his mind wandered from one terrible memory to the next.

"Hey," I said, putting a hand on his arm. "I wasn't just trying to be nice before. I don't blame you for any of this. I *am* angry and terrified, but I don't blame you."

He took a deep breath. Almost instantly, he stood taller. He rolled his shoulders back, and his face became warm and calm.

"This is not about me," he said. Then his lips pulled up at the corners. "I will be okay. I've been dealing with all of this for a long time, and I've grown incredibly good at compartmentalizing trauma. Plus, I have all of eternity to sort it out. So, truly, let's focus on you. What can I do to be here for you? What do you need?" I couldn't tell him how much I appreciated his words. It had been a long time since a man implied that my needs might be important in some way, and maybe even occasionally a priority. I wanted to punch Steven in the face. I wanted to hold my babies. I wanted Callum to die. And I wanted to reach out, grasp Andras by the shoulders, and tug him into a hug.

"Do you have a weapon I can keep by the bed?" I asked. "I know it's useless because I'm not practically a god, and he is, but it would make me feel a little less helpless. Sometimes, when Steven travels, I keep a knife under the bed where the girls can't find it."

Andras raised his eyebrows.

"Absolutely."

He left the room and returned just as I'd finished changing into sleep shorts and a tank top.

"Here. Will this work?" he asked.

Andras stopped short when he saw me. His gaze raked over me from head to toe so slowly that I nearly blushed. His jaw ticked. Heat flashed across his face; then it was gone. Gently, he pushed the iron poker handle into my hand. I extended my arm out like I was holding a sword, aiming it at the wall behind us. I pointed my front foot forward and turned my back foot to a ninety-degree angle, then lunged forward. Andras grinned.

"Fencing?" he asked.

"My parents insisted I did it for almost a decade growing up, hoping it would get me into an Ivy League school."

"And did it?"

"Yes. But I chose not to go. *That* was a scandal."

He tilted his head to the side, raising one eyebrow.

"Why didn't you go?"

"I don't know. Maybe a little to get back at my mom because that was all that she cared about. Our relationship was about her teaching us how to be better than everyone else every second of every day. I was tired of the pressure, the competition, and the bullshit. I still went to a good college, but not the one my mom or dad had picked for me. Plus, I didn't want to be that far from Jess after my dad died. So we chose colleges that were a quick trip from each other. Jess went to Stanford, and I went to Whitman College, a small liberal arts school in Washington."

I brought my hand to my mouth and yawned again. I didn't want to be tired, but every time my nerves eased a little, the exhaustion swept in and tried to take me.

Andras leaned down so that his face was only a few inches from mine. He smiled and whispered, "Let's go to bed."

I frowned. Let's? As in, both of us go to bed together? Andras immediately noticed my shock and confusion, threw his head back, and chuckled warmly. It was a sensual, smooth laugh.

"Is the idea of sleeping next to me that appalling?"

"Of course it isn't," I shot him a look, "but given the circumstances..."

Andras paused for a heartbeat as his smile faded, his face relaxing into something more focused and predatory. He gazed at me with his bedroom eyes and took a step, closing the space between us.

Towering above me, he drawled,

"I'd love to slip that sweater off of you and pull down your pants to touch you, taste you, and press my body against yours and into yours," he smiled. His warm breath tickled my forehead. "But I would never use a situation like this as an opportunity to do any of that. Unless, of course, you asked me to."

I gaped up at him, surprised.

"We need to share a room," he continued, "because if Callum comes tonight, he could kill you faster than I'd reach you, even in the next room."

I nodded that I understood, then silently walked around the bed to rest the poker against the wall where I could reach it. I pulled back the quilts and slid silently between the soft flannel sheets.

"May I?" Andras asked, gesturing to the light switch.

"Yes."

The room went black except for the moonlight glowing around the edges of the heavy forest-green curtains. I couldn't make out the furniture in the room, but I knew that Andras could see perfectly. Their kind was made for the night, even if they could walk outside during the day. The quilt tugged gently on the other side of the bed, and then the mattress sunk with his weight.

"Goodnight," I said.

I turned my back to him and tried with everything in my power to focus on my breathing so that I could find sleep. It was difficult to battle the intrusive thoughts and images, a slideshow of despair and suffering. It wasn't easy to know that Andras lay just a few feet from me, and I couldn't stop thinking about how good it would feel to touch that perfect skin, to run my hand down the defined muscles of his abdomen. The more my brain filled with a circus of terror, the more I needed a distraction.

"Andras?" I whispered in the dark, into the silence.

A LOVER'S PURR

I regretted saying his name in the dark immediately. My body went rigid as if I could play dead and pretend it didn't happen. Maybe he hadn't heard me? Hopefully, he'd already fallen asleep. Because what if he wasn't interested? I couldn't imagine that any of this was easy for him. But what if he wanted a distraction, too? Too complicated. Everything felt too complex.

So many conflicting needs and concerns raced through my mind. I should leave him alone. He probably needs his rest for strength. After all, he planned to kill Callum, whenever he showed up. I was simply having a moment of weakness, beckoning to him in the dark like a jackass, toying with the idea of doing something idiotic. Although, we were on the brink of death. Maybe if there was ever a time to make ridiculous decisions, it was now; we might not survive this. I would fight and claw until the bitter end to get back to my children, so I could be there for them. So they didn't have to mourn me. But I was human, and even if Andras promised to keep me in one piece, Calum was far older and sounded far more vicious.

"Yes?" Andras asked, and I startled, even though his voice was seductive, a lover's purr–like smoke, and midnight, and gin.

He sounded wide awake. Did he even need to sleep? In movies and books, some of them slept all day in coffins, optionally watched over by some sort of ghoul. Others didn't sleep at all, spending their days going to high school and nights finding a food source, or maybe creepily watching *others* sleep.

"Do you need to sleep?" I blurted out.

"I do. But not that much. We typically need a few hours at night and maybe a few hours during the day. It's more like we need a couple of naps for each earthly rotation, instead of a full night's rest. However, we can sleep more if we like, and there have been many periods in my life when I was so godsdamn bored that I slept quite a bit. I barely remember the nineteen-fifties."

I laughed softly.

"Your life is incredible. I still can't believe you're a...that you're–"

"I know. I still don't believe it, and it's been six hundred years." He hummed a laugh.

I turned towards him. I could just make out the shadowy silhouette of his face, the straight nose, and full lips. His chest rose and fell. Jess and I grew up obsessed with faeries and vampires and other fantastical things from books, but never in my wildest dreams did I think I'd be sharing a bed with one. Gods, he was so beautiful, and I could smell him, his scent, mixed with whatever that deep, woodsy scent.

"Having trouble sleeping?" he asked.

"Yeah."

"Do you want to talk for a bit, then?"

"That would be nice. If you're not too tired, of course."

"I'm not tired at all."

He shifted in the bed again, and the mattress tremored. He raised himself up on his elbow, head resting on his hand. *Was he looking at me?* I crossed my eyes at him, and he laughed softly.

"Testing my vision?" He asked so quietly I could barely hear him.

"How did you know?"

"Just a guess," he sighed. I could hear the smile in his words. "And yes," he continued, "I saw that. I can see everything as clearly as the day. I can see your yellow-green eyes and those long lashes. Your pretty olive skin, your high cheekbones and wild, beautiful hair fanned across the pillow. Now I'm picturing your lovely, full breasts, the beautiful soft scar on your lower belly, and the curve of your hips. I haven't stopped thinking about any of it, actually, since that night."

I tried to swallow, but my mouth had gone dry.

"Me either," I admitted quietly.

I wanted to reach out and touch him. I slowly pulled my hand out from underneath the sheets and slid it across the comforter towards him until the bed shifted and a large hand rested gently over it. His long soft fingers roamed the back of my hand and the top of my wrist, lightly tickling the skin. I inhaled sharply. My entire body went motionless before melting into the sheets.

"Andras?"

"Yes?"

"Will you kiss me?"

The bed shifted as he closed the distance between us. A hand gently brushed my cheek, warm breath tickled my forehead before soft lips pressed there. Fingers caressed my neck, then found their way across my chest, down my side, where they stayed, tracing long lines from my ribs to my hips. He placed a kiss on my temple, and then on each of my cheeks, where his lips lingered for some time. I could hardly breathe as my body came to life for him; electricity built in my chest, a tingling shot down my spine, collected in my lower belly, then flowed like warm honey toward the center of me. I could feel him hover above my mouth, his breath jagged and quick. Slowly, his full lips pressed into mine with painful gentleness, as if the self-restraint was part of the act for him. I wrapped one arm around his back, the other around his neck, and let my fingers drift upward to rake through his dark hair, pulling him down to me, and his lips pressed harder, then his mouth parted. His tongue flicked and teased mine, which sailed across his as I explored his mouth, his full lips, and something sharp...

A canine. I pulled back to study his face, still concealed by the shadows. I could just make out his features. He grinned wickedly, both fangs fully extended, then shrugged.

"Sorry," he whispered, not sorry at all.

My breathing hitched. He sat back onto his knees and reached, slowly, for the hem of my shirt.

"Is this okay?" he asked, his fingers hovering just above the fabric.

Yes," I rasped.

Then my shirt was off, and then my shorts and underwear, all at once. Then his. Our naked bodies tangled under the comforter as he placed himself between my legs. My fingers wandered across the pits and valleys between the hard muscles of his chest and stomach, formed from centuries of training as a soldier. I wanted him. I needed him. I moaned, and my hand wandered lower until I reached the hardest part of him.

Taking him into my palm, I stroked lightly up and down the shaft, exploring the impressive size. A low growl rumbled from within him, and I swore for a second that his blue eyes flashed gold. His tongue flicked across my neck, then down my chest, lingering on each breast, where he teased the sensitive peaks of my hard nipples. His fingers found the slickness between my legs, and my clit, where he made gentle, artful circles with the kind of expertise that could only come be the result of hundreds of years of fucking. My back arched, and my legs widened for him as he moved lower until his mouth lingered just above my entrance, where he let his breath tickle and taunt me until I felt like I might die. Then he licked up my entire center. I cried out and grabbed his hair. His tongue moved up and down, fast, quickly bringing me almost to the edge, and then he slowed until my body cooled just a little, before quickening the pace.

He pressed his tongue into me, pushing in and out, pinning my hips down with his arm as my body writhed against him. He moved up to my clit again, sucking gently, pushing two fingers into me, and moving them slowly back and forth until I teetered on the edge again.

Then he stilled.

"No, please," I whimpered.

He chuckled darkly, climbing over me, licking and nipping, until he lay next to me, and I panicked, thinking he was going to leave me there feeling empty and unfulfilled. I'd beg. He slid his arm under my back, gripped my hip with his fingers, and flipped me onto my side. I ground my ass against his hard cock as he positioned himself behind me. I instinctively spread my legs, and he licked up my neck as he positioned the head of his cock against my entrance.

"May I?" he whispered into my ear.

"Oh Gods, please," I moaned.

"Yes?"

"YES!"

He pushed his cock into me, and in, deeper and deeper. I gasped and reached my arm around his back to pull him closer until it was impossible to tell where my body began, and his ended. The fingers of his right hand found my sex again, impossibly slick and ready, and began caressing in gentle circles as he pulled out halfway, then plunged in again. My lower belly tingled and burned with pleasure. He took me to the edge and then held me there.

"Is this okay," he whispered into my ear, and I felt sharp canines graze my neck. My head fell back, my mind wild with need, my body full of him, of him, of him... "Yes!" I moaned. Then there was pressure on my neck, a burning pain, followed by absolute, mind-bending euphoria. I gasped as if I were releasing decades of tension and pain. He could bleed me dry and I'd thank him for it. I went over the edge, screaming his name as I trembled and spasmed around him. He sped up, pounding harder, deeper, until a low growl escaped him as he sucked gently at my neck while his cock pulsed inside of me. Then he released my neck and licked the wound. He slid out of me a few moments later, and we lay there, side by side, panting.

FOR FUCK'S SAKE, JANET.

My eyes flew open as my leg brushed against a strong calf patterned with soft, dark hair. *Oh no.* Staring up at the ceiling, I noted every place where our naked flesh touched, his firm, muscled body draped partially over mine. The aroma of coffee wafting in from the kitchen mingled with our scent—rose, jasmine, cedar, and sex. Blood rushed to my cheeks and plenty of other places just thinking about it. A cell phone buzzed to life on the nightstand, vibrating across the oak stand until it thudded into the rug. Andras's head jerked up from the pillow, his eyes wild, lips pulled back to reveal two razor-sharp fangs fully descended. He scanned the room and then glanced down at me, his eyes raking over our intertwined bodies. Calm fell over his face, and a delighted grin replaced the violent sneer.

"Good morning," he drawled, his lip kicking up on one side. "You look beautiful."

I smiled tightly up at him. My mind whirled from the previous night. Fear filled my core, remembering the reason we were posted up in this cabin together; just above that, wonder sparked and flitted around my ribcage, thinking of our long, long night together, tumbling in the sheets.

His eyes slid down our joined bodies again; then, surprise flashed across his face.

"Oh, pardon," he said, hurriedly, flipping onto his back and off of me. I stifled a laugh and turned to him with raised eyebrows. Andras shrugged, then winked. Stretching my arms slowly above my head, I arched into a stretch, extended my legs, and pointed my toes. Soreness shot through me; muscles ached that I didn't even know existed. My lips felt raw, and the space between my legs, too. *How many times did we...?* Gods, I didn't even know. Everywhere our bodies touched tingled with a persistent need.

The phone buzzed on the floor again. Leaning off the bed, my fingers fumbled to grab at the buzzing menace without slipping out of the sheets into the cold room. I didn't recognize the number, but still answered, just in case it was important— in case it somehow involved my girls. I inhaled sharply, suddenly hit by a pang of nerves.

"Hello?"

"Are you okay?" a female voice asked, an acidic tang in her tone.

It took a moment for me to place it. Janet. Janet from the PTA, who I'd seen yesterday in front of my house and barked at to fuck off before speeding for the hills.

"Hi, Janet," I said, rolling my eyes. "I can't get the socks to you right now. I'm very sick and dealing with some personal...family things. I can–"

"–Look. I don't appreciate you signing up to help and then being yelled at. What is going on with you? Bethany said she saw your husband go in the front gates of your mother's estate yesterday when she was visiting her parents and—"

I swallowed. "Janet, I will get you the donation or whatever. I will get you all the things in the entire world. I'm sorry I yelled at you, but it's none of your goddamn business what's going on in my personal life, and please..." I paused–*do I ask her to stop getting her information from Bethany?* "I beg you, Janet, tell Bethany to jump off a fucking cliff. Okay?"

Janet gasped, no doubt clutching her pearls.

"Have a good day," I added, before hanging up.

With a flick of my wrist, the phone flew across the bed and disappeared into the comforter. Andras said nothing, only looked at me sidelong, as if he were too nervous to speak. Groaning, I sat up, flinging the blankets off as a low growl escaped my throat, then marched to my overnight bag stark nude. I huffed the thing over my shoulder and headed to the ensuite bathroom, my backside fully exposed, in what was easily the least sexy thing I'd ever done in my life. Anger built as my skin erupted in goosebumps from the ice-cold floor beneath my bare feet. I gently closed the door behind me and felt panic. The shadows of night no longer cocooned us. Andras was no longer buried inside of me, no longer a source of escape, of distraction. Janet's phone call abruptly brought me back to reality, where I was being hunted for vengeance, jealousy, and socks.

After showering, I quickly picked through the outfits I'd haphazardly thrown together in my panic-stricken rush to get here after Callum stopped by my house three days ago. What does one wear to fight (or be murdered by) an ancient immortal? *What the fuck is happening in my life right now?* Recalling the action scenes of my favorite films and books, I plucked black leggings, a black knit sweater, and white sneakers from the pile—so I could, what, run fast and bend easily? All of it was totally useless; Callum was a thousand times faster and had been a general in one of the largest and arguably cruelest empires in history. Shuddering, I gathered my waves into a low ponytail. While watching myself dab on some tinted moisturizer and gloss in the mirror, I suddenly remembered that Andras had bitten me. My fingers searched my neck for proof, but all I could feel was smooth skin. Pulling at the neck of my sweater and leaning into the mirror for a closer look still revealed nothing—no puncture marks, no scabs, only a faint purplish bruise that could have easily come from all the kissing.

Had I imagined it? No. It had been real, and my blood warmed at the memory of being flooded with blinding euphoria when he'd sunk his teeth in, followed by the incredible relief after a few seconds of searing pain. But how did that work? I made a mental note to ask Andras or Nadia about it.

The bed was empty but made when I came out of the bathroom, my pajamas folded at the foot of the bed with my phone gently resting on top. Did we have maid service? I snatched up my phone to text Steven a short message:

"How is everything?"

"Fine," he said flatly "The girls have spent most of the day in the main house with your mom, and I've been holed up in the guest house avoiding her. When will you be better?"

I shook my head, and could not have been more happy to be divorced from him.

"I don't know. I'm still very sick. But I hope soon."

Pacing the length of the bed, I waited for a response for a few minutes before giving up and moving toward the bedroom door. I paused at the handle. Back straight, chin up, deep inhale—I pulled the door open and wandered toward the kitchen, toward the murmuring that stopped the second my feet hit the hallway.

Nadia and Andras were still in sweatpants and sweaters, cozied up at the small high-top café table nestled against a snow-specked window, pretending to concentrate on their coffee mugs when I entered the room. I knew that Nadia had heard us last night. Anyone would have, but with vampire-level hearing, she might as well have been in the room. Still, I refused to blush, refused to feel embarrassed. I was tired of wasting time feeling any kind of way but self-assured, and if I survived this weekend, I'd be heading home to purge my life of all kinds of bullshit.

"Is there any more coffee?" I asked, pausing at the doorway. Nadia and Andras snapped their attention to me.

A crooked grin lit up Andras's face. "Let me get it," he offered. Like the wind, he moved from his chair to the other side of the kitchen, where the coffee maker was, so fast my eyes couldn't fully register the movement. One moment, he was sitting; the next, he was across the room, pouring steaming black coffee into a large red mug. Andras was tall, but in that cozy kitchen, he was towering. And in those black sweatpants that fit him perfectly? Devastating. I dragged my eyes from his backside to Nadia, who had been watching me watch him with wicked delight.

"Good morning," she sang.

"Good morning," I replied, as I sauntered over to the table where she sat. "Did you sleep well?" I asked.

"A couple of hours."

"Same."

Nadia's eyebrows lifted ever so slightly as if she wanted to tease, or inquire further, but she stopped herself. Andras appeared at my side a heartbeat later, sliding the mug in front of me on the table. Looking up at him, my lips kicked up at the corners.

"Thank you," I said.

"Cream and sugar?"

"No, thank you."

I took the mug into my hands and brought it slowly to my mouth to sip, both of them watching me carefully.

"Is everything okay?" I asked.

"Nadia and I were talking about what to do if Callum doesn't come. There's a chance that he knows it's a trap, that we're expecting him. If that's the case, he'll bide his time until we're each alone," Andras said.

Fear shot through me.

"No," I said. "My daughters and everyone I come into contact with would be in danger. My sister. Everyone. That's not an option. If he doesn't come for us, we have to go and find him." My hands shook as I set the mug back on the table.

"I won't let anything happen to you or the girls," Andras assured, eyes darkening, as he reached out to put a large, warm hand over mine. "I will shadow you until the end of time to make sure that doesn't happen."

"I agree with Danny," Nadia said, shaking her hair away from her face. She leaned back, resting an elbow on the back of her chair. "If he doesn't show today, I'll hunt him down. None of us can live a particularly peaceful life knowing he's out there."

"So what do we do?" I wondered out loud, wringing my hands in my lap, trying to will the twisted knots in my gut to loosen.

"Well, for today, we wait," Andras intoned gently. "We spend the day and tonight here, hoping he comes. If not, we'll figure it out tomorrow morning."

"Okay," I said. "In the meantime, is there somewhere to get food?" I hadn't eaten since breakfast the day before, too sick with worry to even think about it.

"Oh, shit," Andras swore, looking at Nadia wide-eyed. "I forgot to get food." He turned to me, "I cannot believe I did that. I'm so sorry. Let's go right now. There's a small mountain store not far down the road. I'll get dressed. Is that alright?"

"You don't have to apologize. You guys don't have to eat, right?"

"We *can* eat food, and we *like* to eat food. But we don't *have* to," Nadia said, raising up her cup of coffee.

Andras rose to his feet in one smooth motion. In a few long, graceful steps, he disappeared around the corner and down the hall. Nadia turned to me, a sly jester's smile on her lips.

"So," she crooned.

I shot her a look that conveyed, "No, we are definitely not talking about *that*." She shrugged as if to say, *"Fine by me."*

"Come sit by the fire while we wait," she offered, yawning. "It's much better than by this freezing window."

She slid out of her chair, a pretty blue mug in hand, and sauntered toward the living room. I followed.

I sank back into the armchair near the crackling fire, as Nadia lowered herself onto the sofa with the grace of a ballerina and the regal confidence of a queen. She stared at me as if there was something she wanted to say but was holding back for some reason. I waited for her to start.

"I like you," she said after a few heartbeats. "You're brave. Kind. All of this is, well, a lot, and you haven't hesitated or balked. When you suggested we go after Callum, you meant that. You'd kill him to protect your family."

"Yeah," I agreed, "I would. I'd do anything for them."

"I can feel your fear. That's the reason a mother's love is so fierce, not because she's never afraid, but because she moves forward despite it."

Nadia searched my face for a moment, her lips a tight line like she was reading something there. I smiled tightly.

"What did you mean? You can feel my fear...because you're a vampire?"

She hummed in agreement. "Kind of," she said. "It's like how Andras can mindweave. I can feel how other people are feeling, like I'm experiencing it myself. And I can affect their emotions a bit, too."

"Well, that's rough," I blew out a breath. "That sounds like empathy on steroids. Isn't it hard to manage all the time?"

"Oh, after all these years, you figure it out. It has its uses, too. Like knowing that you're a brave, honest, and kind person. And I know that Andras, well, he's happy around you, in a way I've never seen. He's at ease, and content."

Hearing her words sparked something like giddy pride inside of me, even if I wasn't entirely sure her praise was deserved. Andras *always* seemed at ease and content, prowling the neighborhood at night with random dates, casually draped over the bar at Blotto, striding around with his hands in his coat pockets.

If I were to describe him, I'd say he was "at ease" most of the time. Still, the idea that I might affect him made me smile.

"I like you, too," I admitted, finally.

We drank our coffee in silence, and both of us focused on the flames licking the edges of a log in the fireplace. I didn't know much about Nadia, outside of how she'd met Andras and how they'd been forced to deal with Callum.

"Do you still live mostly in England?" I asked.

"I do. Well, I bounce around between England, Northern France, and random warmer climates when I tire of the cold. I was born in Anatolia."

I frowned, trying to picture it on a map. Had I truly been out of school for so long I'd entirely forgotten geography?

"Turkey is what it's called now," she added.

"Oh, okay. Thank you."

I wondered what it must have been like for them to have witnessed countries rise and fall and change. Nadia stretched her legs out on the sofa and lay back to rest her head on a throw pillow. She looked like royalty in her silk pink pajamas, her sleek hair fanning around her head like a crown.

"You want to ask me questions. Yes? There is nothing much to know, honestly. My family were merchants. We fled when the Roman Empire weakened and the Ottomans invaded. There was an opportunity for me to get separated from my very Christian family, and I took it. I was made not long after by a woman I met along the way, but I didn't find myself in the same predicament as Andras, *thankfully*. She and I had our fun, we parted ways amicably, and that's that. I've lived a dozen lives since. In one of those lives, I met Andras, we buried Callum, and then I lived a few more lives after that. Now here we are."

She rotated her wrist and fanned her fingers, gesturing to the ceiling, as if to reveal a magic trick of some kind. As if to say, ta-da!

"The person who made you—"

"Such a long story, and I can barely remember her face anymore. She was beautiful, strong, and terribly old. Maybe one of the oldest of us."

"The oldest? You mean...you know where vampires come from?"

"The same place everything else comes from, I suppose. We're not human, but we're of this world. There are many things in this world that exist outside of human reality but we'll get to all of that another time."

Her eyes flicked up to something behind me.

"Are you ready to go?" Andras asked.

He'd entered the room and leaned against the doorframe, hands in the pockets of his long coat, without me hearing a thing. *Silent as the night, and just as deadly*, I thought.

I set my empty coffee mug on the table and untangled my legs to get to my feet. My chin dipped once. Andras pushed off the frame to step toward us.

"Coming?" He raised a brow at Nadia.

"No, no. Go on without me." She got to her feet and began stretching her legs. "I'm going hunting."

I glanced at Andras for an explanation, and Nadia caught me.

"For deer blood," she said. "Human blood is too...complicated." She wrinkled her nose in disgust.

Andras shot her an incredulous look.

"I have one human source," Nadia breathed mid-stretch, "she's magnificent, otherwise I don't touch the stuff."

Andras looked amused. "Have fun," he sang, then paused, waiting for me to walk ahead of him and we headed for his car.

In Andras's black sedan, we sped past blurry trees with mostly bald branches. A few stubborn patches of fire-colored leaves clung to branches here and there. We went faster than I'd ever gone in a car. His heightened senses allowed him to race through the hills without a care in the world. Every so often, our eyes would meet, and Andras would grin at me, as if this were something he'd always wanted to do and was overjoyed to be doing—just taking a drive together.

The country store smelled of beef jerky and apple spice potpourri plug-ins. A display of stuffed grizzly bears in overalls took up space next to the cash register. Corn dogs, potato logs, and donuts were for sale at the counter. Fresh cheese curds could be found in the refrigerator section near the back, next to the soda, chocolate milk, and glass bottles of fresh cow's milk. A small fridge hummed near another wall, selling "night crawlers for two dollars" in small styrofoam containers.

I grabbed a few cans of soup, a loaf of crusty bread, some green apples, and three peach pastries. Just enough food to get us through the day, because after tomorrow, if Callum doesn't come for us, we'd start hunting him. I swallowed hard at the thought. I'd take chasing him to the ends of the earth any day over letting him roam free, lurking in every shadow, ready to pounce. Andras casually wandered the store with his hands in his pockets, taking in the local small-town fare, pausing before a small display of travel keychains. I tilted my head in question, ready to open my mouth to ask what he was searching for, when a tall man stalked past us, bumping into me with his shoulder, hard enough to send me sprawling into the keychain stand–if Andras hadn't been there to catch me. The man smelled like he'd taken a bath in lager. Andras held me gently around the waist to steady me on my feet, his eyes searching for the slightest injury.

"I'm okay," I said quietly. I glanced over his shoulder at the stumbling man, who turned to sneer at us.

"Watch where you're going," he slurred, clumsily backing up into the candy bars and sending tiny boxes crashing to the floor.

Andras went wholly still, his dancing sapphire eyes now dark and violent, locked on the drunk man.

"What are you lookin' at?" the man barked, his ruddy face twisted into a rabid glower.

"You should apologize to her," Andras instructed, calmly–too calm–his hands sliding into his pockets.

"Fuck you," the man barked, "and fuck your bitch."

Andras tilted his head casually to the side, grinning wickedly. He tsked. "I'm not having a great week, friend," he began, "and that was the wrong thing to say." He rolled his shoulders.

"When you hurt someone, you apologize." He nodded towards me, "see this woman here? If you so much as glance at her again," the grin melted into something far more menacing and his voice became low, the sound of shadows and wrath, "I will rip your still-beating heart out of your fucking chest."

He stepped toward the man, and his eyes darkened, all the blue eaten up by inky black. The man jerked back, his face white as snow, then froze. His breathing sped up, faster and faster; his chest heaved, but his eyes were vacant. I knew, right then, what Andras was doing. He'd pulled that man into his mind, conjuring up a place of terror, of nightmares. Then the man's shoulders slumped forward and his breathing slowed, as Andras said flatly, "Off you go, then. Go sober up, get some therapy, turn your life around."

The man looked like he'd woken up from a bad dream, blinking frantically and looking lost. The black receded from Andras's eyes. Then the man launched into movement, fell backward onto his ass, scrambled to his feet, and ran from Andras in utter panic, tripping through the front door and looking over his shoulder as he scattered across the parking lot. Still holding my soup cans and groceries, I glanced at Andras, eyebrows raised.

"Seriously?"

"What?" he asked innocently.

He gathered most of what I had in my hands before heading toward the cashier, who had found something really interesting on a beef jerky package, with me by his side.

In the car, I waited for him to speak, but a hundred heartbeats went by, and we sat in silence.

"Andras?"

"Yes?"

"You okay?"

"Yes. And no. I'm furious that man touched you. I didn't see it coming, and just...the thought of someone hurting you..."

"I can stick up for myself," I reproached.

The last thing I wanted was for Andras to go crazy on everyone who insulted me from now until the end of time. *The end of time?* Why was I thinking about him in the long term? *He* had until the end of time, but I would age, and die. I had children to raise, and they certainly wouldn't grow up in the world Andras and Nadia lived in. One with ancient enemies, and...fuck. If someone like Callum exists and is just roaming free, I realized, there must be others, some undoubtedly worse than him. I felt sick.

"I know you can," Andras agreed. "I didn't do that because I think of you as helpless, or because I think you're my property, or even because you're a woman, or because I lo...*care* about you."

My breathing hitched on his stumbled words. Was he going to say something else, something far more damning?

"Standing up for people," he continued, "just feels like the right thing to do. Hell, Nadia could have killed him with a wink, with half a thought, and I would still have defended her. And she would have done the same for me. She *has* done the same for me. Because we're friends."

I smiled warmly up at him in understanding. Friends. We were friends. He cared about me, and I cared about him, complicated though it may be. A deer alongside near the road, and I remembered that Nadia was out hunting. My nose scrunched up at the thought of her, in her long-limbed elegance, pouncing on a doe somewhere in the powdery snow, and ripping its throat out. Ack.

"You gonna tell me what you *did* to the guy at least?" I asked.

"Oh, definitely not," Andras laughed, with notes of wicked delight in the sound, and on his face.

I shook my head at him in mock reprimand, then turned my attention to the valleys and peaks dusted with snow, to Nadia, and then beyond to Jess, and my girls. A few months ago, I'd wanted a little excitement: to feel seen, to be heard. I wanted to be a good mother, to learn everything I could about how to raise them "the best way," and for my husband to love me again, to smile warmly at me. For us to laugh together about our days and our children's antics while rocking on our porch swing. Now...well, I could barely believe it. I was tearing through the mountains with a powerful vampire who looked like a lord of the night on our way back to a cabin where we were waiting for some ancient sadistic prick to come for us. I had filed for divorce, and my little girls were holed up at my mother's manor, playing among the old maples and oaks, on grounds haunted by the memory of my father.

Music, full of vibrating bass sounds, repeating soft and then hard notes, greeted us as we neared the cabin.

Inside, we toed off our boots, and I put the groceries away while Andras went into the living room to say hello to Nadia.

I popped my head into the living room.

"Do either of you want soup?" I asked. "Or are you too full of Bambi?"

Nadia glared at me but I could see the corner of her mouth tugging up. She swayed to the music, her cheeks flushed with the fresh animal blood that coursed through her veins. She wore loose black slacks and a pretty floral blouse with heeled boots.

"Soup would be great," they answered in unison. Andras had casually draped himself over the sofa, a book in hand. Nadia continued to twirl and sway to the music, her lips turned up slightly at the corners.

"Please," Andras added, looking up from his book with a grin.

Minestrone plopped from the can into the saucepan. Stirring it with a wooden spoon, I watched the snow coming down again outside in fat flakes. I was so tired, and it was getting late. I wanted to go to bed, yet the thought of laying next to him, touching him, and feeling him inside of me made my cheeks hot and my stomach curl.

He was so many things. Beautiful, tender, and absolutely deadly. I wanted to stay in this world with him forever, spend eternity getting to know him and studying layer upon complicated layer. But I wanted to get back to my girls, and I wanted that even more. I ached for them like a part of my soul had gone missing. And I knew, *I knew* I couldn't have him and them.

A pit formed in my stomach. I caught a glimpse of my reflection in the glass, and the raw despair on my face startled me. There was something else, too, something beyond my reflection, near the woods. A shadowed blur.

THE HALFLINGS ATTACK

I ran for the living room, stopping short at the entrance as Nadia whirled from the fireplace towards Andras, who was stretched out on the couch.

"Andras. Callum is *here*," she warned, her voice cold and commanding. "I know it because my mood has gone to absolute shit."

Taking a step, I looked between them, "I just saw something near the woods–a shadow. A very fast-moving shadow," I blurted out. I wrung my hands together, unsure what else to do with them.

Andras sat up slowly, tilting his head, listening intently. He sniffed the air and then went utterly still. A nod to each of us, his gaze lifted to the ceiling—something was up there. With cat-like stealth, Andras rose to his feet, inching silently toward me. Nadia slid the fire poker free from its stand, crouching low, one hand on the floor for balance, the other aiming the iron into the air. The fire crackled. Without warning, she sprang toward the ceiling, thrusting the poker upward before landing back into a crouch with a soft thud. She checked the tip for blood, cursing when it came up clean. Then all hell broke loose. Andras twisted, pulling me close as glass shattered. A dark figure exploded through the window, slamming into Nadia. She pivoted out of the shadow's claws, rolling into the wall. Instantly back on her feet, ready to strike, Nadia's eyes locked on the darkness rising in the corner of the room. The figure stepped into the firelight—a young man with brown eyes and sneering, pale lips.

"Andras," I whispered, his arm still around me. My voice cracked as my body began to shake. "It's *him*..." I whispered.

Andras froze in a way only an immortal could. He gently unwrapped himself from me and stepped away. Then, in a blur, Andras shot toward the man who had broken into my home, who had dragged me through my living room by my hair. Rage seared through my chest, so intense I thought it might kill me. *Am I having a heart attack, right now?* Andras' hand snapped out like a viper, seizing the man by the throat and squeezing. "Who the fuck are you?" Andras asked, his voice calm, quiet, lethal, with his fangs fully visible and terrifying. A groan escaped the enormous man, his bulging eyes darting toward the window, toward the outside.

"C-Callum," he choked out, "sent me to follow you." He was struggling, gasping. "I saw you talk to her," his swollen eyes slid to mine, "so I snuck in to find out who she was. I thought the house was empty. But then, she was there, and I was...so hungry."

A shiver shot up my spine and a cold like I'd never known before traveled through my limbs. Had that been why Andras had looked so worried when he'd stared into this man's face that night? Because he suspected he might be a vampire?

A chilly, emotionless calm settled over Andras's striking face, half in shadow, half illuminated by the glow of the fire. He let go of the man's throat, cocking back his elbow as if he were loading a punch, then his fist thrust forward into the man's barrel chest with a thunderous crack, and his hand–his *whole hand*–buried itself inside. I inhaled sharply, covering my mouth. I was going to be sick. The man's eyes widened in disbelief. He gasped, mouth opening and closing like a fish suffocating out of water. Andras growled and yanked his hand free, the squelch and crack echoed through the room. Something slipped from his grip and landed on the floor with a wet thud. I startled. The man's face froze as he went boneless, collapsing to the ground in a heap. Blood trickled from Andras's hand down to the hardwood. Drip. Drip. Drip.

He ran the bloodied hand through this dark hair, face still impassive, detached, the face of a former enforcer, a soldier, a killer. Red streaked his forehead and coated his already disheveled strands. One breath, I was watching him, unable to look away, the next breath, he appeared at my side, his sticky red hand slack at his side. My stomach turned, and I nearly wretched, until Nadia started to rub small circles on my back.

"Try to breathe," she gently encouraged. She must have sensed that I felt sick and faint at the sound of the cracking, and all that blood, and the memory of my father's study, and the dried splatters that crusted the ceiling. I inhaled deeply and exhaled slowly. After all of this was over, if we survived, I did not want to feel this way ever again. I would not feel powerless or trapped ever again.

"I'm sorry," Andras apologized, shaking his head.

My gaze flicked up to his, and I frowned. "I knew what I was getting into," I said. I knew it would be like this, and I'm not here to be coddled." There was a pause. I don't know why this popped into my head, but it did, and I couldn't stop myself from saying it. I smiled tightly, "Plus, I read all of the Anne Rice books, so I feel *pretty prepared*."

Nadia and Andras both scoffed. I threw up my hands in mock offense. I knew that I'd made the joke to stop myself from crying. The way I'd always done, deflected how I felt through humor.

Andras looked between me and Nadia,

"That was a halfling," he said.

"Yeah," she agreed.

She blew out a breath and swore.

A halfling? I tried to remember if I'd ever heard that term before. Nothing came to mind.

"What's that?" I finally asked, looking between them.

Nadia hummed a thought, then said, "it's a creature who is not fully made. Not human, not a vampire. So, still mortal, but with speed and strength. They don't live long between worlds, and it's very uncommon to see them. Except in war."

Andras's expression hardened.

"An army." He muttered, "fuck."

"He knew it was a trap," Nadia said, disgust lacing her words. "It took him a while to come because the bastard was preparing for–."

An explosion reverberated from the back of the cabin. Andras grabbed me around the waist and pulled me behind him at the same time that my eyes caught the fire poker, and I snatched it up just in time. Nadia had already vanished down the hallway. Pans clanged to the ground in the kitchen, drawers rattled open, and someone grunted—then a heavy thud against the wall, followed by a low, agonized groan. A body crashed into the hall, then was hurled into the living room, landing near us. A petite woman with short blond hair scrambled to her feet and bolted back toward the kitchen, toward Nadia. A sharp crack echoed, and then, silence. Slow, deliberate footsteps approached through the shadows until Nadia emerged, leaning casually against the doorframe. "These ones? They're like five minutes old."

"Does that mean super strong or super weak?" I asked. "Because in some books that means–"

"They're strong but feral," Nadia explained. "They don't know how to use their bodies yet. It's honestly kinda sad...and I can't help but feel like this is a distraction. Callum knows damn well that they couldn't possibly do much damage."

"He's up to something," Andras mused.

From outside, a voice bellowed into the night, full of hollow darkness: "I can *hear* you." Andras and Nadia went still. "Are you going to come out here in this freezing bullshit snow, or would you prefer that I join you in there?"

We exchanged tense, wordless glances before slowly approaching the shattered window. Jagged shards framing the scene beyond were as sharp as the fear tightening in my chest. The once-pristine snow was marred and violated by the presence of dozens of figures cloaked in the shadows, their movements strange and menacing. They were spread out across the field, closing in on the cabin and threatening violence.

"Fucking prick," Nadia cursed.

"I heard that," Callum cooed, tsking at her.

Andras's gaze swept over the halflings, then lingered on the trees bordering the clearing, before darting back inside the cabin. His expression hardened, and with cold determination, he squared his shoulders and stalked toward the hallway. Nadia flashed me a smile, her eyes gleaming with a disturbing excitement, as if she were utterly thrilled that things were finally about to get interesting. She followed him, and I trailed close behind. Andras was already rifling through a bag in the bedroom, the tension between us sharp and electric. He pulled out three sets of leather straps, tossing them without a word. I caught mine, my fingers trembling slightly as I turned it over in my hands. The air seemed to grow heavier as he reached deeper into the bag, extracting swords and two gleaming handguns, the cold weight of what was coming settling like a stone in my chest.

"Bullets won't kill them, but they'll slow them down," Andras instructed, "aim for the head." His voice was low and urgent. He fastened the leather straps around his chest with practiced speed. In one swift motion, he grabbed two short swords, sliding them into place on his back with a quiet, deadly efficiency. Nadia followed suit, her movements quick, almost eager. Then Andras turned to me, stepping close as his hands worked to secure the leather holsters around my hips. Each click of the buckle felt like a countdown. My breath hitched as he slid the handguns into place, their weight suddenly all too real.

"Have you used a gun before?"

I nodded.

"Yes, for target practice when I was younger. But I'm better with a sword. Fencing. My parents wanted me to go to Harvard. Remember?"

"You are full of surprises," he chuckled, one side of his lip lifting. Then he tilted his head, "alright, aim for the head to stun, but if you get a chance, cut the damn thing off. That will actually kill them. Even Callum. Nadia and I will go to the clearing; you stay here and– "

"No. I'm coming with you out there. I know I'm more likely to be killed, but I'm more afraid of dying here in one of these rooms on a crocheted pillow," I said, and I meant it. I couldn't stop thinking about one of the halflings getting in here and ripping my throat out on the oak bed, blood seeping into the quilts and making the needlework illegible, gruesome—a terrible way to be found. I'd rather die in the snow, fighting.

My eyes met Andras's, and we stayed that way for a heartbeat. His pupils were larger than usual, the black spreading and eating up the blue, sapphire turning to onyx. He was stunning in a way that only dangerous things can be, with his full lips, sweeping lashes, and the promise of violence in the tick of his jaw.

"Okay. You come then."

Nadia handed one of her swords to me. "Take this," she said. "I'm better with just one, anyway. Keeps my other hand free for…other things."

I raised my eyebrows at her in question. Her lips curled up at the corners to reveal straight teeth and lengthening canines.

"So you're ready, then?" Andras asked Nadia.

"Please," she scoffed, rolling her eyes, then pretended to examine her nails in feigned boredom.

"And you?" he asked, his voice heavy as a grave expression settled over his features.

I wasn't. There was nothing that could prepare me for what we were about to do, no amount of training, or deep breaths, not all of the vampire movies or books in the world. Dipping my chin once was the only confirmation I could give, worried that if I opened my mouth, I'd vomit. We surveyed each other for a moment, taking it all in. Andras wore all black, and the leather straps across his wide chest, the swords on his back, and that classically handsome face made him look like a God of death. He was gorgeous and terrifying in a way that was so wholly ethereal and not at all human. Despite the beauty and otherworldly grace, you could tell he was a soldier, trained to kill, by the way he stood with his shoulders back, jaw set, and eyes wholly fearless. A creature of death.

Nadia, for all of her elegance and beauty, looked far too casual for bloodshed, which made her that much more intimidating. Wearing a blouse and heeled boots to a battle required a level of confidence I couldn't even fathom. Her dark brown eyes were cold and determined. She hadn't bothered to sheath her sword, and instead gripped it with white knuckles, like it was an extension of her arm. Then there was me, in leggings and a sweater, a mother of two who spent a ridiculous amount of time planning cute notes to put into barely literate children's lunch boxes. Yes, I knew how to use a sword, *to win competitions.* Not to smite my enemies. I knew how to use a gun, *to hit a piece of paper.* Not a person.

I should not be here.

Andras inhaled sharply, then spun on his heel, striding purposefully toward the hall. We fell in behind him without a word. My hands trembled violently, the weight of the hilt slipping in my grip as we headed for the cold and perhaps to our deaths.

SNOW-CAPPED CARNAGE

The snow crunched beneath us as my sneakers—a poor shoe choice for warring—sank into the powder almost up to my knees. Unbearable dread squatted in my gut as I slipped into the clearing on shaky legs like a newborn fawn. *I don't belong here.* Andras and Nadia, on the other hand, prowled toward the disheveled creatures littering the clearing like it was any old Thursday. The gap between us and them closed, now less than a hundred feet. Andras and Nadia glided over the snow like it wasn't even there, while I fought to keep pace, my feet heavy and clumsy

The gaunt faces of the closest halflings came into view as we approached. Some sneered at us, others had wild, unfocused expressions. They all had pallid skin. Callum was nowhere to be seen. We stopped no more than fifty feet from the closest halflings, with Andras and Nadia flanking me. I lifted my chin and pushed my shoulders back, careful to look every bit the part of someone who might be dangerous, of someone who belonged there, even if I felt like my nerves were going to combust and turn me to ash.

Snowflakes clung to my lashes, blurring my vision, and I could barely feel my feet—numb from the cold or maybe from the rising fear. My right hand gripped the sword, much heavier than the foil I'd spent years fencing with, while my left hovered over the gun holster on my hip, fingers twitching over a weapon I barely knew how to use. I prayed silently to the universe: keep me alive, let me go home to my babies, let me raise my girls.

My girls. I saw their faces—dark, curly hair like mine, their tiny hands in mine—and something shifted inside me. Fire and wrath ignited in my core, spreading like a storm through every fiber of my being. My hands steadied, and I lifted the sword just as a halfling man with salt-and-pepper hair and a hooked nose hissed and charged.

Nadia met him head-on, her movements fluid and fierce. Without hesitation, she vaulted up his body, her legs wrapping around his neck. With a brutal twist, she snapped it, sending him crashing into the snow, which exploded on impact. In a seamless motion, she spun off him, raised her sword high, and severed his head. Blood spilled, dark against the snow.

I waited for the urge to gag, for the flashbacks of my father's office to hit me, but nothing came. I felt nothing. Even as five more halflings sprinted toward us—so fast their movements blurred to my painfully slow mortal eyes—I was steady.

Andras darted away from my side as a halfling erupted in a burst of snow. I saw nothing but a blur of shadow, blood spraying, something wet and heavy rolling across the ground. Another explosion of snow followed, and a headless body crumpled into the endless white. Nadia shot forward, hooking her finger inside one of their mouths, using the momentum to propel herself behind him. Her sword flashed in the sunlight, and in an instant, his body collapsed, decapitated like so many others.

I was so captivated by Andras and Nadia's effortless death dance that I didn't notice the halfling on my right until it was too late. The creature slammed into me with bone-crushing force, knocking the air from my lungs and sending me sprawling. We flew through the air until my back collided with a fallen tree, pain ripping up my spine. A rabid elderly woman in a cat-themed moo-moo landed on top of me, her gums gnashing at my face and throat, two fangs (her only teeth) gleaming like a rattlesnake's.

I barely managed to block her attack with my forearms, twisting desperately to throw her off. Despite her frail appearance, she was terrifyingly strong. I headbutted her hard, feeling the crunch of her nose breaking beneath the blow, yet she barely flinched. Blood dripped from her crooked nose, warm and sticky, but it only seemed to fuel her frenzy.

Panicking, I jabbed my thumbs toward her glassy gray eyes, making her recoil. She struck back, her delicate hand slamming into my left eye with the force of a boulder. Pain exploded behind my eyelids, stars dancing in my vision as tears streamed down my cheeks.

Suddenly, a large male hand gripped her throat and yanked her off me. I gasped, rolling onto my stomach, clutching a handful of snow to press over my throbbing eye as I scrambled to my feet. Behind me, I heard bones crack, followed by a short, piercing cry. Then, silence.

"Are you hurt?" Andras's voice came from behind me, his large, warm hand settling gently on my shoulder. "Let me see you."

I turned slowly, one eye half-closed and swelling. His lips tightened as his gaze swept over my face, then down the length of my body, checking for harm, checking to make sure I was still whole. He winced as he took in the wound on my arm, but his touch was unbearably gentle as he took my hand. Without a word, he raised it to his mouth, his jaw working, tensing, as he hovered over the marred flesh left by the old woman's bite. Then, ever so slowly, he lowered his lips to my skin, his bloody tongue tracing over the bite. A tingling sensation spread through my arm as I watched the damaged flesh begin to knit itself back together.

"You bit your tongue?" I asked, my voice a mixture of curiosity and awe.

He dipped his chin once. "Our blood can heal, remember? Close your eyes."

I obeyed, and a moment later, felt the warmth of his tongue glide up the side of my face and over my swollen eyelid. The same tingling sensation followed, and just like with my arm, the swelling vanished as if nothing had ever happened. I wiped the moisture from my face with my sleeve, staring up at Andras. His blood-splattered golden skin was a sight to behold, and his blue eyes, filled with sorrow and worry, locked onto mine.

"I'm okay. Thank you."

He opened his mouth, hesitating. "I'm so—"

"I'm okay," I interrupted, squeezing his hand and pressing a kiss to his palm.

A crooked smile tugged at his lips. "If you kiss me again, I won't be able to fight. I'll be too distracted by thoughts of burying myself inside you," he purred, his voice deep and husky.

"Alright, Casanova," I chuckled softly. "Get back out there. I'll be fine—and Nadia looks like she could use some help."

In the clearing, Nadia was completely surrounded, her blade a blur as she slashed through the halflings closing in on her. Her movements were fierce and precise, the conductor of a brutal symphony, a cacophony of growls and screams rising all around her.

He searched my face for a moment, looking for something—maybe a sign that I'd actually be okay. A warm smile tugged at the corner of his lips as he bent to kiss my forehead, lingering as though time stood still and he had nowhere else to be. He backed away and, with a wink, spun towards the fight, cocking his head to the side, a predator locking onto prey. Icy winds swept loose tendrils of hair into my face. I blinked. That fast, Andras had joined the fray. Only this time, the fighting looked different. He stood next to Nadia, hands in his pockets, utterly still. Around him, halflings fell to the snow, clawing at things that weren't there, screaming as if they were afraid of some invisible demon. Some new hell had brought them to their knees and made them beg, cry, and howl. The sounds were unbearable. Nadia seemed almost bored as she took in the chaos. Her face was impassive, one hand on her hip, the other hand clenched on the hilt of her sword, the blade resting casually on her shoulder. But her chest heaved. Was she scared of something, too? *Or was she feeling their terror, because that's her gift?* Andras had become a statue: alive but not, there, but not. Alive, but not. His eyes were as black as the midnight sky, dark as obsidian stones, unfocused, unmoving, otherworldly. *Mindweaving*, I realized. *He's using mindweaving to pull them into a nightmare.*

And then Nadia was upon them. While they screeched and writhed in the snow, lost to some horror, she cut them down.

I inhaled a shuddering breath as a halfling stepped into my line of sight, teeth bared, eyes frantic with bloodlust. Instinctively, my left leg slid back into first position as I raised my sword, the point aimed at the creature barreling toward me, his long black hair whipping behind him in a tangled mess. He closed in fast, claws slashing through the air, grabbing at my hair, my clothes. Each time he lunged, I met him with the blade, slashing violently at his hands and arms until, finally, I saw my opening. Without hesitating, I drove the sword forward, aiming for his chest. Flesh and muscle gave way as I plunged the blade in, grinding sickeningly against bone. Dark blood spurted from the wound, and for a moment, I froze, staring at the gushing stream in shock. But I knew I had only seconds before the stunned halfling would recover and strike again. Planting my feet, I went for the neck and slashed, throwing all of my strength into it. Blood splattered and pumped as the creature's head flopped back, a gruesome gaping wound across his throat, but his head, covered in flowing onyx hair...*Oh fuck, no, no, no,*

I didn't cut all the way through. Wincing, I tried again, this time knocking him to the ground, where he writhed and flailed, blood pumping from his slit throat, head still somehow attached. Looking down upon him, I hacked, my blade scraping bone. Again. Again. Again! At last, my sword went clean through, into the icy red ground.

Blood splatter smeared my lips, mingling with the melting snowflakes on my skin. I could feel the droplets running down my face, but I barely registered them. Andras and Nadia had both paused to watch me—Andras, his brows raised, mouth slightly parted in shock, while Nadia's lips curved into a tight smile, her eyes flickering with amusement. I shrugged. What would they have me do? But before I could catch my breath, another halfling charged—a tall female with hair-like burning embers.

I went for the gun on my hip and aimed with unsteady hands for the creature's pretty, pale forehead. I fired as she zig zagged out of the way. I fired again and missed. *No! No! No!* I held my breath and begged the universe–the stars, the moon, even the energy beneath my feet–for the bullet to find its mark. I fired again and struck true. She jerked to a stop. I fired once more, this time hitting her in the face. No longer pretty, her peach lips pulled back in a sneer, revealing long, white fangs, before she crumpled into the snow.

Her head came off a little bit easier.

I tried not to think about who she'd been before this. Did she have children? A favorite book? I knew these questions would haunt me forever, and now was not the time. I forced myself to shove the thoughts away, burying them deep. I stood frozen in the clearing, watching as Nadia and Andras effortlessly cut down the remaining two dozen halflings, their movements swift and brutal.

Before, when I'd known Andras simply as the hot new neighbor, I would never have guessed he'd been an army general and mercenary in another life, long ago. But seeing him spin and slash, whirl and duck, I couldn't imagine him as anything else. A burst of snow, then blood and death.

Three halflings were on Andras. He crossed his swords at the base of one of their throats and flung the swords outward as the body collapsed, headless. Sheathing the swords on his back, he punched into the chest of the halfling on his right, yanking out its heart. He let it roll off of his fingers into the powder, then did the same to the one on his left. In three moves, in three seconds, all three halflings were dead.

Nadia was no less lethal, but she took her time, and fought with deadly grace–pivoting, spinning, leaping–as if this were a sort of ballet. I wondered what her life had been like over these past centuries, to have become so *good* at killing that it was almost an art.

Once the last of the creatures had fallen, the fresh snow now muddy and streaked with scarlet, Andras and Nadia strode toward me, drenched in dirt and caked with blood. Andras's dark hair glistened with a crimson sheen where his bloody hands had raked through it, and Nadia's blade, like mine, dripped steadily at her side.

"Where the fuck is he?" Nadia snapped as they reached me, her voice sharp.

"I don't know," Andras muttered, his eyes searching the tree line.

Nadia's eyes narrowed, her body tense. "I can feel him," she said, her voice dropping into a low growl. "You're an angry piece of shit, Callum!" she shouted towards the woods.

"I can smell him," Andras muttered. His jaw ticked as he continued to scan the horizon.

"Come out, you prick!" he finally snarled, his voice dark and commanding. The sheer force of it made me flinch.

A slow clap sounded behind us. *Clap, clap, clap.*

"Bravo."

A voice made of gravel followed, laced with that strange, unplaceable accent. We spun around to find Callum lounging on the cabin steps, his elbows propped casually on the stairs, legs crossed at the knee. He looked both ancient and unsettlingly modern, clad in a bizarre mix of Roman military armor and contemporary clothing—a golden breastplate over a black tunic, sleek black trousers, and leather boots. His lips curled into a mocking, hateful smile.

His eyes gleamed with malice as he turned his hateful gaze to Andras.

"Az, I see you're enjoying yourself," he crooned. "Look at that! You killed them all! Men, women—just like the glorious old days of Rome, before everything became so dull. Revertere me ad illud tempus."

"Ire ad inferos!" Andras spat.

An eerie silence settled over us as Callum narrowed his dark brown eyes, locking them on Andras with unhinged intensity. Nadia again rested her sword casually on her shoulder, legs spread in a wide stance, ready. A scowl creased her face, her full mauve lips curled into a sneer. Andras, seemingly unaffected, simply tilted his head, his beautiful features a mask of perfect indifference. My right eyelid twitched from nerves, and my chest heaved with each breath, the pounding of my heart unmistakable even from twenty feet away. The fear that had momentarily left me during the fight surged back, stronger than before, knowing that this evil shithead was poised to unleash himself on us.

"What is it you want, Callum?" Andras asked coldly.

"Want? I want you to *pay*. I want you to *hurt*. I want you to *die*. You trapped me in half-conscious hell for centuries, Andras, *centuries*. I went completely mad and spent day after day dreaming of clever ways to ruin you."

"Oh, you were mad long before that, Callum," Nadia taunted.

"Shut up, bitch," Callum snarled.

"Careful, Callum," Andras ground out. "You deserved what you got, and worse, after everything you did. Much worse."

"What is it that I did, Andras? Gifted you immortality? An army to lead? A castle to live in?"

Andras sighed loudly. "Tsk-tsk," he began taunting, "all of that time to self-reflect, for naught. What a waste. You're conveniently leaving out the murder, the torture, the psychotic fits of rage..."

Callum scoffed.

He pushed off of the steps, slowly stalking towards us.

"You were always so fucking dramatic," he sneered, unsheathing an iron sword. "I'm tired of talking. I'm going to kill *her*," he pointed his sword at Nadia, who smiled wide, as though she were counting on it, "and then *her*," he pointed the sword at me and I inhaled sharply, feeling dizzy, "and I'm going to take my time with the human one, carving her up while you watch."

Fear and rage slammed into me. I fumbled for the gun on my left side again, my grip loosening on the hilt of the sword on my right.

In a blink, Callum lunged for Nadia, but Andras stepped between them, shoving Callum back before launching into a flurry of strikes. Their swords clashed, gleaming in the dusk light, the sound sharp and relentless. Callum bared his teeth and went for Andras's throat, but Andras blocked, spun free, and wrapped his arm around Callum's neck, squeezing as if he meant to rip his head off. Callum regained the advantage, throwing Andras over his shoulder as if he weighed nothing, right as Nadia charged in, slashing at Callum with her sword. He dodged her advances and landed a blow, slicing her leg. Blood oozed as she scrambled up, limping, bright red trailing behind.

The fight blurred into a whirlwind of grunts and slashes. Nadia and Andras tried to flank Callum, but he moved with supernatural ease, outmaneuvering them both. Panic surged. He was going to massacre us, find my family, my children, and...

No. My legs were moving before I could stop myself. I pulled my gun, fired, and missed. Without thinking, I fired again—this time hitting his thigh. Callum's face jerked toward me, snarling, teeth bared. I fired again.

Click. *Empty.*

My heart pounded. I tossed the gun to the side and ran toward him with my sword ready to strike. Steel clashed into iron, but everything I sent his way, he parried with ease, knocking my sword from my hand. He lunged to jab, and I braced for the impact of his blade in my gut, waiting for the pain, and death. I would never see my children again. What would they tell my family when they find me disemboweled in the snow? Nadia roared as her sword crashed down onto Callum's, knocking it off course and sparing me. I recoiled, stumbling back as Callum came for me again, wildly searching the ground for something, anything to protect myself. Andras appeared between us and blocked Callum's next blow, and the next, and the next, getting closer and closer until the tip of Callum's sword struck his chest, cutting deep.

Andras cursed and staggered back, bleeding.

"Andras!" I screamed.

Callum lunged again, without hesitation. Time slowed as he raised his sword for the kill, muscles tensing in his jaw, Andras leaning back out of the reach of the blade. I knew I had to do something. I had to do something fast.

I sprang forward, roaring as I slammed both of my hands into Callum's chest. My body felt hot, molten. I could feel power flooding through me. Both our eyes went wide as electricity surged from my palms into him, sending him careening back and into the snow. Gasping, I examined my palms in disbelief. Callum panted as he sat up and crawled onto his hands and knees like a wild animal ready to charge. I inched back.

Blood had bloomed from Andras' chest. But the red sticky stream that had trickled down his abdomen and seeped through his t-shirt was already slowing as he healed. He observed me, eyes darting all over my body before settling onto my hands. Then those dark blue eyes, bloodshot with blown-out pupils, flicked up to mine in question. I shrugged, having no fucking idea what just happened. But Nadia smiled widely at both of us, like she understood something we didn't.

It had happened before, when that creature had attacked me in my home, but I thought I'd imagined it, thought it had something to do with adrenaline. This time I had witnesses, and they'd seen the power, the raw energy, that had come from me. My heart raced. It didn't make sense. Nothing made sense. I was in a foreign body, in a new reality. Who was I? *What* was I?

Before any of us could register what was happening, Callum seized Nadia from behind, fast. So unbelievably fast. A crack sounded as he snapped her neck, and let her crumble to the ground. Andras howled, "NADIA!" and charged at Callum, who twirled out of reach, grabbed Andras's arm, and plunged his sword into Andras's side. Andras panted and winced, falling to his knees.

"No!" I cried out.

We're dead. We are all dead.

The sun had disappeared fully just beyond the hills, and the valley was quiet and cloaked in shadow. I could see Andras's quick, shallow breaths in the frigid air. Callum leaned down close, grasping his sword at the hilt, and whispered, "That's for betraying me for *her* all those years ago," he gestured at Nadia, "for choosing her after I gave you *everything*." He pulled his sword free from Andras's body, then shoved it back in, "and that's for stabbing me the other day, you prick." Andras growled through clenched teeth. Callum studied Andras's face. His rage softened, black eyes glistening as he whispered, barely audible, "I loved you."

Andras stared back at him, his blue eyes glossy from the pain. "I thought I loved you, too," he grunted out. Then his pupils swelled, and Callum went utterly still, his gaze vacant.

Realization dawned on me. Andras had pulled Callum into his mind–a distraction.

It was my only shot.

I moved. As fast as I could run, I seized my sword from the snow and was upon them in a few steps. I had seconds, just a few heartbeats, to do it. To end this. Positioning myself behind Callum, I realized that if I swung even slightly off, I'd hit Andras, too. Raising the blade with unsteady hands, I widened my legs and spread my toes, anchoring myself to the frozen ground–just like I'd been taught by my fencing coach more than a decade ago. Any moment Callum would rip himself free of whatever illusion he'd found himself trapped in. Panic began to take hold of me. *Go now*, I willed myself. *Go NOW.* Breathing deeply, my lungs expanding until they ached, I exhaled and brought the sword down hard, with everything I was, everything I wanted to be, and everything I'd ever been, slicing through bone, through muscle, until the blade met the snow and something rolled off to the side with a horrible, wet thud. Callum's body turned black and then disintegrated into ash, carried away on an icy breeze.

Still on his knees, Andras blinked, staring at the place where Callum's body had been. Then he turned, wincing from his wounds, looking me up and down.

"Thanks, darling," he whispered.

Nadia still lay unconscious nearby, a thin veil of flakes covering her, clinging to her delicate blouse, her dark rose lips parted just so, as if she were having a peaceful nap. Kneeling beside her, I finally let the blood-stained sword fall from my hand. I leaned over her to examine her neck, craned at an odd angle. The sound of her broken body hung in the air, thrumming in my ears, while my hand gently caressed her cheek.

"Nadia? Nadia, can you hear me?"

I didn't know the first thing about vampire healing or how long it might take for one of their kind to recover from a broken neck—or if they even could. The snow sank to our left as Andras knelt there, scooping his long, muscled arms underneath Nadia's back and legs before hoisting her up close to his chest. He got to his feet with her in his arms as if she were the size of a doll.

"Let's go inside where it's warm," he said gently.

"What about all of this?"

I gestured to the mud and gore, the headless bodies strewn for hundreds of yards around us, haunting and polluting the otherwise undisturbed beauty of these mountains.

"Halflings don't turn to ash right away, like we do. But they can't go in the sunlight until they're fully made. The sunrise will take care of this, of them."

I surveyed the carnage one last time and swallowed hard to stifle nausea as I climbed to my feet. The sword I'd dropped had sunk nearly out of sight, and ice nipped at my already frozen fingers as I freed the steel. The hilt biting into my hand, I led the way back to the cabin.

A FITFUL SLEEP

I bolted upright, sweaty, heart thundering, as a nightmare tore me from sleep. There had been so much blood in my dream, pools of it, against the stark snow. I gasped, clutching my pajama top in my fist. For a dozen heartbeats, the room was unfamiliar, and panic was beginning to set in when it all clicked into place. The cabin. We were in the cabin. And it was barely dawn, from the looks of the cold gray light seeping in around the curtains. How did I get into this bed? The last thing I remembered was sitting on the couch, fussing over Nadia. Then a soothing voice cooing into my ear, "let's get you to bed, Darling," and then strong male arms holding the weight of my aching back and legs. Andras must have carried me to bed after I passed out on the couch.

I lay down, pulling the blankets up tight around my chin as I curled into the fetal position, noticing all of the muscles that were generally unused, now left aching from the fight.

Details from the night before came pouring in. After we brought Nadia in from the snow, Andras had set her down on a blanket by the fire with painful gentleness. He'd made some tea, then presented me with a pretty rose-embossed mug, his hand still crusted in dried blood and gore. His blue eyes were weary and as tumultuous as a midnight sea. When I finished my tea, he'd led me to a hot bath and left me alone, a fresh towel and my clean pajamas waiting for me on the bed when I stepped out a half-hour later. He must have gone to shower while I'd bathed, because when I found him again in the living room, lounging in the chair closest to the fire, his hands and hair were no longer rust-tinted or caked in mud, and he'd changed into black joggers and a gray thermal shirt that showed off his muscled body. I'd thanked him for drawing my bath and laying out my pajamas, then settled on the couch across from him. He crossed and uncrossed his legs at the knee, smiling warmly at me, but something dark shaded his eyes, something I couldn't pin down.

"Are you alright?" I asked, instantly regretting it. Of course he wasn't alright. I no longer loved Steven, and I would be happy to never see him again, but I'd still feel *something* if I had to decapitate him—even if it were wholly justified, even if he were trying to kill me—because at one time I *had* loved him.

"No," Andras admitted.

"I'm sorry," I whispered.

His lips pulled up at the corners, but his eyes were elsewhere.

"Can I ask you something?" I ventured

"Anything."

"When you pulled him into your mind...what did you show him?"

A few heartbeats passed, and I was about to tell him that he didn't have to share, to just forget about it, when he cleared his throat.

"A tomb," he said softly.

My brows furrowed.

"Of cement," he added, eyes flicking to mine.

"That's..."

"Monstrous."

"I was going to say...metal."

He huffed a laugh. Slowly, I edged off of the couch and went to him. Without saying a word, I bent down to kiss him gently on the cheek, wrapped my arms around his shoulders, and breathed in the scent of him, warm woods, and a metallic something else.

"I'm sorry you had to..." I told him, trailing off.

He placed his thumb gently on my chin to guide my face to his so he could look me in the eyes while he sweetly stroked my cheek.

"I'm not sorry about him. But I am sorry for you. I am sorry that you were threatened, and scared, and hurt, and worried for your children. I am truly so sorry."

A small smile was all that I could offer in the moment to accept his apology. My body was so tired. And I didn't blame him, but I didn't have the energy to say that.

Andras took my hand and gently pulled me into his lap, where he held me tight, and we sat in silence, watching Nadia, still as death, for what felt like hours. When I wrung my hands for the two-hundredth time, Andras reassured me that she'd wake up, that broken bones took a few hours to heal for their kind and she just needed rest and time. My cheek on his chest, and my legs tucked in tight, I must have fallen asleep on him. And he must have put me to bed.

Now, the morning after, I was a mess. Images and conversations from last night flooded me as I lay in that bedroom in the dark. My clothes were still damp from the nightmare that had jolted me awake, the one with the blood, the snow, and the...bodies. The shock had worn off, and my thoughts were racing. Images of bloodied maws and wild eyes as the halflings charged. The sound of bone breaking. Andras, the warrior, cutting down his enemies with brutal efficiency. Andras, my lover, stopping mid-fight to literally lick my wounds.

I struggled to reconcile the day before with my real life. I'd spent my night shooting and stabbing creatures, and now I would return, although I didn't know how or in what capacity, to being a mother, to flipping pancakes and answering emails from the damned PTA. When I returned to Denver, I would continue on as a single mother.

I felt confident in that decision, but still mourned the years lost, the time spent feeling so unlovable. It pained me to think about the fact that maybe, for all of these years, I'd missed out on a partner as kind and loving as Andras. I knew it didn't benefit anyone to rummage in the past, but still, it was damn hard not to. Steven hadn't been able to offer basic, common decency for whatever reason. I must not have felt like I deserved it because if I did...maybe...maybe I wouldn't have allowed it to go on for so long. Regret and rage swept through me, followed by grief. I'd lost myself, and in the process of finding myself, I'd met someone who liked me for me, but I couldn't have him. I wouldn't.

Because I had my girls, and my girls were my heart, and the stars, and the moon. As much as I'd love to spend my life with a kind, brave man, who would stay eternally gorgeous, I couldn't. Not only because I'd grow old and die while he lived on for a dozen more lifetimes, but because it was too damn dangerous. Everything with Callum was proof of that. That centuries-old garbage person had been as far as the threshold of my home, had scented my family and peered into our world. He was that close to being able to harm my kids. I shuddered, and my stomach roiled. Never again.

Pushing back the heavy drapes around the window, I saw hot pink sunlight peeking over a distant mountain through clouds, evergreens, and pines. New snow had fallen, covering the dead. The semi-turned halflings, blind with bloodlust, victims of an ancient grudge would rest there forever. The sun crept higher, a silver light spreading over the clearing, and wherever the light made contact with the ground, ash floated up and away on a phantom wind.

Murmuring down the hall drew my attention from the solar cremation outside, but my lazy human ears couldn't pick up what was being said, so I padded towards the door where I could faintly make out Andras's voice.

"She's never going to talk to me again once we get back," he said, barely above a whisper.

"Danny doesn't hate you, love," Nadia said, her voice gentle.

Relief washed over me upon hearing her. She'd finally woken up, and from the sound of it, she'd made a full recovery.

"I could have gotten her killed. Her family..." Andras went on.

"Yes, you could have. But you didn't. Andras, you couldn't have prevented this. You're a vampire, not a god, not a weaver of destiny. I know you think highly of yourself but this was out of your powe–don't you roll your eyes at me! We're going to have to tell her, to explain to her what happened out there. What she did, and what she is...I *do* think you two are fated, and more–that she's fated for something big—"

"Could we please talk about this later?" Andras asked, hushed and hurried.

I felt ridiculous, with my ear pressed against the door, and hoped that I'd misheard them or misunderstood. Fated? Fated for *what*? I opened the door quietly enough, hoping to get a little closer and hear them better, but the house went silent as soon as I stepped into the hallway. I rolled my eyes. Vampire hearing. Of course.

Nadia and Andras were in the kitchen, seated at the little table by the windows, just like the first morning, drinking coffee out of ceramic mugs. They both rested their crossed arms on the table in front of them, leaning in so they could talk about me and whether or not I was something or another. A small part of me danced with delight to learn that he cared whether or not I would talk to him again, whether or not I was upset with him. But then it hardly mattered, because after this…he was right: we couldn't talk anymore.

"Good morning," I said, leaning against the doorway. "I'm glad you're okay, Nadia."

She grinned, performing an airy gesture as if to say *of course I am*.

"Terribly achy, but otherwise completely fine. Andras told me that you watched over me most of the night. Thank you."

I nodded.

Andras surveyed me carefully, his dark blue eyes crawling down my body, scanning for something, searching. He opened his mouth to speak but stopped himself.

A pause.

"Good morning," he finally said, a bit weakly. "Did you sleep okay?"

"I did." The corners of my mouth tugged up. "Thank you for tucking me in."

"Any time," he purred, trying to flirt, but underneath the lilt of his voice, I could make out the concern. I played along, though, and shook my head in mock disapproval.

I wandered over to the cabinet of mugs, choosing a light blue one and setting it on the counter. Hot coffee filled the cup, the steam writhing up to fill the air with caramel and chocolate notes. I cleared my throat gently.

"I have to leave after I get dressed to get back to Liv and Ria."

"Of course," Andras agreed. He smiled, but it didn't reach his eyes. "What can we do to help?"

"I don't know."

"I'll start clearing the snow away from the car while you're getting your things ready," Nadia offered.

"That's very sweet. Thank you."

Leaning against the counter, I sipped the steaming coffee. It scalded my tongue, and I winced. The floor was cold against my bare feet. I gently raised up onto my toes, lightly bouncing from one foot to the other. My eyes were glued to the mug cupped in my hands because I had no idea what to say to either of them. Yesterday, I woke up entangled with Andras's naked, muscled body, content to stay there forever, his hot skin and breath mingling with mine. But last night...last night I fell asleep with dried blood under my fingernails, haunted by the horrific images of the day, of gnashing jaws, of disembodied heads. Yesterday, I killed people. *We* had killed people. Or...halflings–who had tried to kill us!--but the halflings *had been* alive. They'd once been human, they had families, and friends, and I was still sorting out how I felt about any of it. Scared? Grief-stricken. Nothing at all. The apathy was the hardest to swallow; the brief moments where it felt like it was "all in a day's work" especially scared me. *What a terrible, inhuman way to cope*, I thought.

Andras laughed at something that Nadia said and my eyes flicked up to his face. That perfect godsdamn face! The sun-tanned skin, the shocking blue eyes, the full lips and the…

"What in the world are you thinking about, Danny?" Nadia asked, clearly holding back a laugh.

I ignored her and took another sip of the scalding coffee.

Since that first night on my porch, when I'd met Andras, something started changing in me; the energy just under my skin began to build. I'd noticed it at certain times and thought to myself, *Ah, good, the depression is fading, I can see clearly now*. But it was more than that, so much more than that. He made me want things for myself again. Through knowing him, I remembered that I was a fiercely capable creature and more than just a means to an end, but the end *and* the beginning, in and of myself. And sex with him had been, well, otherworldly.

But the greatest gift had been trust. After losing my father and after my marriage with Steven, I didn't think it was possible to trust another human or to trust *myself* with another person. But I did trust Andras. And I wanted him so much, wanted this one selfish slice of happiness so much. I was pretty sure I love–.

"–interesting," Nadia spoke into her coffee cup, interrupting my thoughts. Our eyes met, and hers were *knowing*. Oh shit, she could feel emotions. I shot her a look that communicated to kindly keep it to her godsdamn self. She merely smiled sweetly.

Andras, being a vampire and just generally perceptive as hell, noticed our silent exchange.

"Am I missing something?" he questioned, an eyebrow raised as he glanced between us.

"No," we both echoed each other.

"I should go pack," I announced, shoving away from the counter.

Cupping the coffee mug in my hands, I slowly walked down the hallway to the guest room. I had just set the mug down on one of the bedside tables and started repacking my bag when I felt someone behind me and stilled.

"It's just me," Nadia said.

She came around to the bed and sat next to the small pile of clothes I'd gathered there, patting them in place. Nadia pulled one foot up and angled it so her heel rested against her thigh. Just two girlfriends chatting in their pajamas, it would seem to a stranger. I raised an eyebrow at her in question while I made quick work of folding a sweater.

"You can tell me to mind my own business at any point," Nadia said, smiling tightly, "but I know how you feel about him, and I can sense the conflict there, too. I understand, maybe more than you can imagine. But I just wanted to say, hold on to the people who make you feel at ease and celebrate you being you."

I forced a smile but didn't respond. I didn't know how. Nadia sat quietly for a moment, searching my face, before gathering herself up and heading to the door. "I'll give you some peace while you pack," she said quietly, then paused with her hand on the doorknob, and without turning around, she said, "I'm glad to have met you. If this is the last time we ever see each other, I just want you to know that." She turned the knob and hesitated, keeping her eyes on the door.

"You didn't imagine the electricity in your hands, Danny. You're more powerful than you know, and I suspect that your family knows. I suspect they have the answers to your questions. Just be careful who you ask and who you tell. And come find me, when you need help."

I frowned, caught off guard and confused.

"Nadia, I don't know what—"

"Give yourself some time to process this shitshow before you start down that road because it might be a long one. Just remember what I said."

She opened the door, and as she passed through the threshold, I whispered, "thank you, Nadia."

Her bare feet padded down the hallway, almost as quiet as death, as the icy mountain itself. I continued to pack, struggling to focus on the task at hand. Her cryptic words echoed in my thoughts: "I suspect your family knows."

THE WAY HOME

Slouched on my porch swing, I chipped away at the last remnants of my white nail polish, my eyes anxiously scanning the road for a familiar car. My hands ached from aggressively wringing them for the past hour, and no matter how much water I gulped down, my throat felt dry as sand. There was too much inside—too much fear, too much confusion, too much regret, and far too much grief.

I'd left the cabin in a frenzy that morning, my emotions raw and tangled. I kissed Nadia on the cheek and hugged Andras tightly, letting his cedar scent wash over me, wishing I didn't have to let go. He pressed his lips gently to the top of my head, then my cheek, and finally my lips, and I melted into him. I nearly whimpered at the thought of stepping out of his arms, out of the only warmth I'd felt from a man in such a long time. After everything I'd been through, I *needed* that hug; needed to be enveloped in something good, even if only for a fleeting moment.

Then I backed away, frowning at how cold I felt without him next to me, turned on my heel, and left. I got into my car and drove, feeling an emptiness close in.

I'd sped down the canyon, away from the cabin, away from the place where Callum and a dozen halflings had taken their last breaths. My knuckles whitened as I gripped the steering wheel, my mind splintering with memories, trying to piece together the chaos of the last forty-eight hours. Unlike the woman I'd been a decade ago—a master of distraction and disassociation—I let myself feel every terrible, difficult, unbearable thing.

When my father died, I couldn't face it, so I didn't. After the initial shock and tears, I spent years not thinking about his death and seeing that as evidence that I had coped well. Now, in retrospect, I could see I hadn't coped at all. Instead, I'd squatted in a gilded cage of my own making, in order to feel normal and safe. I'd married Steven because he felt so *boring*, so *opposite* of me, so *stable*. Where I felt every emotion so strongly, all the time, he seemed to feel so little. Where I was passionate and a little wild, he was, according to himself, "practical" and honestly kind of dead inside. Where my dad had "left" without warning, Steven, for all of his flaws, would never leave. He'd grown controlling, bitter, and cruel, letting the worst parts of himself fester for years, but he hadn't left. I'd had to be the one to make the call to end it. I let the tears fall. I let myself ugly cry and scream and roar all the way home.

Fear crashed into me. I'd headbutted an elderly woman in the face and beheaded—*beheaded*—people, people whose names I didn't know and never would. I'd been coated in blood splatter and gore. And something had happened with my hands, some kind of power, something that felt like electricity, powerful enough to send an immortal soldier sprawling in the snow. It had taken half a thought, no effort at all.

What did it mean? What did it mean?

Something inside me had awoken, something that had lain dormant for years, and my intuition told me that Nadia was right, that once I went down the road of figuring it out, there'd be no going back.

It could wait. It had to wait. Back in the real world—the non-vampire real world—I was a newly divorced single mom, about to step into a new life, and I was scared out of my mind. Then, there was Andras, a man who had not yet abandoned kindness or respect in his long and brutal life. A man who saw me, really saw me, at a time when I felt unbearably invisible. Of all the things that had happened, to my horror, saying goodbye to feeling understood made me cry the hardest. I desperately needed to be known to feel real.

As I'd zigged and zagged home through the tight canyon turns, hail pounded the windows, and I missed my girls so much it hurt. I felt thankful they'd stayed safe, and hoped that the long weekend at my mother's sterile estate hadn't caused a different sort of trauma, like being subjected to afternoon tea with mom. The need to hold them, to feel the weight of their warm little bodies in my arms, had herded me home, pulling me toward them with an urgency I couldn't deny.

After pulling up to my house, I'd done my best to find my bearings, to center myself enough that the world stopped tilting under me. I meditated, or tried to, distracted by the fact that the last time I'd tried mindfulness had been to deceive Callum, who'd stood on my porch leaking deadly vengeance into the air like chlorine gas. I abandoned meditation and took a steaming hot bath instead, letting the liquid blaze bring me back to my body, and fell asleep there. I awoke sometime later in freezing water, splashed and howled my way out of the tub, then wrapped myself up in a robe and slept a little while longer under a pile of blankets in my bed, tossing and turning, and jolting awake over, and over, and over, a new nightmare every time I drifted back to sleep.

In the morning, I'd wandered out to the porch in a cozy fleece lounge set I'd purchased three sizes too big for "extra comfort," my head in a daze I couldn't shake, and grabbed a cigarette from the usual hiding spot under the cushion of the porch swing. It was the middle of the day and anyone walking by could see me, but I couldn't bring myself to care. I was a killer now, a suburban warrior, a soccer mom by day, an interloper in a seedy underworld of immortals by night. In the blink of an eye, I'd gone from PTA sock drives to being hopped up on electricity…that I could apparently use to smite enemies? I wondered what a little zap would do to Bethany? Maybe murder *did* run in the family. Maybe my mother had been the one to kill my father. Laughter bubbled out of me, edged with hysteria. I laughed, and laughed, and laughed. Once I settled, I wiped the tears from my eyes. *Oh Gods, I am losing it.*

I stared at the cigarette balanced between my fingers while I waited for that spark of craving or elation that it usually brought, but I felt nothing. The swing swayed forward, back, forward, back, and I couldn't bring myself to light it. Somehow, since the last time I'd snuck out here, smoking had lost all of its allure. I was probably still in shock, still coping. Or maybe I didn't need it anymore, maybe that phase had passed where sneaking a cigarette in the middle of the night provided a sense of control, or a cheap thrill. Maybe I didn't need the same phantom escape or creature comfort anymore. Maybe a cigarette just wouldn't suffice after all I'd witnessed.

The only thing I knew for certain was that things had changed and would never be the same. I'd found a kernel of strength inside of me that had long been dormant, and I'd learned to call on it, to amplify it. I felt like *me* again, like the woman I used to be before I'd lost my voice, lost my way–only I felt stronger now, and far more badass.

The entire box of cigarettes went into the garbage, and I plopped down on the frozen steps, waiting for Ria and Liv to come home to me. The neighbor was shoveling his driveway, and for a moment, I thought I saw patches of red there. I swallowed hard. I needed someone to talk to, but I couldn't talk to anyone. I certainly couldn't bring up vampire wars in therapy, at least not without being hauled away to a psychiatric ward.

Steven's black Subaru crept down our street and pulled up in front of my house. Victoria threw open the car door, flung open the gate, and sprinted up the pathway towards me, her curls and black dress bouncing, snow boots crunching over the salted snow and stones.

"Momma! Momma! Are you okay?" she called out to me, slowing to ascend the stairs until she was upon me, arms around my neck. My eyes stung as I held her, feeling her healthy, strong body against mine. Steven set Olivia down on the path, and she clumsily darted toward us. I beamed as she ambled up the steps and then tackled me; the force nearly knocked me over, but I steadied myself and pulled her into a hug, smelling the lavender and vanilla scent of her hair mixed with that earthy, jammy combination of child grime. My vision blurred and then tears streamed and tickled my cheeks.

"You're squishing me!" Victoria squealed.

"Sorry, honey," I apologized, loosening my grip.

Olivia pointed to my face with an avocado in her fist. "Why are you crying, mamma?" she wondered, tilting her head slightly, brown curls falling across her forehead.

"I just missed you both so much!" I said. "I'm happy! They're happy tears!"

"I have an Avocado!" she announced, waving her green fruit in the air above her head.

"Wow!" I said.

They're safe. They're safe. They're safe. I held back a sob as Olivia's sticky fingers twisted and tugged at my hair. Steven had stopped at the bottom of the steps. He studied me and the girls, waiting to speak until we'd had a moment to ourselves.

"Are you feeling better?" he asked, genuine concern in his face. His overnight bag hung at his side.

"Yeah, I am," I said, gently patting at my eyes with my fingertips. "That was so weird. I have no idea what happened," I lied, gesturing to the tears. "I was in a bad place for a solid forty-eight hours, though," I said, a half-truth. "Thank you for taking the girls and keeping them safe. How was everything? How was my mother?"

"You're mother?" He gave me a look that told me all I needed to know. Then he held up a finger, and mouthed "work" before pointing to his earbud. He tossed his bag on the bottom step and turned to walk down the path.

I grunted as I got to my feet, a daughter on either hip.

Steven yelled to whoever was on the other line, "I understand that, Lee! But it's not going to work for us."

I set the girls down, taking each one by their little hand. "Who wants to paint?" I asked.

"WE DO!" they chimed in unison, hopping about like bunnies.

"Great. Go grab your painting smocks and meet me in the studio!"

The girls dashed into the house, thunderous little footsteps sounding down the hall. I stood with my hands on my hips, scanning the street, the yard, and the herbs in the planter boxes, which had wilted and yellowed in the cold. I pushed away the memory of Andras standing there a few months ago, asking me about my favorite plant.

I turned to go into the house, and my phone vibrated with a text message from Jess:

"Were you actually sick, or did you banish the fam to mom's house so you could fuck the hot neighbor? Also, I had the world's hottest date. Must tell you about it. Can I come over tomorrow night? Are we still on for movie night?"

I chuckled, a small weight lifting from my shoulders with this tiny, symbolic return to normalcy.

I responded quickly, "yes, of course."

I desperately wanted to tell Jess everything. Everything about Andras, about Callum, the past few months, weeks, and days, and the strange thing that happened with my hands. If anyone knew what it could be, it would be her—the family's obsessive researcher and knower of all things ancestral. Yet I knew I couldn't do it. I absolutely could not talk to her about this. Still, even if I couldn't tell her anything, even if I couldn't confide in her about all the beauty and horror of my situation, I very much needed a hug. A sister hug, specifically. We could share that, at least, and a movie. Although...Gods, how the fuck was I going to sit through a vampire movie tomorrow night without losing my mind?

My phone buzzed again:

"Hello, Danny. I hope it's okay that I'm writing you," I read, and my stomach twisted. Andras. *Andras*. "Did you make it back home safely? And your children, too? Do you need anything?"

I inhaled sharply, silenced his notifications until later, then slid my phone back into the pocket of my pants, closed my eyes, and counted backward from ten.

"9...8...7...6...5...4...3–"

The girls burst onto the porch, each kiddo clutching their own smock in hand.

"Ta-da!" Olivia sang, twirling and waiving hers in the air.

I put on their smocks over their clothes with no small effort. We walked together towards the studio, where I kept some canvases and fingerpaints just for them. I couldn't stop smiling, just being there with them: my girls, my life, and my eternal heart. They were safe, and I was safe, and we were going to be okay. In fact, something told me that despite everything, we were going to be more than okay.

EVERYONE'S SECRETS AND LIES

I sat at the easel in my studio, working to get some painting done before Jess arrived for movie night. The girls were asleep in their room, tucked in tight, and snoring peacefully. My latest commission, a fridge-size portrait of a Peruvian Guinea Pig named Theodore, was in its early stages. Tilting my head to the side, I contemplated the owner's insistence that I "capture the essence" of Theodore's personality, "especially his sense of humor." Sighing, I glanced longingly at a few mostly-finished, mixed-media pieces against the far wall. Those pieces were mine, made up of my own thoughts, imagination, and heart. Pieces that I'd poured my blood, sweat, tears, and soul into. They were my mind given form, calling to me to finish them. And I would. I promised myself that I would. Just not tonight.

I stared into Theodore's glossy black eyes that shone like the onyx stones I kept in my daughters' nightstands for protection. I blinked, and for just a moment, I saw Andras in the clearing by the cabin, eyes as black as night, his blood-flecked golden face seething with violence as he cut down one halfling after another. *Thrack. Thrack. Thrack.* I shook the image out of my head, picked up a brush, and then froze, fighting against the sudden tightness in my chest. My paintbrush clattered to the floor, splattering black paint across the cement. Tears fell in tiny rivulets down my cheeks and dripped into my lap, darkening my paint-stained smock. I hadn't even realized I was crying.

My phone buzzed.

"I'm here," Jess texted.

I patted my damp and puffy face and picked my brush up from the floor to put it back in its rightful place. I wiped my still-shaking hands on my smock and hung it up on its hook on my easel. Then, I wandered slowly out of the studio and back into my house to let Jess in.

***

Jess and I were drinking a much-needed bottle of white wine in my living room, cozied up on the rug with blankets and snacks as usual, watching Dracula with the sound off–the part where the actor is shirtless and sensual in all of his evil glory. I couldn't help but think of Callum, and those depthless black eyes of his. Jess bounced her thick eyebrows playfully and adjusted the collar of her sleep shirt as she continued the story of her date: "So we're getting hot and heavy, and we're kissing, and it's amazing, and I'm unbuttoning her blouse and going in for some boob action, and—"

I wrinkled my nose and interrupted, "—you know that you sound like a frat bro when you talk about sex, right?" I threw a piece of popcorn at her, and she caught it in her mouth and then flashed a winning grin.

She playfully chewed, swallowed, and cleared her throat dramatically.

"As I was saying," she went on, "before being so *rudely* interrupted by my prudish sister...I was caressing her gorgeous *breasts*." She paused to let it sink in, "when I swear I saw fangs, and I realized that maybe we should lay off of the movies for a while," she quirked her mouth to the side, "that, or I need to smoke less weed."

My whole body went rigid. Fangs? I leaned into Jess, closing the distance between us. "What do you mean *fangs*?" I whispered.

Jess frowned. "Dude, are you okay? Why are you whispering? And why do you suddenly look so...peaky? You're acting so...off...today."

"Jess, seriously, what do you mean she looked like she had fangs?" I pressed.

"I don't know, like fangs. Like, hiiiiiisssss," she held up her hand with her pointer finger and middle finger curled into a "V" shape, "like, you know, fangs." She kept talking but her voice suddenly sounded so far away. "I thought I caught a glimpse, but obviously, it was just the angle and the moonlight because when I looked closer, nothing was there, and also, that's just crazy. Anyway, we definitely fucked, and it was awesome, and I thought you'd be proud because it's been *forever*. Like, I almost worried that she'd find cobwebs in there."

She gestured to her crotch.

I couldn't breathe. My mind raced. It was probably nothing. What were the odds she'd meet another one? Andras said there weren't many. Should I ask him? After avoiding him for two days? Just forty-eight hours ago, I'd been in a cabin in the mountains with him, in a state of both terror and ecstasy, but that already felt like another life, somehow–like it had happened in another realm. Jess slowly passed a hand in front of my face.

I twisted and gave her a flat, unamused look, my head inclined to the side.

"Sis? I'm getting worried about you. Is everything alright?" she asked me, her face pinched with concern.

"I'm fine. Yeah, I'm fine." I cleared my throat and forced a smile. "Anyway, show me a picture of this super babe."

Jess grinned as she flipped through her phone before handing it to me, screen up. "Here she is," she sang.

I took the phone, smiling back. Then my gaze landed on the screen, and the room tilted. The walls closed in, and I had to steady myself on the rug as my breath quickened. I knew that woman. Those big almond eyes, lined with thick black eyeliner, those high cheekbones, that sharp nose—I knew her.

Nadia. I was looking at a picture of fucking Nadia. But the name on her profile said "Raven." Raven, my ass.

"Sis?" Jess called to me softly, her hand moving to rest gently on my shoulder. I jumped, the warmth slowly draining from my face and limbs. Why was Nadia going after my sister? Other than my children, Jess was the most important person in my life, and if something happened to her...if someone hurt her...I ground my teeth at the thought. Panic turned to rage, and I was on my feet, stomping to my phone, leaving Jess sitting on the carpet looking bewildered and concerned. I snatched my phone from my bag and called Andras.

"Danny?" he answered, voice ragged as though he'd been crying.

"Why the fuck did Nadia go out with my sister?" I snapped.

My eyes narrowed as I saw red and felt my blood roil in my veins, felt my legs buzz into action, felt...felt...oh *fuck*–I felt electricity in my hands. *I am going to fry her.*

"Wait, what?" Andras asked, incredulous. "I didn't know that she...she's here, let me ask her–"

I didn't wait for him to answer.

"We're coming over," I barked and hung up.

I spun to face my wide-eyed sister.

"Brace yourself, Jess," I said, "I have so much to tell you."

conclusion

This concludes the House of Secrets, Book One of the Bloodborne Trilogy. Book Two, House of Blood, will be released in the fall of 2025.

Please consider leaving a review wherever you purchased your copy and/or Goodreads.

Subscribe to our list at ME-Evans.com for book updates and author events. You can also follow M.E. Evans on social media: Instagram @YGBG_books or TikTok @meevans_reads_writes

Acknowledgments

I'd like to thank my friends. Your love, support, and friendship have been one of the greatest gifts of my life. My mom, for always supporting my dreams (even when maybe she shouldn't have). My kiddo, for teaching me to love selflessly and fiercely. I'd like to thank my favorite authors; your books have healed parts of me that desperately needed to be healed. Thank you for providing an escape that I desperately needed during all of the dark times of my life. And thank you, Sarah, for your amazing editing skills. And last but not least, thank you, *all of you*, for supporting me by reading my work. Without you, I wouldn't have dared. This book is for you (the smut and all).

Printed in the USA
CPSIA information can be obtained
at www.ICGtesting.com
CBHW051600181124
17600CB00036B/375